THE PARTY AT JACK'S

· · ·

The
University of
North Carolina
Press

. . .

Chapel Hill &
London

THOMAS WOLFE

. . .

THE PARTY AT JACK'S

. . .

Edited and with an introduction by

SUZANNE STUTMAN & JOHN L. IDOL, Jr.

© 1995 The University of

North Carolina Press and Paul Gitlin, Administrator, C.T.A.,

Estate of Thomas Wolfe.

By permission of the Houghton Library, Harvard University

Introduction by Suzanne Stutman and John L. Idol, Jr.

© 1995 The University of North Carolina Press

Manufactured in the United States of America

The paper in this book meets the guidelines for permanence and

durability of the Committee on Production Guidelines for Book Longevity

of the Council on Library Resources.

Title page illustration by Ed Lindlof

Library of Congress Cataloging-in-Publication Data

Wolfe, Thomas, 1900–1938.

The party at Jack's / by Thomas Wolfe; edited and with an introduction by

Suzanne Stutman and John L. Idol, Jr.

p.   cm.

ISBN 0-8078-2206-X

1. New York (N.Y.)—Social life and customs—20th century—Fiction.

2. Apartment houses—New York (N.Y.)—Fiction. 3. Entertaining—New York

(N.Y.)—Fiction. 4. Fires—New York (N.Y.)—Fiction. I. Stutman, Suzanne.

II. Idol, John L. III. Title.

PS3545.O337P37   1995

813'.52—dc20

94-34179

CIP

99 98 97 96 95   5 4 3 2 1

FOR LOUIS D. RUBIN, JR.,

keeper of the torch

and

FOR RICHARD S. KENNEDY,

who made it all possible

CONTENTS

. . .

INTRODUCTION

. . .

Background

At Oteen in the North Carolina mountains during the summer of 1937, where he was busily revising a piece for which he had made notebook entries in 1930, Thomas Wolfe started adding fresh material. Pleased with his efforts, despite numerous interruptions from kinfolk and literary lion hunters, Wolfe wrote to his literary agent, Elizabeth Nowell, to report how his work was going:

> I have completely rewritten it and rewoven it. It is a very difficult piece of work, but I think it is now a single thing, as much a single thing as anything I've ever written. I am not through with it yet. There is a great deal more revision to be done, but I am sending it to you anyway to let you see what I have done, and I think you will be able to see what it may be like when I'm finished with it. (Nowell, ed., *The Letters of Thomas Wolfe* [New York: Scribner's, 1956], 651)

The piece was *The Party at Jack's*, portions of which have seen print through the efforts of Elizabeth Nowell and Edward Aswell, Wolfe's editor at Harper's, who included portions of it in *You Can't Go Home Again*.

Just when he first wrote the parts he was now rewriting cannot be fixed precisely. Besides bits of dialogue done as early as 1930, the earliest definite outline of a chronological sequence for the events occurring on the day of the party appeared on a manila envelope dating to the fall of 1932. Here Wolfe scrawled

I   Jacobs–German background–Schoolboy scene
II   Jacobs Awake
III Esther and the Maid
IV   Jacobs and Esther.

Since Wolfe used such outlines both to show what he wanted to write and to list those pieces already done for some project he had in mind, it is impossible to claim that the present outline launched what he would in time call *The Party at Jack's*.

Whatever came first, manuscript drafts of the story as he conceived it or the outline recounting what he had done, papers in the Wisdom Collection in the Houghton Library reveal that he set to work to create accounts of Frederick and Esther Jacobs and one of Esther's maids, Katy Fogarty. Frederick (Fritz), a German Jew, dreams about his schoolboy days and his return to the Rhineland after becoming fabulously rich in America. He awakens to luxuriate in his princely Park Avenue apartment (bMS Am 1883 [932]). Esther awakens in the tastefully furnished Jacobs household to enjoy her awareness of her body and to chastise Katy for becoming a victim of strong drink. This episode ends with Esther musing further on what she's made of her life and the wonder she feels about her lot as a beautiful, talented, admired woman (bMS Am 1883 [933]). Following their separate awakenings, Fritz and Esther come together. He proudly reads reviews of her stage designs for an otherwise undistinguished play. Together, they revel in her success. On his way to his office, he thinks about the lies, thefts, and chicanery of his driver, dismissing his behavior as typical of servants. Upon reaching his office, he meets a fellow broker, Rosenthal, who is a bona fide crackpot. Tales of Rosenthal's crazy behavior are told by his Irish secretary (bMS Am 1883 [934]).

As arranged in the Wisdom Collection, the next manuscript indicates further development of the story.

        Synopsis
          1. Before sunrise
          2. Morning [Jacob's Dream
                 [Character of Jacobs The Day
                 [Jacobs getting up
                 Mrs. Esther Jacobs
                 Esther with Jacobs

Esther's morning–canceled
Esther with Alma, Edith, Freddy
Esther's morning
3. Noon
4. Afternoon
5. Evening

The chronological scheme set down here would hold throughout Wolfe's many revisions and provide a classic touch to his use of time, less than twenty-four hours from the awakening scenes to George Webber's farewell words to Esther Jack. In outline form as Wolfe looked forward to embodying this material in his chronicle of his new protagonist's (George Webber's) life, that scheme appears in the William Wisdom Collection of Wolfe manuscripts at the Houghton Library under the index bMS Am 1883 (1336).

Part IV
You Can't Go Home Again
(1930–1938)
Book
The Party at Jack's (1930)

Chapters:
Morning
Morning: Jack Asleep
Morning: Jack Erect
Morning: Jack Afloat
Morning: Mrs. Jack Awake
Morning: Mrs. Jack And The Maid
Morning: Jack And His Wife
Morning: The World That Jack Built
The Great Building (April, 1930)
The Elevator Men
Before The Party (Mrs. Jack And The Maids)
Piggy Logan
The Family (Mrs. Jack, Alma, etc.)
The Party Beginning
The Guests Arriving
The Lover
Mr. Hirsch Was Wounded Sorrowfully
Piggy Logan's Circus

The Guests Departing: The Fire
The Fire: The Outpouring of the Honeycomb
The Fire: The Tunneled Rock
After The Fire: These Two Together

This outline probably reflects the story as Wolfe had shaped it before leaving New York for a speaking engagement at Purdue University in 1938. (It is the basis of our reconstruction of *The Party at Jack's*.)

Exactly how Wolfe arrived at this scheme cannot be precisely traced in surviving versions of the story. The central event, a party and fire at the Park Avenue apartment of Aline Bernstein, his mistress and patron, occurred on 3 January 1930 and was to be included as part of Eugene Gant's story. But over a period of years, Wolfe added actions and characters, finally reshaping the story to show shifts in characterization, symbolic import, and values (more about these later). Although he had settled on a time scheme, he remained uncertain about whether his fictional surrogate would attend the party and witness the fire. One draft (bMS Am 1883 [985]) follows the storyline from preparation for the party through Piggy Logan's circus on to the fire and its aftermath. In this version, Esther telephones her lover to report on the party and to tell him about the unexpected fire. With George Webber not on the scene, Stephen Hook figures more prominently here than in the version where Esther's lover makes a belated appearance at the party. As he filled out the action, Wolfe faced decisions about what his surrogate would do once Wolfe had decided to have him appear. How would he show his resentment that Esther had insisted that he be there? With whom would he converse? How much would he eat and drink? How would he respond to Piggy Logan and his wire circus act? What would he do during the fire and its aftermath? How would he reveal his decision to break with Esther? In one episode involving Esther's lover—not called George or Eugene—Esther, seeing her lover and Lily Mandell talking together, comes to them, calls them her best friends, and wishes they could know each other better. She senses the raw sexual attraction between Lily and her lover and leads them off to a bedroom, where they become the two-backed animal. This episode (bMS Am 1883 [938]) complicates Esther's character considerably. Interpreted charitably, it reveals her as someone capable of rising above sexual possessiveness in order to foster friendship. Read uncharitably, it reduces her to a panderer, a wily spider spinning a web of iniquity, showing her to be no better morally than the decadent, privileged crowd she has invited to her party.

Having opted to include Esther's lover at the party, Wolfe makes him largely a guest among many, many guests until the outbreak of the fire and the hurried departure of most of the other partygoers. Those partygoers and their interactions would come to constitute the central portions of his novel. Their numbers could swell or shrink as Wolfe's needs and purposes changed. (They could also dwindle—and did—when Elizabeth Nowell and Edward Aswell shaped the material for its appearance in *Scribner's Magazine* and *You Can't Go Home Again*.) Prominent among those added is Roy Farley, a homosexual, whose mincing ways create laughter and applause. Like Saul Levinson and his wife and a sculptor named Krock, Farley would not survive as a partygoer when Nowell and Aswell edited Wolfe's various drafts for publication. Cut from the guest list, with some of his traits then assigned to his father, was Freddie Jack, his removal being made with Wolfe's consent as Nowell began to condense the story for periodical publication. (She later suggested to Aswell that Freddie be restored in order to correct some inconsistencies in Fritz Jack's character, a suggestion Aswell chose to ignore.)

Wolfe's potential list of partygoers originated in the guests gathered at Aline Bernstein's home to enjoy a performance of Alexander Calder's celebrated wire circus. Excepting such respected persons as Thomas Beer and his sister, Wolfe cast a satiric eye at most of Bernstein's guests, largely an assemblage of New York's financial and artistic elite. True to his longtime practice, he sometimes used real names in early drafts, a factor that forced Aswell later to check with Bernstein to learn who could possibly bring a libel suit against Harper's. Aswell's concern probably stemmed from conversations with Nowell. She had earlier told Maxwell Perkins that the longer version of the story "may be libelous since it tells the dirt on the private lives of practically every person at the party" (personal letter from Nowell to Perkins, Dec. 1938). However long or short the final list, Wolfe obviously meant to present Esther Jack's guests, in the main, as privileged, corrupt, decadent, hypocritical, and hostile to the true artist.

A further stage of development, the introduction of working-class characters, first involved two elevator men, one young, the other elderly. The older man, John Enborg (the surname finally chosen), grateful to have a job, defends his privileged employers. His reasons to speak for them are challenged by a third representative of the working class, Hank, who apparently emerged as the voice of organized labor when Wolfe reworked his material at Oteen. In the handwritten pages dating from Oteen and in typed pages done in New York after Wolfe's return to the city, these working-class men are both individualized and, except for Hank, made more sympathetic. If Wolfe were to have his surrogate cast his lot with the working class, proletarian traits and ideas needed to be understood. To make the proletarian pill less easy to swallow, Wolfe coated Hank with more than a little sourness. If he were to show that old loyalties to the upper classes were no longer fitting in a greedy, corrupt age, he needed someone to provide tough arguments against John Enborg's nostalgic attachment to such wealthy people as the Jacks.

Wolfe came to see, as Richard S. Kennedy convincingly argued, that the building in which the workers served the wealthy could be presented as a symbol of the American economic system. Efficient, strong, durable, and secure as it seemed to be, the building was honeycombed with shafts and situated on tunnels connecting it, by rail, to the rest of the nation. Problems in the shafts or tunnels could weaken or undermine it. Without the workers, the building could not operate effectively. The more he became socially and economically aware, the more Wolfe believed he must fashion a story capable of addressing some of the nation's ills. Thus as *The Party at Jack's* evolved from its first drafts through those portions written at Oteen and later in New York, Wolfe was not content to have his surrogate reject Esther's world because it was artistically decadent and, at bottom, hostile to the creative spirit: Now he would warn his fellow citizens about the callousness, greed, and hypocrisy of the privileged.

His story now had the three unities: a single setting at the Jacks' Park Avenue apartment, a party interrupted by a fire and its aftermath, and time running from the Jacks' awakening until their retiring to bed. Until the material could take its place in some work in progress, the narrative of Eugene Gant's and George Webber's discoveries and deeds, Wolfe frequently listed episodes and tallied his word count, giving variously 18,000, 35,000, and 60,000, the last a reckoning taken as he recorded pieces completed after 1935 and 1936. The variations perhaps resulted from additions made to the story over the years or possibly, for the lowest number, the maximum that Nowell considered marketable to a periodical. In her effort to help him place the story before he went to Oteen, Nowell trimmed it to 25,000 words. (She later submitted a 26,000-word version to *Redbook* and after its rejection there slashed more than 10,000 more words to make it acceptable to *Scribner's*, where it appeared in May 1939.)

Although Wolfe had participated in trimming the version sent to *Redbook*, he was by no means ready to put the story aside. Settled in at Oteen, he turned to it once more, restoring text that he and Nowell had sliced for *Redbook* and adding to it, thinking as he did so that it would be "very long, difficult and closely woven." He went on to tell Hamilton Basso,

> I don't know how it's going to turn out, but if I succeed with it, it ought to be good. It is one of the most curious and difficult problems I have been faced with in a long time and maybe I shall learn something from it. It is a story that in its essence and without trying or intending to be, has got to be somewhat Proustian—that is to say its life depends upon the most thorough and comprehensive investigation of character—or characters, for there are more than thirty characters in it. In addition, however, there is a tremendous amount of submerged action which involves the lives of all these people and which includes not only the life of a great apartment house but also a fire and the death of two people. I suppose really a whole book could be made out of it but I am trying to do it in a story. (*Letters of Thomas Wolfe*, 631)

A few days later (29 July 1937) he told Nowell much the same thing and then, sometime in late August, that he was sending the story to her, adding that he now considered it "a single thing" but still in need of revision. Back in New York, he resumed work on it, eventually producing a typescript from which Aswell shaped the portion of *You Can't Go Home Again* that he called "The World That Jack Built." From the various drafts in the Wisdom Collection, we have attempted to restore to Wolfe and American literature the "single thing" that Wolfe named *The Party at Jack's*.

Themes and Characters

Many filaments in Wolfe's complex web of themes—those that he spins out time after time—coalesce to make this work one of his richest. Here he spreads before readers a table so groaning with food that both Bacchus and Brueghel would surely rush to pay compliments to Esther and her cook and maids. Here he gives such meticulous attention to clothing, furnishings, and wall hangings that the swankiness of the Jacks' Park

Avenue apartment becomes palpably real, the fullness of Wolfe's description rivaling his detailing of the Pierces' luxurious Hudson River mansion. This attention to how well, how sumptuously, and how far above the struggles and worries of the working class the Jacks live affords Wolfe another chance to chronicle life among the privileged class. His account stretches from the dream of wealth, power, and fame of Frederick Jack in Germany through Frederick's and Esther's awakening voluptuously in quarters where his dream has become a proud reality. In relation to Wolfe's thematic interests in the present work and elsewhere in his canon, Frederick's rise from the status of an immigrant German Jew to his position as a lord of wealth and sophistication invites contrastive and comparative looks at the yearnings of another provincial, George Webber. Comfortable and secure though the Jacks appear in their Park Avenue surroundings, Wolfe provides hints of coming trouble by having trains send tremors through their building. Unlike trains in other passages in his canon, where Wolfe tends to be lyrical about their size and might, trains in this work are associated with the potential collapse of structures that could be taken as symbolic of the nation's capitalistic economy. More than that, the tracks carrying them beneath the proud towers of Manhattan come to represent here the ties existing between the rich, the poor, and those in between. In a sense, the tracks parallel Herman Melville's monkeyrope as a symbol of men's interconnections.

Wolfe's emphasis on wealth and the power, corruption, and decadence it affords the Jacks and their circle enables him to trace the ignoble use of money and position among the privileged class. While they show themselves to be the apes of fashion—by wanting to see Piggy Logan perform—and tolerant of crimes both petty and major among their servants, they have little genuine interest in promoting art that has stood the test of time and fail to dismiss or prosecute their thieving and conniving servants. All the wrongs and decadence laid bare here add proof that Libya Hill, the microcosm of corrupt economic and cultural life presented early in the Webber cycle, has its sordid counterpart in bustling and greed-driven Manhattan. As an artist, Wolfe wanted to show that he was just as obliged to expose and revile corruption in the nation's greatest city as he was to set forth the dark deeds of Judge Rumford Bland and others living or working on the square of Libya Hill. His protagonist must assume the role of Hercules, attempting to lead the nation to join him in cleansing this American version of the Aegean stables. To perform that labor meant that his protagonist would arouse the ire of Libya Hillians and New Yorkers. To find the strength, time, and, more important, freedom to combat the forces threatening to undermine the nation, Wolfe asked George Webber to cast aside his hope for fame and love. Speaking the truth carried a heavy price, Webber had learned upon publishing his first novel, and another sacrifice he must make if he is to continue to expose the hypocrisy of the Jacks' circle is Esther's love and support. Here, then, is how the episodes making up this work fulfill Wolfe's plan (expressed in Statement of Purpose for the Webber cycle) of illustrating "essential elements of any man's progress and discovery of life and as they illustrate the world itself, not in the terms of personal and self-centered conflict with the world, but in terms of ever-increasing discovery of life and the world, with a consequent diminution of the more personal and self-centered vision of the world which a young man has."

Here Wolfe tries hard—but not always successfully—to cast off self-centeredness, the Eugene Gant-i-ness of his first two novels. (Something of Eugene Gant remains because portions of the present work come, with little or no revision, from "The October Fair," that portion of his grand plan for a series of novels treating his love affair with Aline Bernstein, the model for Esther Jack.) An early draft of the farewell scene with Esther Jack has the young hero speaking like some Faustian aesthete—the Jacks and their peers are represented as deadly enemies from whom the artist must escape if he is to render the world at large, the privileged and the wretched of the world, "with a young man's mind, with that wonderful, active, hungry, flaming, seething mind of a young man." A later draft portrays a socially conscious artist, one capable of seeing the dross behind the glitter, the self-serving motive underlying a show of compassion, and the moral and intellectual emptiness masked by a push to be up-to-date in everything. To do the job awaiting him as a champion of the working class, he swallowed a bitter pill, a farewell to love, and departed knowing that "there were new lands; dark windings, strange and subtle webs there in the deep delved earth, a tide was running in the hearts of men—and he must go." As *George*, he would choose sides with men of the earth and help them reveal the fact that the privileged class merely occupied a structure supported by the sweat, agony, and deprivation of the common men; as *Webber* he would be the artist helping the common man understand the value of his work, thought, and talents. Ultimately, the party he chose was not one of jack—money and the power and the privileges it brings—but one of honest toil.

In effect, the opening dream sequence prefigures the many themes that Wolfe presented throughout his entire book-length manuscript. Indeed, it seems as if humanity itself takes a haunted ride down the river of time and memory into its deepest soul to examine the profoundest truths of mankind with Frederick in his moments before awakening. Frederick Jack, and the life he has created, seems to rest like some enfabled city, with which he is so much in tune, on solid ground. Yet in his dream, Frederick is trapped in time suspended. In this nether world of his mind's creation he has neither power nor control, as past and present surrealistically form their own strange reality. The classmates who taunt him about his Jewishness and who pursue him with a violent anti-Semitism are prophetic of Germany's hate-filled future, a future that George Webber encounters in the latter portion of *You Can't Go Home Again*.

In his dream, Frederick finds that his family treats him as if he were a child, not the adult he has become, and their smothering attention suffocates him, much like the adult Wolfe found himself to be when he returned to Asheville. To assert his power and "manliness," Frederick recounts his wealth and ownership, much like King Midas counting his gold. Yet the ancient cobbled streets and his connection with the past fill him with exquisite happiness. When he encounters his old schoolmates, whom he feels somehow destined to meet, they are old and battered, and he knows that they have all suffered blows from life. He feels a sense of unity with his enemies and, indeed, with all mankind. He longs to tell them of his life in America after he left Germany, of his loneliness and poverty in his early years, and of his empty success. He yearns to tell them how he gained power yet somehow lost the dream, how like smoke and sand the boy's dream has vanished.

Like the characters who come and go at the Jacks' party that very evening, Frederick has become one of the hollow men, possessing a "suave and kindly cynicism" and "the varnish of complaisance." Like J. Alfred Prufrock, who lived in the world between the real and the unreal, between imagination and reality—who lived a life stunted and dulled and full of emptiness in that great city London—Frederick Jack stood, in the final moments of his dream, looking toward the water, rocking in time's harbor and listening to the mermaids sing.

In the next four chapters, Wolfe sets about establishing his themes and further developing his characterization of Frederick and Esther Jack. Frederick (Fritz) believes that he is in total control of his world. Like a Roman emperor, he sensuously luxuriates in his sumptuous surroundings, narcissistically adoring his own health and vigor. He possesses not only the luxury of wealth but that of time as well, time enough to reflect from his height and distance upon the antlike populace who "swarm" to and fro, both literally and figuratively beneath him. Yet, from the beginning, the almost imperceptible tremor coming from deep within the rock below causes him a vague sense of foreboding and apprehension. The natural world seems overshadowed by the cruel, piercing dominance of these lifeless, monstrous buildings. Indeed, his connection with nature is an artificial one, experienced through the "expensive" sport of golf. He walks upon the "rich velvet of the greens" and "luxuriates" upon the "cool veranda of the club." Even nature has been tamed for his rich men's pursuits. The artificiality of the buildings mock the golden light of the day, an imitation of gold and silver: "silver-burnished steel and cliffs of harsh white-yellow brick, haggard in young light," imagery of false idols, craven images. Indeed, "the immense and vertical shapes of the great buildings . . . dwindled to glittering needles of cold silver [as] light cut sharply the crystal weather of a blue shell-fragile sky." Nature seems to bleed, indeed, to face destruction from these needlelike buildings. The creatures of the city seem to be miniature representations of this lifeless creation. Their cabs are like "hard-shelled prehistoric beasts emerging from Grand Central projectile-like in solid beetle-bullet flight." Mr. Jack has paid for this sense of order and power out of chaos "with the ransom of an emperor." He has indeed paid dearly, with his very soul. The window of his apartment building is paralleled by the window of his eye from which the narrowness of his vision is reflected. He worships illusion—the illusion of power, the illusion of youth, the illusion of eternal potency—and "in that insolent boast of steel and stone [he sees] . . . a permanence surviving every danger, an answer, crushing and convulsive in its silence, to every doubt."

Frederick is characterized as a hollow man, fragmented and full of self-delusion. In contrast, Esther is characterized as a woman possessing a sense of oneness, a connectedness with life, past and present, rich and poor, old and young. Through Esther is "always the clear design, the line of life, running like a thread of gold" from childhood to the present. Her beauty is real, not artificial. Her face reveals complex emotions; it is not smooth and controlled as is Frederick's. Esther is capable of genuine sorrow and depth of feeling. She does not merely take from others, as does Fritz and others like him, for her own gain. She is an artist, a creator. She possesses the ability to create real gold, to transform people and to give them hope. In fact, Esther is like nature herself: "that one deathless flower of a face that bloomed among so many millions of the dead." Like a fertility goddess, she offers hope in the wasteland of modern society.

In these chapters, Wolfe satirizes capitalistic waste and greed, tellingly representative of both the privileged class and their poorer counterparts. Both patron and servant are alike, the only difference being the degree of wealth and power each possesses. Above all else, the goal is to win, and corruption trickles down through the hive, the honeycomb. This corruption is represented, respectively, by the relationship between Esther and her maid and between Frederick and his chauffeur. In words reminiscent of a song of the period and used in *The Great Gatsby*, "the rich get rich and the poor get children." Within the Jacks' household, privilege and dishonesty are paralleled within the city at large.

Wolfe develops a universal theme of blindness and despair in which the false values and self-interest of society at large preshadow, much like the tremor below the earth, the coming apocalypse that Frederick and his united family will experience. The narrator foresees that when financial calamity strikes, Frederick's "gaudy bubble" will explode "overnight before his eye." For all his plumpness, ruddiness, and assurance, he will "shrink and wither visibly in three days' time into withered and palsied senility."

Yet another representative of the falsehood and sterility worshiped in this hollow and anchorless society is Piggy Logan. He is contrasted to Esther, Wolfe's symbol of the "true" artist. His attire and demeanor are artificial, and he is described as being almost inhuman. His round and heavy face smudged darkly with the shaven grain of a thick beard, he seems like the brutal, ignorant characters in the earlier dream sequence. His forehead is "corrugated" and his close-cropped hair is composed of "stiff black bristles, mounting to a little brush-like pompadour" like the lifeless wire dolls he creates. In this upside-down world the real is perceived as artificial and the trivial superb, so that great writers, like Dickens and Balzac, have been found to be "largely composed of straw wadding" by both critics and readers at large. The partygoers, like the people of the wasteland, are indeed people living in a damned world, bored with all of the elements of life. They are bored with love and hate and life and death, but not with Piggy Logan and his wire dolls, at least not so long as his wire circus remains fashionable.

Like Virginia Woolf's Mrs. Dalloway, Esther has within her an ability to bring people together into a magical confluence, a "wonderful harmony." Indeed, the party seems to take on its own separate life, creating a world of enchantment in which all assembled seem like creatures from a land where only wealth, joy, and beauty reside. Esther's heart and soul infuse her world with splendor: "the warm heart and the wise, the subtle childlike spirit that was Mrs. Jack." She is able to do what few others in her world—or any—are able to do: to create unity out of chaos. The characters in this dramatic sequence—for the party scene is dramatic in form—are introduced almost as through a receiving line, like the characters in a play. It is her very humanity that saves Esther from the death-in-life surrounding her in this Wolfean version of wasteland. She possesses "the common heart of life" and thus can associate easily with the wealthy and celebrated as well as with her servants and co-workers. She escapes the sterile and limited lives of her family and guests by unifying all classes, all time. She remembers the sorrow of her youth, and her recollections enrich her. Yet, she is still part of this world and is corrupted by it, so that she is unable to reject the hollowness at its core.

It remains for her lover, George Webber, to view the party and the behavior of her guests from the perspective of an observer. He can see what she will not, or cannot, see. George moves in and out of the activities of the party, but ultimately he is more clearly a Proustian onlooker than a participant. He penetrates the surface glitter of this wealthy, sophisticated gathering and sees Esther's guests as they really are. His growing awareness of the guests' corruption—and of his own potential for being swept down into their moral cesspool—enables him, finally, to leave this illusory world, even though he must sacrifice his love for Esther in going his own way. He now perceives that he faces the disillusionment of youth and the aching knocks of experience: "To see the starred face of the night with a high soul of exaltation and of noble aspiration, to dream great dreams, to think great thoughts. And in that instant have the selfless grandeur turn to dust, and to see great night itself, a reptile coiled and waiting in the nocturnal blood of life." In lifting the veil and seeing the ugliness and inherent danger of this world, George catches more than a glimpse of the serpent in Esther's paradise of love and chooses to cast himself out while he still has the will to do so.

George's keen vision helps readers see each character with penetrating awareness: The beautiful and seductive Lily Mandell is "corrupt and immodest." Stephen Hook, damned and tormented, assumes a mask of disdain and boredom and is too self-conscious to allow himself to respond honestly to Esther's delight and gratitude at his generous gift of a book of Brueghel's drawings. Roberta Heilprinn is cool and manipulative, acting not spontaneously but out of some planned strategy to exert her control over others. Even Esther, George notes, like her friend and counterpart, Roberta, manipulates others with her deceptive innocence. It is Amy Van Leer who symbolizes the tragic waste and corruption of this decadent age, her broken and fragmented speech and consequent inability to communicate except by frenzied, half-articulated phrases personifying a corruption and impending decay almost as old as civilization itself: "her life seemed to go back through aeons of iniquity, through centuries of vice and dissipation . . . [like] the dread Medusa . . . some ageless creature, some enchantress of Circean cunning whose life was older than the ages and whose heart was old as Hell." Wolfe leaves no doubt that the serpent has wholly claimed this wastelandish flapper.

He worked tirelessly on the chapter entitled "Mr. Hirsch Was Wounded Sorrowfully," creating several variants until he was satisfied with his cutting counterpoint depicting the tired lust and bored ennui of the partygoers. The social chatter of the rich whose indiscriminate lust for wealth and power creates the misery of the poor rings with "political correctness." Only Mr. Robert Ahrens is depicted as a genuine human being. He does not engage in empty conversation and refuses to be baited by Lily Mandell when she asks him about the writer Beddoes. Ahrens's knowledge is real, not a contrived pastiche like that of Lawrence Hirsch. Amidst the glitter and meaningless chatter, he moves quietly, not engaging in conversation but actually browsing through books in Esther's library, in contrast to Piggy Logan, who pulls volumes from the shelves and hurls them to the floor.

Young and old, man and woman, they were an ark of lost humanity drifting, doomed, toward some eventual disaster:

> Well, here they were then, three dozen of the highest and the best, with shimmer of silk, and ripple of laughter, with the tumultuous babel of fine voices, with tinkle of ice in shell-thin glasses, and with silvern clatter, in thronging webs of beauty, wit and loveliness—as much passion, joy, and hope, and fear, as much triumph and defeat, as much anguish and despair and victory, as much sin, viciousness, cruelty and pride, as much base intrigue and ignoble striving, as

much unnoble aspiration as flesh and blood can know, or as a room can hold—enough, God knows, to people hell, inhabit heaven, or fill out the universe—were all here, now, miraculously composed, in magic interweft—at Jack's.

As Piggy Logan prepares his wire circus, his admiring claque of socialites rudely enters the Jacks' apartment. Amy, offended by their slight of her beloved Esther, utters her only complete sentences of the evening: "Six little vaginas standing in a row and not a grain of difference between them. Chapin's School last year. Harvard and their first—this! All these little Junior League bitches." Piggy Logan's circus is a grotesque parody of art. His "celebrated sword swallowing act" is a brutal display of ignorance, obscene in its banality. Indeed, the guests themselves seem to be little more than hollow dummies: the young society girl speaking through motionless lips; Krock, the depraved sculptor, making crudely aggressive sexual advances; and even Esther herself forcing George and her closest friend upon each other and enticing them to engage in sexual promiscuity. Finally, the depravity of the party-goers becomes too much for George to endure. He understands that if he remains in this jaded world of illusion and glitter, he too will be destroyed.

After the party, the noises of the great city once again enter the Jacks' apartment; the cause is the outbreak of a fire in the building. Almost immediately the intimate little group remaining with Esther undergoes some frenzy when it hears the sirens and smells smoke, but eventually everyone joins the "ghostly" procession and leaves the building. The honeycomb of the apartment building takes on an atmosphere of unreality as the dim lights and thick, acrid smoke cast a haze over this world. Wolfe makes this frightening ordeal of escape a kind of hell. From this strange world, a "tide of refugees . . . marched steadily" out of the building. It seems as if, the old order destroyed as in Frederick's dream, all humanity comes together in "an extraordinary and bizarre conglomeration—a parade of such fantastic quality as had never been witnessed in the world before." The lover is moved by this "enormous honeycomb of life," young and old, rich and poor, speaking together a babel of languages representative of all the languages of mankind. Indeed, the apartment building itself seems a little world representative of the larger world of the city, "with a whole universe of flesh, and blood, a world incarnate with all the ecstasy, anguish, hatred, joy, and vexed intrigue that life could know." Only a great writer or painter like Shakespeare or

Brueghel (or Wolfe perhaps) can present the enormity of such a spectacle. George realizes that this great event unraveling before him, this symphonic sweep of brotherhood and humanity, seems to take on the majesty of a vision, and he notes as well a sense of prophetic doom. For this mass of humanity gathered before him seems like victims of some great shipwreck, like the *Titanic*, "all the huge honeycomb of life . . . assembled now, at this last hour of peril, in a living fellowship—the whole family of earth, and all its classes, at length united on these slanting decks." Man is indeed united in the vast honeycomb of life, and every action is ineluctably interwoven.

Eventually the fire is brought under control and the crowd is dispersed, but there is a sense of foreboding within the small group taking refuge in a little drugstore nearby. These "lords and masters of the earth" have for a moment relinquished the illusion of control to which they have become accustomed. They are like "shipwrecked voyagers . . . caught up and borne onwards, as unwitting of the power that ruled them as blind flies fastened to the revolutions of a wheel." Like Hemingway's ants upon a burning log, Wolfe's inhabitants are little more than insects blinded to the larger world beyond their small realities and propelled from life to death by forces greater than their own.

The various cells in which concurrent action is taking place are exposed for us to see. For example, in the vast hive of the tunnels beneath the apartment building decisions are being made that will affect the lives of 500 train passengers traveling outward to their individual destinies, and some design begins to formulate itself: "lights changed and flashed . . . poignant as remembered grief, burned there upon the checkerboard of the eternal dark." As the men in the train tunnel work to restore "order," firemen free the bodies of two trapped elevator operators whose deaths will be noted by a hardened reporter in the few lines he files with his newspaper.

Faced with a common danger, these Park Avenue apartment dwellers and their high-society guests had mingled with maids, butlers, cooks, and other workers and had briefly felt a common bond of humanity. With the all-clear signal, the privileged class returns to the building with the assorted retainers. The old order is quickly reestablished. Nothing has really changed; the sense of brotherhood, indeed, the prophetic hope for the future, has vanished like smoke from the extinguished fire, as the old "ordered formality" and "cold restraint" once more prevail. Class animosity boils up again when Esther feels bruised by Henry's cold and unyielding lack of response. She longs for what she will probably never again have, the cordial and familiar humanity of someone like John Enborg and Herbert Anderson.

Like her lover, Esther is aware that something great and perilous has happened, something that somehow threatens their very lives: "When you think of how sort of *big*—things have got— . . . And how a fire can break out in the same building where you live and you won't even know about it—I mean, there's something sort of *terrible* about it, isn't there?" She is aware as well of the greatness of the spectacle in which both she and George have been participants and observers. But when she attempts to return the world to just the two of them, to the fantasy of the "good child's" dream, George realizes that he has already left her behind.

George now knows that his allegiances lie elsewhere. George must search for that vaster world, the world of fellowship, deprivation, and social injustice awaiting an articulate voice. Esther is indeed noble and worthy of his love if viewed in isolation from her class, but she is doomed like the others; and if George stays, he too will perish. Two good men have already perished, their deaths the direct result of their eagerness to serve the class that the Jacks represent. "The dark green wagon . . . with a softly throbbing motor" that removes the bodies of the dead is reminiscent of the earlier imagery of automobiles, vehicles associated with the frenzied life of a money-grubbing city. As Mr. Jack prepares for sleep, he feels that peace has been restored. "It was so solid, splendid, everlasting and so good. And it was all as if it had always been—all so magically itself as it must be saved for its magical increasements, forever." Yet the reader, remembering the tremors that Frederick has felt before and now senses again, understands that all is not the same. The world that Jack has built, the world of moneyed luxury and power, is an endangered world, precipitously resting on a foundation now cracking apart.

In *The Party at Jack's*, Thomas Wolfe conceived and wrought to a virtually complete state a social fable of universal proportions, a work prefiguring other socially conscious themes and images in the Webber cycle, a work offering powerful and prophetic testimony of the writer he was striving to become.

EDITORIAL POLICY AND TEXT

. . .

To present *The Party at Jack's* as Wolfe left it in the hands of his new editor at Harpers's, Edward Aswell, we had two major questions to answer: What material should we include? What kinds of textual flaws should we silently correct? Otherwise, we intended to reproduce Wolfe's words as we found them. Although Wolfe thought of this work as his "most densely woven piece of writing" (*Letters of Thomas Wolfe*, 653), it has never been published in its entirety. The piece by that title appearing in *Scribner's Magazine* (May 1939) was trimmed to fewer than 17,000 words by his agent, Elizabeth Nowell, and Aswell used a truncated version in *You Can't Go Home Again*.

Our silent corrections cover such typographical errors as transposed letters, missing letters, and the typists' failure to include opening or closing quotation marks. We silently corrected misspelled words (e.g., *ecstasy* for *ecstacy*) and changed commas to semicolons if, in our judgment, a comma splice created a misreading. We added capitals to proper nouns where lower-case letters appeared; we italicized the titles of books; we changed *Jacobs* to *Jack* and *Alice* to *Esther* in accordance with Wolfe's decision to use a different surname and given name in those instances where that change had not been made in the text; we added accent marks to foreign words and phrases as required by convention; we marked an ellipsis by three spaced periods instead of following the inconsistent practice of Wolfe's typists in their use of two to ten unspaced periods or two or more widely spaced hyphens; we added terminal periods that had not been typed, and we supplied, as needed,

commas before nouns of direct address. Although the name of the Jacks'
maid sometimes appeared as *Katy*, we used *Molly* throughout in accordance with Wolfe's greater frequency of use of the latter. After debating
whether to hold to the name *Will* for the elevator operator that the Jacks
attempt to have carry them to safety, we decided to use *John* in accordance with Wolfe's statement that elevator operators named *John* and
Herbert had died during the fire.

Our most substantial editorial act was to delete repetitive passages
occasioned by Wolfe's practice of rewriting an episode or section as he
added fresh material. Our guide through a maze of drafts was Wolfe's
outline as given in the Introduction. That outline, we are convinced,
forms the basis of the "single thing" Wolfe came to see as he reworked
the piece.

We incorporated Wolfe's handwritten corrections and followed his
directions for inserting additional handwritten or typed material, with
one exception. At the end of the typescript where Wolfe had changed
Mr. Jack to *Mrs. Jack*, and the pronouns accordingly, we left the wording
as it appeared in the typescript. From Nowell's notes to Aswell, we knew
that Wolfe's changes there were prompted by his hope of cutting the
piece for *Redbook*. Restoring the passage to its original state has the
added advantage of giving the piece the powerful thematic closure that
Wolfe intended.

Manuscript copy in the Wisdom Collection, some of it perhaps dating as early as 1930, begins with a draft of Frederick Jacobs's dream of his
boyhood days in Germany (bMS Am 1883 [932]) and continues through
fifteen additional sets (933–49), ending with lists of characters attending
the party, notes on the tunnels and cellars beneath the solid-looking
building on Park Avenue, and a page narrating Mrs. Jack's emergence
from her room to see whether everything is ready for her party. Most of
these hundreds of manuscript pages were later given to typists. Where
typists mistakenly read a word or phrase, Wolfe made corrections. On
these typewritten pages he sometimes added text interlinearly or in the
margins. Occasionally, he struck out words or sentences. Pages containing corrections and additions or deletions would then be retyped. Once
he reached this state, Wolfe rarely did more than correct typographical
errors. The two major exceptions to this practice occurred when he
sought to develop the characters and ideas of the elevator men more
fully and to introduce more guests at Esther's party. For these and
shorter passages elsewhere, he wrote additional copy, had it typed, and

marked in the original where in should be inserted. Occupied with these revisions at Oteen, he wrote Nowell in New York, "I am working on 'The Party at Jack's.' I have changed and revised it a great deal with an effort to weave it together better and to get it to move more quickly" (*Letters of Thomas Wolfe*, 635).

Copy text for this edition comes from material indexed in the Wisdom Collections as bMS Am 1883 (982), (983), (984), and (986). Material indexed under (985) apparently includes additions and revisions undertaken during Wolfe's Oteen sojourn and after his return to New York. Much of that revised material appears in the pages indexed as (986). It was from these pages that Nowell extracted the story published in *Scribner's Magazine*. Her choice of that draft indicates to us that it represents Wolfe's intent to use it as copy text in Part IV of the projected *You Can't Go Home Again*. Groupings (985) and (986) reflect changes representing Wolfe's decision to rework material originally written for "The October Fair" and that portion of it detailing Eugene Gant's break with Esther and her circle. Consequently, stylistic practices in (986) are in accord with the simpler, less poetic, leaner prose of his final period. Copy text for Book II of *You Can't Go Home Again*, as cut and revised by Aswell, comes from (982), (983), (984), and (986). A comparison of these pages with page proofs of the novel reveals that Aswell decided not to restore the Jacks' son to the story. He changed the names Amy Van Leer to Amy Carleton, Robert Fetzer to Samuel Fetzer, and Katy Fogarty to Nora Fogarty. He gave words that Wolfe had put in Mr. Jack's mouth to Mrs. Jack, and he added clarifying passages. For example, "Janie and May and Lily, in their trim, crisp uniforms and with their smiling, pink faces, were really awfully pretty" becomes "Janie and May, passing back and forth between the kitchen and the maids' sitting room in their trim, crisp uniforms and their smiling, pink faces, were really awfully pretty." He dropped a few of the guests that Wolfe had on hand for the party, perhaps because he feared legal action if he kept them in. Our text is entire and untouched except for the silent corrections and omissions of repetitive passages.

We find in these pages as reassembled what Wolfe hoped Nowell would discover when he mailed his revisions back to her from Oteen— "unity and the direction of a single thing" (*Letters of Thomas Wolfe*, 653).

ACKNOWLEDGMENTS

. . .

Our indebtedness to persons and institutions for help, encouragement, and funding begins with Paul Gitlin, administrator of the Thomas Wolfe estate. To him we are deeply grateful. Various administrators at our universities, Pennsylvania State and Clemson, supported our efforts: from Penn State, English department head Robert Secor, Deans Margaret Leidy, Raymond Lombra, Leonard Mustazza, and Jack Royer; from Clemson, Dean Robert Waller and English department head James Andreas. Not the least of their commitments to this project were the sabbatical leaves we enjoyed. We express our thanks to Richard S. Kennedy, Aldo P. Magi, Harold Woodell, Carol Johnston, James Clark, David Strange, Ted Mitchell, Melinda M. Ponder, Darlene O'Dell, Susan Hilligoss, and the Houghton Reading Room staff.

For her belief in the worth of this project, we thankfully acknowledge the encouragement we received from Sandra Eisdorfer of the University of North Carolina Press.

John Idol expresses personal gratitude to Clemson's English department for granting him one of the John Lane awards, to the National Endowment for the Humanities for a travel grant, to the Thomas Wolfe Society for a William B. Wisdom Grant in Aid of Research, and to Adelaide Wisdom Benjamin for the gift that funded the Wisdom Grant.

Suzanne Stutman expresses her thanks to Penn State's Institute for the Arts and Humanistic Studies, the Research and Graduate Studies

Office, and the Office of the Associate Dean of the CES system for the grants that made this research possible.

Finally, we thank our families. Once again Fred and Marjorie proved themselves to be patient, understanding, interested, and wholly supportive.

THE PARTY AT JACK'S

. . .

MORNING

· · ·

"Hartmann!"

"Hier, Herr Professor."

"Das wort für *garten*."

"*Hortus*, Herr Professor."

"Deklination?"

"Zweite."

"Geschlecht?"

"Maskulinum, Herr Professor."

"Deklinieren!"

Hartmann stiffened his shoulders slightly, drew a deep breath, and, looking straight before him with a wooden expression, rapidly recited in an expressionless sing-song tone:

"Hortus, horti, horto, hortum, horte, horto; horti, hortorum, hortis, hortos, horti, hortis."

"So. Setzen sie, Hartmann."

Hartmann sat down blowing slightly at the corners of his thick mouth. For a moment he held his rigid posture, then he relaxed warily, his little eyes wavered craftily from side to side, he stole a look of triumph and of satisfaction at his comrades.

He was only a child in years, but his limbs and features held in miniature the mature lineaments of a man. He seemed never to have been young or child-like. His face was tough, sallow and colorless: the skin looked as thick and rough as a man's and it was covered unpleasantly with thick white hair which was not visible until one came close to him. His eyes were small, red, and watery looking and thickly lashed and

3

browed with the same silken, unpleasantly white, hair. His features were small, blunted, and brutal: the nose small and turned up and flattened at the tip, so that the nostrils had a wide flaring appearance, the mouth was coarse, blurred and indefinite, and the cheekbones also had a blunted flattened-out appearance.

Hartmann's head was shaved, a bluish stubble of hair covered it evenly, and the structure of the skull was ugly, mean, and somehow repellent: it seemed to slant forward and downward from the bony cage at the back of the brain to a pinched and painful brow. Finally Hartmann's body was meagre and stringy looking, but immensely tough, his hands were disproportionately large and raw, and dangled crudely and clumsily at his sides. Brutal in mind and body, neither his person nor his character was pleasing, and Frederick hated him. And this hatred Hartmann returned on him with cordial measure.

"Jack!"

Frederick did not hear that word of harsh command. His dark eye brooded into vacancy, his mind was fixed and lost in stellar distances, his spirit was soaring far away across the surging blue, the immense and shiny wink of an ocean that washed the shores of all the earth. And a channel of bright water led him straight to the goal of all his dreaming. Upon the decks of clean white river-steamers he went down the river Rhine. He went from Koblenz on to Bonn, from Bonn, to Köln, from Köln to Düsseldorf, and then through Holland to the sea. And then he put out to sea upon another mightier ship. The sea was blue and shining, but there was also gold upon it: it was never grey. The great ship foamed and lifted with a lordly prancing motion, like a horse, he felt the rock and swell, the infinite plangent undulance of the sea beneath that foaming keel, and the great ship rushed onward day by day into the west.

And now, after many days, Frederick saw before him the outposts of the land. He smelled the brave familiar fragrance of the land, the spermy sea-wrack and the warmth of earth, and he saw before him first pale streaks of sand, a low coast, and then faint pallid greens, and little towns and houses. Now, the ship entered the narrow gateways of the harbor, and now Frederick saw before him a great harbor busy with the play and traffic of a thousand boats. And he saw before him, at the harbor's base, a fabulous city, built upon an island. It swept upward from an opalescent cloud, from which it seemed to grow, on which it was upborne lightly, and as magical as a vision, and yet it was real and shining, and as solid as the rock on which it had been founded. And by the city flowed a river—"ein Fluss viel schoner als den Rhein"—a thing almost incredible, and yet it must be so, for Uncle Max had seen it, and sworn just the night before that it was true. Beyond the city was an immense, fertile, and enchanted land—"ein Land von unbegrenzte möglich keiten," Uncle Max had sworn, and surely Uncle Max had known, for he had come back from that country speaking its strange nasal accents, wearing its strange garments, rich with the tribute of its enormous bounty. And he had said that some day he would come and take Frederick back with him, and Frederick, dreaming of the wealth, the gold, the glory and the magic of that far shining city that floated upward from its cloud of mist hoped for this more than for anything on earth.

"Jack! Jack! Ist Friedrich Jack hier?"

He came to with a sharp start of confusion as that harsh and choleric voice broke in upon his revery, and the class whose attention had been riveted for some seconds on his dreaming face burst into a sharp and sudden yelp of glee as he scrambled frantically to his feet, straightened his shoulders, and stammered out confusedly,

"Hier, bitte. Ja. Ich bin hier."

That high and hateful face, hairless, skull-like, seamed and parchment dry, scarred hideously upon one sallow cheek, with its livid scorpion of saber wounds, and with thin convulsive lips drawn back above a row of big yellow teeth, now peered at him above its glasses with a stare of wall-eyed fury. In a moment the stringy tendons of the neck craned hideously above the choker collar, and the harsh voice rasped with fury as old Kugel's ramrod form bowed with a slightly ironic courtesy in its frock coat sheathing of funereal black.

"Wenn sie sind fertig, Excellenz," he said.

"Ja—Ja—fertig," Frederick stammered foolishly and incoherently, wondering desperately what the question was, and if it had already been asked. The class tittered with expectancy, and already unnerved by his shock and confusion, Frederick blurted out with no sense at all of what he was saying: "Ich meine—Ich bin fertig—Onkel!"

A sickening wave of shame and mortification swept over him the moment that he spoke the words, and as the instant roar of the class brought to him the knowledge of his hideous blunder. Onkel! Would he ever hear the end of this? And how could he have been such a fool as to identify, even in a moment of forgetfulness, this cruel and ugly old ape with the princely and heroic figure of his Uncle Max. Tears of shame welled in his eyes, he stammered out incoherent apologies and explanations that went unheard in the furious uproar of the class, but he could have bitten his tongue out for rage and mortification.

As for Kugel, he stood stock still, his eyes staring with horror, like a man who has just received a paralytic stroke. In a moment, recovering his powers of speech, and torn with fury between the roaring class and the culprit who stood trembling before him, he snatched up a heavy book, lifted it high above his head in two dry, freckled hands, and smashed it down upon the table with terrific force.

"Schweig!" he yelled. "Schweigen sie!" a command that was no longer necessary, since all of them had subsided instantly into a stunned cowed silence.

He tried to speak but could not find the words he wanted. In a moment, pointing a parched trembling finger at Frederick, he said in a small choked whisper of a voice:

"Das wort—das wort—für Bauer." He craned convulsively above his collar as if he was strangling.

Frederick gulped, opened his mouth and gaped wordlessly.

"Was?" screamed Kugel taking a step toward him.

"Ag-ag-ag!" he stuttered like a miserable idiot.

"Was!"

He had known the word a moment before—he knew it still, he tried frantically to recall it, but now, his fright, shame, and confusion were so great that he could not have pronounced it if he had had it written out before him on a piece of paper.

Desperately he tried again.

"Ag-ag-ag," but at the titter of laughter that began to run across the class again, he subsided helplessly, completely disorganized and unable to continue.

Kugel stared at him a moment over the rims of his thick glasses, his yellow bulging eyeballs fixed in an expression of hatred and contempt.

"Ag-ag-ag!" he sneered, with hateful mimicry. "Erst es war *onkel*— und jetzt müsst er den Schlucken haben!"

He regarded Frederick a moment longer with cold hate, and then dismissed him.

"Schafskopf! Setzen sie," he said.

Frederick sat down.

*　*　*　*　*

That day as the children were going away from school, he heard steps pounding after him and a voice calling to him, a word of command and warning raucous, surly, hoarse. He knew it was Albert Hartmann, and he did not stop. He quickened his step a little and walked on doggedly. Hartmann called again, this time with menace in his voice.

"Hey—Jack!" Frederick did not pause. "Excellenz! Onkel!" it cried with a jeering note.

"Ag—ag! Schafskopf!" At the last word, Frederick stopped abruptly and turned, his face flushed with anger. He was a small neat figure of a boy, well-kept, round-featured, with straight black hair and the dark liquid eyes of his race. His somewhat chubby face was ruddy and fresh colored, his neat blue jacket and his flat student's cap were of far better cut and quality than Albert Hartmann's, which were poorly made and of mean material, and his firm plump features had in them a touch of the worldly assurance and scornful complacency, the sense of material appraisal that the children of wealthy merchants sometimes have.

Hartmann pounded up, breathing thickly and noisily through the corners of his blunt ugly mouth. Then he seized Frederick roughly by the sleeve, and said:

"Well, Ag-ag, do you think you'll know the word next time he asks you? Have you learned your lesson? Hey?"

Frederick detached his sleeve from Albert Hartmann's grasp, and surveyed him coldly. He did not answer him. At this moment, Walter Grauschmidt, another of the boys in the class, came up and joined them. Albert Hartmann turned and spoke to him with an ugly grin.

"I was asking Ag—Ag here if he'd know the word for farmer the next time Kugel calls on him," he said.

"No. He'll never know the word for farmer," Walter Grauschmidt answered calmly, and with assurance. "He'll know the word for money. He'll know the word for cash. He'll know the word for interest and loan in every language in the world. But he'll never know the word for farmer."

"Why?" said Albert Hartmann looking at his more gifted and intelligent companion with a stupid stare.

"Why," said Walter Grauschmidt deliberately, "because he is a Jew, that's why. A farmer has to work hard with his hands. And there never was a Jew who would work hard with his hands if he could help it. He lets the others do that sort of work, while he sits back and takes the money in. They are a race of pawnbrokers and money lenders. My father told me." He turned to Frederick and spoke quietly and insultingly to him. "That's right, isn't it? You don't deny it, do you?"

"Ja! Ja!" cried Albert Hartmann excitedly, now furnished with the words and reasons he had not wit enough to contrive himself. "That's it! That's the way it is! A Jew! That's what you are!" he cried to Frederick. "You never worked with your hands in your life! You wouldn't know a farmer if you saw one!"

Frederick looked at them both silently, and with contempt. Then he turned and walked away from them.

"Yah! Pawnbroker! Your people got their start by cheating other people out of money! Yah!"

The hoarse and inept jibes followed him until he turned the corner of the street in which he lived. It was a narrow cobbled street of ancient gabled houses, some of which hung out with such a crazy Gothic overhang that they almost touched each other across the street. But the street was always neat and tidy. The houses were painted with bright rich colors and there were little shops with faded Gothic signs above them. The old irregular cobbles had a clean swept appearance, and the old houses were spotless in their appearance. The stones and brasses seemed always to have been freshly scrubbed and polished, the windows glittered like flat polished mirrors, and the curtains in the windows were always crisp, fresh and dainty looking. In Spring and Summer, the window ledges were gay with flower boxes of bright geraniums.

In an old four-story house half way down this little street, Frederick lived with his mother, a sister, his uncle and his aunt. His father had died several years before, and had left his family a comfortable, although not a great, inheritance. And now his uncle carried on the family business.

They were a firm of private bankers and they had always borne a respected name. Beginning with Frederick's grandfather, over sixty years before, the firm had carried on its business in the town of Koblenz. And it had always been assumed, without discussion, that Frederick also would go into the firm when he had finished school.

Frederick went along the pleasant ancient street until he came to the old house where he lived. In this house, members of his family had lived for eighty years. His bedroom was on the top floor of the house. It was a little gabled room below the eaves and at night before he went to sleep he could hear the voices of people passing in the street, sometimes a woman's laughter suddenly, and sometimes nothing but footsteps which approached, passed, and faded with a lonely echoing sound.

The street ended in a broad tree-shaded promenade that crossed it at right angles and which was one of the leading thoroughfares of the town.

Beyond that was the river Rhine.

MORNING

· · ·

JACK ASLEEP

· · ·

Jack thought he had gone back home to visit his family. Although his uncle had been dead for twenty years, and his aunt for twelve, and his sister was now an elderly married woman, with grown-up children of her own, who lived in Frankfort, and his mother was an old woman in the seventies, it seemed to Jack that they were all living in the old house in the Weinfass Gasse, and that none of them had grown any older. He was himself a spruce, smartly groomed, grey-haired man, but no one seemed to notice this. Everyone treated him as if he was a child, and as if he had been away from home for forty days, instead of forty years.

But now that he was back among them, he was haunted day and night by intolerable images of fear and pity. Nothing around him seemed to have changed one jot. The old house in the Wine-Cask Street looked just the same as it had always looked, and when he entered a room it leaped instantly into all its former life for him and he remembered the place of every minute object in it, even the place in an old wooden clock where the winding-key was kept, although these were things he had not thought of for many years. And the heavy deliberate tock of the old clock in the silent room suddenly awoke, with its own single character of time, the memory of a thousand winter evenings when he had bent above his book under the warm light of the table lamp, and had felt time slowly wear away around him, the grey ash of its slow intolerable fire.

9

These images of the past returned to him instantly, and they filled him with weariness and horror. Everything was as familiar as it was the day he left it, and yet it was stranger than a dream. He had returned to all that he had known and was part of, and yet it no longer seemed a part of him. It seemed incredible that it had ever been a part of him, and its very familiarity filled his soul with terror and unbelief. And this same doubt and terror chilled his heart when he thought of all the years since childhood that he had spent in America, and of the life he had lived there. The old life of his youth had instantly possessed him with all its terror of strangeness and familiarity and now it seemed impossible to believe that he had ever been away.

Then, Jack thought he went to bed in the little room of his childhood and that he dreamed he had gone to America, and that all his life there had been nothing but a dream. He thought he awoke suddenly at dawn to hear a cart rumbling on the narrow cobbled street below and to think for a moment that he was in New York. Then he would sweat with horror for it seemed that he belonged to nothing he had known, and could never tell whether his life had been a dream or a reality, or whether he had ever known a home or made a voyage. And it seemed to him that he was doomed forever to be a traveller upon the illimitable and protean ocean of time, borne constantly across its stormy seas upon a dark phantasmal ship that never reached a port, haunted forever by dreams of homes and cities he had never known. Grey horror gripped him. The snake of desolation ate his heart.

Yet, it seemed to Jack that his family saw nothing strange in his appearance or demeanour. He had returned to them, but he was still a boy of seventeen to them. He looked into the mirror in his little room, and he saw the grey hair and the worldly features of a man past fifty. This was the self he knew and saw, but his mother, his aunt, his uncle, his sister, his cousin, Karl, and the servant Anna, saw no change in him at all. And just as nothing in the street or house had changed a jot, so all of them looked just the same age as they had looked when he was seventeen.

Moreover when he tried to speak to them, he found he had forgotten his native German tongue. He understood every word they spoke to him, yet when he tried to answer a strange wordless jargon broke harshly from his lips, filling his heart with shame and terror. And yet they seemed to know just what he wished to say, and answered him without surprise.

Alone, with fear slow-feeding with its poisonous lip against his heart, he would try to speak to himself in English, but the words came rustily with a guttural outlandish accent, strange and difficult to his own ears and, he felt, incomprehensible to others. It seemed that he was tongue-less, homeless, and a phantom, that he belonged to nothing, was sure of nothing, and that his whole life might be nothing but an image in the dream of time.

Jack thought he had returned to his own people for only a short visit and yet, at the very instant of returning, he was filled with horror and desolation to the roots of his soul, and with a desire to escape as soon as possible. But, escape where? He was no longer sure of his own life in America, or that he had ever been there, and the thought of his return there filled him with the same doubt, horror, and confusion. And his family treated him as if he had returned to live with them forever, and was still a child. They lavished upon him the kind of tenderness and affection that people lavish on a beloved child who has returned from a long journey, and their incessant kindness, their constant efforts to amuse, interest, and delight him choked him with a sense of furious exasperation and indignity, and at the same time with an unutterable rending pity. Their eager attentions, their constant solicitude, their glee-ful certainty that the childish entertainment they had prepared for him was just the thing that would enrapture him rasped his nerves to a frenzied irritation. Hot and angry words rose to his lips, words of curt refusal, angry requests that he be given an hour's peace and privacy alone, but when he tried to speak them he could not. They were them-selves like children in their eager innocence, and to answer their tender love, to repay their pitiable preparations, with sharp and angry words would have been like meeting the love of children with a blow.

Yet, their well-intentioned kindliness was maddening. On his arrival, they had all insisted on panting up the steps behind him to his room. The little room beneath the gables that he had slept in as a child had been made ready for him, but now it seemed small and cramped. The same bed he had slept in as a boy was spread tightly with clean coarse linen sheets and pillows, and covered with the fat pleated yellow comfor-ter beneath whose warmth he had lain snugly as a child but which would now only warm his feet and legs while his shoulders froze, or cover back and neck, while feet congealed. He wondered how he could ever fit into such a bed, or find repose on the granite hardness of its two thick mattresses, or wash himself out of the little half-pint bowl and pitcher which sat tidily upon its school boy's washstand, or dry his face upon the scrap of towel, or crouch down low enough to see to shave himself in the little square of mirror in whose mottled surface the face blurred, swelled, or contracted with a mercurial uncertainty.

But they all stood around and beamed and winked at one another gleefully as if his heart must be simply bursting with speechless rapture in face of all this luxury. Anna,—Die Grosse Anna—the servant who had worked for his family as long as he could remember waddled heavily to the bed and pranced her stiffened fingers up and down on it a dozen times, turning to look at him triumphantly as if to say: "What do you think of that, hey?"

Then Anna and his mother had made him sit down upon the bed and bounce up and down on it in an experimental manner, while all the others stood and looked on admiringly. He had obliged them dutifully, but suddenly, as he was bouncing up and down there like a fool, he had looked straight into the little mirror and seen his image, bobbing clownishly, reflected there. He saw his face, the plump, ruddy face of a well-kept man of fifty-four, the neat grey moustache, crisply trimmed, and twisted at its ends into waxed points, the clipped grey hair, neatly parted in the middle, the straight square shoulders set-off trimly with a coat that fit him beautifully, the crisp business like style of the collar and the rich dull fabric of his necktie, with the white carnation in his buttonhole. It was the figure of a man of mark and dignity, but now he saw it disfigured by a foolish simpering leer, and prancing up and down upon a bed like an idiot. It was intolerable, intolerable, and suddenly Jack began to choke with speechless rage.

But everyone stood around him goggle eyed and gap-jawed with a look of rapture, and Anna said to him with exultant satisfaction: "Ah, I tell you what! It's good to be back in your own bed again, isn't it, Mr. Freddy? I'll bet you thought of it many's the time while you were gone. Hey? I thought so!" the old fool said triumphantly, although he had said nothing. "Sleeping among all those foreigners," the ignorant woman cried contemptuously, "in beds you don't know who's been in the night before! Well, Mister Freddy," she went on in a bantering tone, "home's not such a bad place after all, is it?" She prodded him stiffly with her thick red fingers, chuckling craftily.

Jack stared at her with an expression of apoplectic horror. *This, this,* Great God, to a man who had gone out and conquered the great world and who had known all the luxury and wealth that world could offer.

This to a man who lived only in the best hotels when he travelled anywhere, whose room at home was a chamber twenty feet each way,—yes, by God, a room twenty feet each way in a city where every foot of space was worth its weight in gold.

Then his cousin Karl, winking at him drolly, had opened the door of the little walnut cabinet beside the bed and sharply rapped a knuckle against the chamber-pot with a mellow echoing ping. All the others had screamed with laughter, coarsely, while he sat there foolishly with a burning face. Were they mad? Was it a clownish joke that they were playing on him? But when he looked into their faces and saw the depth of love and tenderness in them he knew that it was not and the words of hot anger were silenced on his lips.

In the morning, before he was up, he heard Anna toiling heavily up the ancient winding stairs. Broad and red of face and breathing stertorously, she entered, bearing a tray with a silver pot, an enormous cup and saucer of fine thin china, a crispy flaky roll and a pot of jam. Eagerly, Jack seized the handle of the silver pot, tilted the tall frail spout into the cup and then discovered that the pot contained hot thick chocolate instead of the strong black coffee which he had had for thirty years, and must have now. But when he demanded irritably of Anna if she had no coffee, and why she had not brought it to him, she looked at him first with an expression of stupefaction, and then with alarm and reproach.

"Why, Mister Freddy," she said chidingly, "you've always had your chocolate every morning of your life. Surely you haven't gone and started drinking coffee while you were away. Why, what would your mother say if she knew you'd gone and formed the coffee-habit? You know she'd never let you have it. Ach! That's what comes of all this gadding about and going to America," she muttered. "It's Mister Max who got you into this—with all his crazy Yankee ways he's picked up over there—oranges for breakfast, if you please!—Gott!—putting all that acid in your stomach before you've got any solid food in you—I told your mother when you left—I said that something of this sort would happen—'He's not to be trusted with that child!' I said. 'You mark my words, you let him go with Mr. Max and something will happen you'll be sorry for!' Come, now, Freddy" she said coaxingly and with a bantering jocosity that infuriated him, "Drink your nice chocolate that I made for you while it's good and hot. It's just the thing you need." Then, seeing the angry protest in his face, she relented a little, saying: "Well, I'll ask your mother if you can have a cup of coffee for your Second Breakfast. If she says it's all right, I'll make it for you."

Zweite Frühstück! He had forgotten that abomination! At nine o'clock in the morning beer, sausages, sauerkraut, cold cut meats, and liverwurst, pumpernickel, butter, jam—and beer again! Bah! He started to tell her savagely that, so far as he was concerned, there would be no second breakfast; he'd have coffee, toast, two eggs and orange juice right now, or not at all. Yes, by God! And he'd put an end to this Mister Freddy business once for all. Did this old fool think he was a schoolboy that he should have to whine and wheedle like a ninny for a cup of coffee? Ask his mother!

The sense of injury and indignity rose up choking in his throat. Why, damn them all, he'd show them if he was to be treated like a child in arms. He'd show them that they had a grown man to deal with, who had gone out and faced the world alone, and made his own way in a foreign country while the rest of them stayed home and went to seed in a one horse town. Where would they all be now if it hadn't been for him? Who had moved heaven and earth during the war to get food through to them? Who had smuggled, bribed, pulled wires, wrote letters, sweated blood, made use of every stratagem and exerted every influence, and spared no labor and expense to keep them all from starving? Whose money had kept them going in the years that followed the Armistice? Who was it? Oh, they knew, they knew well enough! Mister Freddy was the boy! And was the man who had done all this to ask permission of his mother to drink a cup of coffee? By God, he did not think so!

Yet, when he looked up with a tongue of fierce reproof, he saw Anna's broad red face, which had in it all the love, the loyalty, the concern, and simple trust of those innocent and child-like people who spend their lives in serving others, and whose lives are lived only in the lives of those they serve and love. When Jack saw this, he could not speak the hot and angry words. Instead, his heart was twisted in him with wild nameless pity. It seemed to him that his life had been steeped in all the hard and iniquitous dyes of the great earth, that he could never recapture his lost innocence again, nor make these people understand the man be had become. To them he was still the child who had left them; to him they seemed themselves like children. The strange dark light of time fell over him, and he had no tongue to utter what he wished to say.

Then his mother came and sat beside him, her dark convulsive face marked deep with pride and tenderness. And one by one the others came and stood fondly around his bed; wild fury choked him, shame covered him, pain and pity stabbed his heart, but they stood round him while he dressed.

They were always with him. They were with him in the house and in the garden. They were with him when he went out in the street. They watched him eat, they came to watch him when he bathed. Each night they ushered him to bed, and every morning they were standing round him when he woke. He was never for a moment free of them, he had not a moment's peace or privacy; horror, boredom, a feeling of loss and agony drowned his spirit. He turned on them to curse them with all the fury of his maddened and exasperated flesh, but when he looked into their faces alive with love and tenderness his heart was torn with wild pity, and he could not speak.

In the house it was always night or morning. In the street it was always morning, and under the lime trees in the garden behind the house where bright geraniums grew, it was always afternoon. And they were always with him. They prodded him with gleeful fingers, they winked at him with knowing and secretive winks, they rubbed their hands in exultant anticipation, as they hinted, darkly, at some new delight they had prepared for him. Sometimes it was Anna with something held behind her back: a plate covered with a napkin—"Guess what's here?" He could not. It would be a heavy peach-cake, glutinous with its syrups, and covered with a luscious inch-thick coat of "schlagsahne." And with beer! Great God! With beer! His stomach turned against this richness, his Yankee notions cautioned a trim girth for business men, and careful diets, and his man-like dignity cursed with rage because a mature and worldly man must grin and gloat like a boy over a cookie which a fool of an old woman had given him. Nevertheless, he took it smiling, trying to show the right degree of stupefied surprise and ecstasy the old woman expected him to feel.

Then the others rubbed their hands exultantly as they hinted at surprises, or told him of delights in store for him. On Monday they were invited out to Uncle Abe's for dinner—his heart sank down with leaden weariness; on Wednesday Cousin Jake was coming with his wife for tea—his flesh turned grey with apathy; on Sunday—oh! he'd grin all over when he heard what they had planned for Sunday!—they were taking the Rhine-boat for a picnic in the woods across the river ten miles up, after which they would cross by ferry, and walk home again.

Desolation.

Jack thought that he endured it all—dinner at Uncle Abe's together with young Abie's stamp collections, and songs and selections at the piano by young Lena afterwards; tea with the family and Cousin Jake and his wife Sadie, and all that pompous fool's smart-Aleck questions about America—which he had never visited but which he could talk about, of course, with all his customary conceit, assurance, and un-fathomed ignorance.

Jack endured it all—food, weddings, the interminable family gather-ings, and reunions, funerals, gossip, visits and receptions. He endured all the questions endlessly repeated and patiently answered to circles of dark oily faces, smiling with benignant and approving pride above fat paunches comfortably crossed by hands. He endured the picnics up the river and the long walks back, blistered feet and prehistoric plumbing, beer evenings of a sodden jollity in enormous and cavernous drinking halls, thick with a murk of smoke, glutinous with the warmth and odor of a thousand heavy bodies and roaring with the thick mixed tumults of guttural voices and Wagnerian music.

Jack endured it all, and fear ate like a vulture at his heart, desolation rested in his bowels, and his heart was torn with nameless horror and pity as he saw how like a ghost he had become to all that was a part of him, to everything with which his life was most familiar. And always time lay feeding at his heart. It crept along the channels of his blood, it grew within his flesh and flowered in his brain like a grey and cancerous plant. He lay tranced below its hypnotic pressure, like a rabbit caught and held under the baleful spell of a serpent's eye, he was powerless to act or move, but always he was conscious of his life wasting and consum-ing fatally under the strange dark light of time. In his heart there dwelt forever the horror of a memory, almost captured, of a word almost spoken, of a decision almost understood and made. The knowledge of some great labor left undone, of a terrible duty unfulfilled, of the irrevo-cable years that had been passed and wasted and of friends and works forgot while he lay tranced and stricken by time's sorcery, haunted him day and night, but what the goal, the labor, and the duty were, he could not say.

Smoke! His life was passing like a dream under the strange and terrible visages of time, and Jack sought for some door he could enter, and he found none open. He longed for some goal and home and harbor, and he had nowhere to go.

Then, out of the old house where all lay sleeping he crept one day into the high and ancient street where all the houses tottered and leaned together like conspiring crones and where bright sunlight cut cool depths of Gothic shadows and where it was always morning.

✻   ✻   ✻   ✻   ✻

Now Jack was walking in an ancient cobbled street, but not the one he lived in. The old gabled houses with their mellow timbers, their bright rich colors, and their high Gothic overhang seemed to bend and lean like old live things above the narrow cobbled ways, conferring quietly in all the attitudes of familiar personal intimacy. They had a look of old witch-haggery, crone-like, wise and ancient, and yet unmalign. They were like old benignant wives and gossips of the town huddled above some juicy morsel of town scandal, and yet they seemed innocent and familiar.

Although the street was hundreds of years old, it had a quality that was wonderfully fresh and living. The slow wear and waste of time, the rich alluvial deposits of centuries seemed only to have given to the street a richer and profounder sort of life. This life had not only entered or worked its way into the old houses, it had also got into the cobbles and the narrow pavements before the houses, giving a line of life, a rich and vital color to everything. The old timbers of the houses were seasoned in the hues of time, and even in the warp and wave of ancient walls, in the sag and bend of roofs and basements, there was a rich undulant vitality which only time could bring. Moreover, all harsh lines and angles seemed to have been rubbed and softened by this slow enormous chemistry of time. And this chemistry had given the street a warmth and life which seemed to Jack to make it not only richer in quality, but somehow more young and wholesome than the streets of home.

The street sprang instantly into living unity, with a tone and quality which was incomparable and unique, and yet the houses were richly varied by all the colors and designs of an elfin and capricious architecture. But in comparison to this street, a street at home with its jargon of ugly and meaningless styles, its harsh pale colors broken with gloomy interspersions of dingy grey and rusty brown, the prognathous rawness of apartment houses, lofts, and office buildings of new raw brick or glaring stone, that ranged from dreary shambles of two stories to forty glittering floors of arrogant steel and stone, the ragged confusion of height, and the beaten weariness of grey pavements bleakly worn by a million feet, seemed sterile, raw, and lifeless in its senseless and chaotic fury.

It was morning, the sun cut crisply and yet with an autumnal mellowness into the steep old shadows of the street. The sun felt warm and drowsy, but in the shadows of the houses Jack felt at once the premonitory breath of frost.

Before one of the old houses a woman with thick mottled arms and wide solid-looking hams was down upon her hands and knees, vigorously "going for" the stone step before a door. Jack noticed that the step was of old red stone, worn and hollowed deeply by the feet of four hundred years, and at the same time he noticed that the street and pavement was made of this same red stone, and had been worn, rounded, and enriched by time just as everything else had been. The woman who was scrubbing the stone finished, and got up like a strong clumsy animal. Her face was red, flushed triumphantly by her labor, and with a swift motion of her thick red hand she brushed back some strands of blown hair. Then she seized the bucket of grey sudsy water and dashed it out into the gutter. Finally she began to talk loudly and cheerfully to a woman who was passing along the other side of the street with an enormous market basket on her arm. And Jack felt that all of this was just as it had always been. All his former sensations of strangeness and phantasmal unreality had vanished. He felt secure and certain and exultant. He seemed always to have known this street, and all the people in it, and this knowledge gave him a feeling of the most extraordinary happiness he had ever known.

A man rode slowly by upon a bicycle. The man wore a flat cap, he had a straight stiff collar and wore a stringy necktie. He had on a belted coat, and he wore thick solid shoes and long black woollen stockings. He pedalled with deliberate care, pausing at the apex of his stroke, while his wheel wobbled perilously on the cobbles, and pedalling downward with a strong driving motion that sent him swiftly forward again. The man had a small lean face, a little bristly tuft of moustache, and hard muscular jaws that writhed unpleasantly. Jack was sure he knew this man. And all along the street there were small shops with panes of leaded glass and little bells that tinkled as one entered. Some had old wooden signs that hung out in the streets before them, and some had Gothic lettering of rich faded colors on the wall of the house above the shop. The windows were crammed to bursting with fat succulent looking sausages, rich pastries, chocolate, rolls and bread, flasks of wine or bundles of cigars made of strong coarse looking tobacco. And Jack knew that when one entered the shop the proprietor would greet him with a long, droll, gutturally friendly "Mo-o-o-rgen!"

Jack did not know why he was walking in this street, but he knew that a meeting with someone he had known was impending, and this certain knowledge increased the feeling of joy and security he had already. And suddenly he saw them all about him in the street—the friends and schoolmates of his youth—and he knew instantly why he was there among them.

And now another curious fact appeared. Here were the companions of his early years in the grammar school, and here were those he had known later in the gymnasium. He knew and recognized them instantly, and yet he saw with a sense of sorrow and without surprise that all of them had grown old. He had seen none of them since his childhood, and now the children he had known had grown into old men with worn eyes and wrinkled faces. Jack saw this instantly and yet it caused him no surprise; when he looked at them he could see they were old men but he seemed to look straight through their old faces into the faces of the children he had known. And the moment that he saw them they came to him and grasped him by the hand. They spoke to him with kindly friendship and with no surprise or questioning, and there was something infinitely sorrowful, weary, and resigned in their voices.

Then they were sitting all together at a pleasant table in an old beer house, looking with quiet eyes into the street. The waiter came to take their order, and they ordered beer. Jack saw that the waiter was a heavily built man of middle age who walked with a heavy limp. His head was shaven, he wore a long apron that went from neck to ankles and that had been woven out of a coarse blue thread. The man had a kindly brutal face, and the same quiet and sorrowful eyes the others had. He said "Was soll es sein?" in a gruff and friendly tone, taking their orders with a rough male friendliness and limping away to fill them.

They sat at a table of old dark wood, scored and carved with many deep initials and shining with the cleanliness of countless scrubbings. The place was vast and deep; it was full of old dark woods and cool depths, and the strong wet reek of beer came freshly on the air.

With Jack sitting at the table and looking out into the street were Walter Grauschmidt, Paul Heyst, and Ludwig Berniker. Ludwig had become a mountain of a man, with a bald, shining, completely hairless head and a swinish face. And yet the head and face had also a profound and massive strength, a curious and tragic mixture of swinish gluttony and lonely and sorrowful thought, as if the beast and the angel of the race had come together there. Jack had seen these faces in his youth ten thousand times, and they had haunted his memory with the enigma of their bestial and hateful swinishness and their massive and lonely power and dignity, but now he noticed also that Ludwig's head was disfigured at the temple with a clean bullet hole, bluish and bloodless at the edges, and drilled cleanly through his brain. Then he remembered having heard that Ludwig who had served throughout the war as an officer of infantry had been killed, or it was thought, had killed himself, in the week before the Armistice. Yet neither this fact, nor the clean bullet hole in Ludwig's temple, caused Jack any surprise whatever.

Instead, a quiet and certain knowledge, an old and sorrowful acceptation which had no need or words, seemed to bind them all together as they sat at their pleasant table, looking out into the street. Then, as they sat there at their beer, looking with quiet eyes into the street, Jack saw the figure of his once hated enemy Hartmann, stumping by. And Hartmann, too, had grown old and battered. He also walked with a heavy limp, which he had got in the war, he was poorly and shabbily dressed, and he wore the flat cap of a working man.

Yet Jack knew him instantly, and with the same strange recognition that had no surprise in it. He jumped to his feet crying sharply, "Albert, Albert!", and Hartmann turned slowly, blinking and peering from right to left through small worn rheumy eyes like an old bewildered animal. Then Jack ran out into the street to greet him. But the sense of triumph, the moment of victory, which he thought would be the fruit of the encounter, had vanished. He was conscious only of a feeling of great warmth and affection for Hartmann, and of the sorrowful presence of time. Then Hartmann knew him, and to his horror he saw him make a movement towards his cap as if to take it off. But instead, he rubbed his hand clumsily and hesitantly upon his trousers leg before he grasped the hand that Jack held out to him. Then the two of them together went back into the beer hall and joined their friends where they all sat by the window. Hartmann greeted the rest of them shyly and awkwardly, and at first seemed ill at ease as if he thought this big cafe was much too fine for a working man. An immense weight of sorrow and dejection bowed him down and, at length, shaking his head slightly, he said quietly to Jack:

"Oh, Frederick, Frederick! I have known so much trouble in my life."

For a space the others had said nothing. Then Ludwig took his pipe out of his mouth and held it in the great mutton of his hand upon the table. Then he said quietly, in confirmation, "Ja-a-a. Ich weiss."

It was so quietly spoken that it seemed a whisper rather than a word, and suddenly it seemed to Jack that at the instant it was spoken all the others had confirmed it like an echo, and that in it was all the sorrowful and resigned wisdom of the earth. And yet he could not swear that anyone had spoken. They sat there quietly, in their strange communion of sorrow and kindliness, and resignation, they drew with slow meditation on their pipes and drank their beer.

It seemed to Jack now that all he had wanted to say to them need not be said. A thousand times he had looked forward to such a meeting. He had foreseen their wonderment and awe when they saw how fine a man he had become. It had thrilled him to think of the great figure he would cut among them when he returned and they would see him, not old and shabby and provincial as they were, but a man of urbane and distinguished manner, a man of high position in the great world, a man of power and quiet authority, who sat familiarly at dinner every day with famous people, and who dealt every day with sums of money which would have beggared their whole city. In years, they were no older than he was and yet their flesh was old and loose and sagging, while his was ruddy, plump and firm. Their teeth, clamped on their pipes, were old and blackened and decayed while his were still white and sound, cunningly braced and filled with gold and porcelain by the finest dentists, and everyone could see at once the difference between their cheap ill-fitting clothes and the expensive and "distinguished" garments which had been made for him by a London tailor. Here, for instance, was old Grauschmidt sitting at his side and wearing an incredible wing-collar, a stringy little necktie, a shoddy little suit of an outlandish cut, with a funny little hat of green that had a brush of horsehair at the side of it. If he wore that outfit in New York he would have a crowd of urchins howling at his heels within five minutes, and yet, Jack felt none of the triumph and superiority he had expected to feel.

He had been eager to tell them of his wealth, his great possessions, of the glittering life he lived, and of the fabulous world he lived in. He wanted to tell them of his three expensive motor cars, and of his chauffeur to whom he paid over seven hundred marks a month—yes! with fine food and lodging for his family thrown in!—which was more than most of them could earn in three. He wanted to tell them of the great house he was building in the country which would cost him more than five hundred thousand marks when it was finished, and of the apartment in the city to which he had recently moved, and for which he paid a rent of more than fifty thousand marks a year. And he wanted to tell them of the four maids who got three hundred fifty marks a month apiece, and of his cook—a German woman!—whom he paid five hundred marks a month, and of his offices, where he paid two hundred thousand marks a year in rent, and where even the humblest of his fifty employees—even the office boys—were paid four hundred marks a month.

He had licked his chops in triumph a thousand times as he foresaw the look of stupefaction on their faces when he told this tale of magic. He could see the pipe poised halfway to the gaping mouth, and hear their guttural fascinated grunts of disbelief and wonder as he went on from height to dizzy height, telling his story quietly and modestly, without vain boasting or affectations. He would laugh good-naturedly at their astonishment, and when they asked him if such marvels as he had described were not almost unheard of, even in the legendary country where he lived, he would assure them they were not—that he was nothing but a minnow in an enormous pond, and that he had many friends who considered him a poor man—Ja! who spent and earned more in a month than he did in a year!

With fast-gathering impulse, in a tidal sweep of strong desire thicker and faster than his power to utter them, the images of splendor swept up from his memory. He would tell them of great buildings soaring eighty floors into the sky, and of towns the size of Koblenz housed within a single building. He would tell them of a city built upon a rock, and of tunnels bored below the whole length of the city through which at every moment of the day nameless hordes of men were hurled to destinies in little cells.

Then he would tell them of the night-time world of wealth and art and fashion in which he cut a figure. He would tell them of the style and wit and beauty of his daughter, and of pearl necklaces he gave her, and of money spent upon her clothes in one year's time that would keep a German family comfortably for ten. He would tell of the ability and shrewdness of his wife's sister—as smart a woman as ever lived!—and of her great position as vice president of a fashionable woman's store. He would speak casually of the four trips she made to Paris every year, and of the fortunes which the wives and mistresses of the millionaires spent every year for clothes. He would tell of the business ability of his only son, who was barely twenty-four, but who was prized and trusted like a man of forty by his employers, and who earned four hundred marks a week in a broker's office.

Finally he would tell them of his beautiful and talented wife. He would tell them of the high place she had won for herself in the art-world of the city, and of the famous people who knew her and respected her, and how celebrated men and women came and sat around his table every night, and how they called him "Fritz" and how he called them by their first names, and knew all the ways and secrets of their lives.

Jack had thought and dreamed of this triumphant moment for thirty years, but now that it had come, he could not talk to them. All that he had to say stormed wildly at the gates of speech, but when he tried to speak he could not. Instead, a fast thick jargon broke harshly from his lips, filling his ears with terror, and stirring the air about him with its savage dissonance. He paused, stricken to silence by that unaccustomed sound. He tried again; a speech that was no speech, a sound more brutal than the jargon of a tongueless maniac smote terror to his heart.

Now madness seized him. The veins swelled upon his forehead, his face grew purple with his rage and bafflement, he beat the table and shouted into their faces, he cursed, snarled, and jeered at them, but nothing but a bestial and incoherent jargon came from him. Then he saw that they were all looking at him with quiet and sorrowful eyes, and their look told him that they knew all, understood all that he had wished to say. And at the same moment it seemed to Jack that he heard that strange whispering echo—that sound filled with acquiescence, with the resigned and final knowledge of men who had known all that any men on earth could know—and which seemed to say, although he could not be certain any words were spoken: "Yes. We know."

He said no more. His friends were looking at him with their weary and sorrowful eyes in which there was neither any trace of envy or mockery, nor any of youth's pride or pain or passion. There was only the agreement of an old and final wisdom, an immense and kindly under-standing. Without speaking they seemed to say to him: "We know, we understand you, Frederick, because we have all been young and mad and innocent, and full of hope and anguish. We have seen the way the world goes, and we have seen we could not change it, and now we are old and have seen and known as much of it as men can know."

Now Jack no longer wanted to tell them of his triumphs in the world. He no longer wanted to boast about his wealth, his power, his family, or his high position. Instead, it seemed to him that for the first time in his life, his heart had been cleansed of vanity and pretense. He had for these men a feeling of trust and affection such as he never before had for anyone. And suddenly he wanted to talk to them as he had never talked to anyone, to say and hear the things he had never said and heard.

Like the Mariner who found that he could speak again as soon as he had blessed the living creatures in the sea, so now it seemed to Jack that he could speak and be free again if in penitence and shame he could unpack the sorrowful and secret burden that lay heavy on his heart. He wanted to ask the old men what their own youth had been like and if any of them had known the bitter misery of loneliness and exile in a foreign land. He wanted to tell them the secret dreams and visions of his youth which he had never told to anyone and to hear what dreams and visions they had known. He wanted to tell them of the first years of his life in America, of his little room in a boarding-house, and of the little room he had lived in later in his uncle's house, and how, forlorn, lonely, poor and wretched as his life had been, he had brought into these little rooms all the proud hope and ecstasy youth can know. He wanted to tell them how he had dreamed of growing rich and famous and of how for years a proud and secret image had sustained his spirit with its prophecy of love and triumph.

That image was this: in an ancient cobbled street like this one and in one of the old and elfin houses in this street a woman lived. The woman had the face and figure of a young woman he had seen in Bonn when he had stopped off there for a visit to a kinsman on his way to America. He had seen the woman seated at a table with two men in an old dark tavern such as this one where the students at the university went for beer. She was a great blonde creature, lavish of limb and full and deep of breast. She looked toward him once and smiled and he had seen that her eyes were grey and clear and fathomless. Jack had never forgotten her and in the dream which was to haunt and sustain his spirit during his first years in America he saw himself as a rich, famous, and distinguished man who had returned to find her. And although he had seen this woman just one time and only for a moment and knew nothing more about her he was certain that he would know where she was when he went to find her. He could see the street, the house, even the room where she would be. The street was like the picture of a destiny, and the old red light of fading day that lay quietly on the gables of the houses, resting there briefly without violence or heat, with a fading and unearthly glow, was like the phantasmal light of time and dreams. And Jack watched with prescient certitude to see himself, as he turned in from a corner to the street and approached the house where she was waiting for him. He heard her singing as she combed her long blonde hair and he knew the song and all the words she sang as well as all the words that she would speak to him.

Her lips were red and full, half-parted, living, warm and fragrant as her breath, her hair was like ripe wheat and spun as fine as smoky silk, her eyes as blue and depthless as unfathomed water, and her voice and the song she sang as rich, as strange and haunting as any songs that sirens sang from fabled rocks. Then she received him into her great embrace, he lay drowned in the torrent of her hair, cradled in the fathomless undulance of her great blonde thighs, borne upon the velvet cushion of her belly, engulfed in the lavish bounty of her breasts, and lost to time, to memory, to any other destiny save dark night and the everlasting love of her great flesh to which, a wisp of man, he surrendered blindly with a passionate and willing annihilation.

This was the dream as it had come to him a thousand times in the first years of poverty and exile to fortify his soul with its triumphant music of love and victory and now he wanted to tell his friends about it and ask them if they too had known such dreams as this in youth. He wanted to tell them how he had gained the power and wealth his heart had visioned and how he had lost the dream and he wanted to ask them if they had also known such loss. He wanted to tell them how the loss had not come bitterly and suddenly but how it came insensibly day by day so that man's youth and visions slip away from him without his knowing it and time wears slowly at his life as a drop of water wears at rock. He wanted to ask them if they had learned as he had learned the hard knowledge which the world can give a man and which he must get and live by if he is to draw his breath calmly without pain and not to die maddened, snarling, beaten, full of hate, like a wild beast in a snare.

Jack wanted to ask the old men if they too had found that a boy's dreams and visions passed like smoke and were like sand that slid and vanished through his fingers for all the good that they might do him. He wanted to ask them if they had learned that a suave and kindly cynicism was better than all the tortured protest in the painful and indignant soul of man and a wise and graceful acquiescence to the way of the world more sensible than all the anguish and madness youth can know. He wanted to ask them if they too had found there is no shame too great to be endured but thinking makes it so and that the wise men of the world have eyes to see with when they need them, ears to hear with when they want to use them for that purpose, but neither eyes, ears, tongues or words for what had better not be seen or known or spoken.

He wanted to ask them if they too had found that a hard word breaks no bones, that envy, venom, hatred, lies and slander are poisons to which man's hardy flesh may grow immune and the falseness of one's wife or mistress is an injury less harmful to sound sleep than an ill-cooked meal or a lumpy mattress—yes! far less harmful to the healthy slumber of a man of great affairs than the ravings of a drunken boy upon the telephone in the middle of the night. Such injuries as this were real and not to be endured. But cuckoldry! Why, cuckoldry was nothing, a joke, a thing to be made light of or ignored by people of experience, something sophisticated people laugh about, a subject for light comedy in the theatre, an evil only to some yokel who would not take the world as it was made.

Had they not found it so? Was a serious man to lose his own good sleep because his wife had gone to bed with other men? Was it a matter of moment that a woman gave her body for an hour or so to a lover? What did it matter so long as she behaved herself discreetly and got home in time for dinner. Cuckoldry! Why, a man might even take some pride in it, a kind of secret and illicit joy, if his wife had only made him cuckold with a celebrated man—a famous painter, say, or a distinguished lawyer—yes, even if the lover was only a nameless and infatuated fool of a boy, a man might feel a cynical and urbane amusement, an almost paternal and friendly interest. But to lose sleep, to writhe with jealousy or grow sick with shame, to be tortured by a thousand doubts and fears, to waste in flesh and lose all interest in one's business, to strangle with hatred and choke with murderous fury for revenge, because of the illicit rhythms of a woman's hams, the infidelities of a few inches of hair and gristle—it was a grotesque idiocy, a childish and provincial superstition, and not to be thought of by a grown man. Jack wanted to ask his friends if they had not found it so.

Jack also wanted to know if his friends had steeped and stained their souls in the hard dyes of the earth's iniquity. He wanted to know if they were crusted hide and heart with the hard varnish of complaisance. He wanted to know if they had seen the good man drown and the mad boy perish, if they had held their peace and saved their lives by losing them, buying success at the price of one man's failure or another's folly, paying for position as they went, and sure of nothing except that prizes go to men who yield consent.

The words of shame and penitence rushed to his lips in a hot and choking flood releasing the foul packed burden of his heart of a weight it had not known it bore. Yet when he tried to speak, he could not, no more than when vain boasting filled his mouth. But suddenly he saw their quiet and sorrowful eyes fixed on him, he heard again a strange and wordless whisper full with its weary final knowledge and he knew that they had known all this too and had for him neither reproach nor loathing because of it.

The old men sat there looking with their quiet eyes into the street where it was always morning. Bright sunlight, ancient, sorrowful, and autumnal sunlight, cut into the cool steep shadows of the street and the sunlight was like wine. Between the terraces of October hills, he knew, the Rhine was flowing. Bathed in the sorrowful harvest of that light, premonitory with its sense of death and parting, the wine hills rose steeply from the edges of a fabled river and the river was itself a tide of golden wine.

Then Jack bought the old men wine.

He shouted loudly to the waiter with the brutal and friendly face, and the man came quickly towards the table with his heavy limp. Jack flung great sums of money on the table, and he bought the old men wine. He bought frantically, lavishly, as if he could somehow consummate the only act and answer that was left for him. He bought until the old carved table was covered with tall slender bottles of the golden wine. The old men poured the potent wine into their throats. Again and again they filled their glasses with wild golden wine and drank it down. Then the old men lifted up their lined and worn faces and, looking out into the street with their quiet and sorrowful eyes, which never changed or faltered in their expression of a single and final knowledge, they sang out strongly in the hoarse, worn voices of old men such songs as young men sing, which they had sung themselves in youth. They sang again the songs of love and hope and wandering, of drunkenness and glee, and of wild and strange adventure.

Jack turned his face away into his hand and wept bitterly.

*   *   *   *   *

Now Jack thought he was standing with his mother on the Rhine-boat landing. Bright October sunlight lay upon the terraced hills and filled the river with its light. It was morning, the landing place was swarming with an immense energy of arrival and departure, but the breath of autumn, sorrowful and foreboding, was in the air. Jack felt an immense and nameless excitement stirring in him, and also a sense of incommunicable sadness. The Rhine boat had just come in, people were streaming up the landing from the boat, and other people were streaming into the boat. The porters were diving feverishly among the crowd, loading, unloading, stockily bowed with people's baggage, uttering sharp cries of warning as they rushed on and off the boat. In the crowd Jack saw many people that he knew.

He spoke to his mother, but she did not hear him or answer him. Instead, she stood motionless, looking with a fixed stare at someone who was standing on the top deck of the crowded boat, as if she wanted to fix his image in her mind forever. Jack followed his mother's glance, and he saw that she was looking at a plump fresh skinned boy of seventeen. The boy was neatly dressed in a somewhat comical and countrified fashion, and he was wearing a flat student's cap. He stood looking back at Jack's mother, with the same fixed voracious stare, as if he too was trying to fix forever in his memory this final picture of her. The boy was also trying to smile, but his eyes were glazed and wet with tears and from time to time he turned his plump ruddy face away and wiped furtively at his eyes with the sleeve of his coat. Then he would begin to look at Jack's mother again with the same fixed and ridiculous effort at a smile.

Jack saw that the boy was himself and he began to shout to him in an excited voice. But the boy paid no attention to him and did not seem to hear him. Then the porters pulled the landing bridge back on the landing stage, the whistle sounded sharply twice, the great paddle wheels began to churn, and the white Rhine-boat moved out swiftly into the river. On the top deck the boy stood, a small, plump, forlorn figure, waving frantically with his handkerchief as the boat receded. Jack's mother kept her eyes fixed on that small receding figure until she could see it no more, and the boat had dwindled to a white dot in the distance. Then she turned and began to walk away blindly, with tears streaming down her cheeks and her powerful dark face twisted and contorted in the convulsive mask of sorrow of the Jew. Jack ran after her shouting frantically: "Mother, mother! Here! Look at me! I am here! It is Frederick." But she neither turned nor glanced at him, no more than if he had been a viewless ghost. He shouted to the people around him at the top of his voice. No one heard him. No one looked at him. No one saw him.

*   *   *   *   *

The Rhine-boat was a miracle of shining white and polished brass and glittering glass. All day in the rich fading sunlight of October its dove white breast was feathering the surface of the golden river. The boat was loaded with a crowd of people who sang and drank and ate and shouted constantly. All day long the waiters rushed back and forth across the decks bearing steins of foaming beer, bottles of wine, and trays filled with food and sandwiches. All day long the white Rhine-boats passed along the river, and as they passed the powerful voices of the young men singing rolled across the water and echoed in the hills. And all day long they passed the great Rhine barges churning swiftly down the river towards the sea and Holland, or up the river towards Mainz.

On the ship there were two brothers whose faces were to haunt his dreams forever. They were enormous men of middle age; they were expensively dressed and they drank wine all day long. Their ponderous jowls hung down from their great red faces comically, they had large flowing moustaches, and their eyes were large and brown and gentle as a cow's. They held long folding maps in the great muttons of their hands, and all day long, as the ship went down the river, they looked from time to time at their maps, grunting with a guttural satisfaction of discovery: "Ach—die Lorelei! Ach—das Rheinpfalz!" Then they would return solemnly to their eating and drinking. They were comical in the solemn intentness of their glutting, and yet in their great size, their huge red glowing faces, their thick brown moustaches and their great gentle brown eyes, there was a profound and impressive nobility, such as great well kept bulls might have.

Then day faded on the ancient hills, the ruined turrets melted into dusk, and night came on.

Jack stood alone in darkness watching as the dim white breast of the boat feathered against dark flowing waters, and Jack could hear dark hoofs rushing on the land, and he thought he heard the mermaids singing.

*   *   *   *   *

Then, out of the dream of time into the dream of time, Mr. Frederick Jack awoke with sad defunctive music in his brain, and instantly he knew that it was morning, May the second, nineteen hundred twenty-eight. A fine bright day and spring at last, he thought, with golfer's relish. April's ended.

MORNING

. . .

JACK ERECT

. . .

Mr. Frederick Jack rose quite early in the morning and he liked the sense of power. The best of everything was good enough for him, and he also loved his family dearly. He liked the odor of strong inky news-print together with the sultry and exultant fragrance of black boiling coffee the first thing in the morning. He liked lavish plumbing, richly thick with creamy porcelain and polished silver fixtures, he liked the morning plunge in his great sunken tub, the sensual warmth of clean sudsy water and the sharp aromatic clean-ness of the bath salts. He had a keen eye for aesthetic values, too, and he liked to watch the swarming dance of water spangles in their magic shift and play upon the creamy ceiling of the bathroom. Most of all, he liked to come up pink and dripping, streaked liberally from head to toe all over his plump hairy body with strong wholesome soap-suds, and then he loved the stinging drive and shock of needled spray, the sense of bracing conflict, hardihood, tri-umph and, finally, of abundant glowing health as he stepped forth drain-ing cleanly down upon a thick cork mat and vigorously rubbing himself dry in the folds of a huge crashy bath-towel.

Mr. Jack also liked the opulent bowled depth and richness of the creamy water-basin, and he liked to stand there for a moment with bared lips, regarding with considerable satisfaction the pearly health and hue of his strong front teeth, the solid clamp and bite of the molars edged expensively with gold. Then he liked to brush them earnestly with a brush of stiff hard bristles and an inch of firm thick paste, turning his head strongly from side to side around the brush, and glaring at his image in the glass until he foamed agreeably at the mouth with a lather of pink spittle tinged pleasantly with a fresh and minty taste. This done, he liked to spit it out, soft flop and fall of blobsy bubbled pink into the open basin where clean running water washed it down, and then he liked to rinse his mouth and wash his throat and tonsils with the tonic antiseptic bite of strong pale listerine.

Mr. Jack also liked the tidy crowded array of lotions, creams, unguents; of bottles, tubes, brushes, jars, and shaving implements that covered the shelf of thick blue glass above the basin. He liked to lather his face heavily with a large silver-handled shaving brush, rubbing the lather strongly in with firm stroking finger tips, brushing and stroking till his jaws were covered with a smooth thick layer of warm shaving cream. Then Mr. Jack took the razor in his hand and opened it. He used a long straight razor, murderously sharp, and he always kept it in excellent condition. At the crucial moment, just before the first long downward stroke, Mr. Jack would flourish slightly forward with his plump arms and shoulders, raising the glittering blade aloft in one firm hand, his legs would widen stockily, crouching gently at the knees, and his lathered face would crane carefully to one side and upward, and his eyes would roll aloft, as if he was getting braced and ready underneath a heavy burden. Then holding one cheek delicately between two daintily arched fingers, he would advance deliberately upon it with that gleaming blade. He grunted gently, with satisfaction, at the termination of the stroke. The blade had mown smoothly, from cheek to jowl, an even perfect swath of pink clean flesh across his ruddy face. He exulted in the slight tug and rasping pull of wiry stubble against the smooth and deadly sharpness of the blade, and in the relentless sweep and triumph of the steel. Then he liked to rinse his glowing face first with hot, then with cold water, to dry it in a crisp fresh towel, and to rub face and neck carefully with a soft, fragrant, gently stinging lotion. This done, he stood for a moment, satisfied, regarding his image, softly caressing the velvet texture of shaved ruddy cheeks with gentle finger tips.

Mr. Jack also liked to twist his close-clipped moustache ends into fine waxed points and carefully to part exactly in the middle his grey distinguished-looking hair, which was somewhat thin, and cropped closely up the sides in German fashion.

Elegant in dress, even perhaps a trifle foppish, but always excellently correct, Mr. Jack wore fresh garments every day. No cotton touched him. He wore undergarments of the finest silk and he had over forty suits from London. Every morning he surveyed his wardrobe studiously, and he chose with care and with a good eye for harmony the shoes, socks, shirts and neckties he would wear, and before he chose a suit he was sometimes lost in thought for several minutes. He loved to open wide the door of his great closet and see them hanging there in thick set rows with all their groomed and regimented elegance. He liked the strong clean smell of honest cloth, the rich dull texture of good material, and in those forty several shapes and colors he saw forty pleasing reflections and variations of his own character. They filled him, as did everything about him, with a sense of morning confidence, joy, and vigor.

Mr. Jack also had the best room in the house, although he had not asked for it. It was an immense and spacious chamber, twenty feet each way and twelve feet high, and in these noble proportions was written quietly a message of wealth and power. In the exact centre of the wall that faced the door was placed Mr. Jack's bed, a chaste fourposter of the Revolutionary period. A chest of antique drawers was placed in the centre of another wall, a gate-legged table, with a row of books and the latest magazines, two fine old windsor chairs, a few tasteful French prints on the walls, an old well padded easy chair, another little table at the side of his bed, on which was set a small clock, a book or two and a little electric lamp, and curiously, an enormous chaise longue, such as women use, but of a sober grey hue and long and wide enough to receive the figure of an eight foot man, which stood at the foot of the bed, and in which Mr. Jack liked to stretch himself and read—this was about all the furniture the room had in it. The total effect was one of a modest and almost austere simplicity combined quietly and subtly with a sense of spaciousness, wealth, and power. Finally, the floor was covered with a thick and heavy carpet of dull grey. Mr. Jack liked to walk across it in his bare feet, the floor below it neither creaked nor sagged. It was as solid as if it had been hewn in one single block from the timber of a massive oak.

Mr. Jack liked this. He liked what was solid, rich, and spacious, made to last. He liked the sense of order and security everywhere. He even liked the thick and solid masonry of the walls, through which the sounds of the awaking city all around him came pleasantly to his ears with a dull, sustained, and mounting roar. He liked to look through the broad window of his room into the canyon of the street below, and see the steep cool morning shadows cut cleanly by the young and living light of May. He liked to raise his eyes aloft upon the glittering pinnacle of the building opposite him and see the young light of the morning flame and glitter on the arrogant bright silver of the city's spires and ramparts. He liked to look down upon the oiled bluish ribbon of the street below him and watch the trucks and motors as they began to charge furiously through that narrow gulch in ever-growing numbers. The thickening tide of the man-swarm, as it began to stream past to its labors in a million little cells, was also pleasing to him. Founded like a rock among these furious, foaming tides of life Mr. Jack saw nothing but security, order, and a radiant harmony wherever he looked.

And all of this, he felt, was just exactly as it should be. He loved the feeling of security and power that great buildings and rich and spacious dwellings gave to him. Even in the furious thrust and jostle of the crowd his soul rejoiced, for he saw order everywhere. It was the order of ten million men who swarmed at morning to their work in little cells, and who swarmed at evening from their work to little cells. It was an order as inevitable as the seasons, as recurrent as the tides, and in it Mr. Jack read the same harmony and permanence that he saw in the entire visible universe around him. And he liked order. He did not like for things to shake and tremble. When things shook and trembled, a slight frown appeared between his eyes, and an old unquiet feeling, to which he could not give a name or image, stirred faintly in his heart. Once, when he awoke at morning, he thought he felt a faint vibration, a tremor so brief and slight he could not be certain of it, in the massive walls around him. Then Mr. Jack had asked the door man who stood at the street entrance a few questions. The man told him that the building had been built across two depths of railway tunnels, and that all that Mr. Jack had heard was the faint vibration that might have come from the passing of a train twelve depths below him. Then the man assured him it was all quite safe, that the very trembling in the walls, in fact, was just another gauge and proof of safety.

Still, Mr. Jack did not like it. The news disturbed him vaguely. He would have liked it better if the building had been built upon the solid rock.

*   *   *   *   *

For breakfast he liked orange juice, two leghorn eggs, soft boiled, two slices of crisp thin toast, and tasty little segments of pink Praguer ham, which looked so pretty on fresh parsley sprigs, and coffee, coffee, he liked strong fragrant sultry coffee, cup by cup.

With simple comforts such as these Mr. Jack faced the world each morning with strong hope, with joy breast and back as either should be. The smell of the earth was also good, and fortified his soul. Up through the pavements of thick stone, out of the city's iron breast, the smell of the earth was coming somehow, immortal and impalpable, cool, pregnant, moist and flowerful. It was loaded to its lips with the seeds of life and always coming onward, upward, out of steel and stone or subterranean rock, never to be seen or touched and like a miracle as it impended in the bright living morning air in waves of subtle and premonitory fragrance.

Mr. Jack, although city bred, could feel the charm of Mother Earth. Accordingly with eyes half closed, the strong deep volutes of his nostrils trembling gently, he arose and sniffed that living laden air with zestful satisfaction. This was more like it, now. Made him feel like a young colt again. He breathed deeply, slowly, deliberately, his hands pressed with firm tenderness against his swelling diaphragm.

He liked the cultivated forms of nature: the swarded greens of great estates, gay regiments of brilliant gardened flowers, the rich clumped masses of the shrubbery, even the gnarled old apple tree of other times which had been left cunningly by the architect to lend a homely and familiar touch at the angle of the master's room. All this delighted him, the call of the simple life was growing stronger every year, and he was building a big house in Westchester County.

He also liked the ruder and more natural forms of beauty: he liked the deep massed green that billowed on a hillside, the smell of cleanly mown fields, and he liked old shaded roads that wound away to quietness from driven glares of speed and concrete. He knew the values in strange magic lights of green and gold, and he had seen an evening light upon the old red of a mill, and felt deep stillness in his heart (all—could anyone believe it?—within thirty miles of New York City). On those occasions the distressful life of that great and furious city had seemed very far away. And often he had paused to pluck a flower or to stand beside a brook in thought. But after sighing with regret as, among such scenes, he thought of the haste and folly of man's life, Mr. Jack always came back to the city. For life was real, and life was earnest, and Mr. Jack was a business man.

Mr. Jack also liked the more expensive forms of sport. He liked to go out in the country to play golf; he loved bright sunlight and the fresh mown smell of fairways. The rich velvet of the greens delighted him, and afterwards when he had stood below the bracing drive of needled showers, and felt the sweat of competition wash cleanly from his well-set form, he liked to loaf upon the cool veranda of the club, and talk about his score, and joke and laugh, pay or collect his bets, and drink good Scotch with other men of note. And he liked to watch his country's flag flap languidly upon the tall white pole because it looked so pretty there.

It was of golf that Mr. Jack was now thinking as he sniffed the morning air.

Mr. Jack also liked to gamble and he gambled everywhere he could. He gambled every day upon the price of stocks: this was his business. And every night he went and gambled at his club. It was no piker's game he played. He never turned a hair about a thousand dollars. Large sums did not appall him. He counted by the hundred thousand every day; he was not frightened by amount or number. When he saw the man-swarm passing in its million-footed weft he did not sicken in his heart. Neither did his guts stir nauseously, growing grey with horror. And when Mr. Jack saw the ninety story buildings all about him, did he fall down grovelling in the dust? Did he beat a maddened brain against their sides, as he cried out, "Woe! O woe is me!"? No. He did not. The brawling shift and fury of great swarms of people warmed his heart, and beetling cliffs of immense and cruel architectures lapped his soul in strong security. He liked great crowds and every cloud-lost spire of masonry was a talisman of power, the monument to an everlasting empire. It made him feel good. For that empire was his faith, his fortune, and his life. He had a place there. Therefore, the fury of great crowds, the towering menace of great buildings did not oppress his soul. He never felt that he was drowning. A ruddy compact human atom, five feet seven inches tall, he was, he knew, if not a man among a million, at least a man among some thousands.

Yet, his neck was not stiff, nor his eye hard. Neither was he very proud. For he had seen the men who lean upon their sills at evening, and those who swarmed from ratholes in the ground, and often he had wondered what their lives were like.

*   *   *   *   *

Mr. Jack was a wise man, too, who knew the world, the devil, and the city well. He liked the brilliant shock and gaiety of evening and, although kind, he was not averse to a little high-toned cruelty at night. It gave a spice and zest to things, a pleasant tinge of wickedness, and after all, it broke no bones. A nice juicy young yokel, say, fresh from the rural districts, all hands and legs and awkwardness, hooked and wriggling on a cruel and cunning word—a woman's, preferably, because they were so swift and deft in matters of this nature, although there were men as well whose skill was great—some pampered lap-dog of rich houses, to his preference, some fiesty nimble-witted little she-man whose lisping mincing tongue was always good for one or two shrewd thrusts of poison in a hayseed's hide. Or a nice young couple, newly married, say, eager to make their way among smart people and determined to go forward with sophisticated knowingness—to ply their stage fright smoothly with strong drink, until the little woman indiscreetly showed a preference for some insolently handsome youth, who should be present to give a touch of pleasant menace to the evening, was discovered in his arms, say, in a bed room, or sat upon his lap before invited guests, or merely lolled upon him with an intoxicated ardour—why surely moments such as these, even the strained smile, the faint green pallor of the husband's face, were innocent enough, and did no lasting harm to anyone.

Of the two enjoyments, however, Mr. Jack felt he rather liked the wincing of the solitary yokel better: there was something so much like innocence, youth, and morning in the face of a nice freshly baited country boy, as it darkened to a slow dull smouldering glow of shame, surprise, and anger, and as it sought with clumsy and inept words to retort upon the wasp which had stung it and winged away, that Mr. Jack, when he saw it, felt a sense of almost paternal tenderness for its hapless victim, a delightful sense of youth and innocence in himself. It was almost as if he were revisiting his own youth: it was far better than a trip out to the country, and the sight of dewy meadows, or the smells of hay and milk and butter.

But enough was enough. Mr. Jack was neither a cruel nor an immoderate man. He liked the great gay glitter of the night, the thrill and fever of high stakes, and the swift excitements of new pleasures. He liked the theatre and saw all the worthwhile plays, and the better, smarter, wittier revues—the ones with sharp satiric lines, good dancing, and Gershwin music. He liked the shows his wife designed because his wife designed them, he was proud of her, and he also enjoyed these evenings of ripe culture at the Guild. He also went to prize fights in his evening clothes and once when he came home he had the red blood of a champion on the white boiled bosom of his shirt. Few men could say as much.

He liked the social swim, the presence of the better sort of actors, artists, writers, and the wealthy cultivated Jews around his table, he liked the long velvet backs of lovely women, and the flash and play of jewelry about their necks, he liked a little malice and a little spicy scandal deftly hinted in a word. He liked the brilliant chambers of the night with their smooth baleful sparkle of vanity and hate. He breathed their air agreeably, without anguish or confusion. He even liked a little quiet fornication now and then, and all the other things that men are fond of. All this he had enjoyed himself, but decently and quietly, all in its proper time and place, without annoyance to other people, and he expected everyone to act as well as he.

But ripeness with this man was all, and he always knew the time to stop. His ancient and belraic spirit was tempered with an almost classic sense of moderation. He prized the virtue of decorum highly. He knew the value of the middle way. He had a kind heart and a loyal nature. His purse was open to a friend in need. He kept a lavish table and a royal cellar, and his family was the apple of his eye.

He was not a man to wear his heart upon his overcoat, nor risk his life on every corner, nor throw himself away upon a word or at any crosswind of his fancy, nor spend the heart and strength out of his life forever just on the impulse of a moment's wild belief. This was such madness as the Gentiles knew. But, this side idolatry and madness, he would go as far for friendship's sake as any man alive. He would go with a friend up to the edge of his own ruin and defeat, and he would ever try to hold him back from it. But once he saw a man was mad, and not to be persuaded by calm judgment, he was done with him. He would leave him where he was, although regretfully. Are matters helped if the whole crew drown together with a single drunken sailor? He thought not. He could put a world of sincere meaning in the three words: "What a pity!"

Yes, Mr. Frederick Jack was a wise and kind and temperate man, and he had found life pleasant, and won from it the secret of wise living. And the secret of wise living was founded in a graceful compromise, a tolerant acceptance. If a man wanted to live in this world without getting his pockets picked, he had better learn how to use his eyes and ears in what is going on around him. But if he also wanted to live in this world without getting hit over the head, or without all the useless pain, the grief, the terror, and the bitterness that scourges man's sad flesh, he had better learn how *not* to use his eyes and ears, in what is going on around him. This sounds difficult but it had not been so for Mr. Frederick Jack.

Perhaps some great inheritance of pain and suffering, the long dark ordeal of his race, had left him, as a kind of precious distillation, this gift of balanced understanding. At any rate, he had not learned it because it could not be taught. He had been born with it.

Therefore, he was not a man to rip the sheets in darkness or beat his knuckles bloody on a wall. He would not madden furiously in the envenomed passages of night, nor strangle like a mad dog of his hate and misery in the darkness, nor would he ever be carried smashed and bloody from the stews. A woman's falseness, the lover's madness, the pangs of misprized love were no doubt hard to bear, but love's bitter mystery had broken no bones for Mr. Jack and, so far as he was concerned, it could not murder sleep the way an injudicious wiener schnitzel could, or some drunk young Gentile fool ringing the telephone at one A.M.

Mr. Jack's brow was darkened as he thought of it. He muttered wordlessly. If fools are fools, let them be fools where their folly will not injure or impede the slumbers of a serious man.

Yes. Men could rob, lie, murder, swindle, trick, and cheat—the whole world knew as much. And women could be as false as hell and lie their guilt away from now to doomsday with a round rogue's eye of innocence, ten thousand oaths, and floods of tears. And Mr. Jack also had known something of the pain, the madness, and the folly that twists the painful and indignant soul of youth—it was too bad, of course, too bad, but regardless of all this the day was day, and men must work, the night was night, and men must sleep, and it was, he felt intolerable—

Ein!—

Red of face, to tune of tumbling morning water, in big tub, he bent stiffly, with a grunt, a plump pajamaed figure, until his fingers grazed the rich cream tiling of the bathroom floor.

Intolerable!—

Zwei!—

(He straightened sharply with a grunt of satisfaction—)

—that a man with serious work to do—

Drei!

(His firm plump arms shot strongly to full stretching finger tips above his head, and came sharply down again until he held clinched fists against his breast—)

Vier!—

—should be pulled out of his bed in the middle of the night by the ravings of a manic—ja! a crazy young fool—

(His closed fists shot outward in strong driving crosswise movement, and came strongly to his sides again).

Ein!—

—It was intolerable and, by God, he'd tell her so!

(Head to waist, stiff-legged and grunting vigorously, he bent again until his fingers grazed the floor).

MORNING

· · ·

JACK AFLOAT

· · ·

At seven twenty-eight Jack awoke and began to come alive with all his might. He sat upward and yawned strongly, with a stretching and propitiating movement of thick outward-yearning arms, at the same time bending a tousled slumber-swollen face into the plump muscle-hammock of his right shoulder blade, a movement coy and cuddlesome. Eee-a-a-a-ach! He stretched deliciously out of thick rubbery sleep, happily, with regret, and for a moment he sat heavily upright rubbing at his somewhat gummed sleep-reddened eyes the firm clenched backs of his plump fingers. Then he flung back the covers with one determined motion, and swung strongly to the floor. For a moment his short well-kept toes groped blindly in fine grey carpet stuff, smooth as felt, for suave heel-less slippers of red Russian leather. Found and shod he paddled drowsily across the floor's thick noiseless carpeting to the window and stood, yawned strongly, stretched again, as he looked out with sleepy satisfaction at the finest morning of the year.

Nine floors below him Forty-seventh Street lay gulched in steep cool morning shadow, bluish, barren, cleanly ready for the day. A truck roared past with a solid rattling heaviness. An ash can was banged strongly on the pavement with an abrupt slamming racket. Upon the street a man walked swiftly by with lean picketing footsteps, turned the corner into Madison Avenue, and was gone, heading southward towards its work, a little figure

40

foreshortened from above and covered by its neat drab cone of grey. Below Jack the street lay, a narrow bluish lane, between sheer cliffs of solid masonry, but straight before him on the western front of that incredible gulch of steel and stone to which opulently the name Vanderbilt Avenue had been given, the morning sunlight, firm, living, golden, young, immensely strong and delicate, cut with a clean sculptural sharpness at blue walls of shade. The light lay living with a firm, rose-golden, yet unearthly glow of morning upon the soaring upper tiers and summits of immense pale structures that rose terrifically from solid sheeted basal stone and glittering brass, still sunk in the steep blue morning shadow of that incredible gulch. Sharply, and yet with its unearthly rose-golden clarity, the light cut at appalling vertices of glass, and silver-burnished steel and cliffs of harsh white-yellow brick, haggard in young light. It lay clean and fragile, without violence or heat, upon upsoaring cliffs of masonry and on vast retreating pyramids of steel and stone, fumed at their summits with bright fading flaws of smoke. It was an architecture cruel, inhuman, monstrous and Assyrian in its pride and insolence soaring to nauseous pinnacles and cut wedge-like, wall-like, knife-like at a sickening height and depth from a wrought incredible sculpture of shade and light.

The morning light lay with a flat reddened blaze upon ten thousand even equal points of glass; it lay firmly on the upper tiers of great hotels and clubs and on vast office spaces bare of life. Jack looked with pleasure straight into great offices ready for the day: firm morning light shaped clean patterns out of pale-hued desks and swivel chairs of maple, it burnished flimsy thin partition woods and thick glazed office glasses. The offices stood silent, barren, with a clean sterility, in young morning light, empty and absent with a kind of lonely expectation for the life that soon would swarm into their emptiness to fill and use them.

The proud, glittering, vertical arrogance of the city, graven superbly like a triumphant and exulting music out of light and shade, was still touched with this same premonitory solitude of life. From streets yet bare of traffic the buildings rose haggard and incredible in first light, with an almost inhuman desolation, as if all life had been driven or extinguished from the giant city, and as if these inhuman and perfect relics were all that remained of a life that had been fabulous and legendary in its monstrous arrogance. The immense and vertical shapes of the great buildings soared up perfectly into a perfect sky: their pointed spires that dwindled to glittering needles of cold silver light cut sharply the crystal weather of a blue shell-fragile sky. Morning, bright shining morning, blazed incredibly upon their shining spires: the clean soaring shapes were built into a shining air which framed them with a radiant substance of light that was itself as clean as carving and only less material than the spires that carved it.

The cross street straight below him was now empty, but already in the short steep canyon that stretched straight and hard between its sheer terrific walls the trucks were beginning to drive past his vision at the cross street openings, an even savage thunder of machinery going to its work. And lengthways in that furious gulch the glittering bright-hued cabs were drilling past projectile-like in solid beetle-bullet flight to curve, vanish, and emerge again from the arched cab driveways of the Grand Central Station.

And everywhere, through that shining living light and above the solid driving thunder of machinery, Jack could feel the huge vibrant tremor, the slow-mounting roar of furious day. He stood there by his window, a man-mite poised midmost of the shining air upon a shelf of solid masonry, the miracle of God, a proud plump atom of triumphant man's flesh, founded upon a rock of luxury and quietude at the earth's densest and most central web of man-swarm fury, the prince of atoms who bought the luxuries of space, silence, light and iron-walled security out of chaos with the ransom of an emperor, and who exulted in the price he paid for them, a compact tiny tissue of bright blood, a palpable warm motion who gazed upon sky-pointing towers blazing in young light, and did not feel appalled, a grain of living dust who saw the million furious accidents of shape and movement that daily passed the little window of his eye, and felt no doubt or fear or lack of confidence.

Instead, if those appalling shapes had been the monuments of his own special triumph, his sense of confidence, pride, and ownership could hardly have been greater.

My city. Mine.

They filled his heart with certitude and joy because he had learned, like many other men, to see, to marvel, to accept, and not to read, and in that insolent boast of steel and stone he saw a permanence surviving every danger, an answer, crushing and conclusive in its silence, to every doubt.

His eye swept strongly, proudly, with a bright awakened gleam of life along the gulched blue canyon of the avenue until his vision stopped, halted at the end, forced upwards implacably, awfully, along the terrific vertex of the Lincoln Building which rose, a flat frontal wall of sheer appalling height, a height incredible, immeasurable, cut steeply in blue shade.

Then, with firm fingers pressed against his slowly swelling breast, he breathed deliberately, the fresh living air of morning, laden with the sharp thrilling compost of the city, a fragrance, subtly mixed of many things, impalpable and unforgettable, touched with joy and menace. The air was laden with the smell of earth, a quality that was moist and flowerful, it was tinged faintly with the fresh wet reek of tidal waters, a faint fresh river smell, rank, a little rotten, somehow wild with jubilation and the thought of ships. That shining incense-laden air was also spiced impalpably with the sultry and fragrant excitement of strong boiling coffee, and in it was the proud tonic threat of conflict and of danger, and a leaping wine-like prophecy of power, wealth and love. Jack breathed that vital ether slowly, strongly, with the heady joy, the sense of unknown menace and delight it always brought to him. A trembling, faint and instant, passed in the earth below him. He paused, frowning, waiting till it stopped. He smiled.

Great trains pass under me. Morning, bright morning, and the dreams we knew: a boy, the station, and the city first, in morning, living morning. And now—yes, even now!—they come, they pass below me wild with joy, mad with hope, drunk with their thoughts of victory. For what? For what? Glory, huge profit and a girl!

O! Du schöne schöne zauberstadt!

Power. Power. Power.

*   *   *   *   *

Jack breathed the powerful tonic fragrance of shining morning and the city with strong pleasure. Then, thoroughly awake, he turned, moved briskly across his chamber to the bathroom, and let fall with a full stopped thud the heavy silver-headed waste pipe of his lavish sunken tub. He turned the hot water tap on full force and, as the tumbling water began smokily to fill the tub with its thick boiling gurgle, he brushed his teeth and gargled his throat. Then, scuffing suave slippers from his feet, and gripping the thick warm tiling of the floor with strong bare toes, he straightened with a military smartness, drew deeply in a long deter-mined breath, and vigorously began his morning exercises. With stiff-ened legs and straight flexed arms, he bent strongly towards the floor, grunting, as his groping finger tips just grazed the tiling. Then he swung into punctual rhythms, counting, "One—Two—Three—Four," as his body moved, lapsing presently into a mere guttural and native mutter of "Ein—Zwei—Drei—Vier!" as he went on. At length he paused, panting, red, victorious: he turned the water off, tested it gingerly with a finger which he jerked back with a grunt of hurt surprise; he turned the cold water spigot strongly to the left and waited while cold water tumbled, surged up bubbling, seething, milky, sending waves of trembling light across the hot blue surface of the water.

He stripped off rapidly the neat pajama suit, silk-blue, that clad his sturdy figure with a loose soft warmth, and comfort. For a moment he stood in sensual contemplation of his nakedness. He felt with pleasure his firm swelling bicep muscle and observed with keen satisfaction the reflection in the mirror of his plump, hairy, well-conditioned body. Firm, well-moulded, and erect, well-fleshed and solid-looking, there was hardly a trace of unwholesome fat upon him—a little undulance, perhaps, goose-plump, across the kidneys, a suggestion of a roll of flesh about the waist, but not enough to give concern, and far, far less than he had seen on men twenty years his junior. Content, strong, deep and glowing had filled him: he turned his rapt eye away reluctantly and tried the water with a cautious toe. He found it tempered to his liking. He turned off the flow from the cold water pipe, stepped carefully into the tub, and then settled his body slowly in its blue-crystal depths with a slow grunt of apprehension.

A sigh, long, lingering, full of relief and pleasure, expired slowly on his lips. He rolled down slowly in a wallow of complete immersion and came up dripping: with a thick lather of fragrant tarry soap, he soaped himself enthusiastically across his hairy chest and belly, under the armpits, over his shoulders, up his pink solid-looking neck, and into the porches of his reddened ears. He slid under again in a slow bearlike wallow and came up with a cleansed and grateful feeling, filled with the pleasant fragrance of his flesh.

He lolled back in a sensual meditation against the rich cream thickness of the tub and gazed with dreamy rapture at his navel, and at the thick wet hair which floated, waving gently, strong, oily, silken, the sea-frond forest of himself. He looked with brooding tenderness, with strong wonder, at the flower of his sex: short, strong, and wrinkled, velvet to his touch, and circumcised, it floated slowly upward like a fish at rest, gently sustained upon the floating pontoons of his ballocks, gently afloat upon the spread veined mesh of his full floating bag. He grasped it tenderly, soaping it with respectful fingers and with a look of delicate and refined concern upon his face. How are you, sir, this morning? Will that do? Reverently he released it, leaning backward, watching as it swam. A smile broke happily cross his lips: he found life good. Was there, he asked himself rhetorically, life in the old boy yet? Was there? How many men of fifty-four could say as much? Grow old? A laugh, low, deep, guttural, thick with triumph, welled up exultantly in his throat. Grow old! Yes! Grow old, by God, grow old! He almost shouted. Grow old along with me! Oh, he would show old tottering toothless fools what growing old was like.

He would keep groomed and ready for the work of love if it took the treasure of a king and all the cunning in the brain of science. A sensual fantasy, wild and jubilant, possessed him, filling his heart with triumph and exultant certainty. He would be trained and groomed more finely than an athlete for the single goal and end of his desire. He would renew the juice of youth and love within him constantly, if surgeons had to graft into his flesh the genitals of a bull, or if he had to buy the manhood of a youth of twenty-five, to do it. He would be fed and renewed forever on foods and liquors rich with all the energies of love, and he would have them at whatever cost—if hunters had to scour the jungles of the earth to find them, if divers had to go down to the seafloors of the earth to gather them—oh! if a hundred men must lose their lives or shed their blood to keep youth living in him, he would have it, he would keep it— or what was money, what was science, for?

Jack thought of women, seductive, rare and lovely women, bought with gold, and more seductive for the gold that bought them. He no longer thought or cared to think about the lavish Amazon, the blonde creature great of limb and deep of breast who, in the visions of his youth, had waited for him, singing, in an ancient house. Or, if he ever thought of her, it was without regret, without desire: she was an image crude, naive, and youthful, such as children have, as far and lost and buried as the boy who wanted her. But Jack was a modern man, and even styles in woman's flesh had changed. He liked his women cut to fashion: he liked women with long flat hips and unsuspected depth and undulance. He liked women with firm narrow breasts, long necks, long slender legs, and straight flat bellies. He liked their faces long and pale, a little cruel and merciless, he liked thin wicked mouths of red, and long slant eyes, cat-grey, and lidded carefully. He liked ladies with spun hair of bronze-gold wire; he liked a frosted cocktail shaker in a lady's hands, and he liked a voice hoarse-husky, city-wise, a trifle weary, and ironic, faintly insolent, that said: "*Well!* What happened to *you*, darling? I thought that you would never get here."

And thinking so, he flopped suddenly, flatly, with the caught hooked motion of a fish, in the warm soap-lathered water.

Tonight. Tonight.

The water spangles, gold-green, stinging, flashed in a swarming web upon the ceiling.

MORNING

· · ·

MRS. JACK AWAKE

· · ·

Mrs. Jack awoke at eight o'clock. She awoke like a child, completely alert and alive, instantly awake all over and with all sleep shaken clearly from her mind and senses the moment that she opened her eyes. It had been so with her all her life. For a moment she lay flat on her back with eyes wide open, completely awake but staring with a blank, puzzled stare straight up at the ceiling.

Then with a vigorous and jubilant movement she flung the covers back from her small and opulent body, which was clothed with a long sleeveless garment of thin yellow silk. She bent her knees briskly, drew her feet from beneath the cover, and straightened out flat again. For a moment she surveyed her small straight feet, with a look of wonder and delight. The perfect and solid alignment of the little toes, and the healthy shining nails which, save for a slight bluish discoloration at the edge of one great toe were as perfect, healthy, and well kept as her small, strong, and capable hands filled her with pleasure.

With the same expression of childish wonder and vanity, she slowly lifted her left arm and began to revolve it deliberately before her fascinated eye. With a tender concentration she observed how the small and delicate wrist obeyed each movement with a strong suppleness, and then she gazed raptly at the strong, graceful winglike movement of the hand, at the strength, beauty, and firm competence that was legible in its

47

brown narrow back and in the shapely fingers. And filled with delight at the strength and beauty of her hand, she lifted the other arm as well, and now turned both of them upon their graceful wrists, gazing upon both hands with a tender concentration of delight.

"What magic!" she thought. "What magic and strength is in them. God! How beautiful they are, and what things they can do! The design for all of it comes out of me in the most wonderful and exciting way," she thought, with a sense of love and wonder. "It is all distilled and brewed inside of me—and yet nobody ever asks me how it happens! First, it is all one piece—like something solid in the head," she thought comically, now wrinkling her low forehead with an almost animal-like expression of bewildered and painful difficulty. "Then it all breaks up into little particles and somehow arranges itself and then it starts to *move*!" she thought triumphantly.

"First I can feel it coming down along my neck and shoulders, and then it is moving up across my legs and belly, then it meets and joins together like a star ('that art of three sounds not a fourth sound a star!'" she thought) in her image of beautiful faces, such images—"a thread of gold" and "a star" were constantly re[turning]. "Then it flows out into my arms until it reaches down into my finger tips—and then the hand does just what I want it to. It makes a line—and everything I want is in that line—it puts a fold into a piece of cloth, and no one else on earth could put it in that way, or make it look the same—it gives a turn to the spoon, a prod of the fork, a dash of pepper when I cook for him," she thought, "and there's a dish the finest chef on earth can never equal— because it's got me in it, heart and soul and all my love," she thought with modest joy. "Yes! And everything I've ever done has been the same —always the clear design, the line of life, running like a thread of gold all through my life back to the time I was a child," she thought. And at this moment, it really seemed to her that her life, at every time and moment had always had the unity, beauty, and assurance of this "thread of gold."

Now, having surveyed her strong and beautiful hands with an immense and tender satisfaction, the woman began deliberately an inspection of her other members. Craning her head a little to the side, she began to revolve one arm slowly, and it was evident from her dissatisfied and somewhat scornful frown that she did not regard this member with the same pride and pleasure with which she had looked at her hand. Her arm was slender, firm, and strong looking but rather short, and for this reason she did not like it. As she looked at it, she shook her head slightly with a comical gesture of depreciation as she muttered "No." Her arm seemed stumpy, short, and ugly, and with her love of "a clear design," for the swift, beautiful, and incisive character which had shaped her hands, her arm seemed to her to be without any distinction whatever.

Therefore, she turned her discontented look from them, and craning her head downward and staring with a puckered glance of a child, she put her hands beneath her breasts and looked at them. They were the full loose sagging breasts of a woman of middle age who has born children, and their ends were tough, brown, and leathery looking, surrounded by brown areolas of mottled flesh. And curiously, although it was here and here only that the woman's noble and delicate beauty had been marred by age and labor, she regarded her breasts with no sign either of approval or despair. Rather, she held them in her hands and looked at them with the intent rude and somewhat puzzled stare of a child, which was as detached in its curiosity as if they were no part of her.

At length she released them and slid her hands down gently across her waist, which was still small and delicate, and over her hips. Then she drew her hands back slowly over the smooth contours of her thighs and rubbed them with sense of approval and satisfaction on her belly. It was comely, proportionate, and yet bountiful, swelling smoothly with a velvet unction. There was a wide smooth sear upon it and for a moment her finger traced the slick smooth imprint of this sear below her gown. Then the woman put her hands down at her sides again, and for a moment more she lay motionless, toes evenly in line, limbs straight, head front, eyes staring gravely at the ceiling,—a little figure stretched out like a queen for burial, yet still warm, still palpable, immensely grave and beautiful, as she thought: "These are my hands and these are my fingers; these are my legs and hips, this is my velvet belly, and these are my fine feet and my perfect toes:—this is my body."

And suddenly, as if the grave and final estimate of these possessions filled her with an immense joy and satisfaction, she flung the covers jubilantly aside, sat up with a shining face, and swung her body strongly to the floor. She thrust her small feet vigorously into a pair of slippers, stood up, thrust her arms out and brought the hands down again behind her head, yawned and then thrust her bare arms into the sleeves of a yellow quilted dressing gown which was lying across the foot of the bed.

The woman had a rosy, jolly, and delicate face of noble beauty, which was like no one else on earth. The face was small, firm and almost heartshaped, and in it was evident that same strange union of the child and of the woman, which was also visible in her body. The moment anyone met her or saw her for the first time he must instantly have felt: "This woman looks exactly the way she did when she was a child. She has not changed at all." Yet her face also bore the markings of age and maturity of a middle-aged woman: it was when she was talking to someone and when her face was lighted by a merry and eager animation that the child's face was most clearly visible.

When she was at work, her face was likely to have the serious and rather worn concentration of a mature and expert craftsman engaged in an absorbing and exacting labor, and it was at such a time that she looked oldest: It was then that one noticed the somewhat fatigued and minutely wrinkled spaces around her eyes, and some strands of coarse grey that were beginning to sprinkle her dull dark-brown hair.

Finally, in repose, or when she was alone, her face was likely to have a sombre, brooding and almost sorrowful depth. It had at such a time a beauty that was profound, and full of mystery. And it had also in it the troubling quality of something fatal and last of someone who has "lost out" somewhere in life in some priceless and irrecoverable thing; her forehead was low and at such a time could be wrinkled by an almost animal-like look of perplexity, confusion, and even grief. Such a look could trouble a friend or a lover because it suggested a knowledge buried, secret, and fundamental to the life of a person he believed he had come to know. And at such a moment, she looked completely like the woman with no trace of the child about her.

She was three parts a Jewess, and it was at such a time as this that the ancient, dark, and sorrowful quality of her race was most evident. But this was not often, to act, to work, to move and live in the world, with almost furious industry was the way people remembered her best, the very weather of her soul, the way she appeared most often was as a glowing, jolly, indomitably active and eager little creature, in whose delicate and lovely face the image of the child, proud, and with an invincible joyfulness was looking out of the woman's face with an immortal confidence.

Thus, in the woman's face were all the lights and tunes of beauty, grave, gay, or eager, troubled by strange depths and haunted by an obscure and sorrowful perplexity, now the woman, now the child, and now strangely, marvelously, both, she had in her all the enchantment of a beauty that was dark and strange as Asia, and as familiar as the light of day. By night—in the great cliff and glitter of the city night, with all its proud and arrogant dust of gold, its incredible pollens soaring into space of a million sown lights and with its shining edge of menace, its corrupt and sneering faces, the woman's face could glow cruel and brilliant in chambers of the night with a proud, sensual and almost arrogant assurance.

But by day, in the first dear light of morning, or by noon, by the high, sane practical light of golden noon, she had as jolly, a rare and good a face of delicate and noble beauty as any on this earth could be. Her jolly apple-cheeks were glowing with all the health and freshness in the world, and they were as red and tender as a cherry, her mouth was red and tender, as the petals of a rose, her eyes were brown and kind, wise, sharp and eager. When she came into a room she filled it with her exultant health and loveliness and she seemed to give structure, a color of morning joy and life to all the brutal and furious stupefaction of the streets she came from.

So, too, when she went out in the streets at morning, glowing all about her with an eager, merry, and insatiable curiosity, she gave a color to these grey beaten pavements which they had never had before. Her little face, among the spires and ramparts of the cruel and inhuman architectures that beetled all about her was blowing like a deathless flower; among the numberless swarms of desolate and sterile people, thrusting and thronging endlessly up and down a thousand streets with a kind of weary and exacerbated fury, as they urged themselves on to the consummation of their arid and fruitless labor, the sight of that woman's face was like a triumph and a prophecy.

It shone there as the other people thronged about her like the token of a deathless and glorious beauty to people trapped in hell, the man-swarm pressed about her in an incessant tidal grey, grey hats and dead grey flesh, and dark dead eyes. They thronged past her with their accursed hats of cheap grey felt, and their million faces set in the few familiar gestures of an inept hardness, a cunning without an end, a guile without a purpose, a cynical knowledge without faith or wisdom, and with their scrabble of a few harsh oaths and cries dedicated to the sterile and unending repetition of their own knavishness. And against all these million evidences of the vileness, cheapness, and shabby, dingy evil of which men are capable if there was only this evidence of their beauty, and magnificence, it was enough. The woman passed among them, and that one deathless flower of a face that bloomed among so many millions of the dead at once struck music from the shining morning: it gave a tongue to chaos, a music of energy and joy to the vast pulsation of the city's life, a structure of beauty, life, and certitude to everything it passed, —so that even the sterile and grey-faced people thrusting about her everywhere with their harassed and driven eyes, were halted suddenly in the dreary fury of their lives, and looked at her, at the music of health and joy that shone out of her face, and stared after her little figure as it moved briskly along, and which in its opulence, its sense of something fertile, curved, and living as the earth was so different from their own grey and meagre flesh, that they looked at her almost like wretches who are trapped and damned in hell, but to whom for one moment a vision of a living and deathless beauty has been granted.

MORNING

· · ·

MRS. JACK AND THE MAID

· · ·

At this moment, as Mrs. Jack stood there by her bed, her maid servant, Molly, knocked at the door and entered immediately, bearing a tray with a tall silver coffee pot, a small bowl of sugar lumps, a cup, and saucer and a spoon. The maid put the tray down on a little table beside the bed, saying in a thick Irish voice:

"Good maar-nin', Mrs. Jack."

"Oh, Hello, Molly!" the woman answered, crying out in the eager and surprised and rather bewildered tone with which she usually responded to a greeting. "How are you?—Hah?"—clapping her hand to one ear as she phrased this conventional question, as if she was really eagerly concerned, but immediately adding: "Isn't it going to be a nice day? Did you ever see a more beautiful morning in your life?"

"Oh, *beautiful*, Mrs. Jack," Molly answered. "Beautiful!" The maid's voice had a solemn and almost reverential tone of agreement as she answered, but there was in it the undernote of something sly, furtive, sullen and Irish, and the other woman looking at her swiftly now saw the maid's eyes, sullen, drunken, inflamed, and irrationally choleric, staring back at her. The maid's voice was respectful and even unctuously submissive in its agreement but her bleared and angry looking eyes stared back with a sullen and drunken rancour, a resentfulness, whose bold, wilful and wicked defiant glance seemed to be directed not so much at

53

her mistress as at the general family of the earth. Or, if her angry eye did swelter with a glare of spite more personal and direct, her resentment was instinctive, blind and stubborn—it just smouldered in her with an ugly truculence, and she did not know the reason for it. Certainly, it was not based on any feeling of class inferiority, for she was Irish and a papist to the bone, and where social dignities were concerned she had no doubt at all on which side condescension lay.

She had served this woman and her family for more than twenty years, and it must be admitted (for her present defection was a recent one) that she had swindled them, stolen from them, lied to (and for) them, and grown slothful on their bounty with a very affectionate devotion and warmth of old Irish feeling—but she had never doubted for a moment that they would all ultimately go to hell, together with the other pagans and all alien heathen tribes whatever.

Meanwhile, she had done herself pretty well among these prosperous infidels for some twenty years, fattening herself up in a cushy job, wearing the scarcely worn garments of two of the best dressed women on the earth and seeing to it that the constable who came to woo her several times a week should lack for nothing in the way of food and drink to spur him on to fresh accomplishment in the exercise in which, it seemed to her, he excelled—or, as she would have put it, "a [?]."

Meanwhile she had feathered her nest snugly to the tune of several thousand dollars, and kept the old folks back in Clare or Cork or wherever it was she came from, faithfully furnished with a glittering and lascivious chronicle, sprinkled with pious interjections of regret and deprecation and appeals to the Virgin to watch over her and guard her among such infidels of this brave new world that had such pickings in it. No—decidedly this truculent resentment which smouldered in her eye had nothing to do with caste: she had lived here for twenty years a kind of female Marco Polo enjoying the bounty of a very good superior sort of heathen, and growing used and tolerant to almost all their sinful customs, but she had no doubt where the true way and the true light was, and that she would one day find her way back into the more civilized and Christian precincts of her own kind.

Neither did the grievance in the maid's hot eye come from a sense of poverty, the stubborn silent anger of the poor against the rich, the feeling that good decent people like herself must fetch and carry all their lives for lazy idle wasters, that she must drudge with roughened fingers all day long in order that this fine lady might smile brightly and keep beautiful.

No, the maidservant knew full well that there was no task in all the household range of duties—whether of serving, mending, cooking, cleaning or repairing, which her mistress could not do far better and with more dispatch than she.

And she knew further that every day in the great city which roared all about her own dull ears this other woman was going back and forth with the energy of a dynamo, a shining needle flashing through the million repetitions of the earth's dull web, buying, ordering, fitting, cutting, and designing—now on the scaffolds with the painters, beating them at their own business in immense, draughty and rather dismal rooms where her designs were hammered into substance, now sitting cross-legged among great bolts of cloth and plying a needle with a defter finger than any on the dully flashing little hands of the peaked and pallid tailors all about her, now searching and prying about indefatigably through a dozen gloomy little junk shops until she unearthed triumphantly out of the tottering heaps of junk the exact small ornament which she must have— always after her people, always good humoredly but formidably pressing on, keeping the affair in hand, and pushing it to its conclusion (enforcing the structure, the design, the rich incomparable color of her own life on the incompetent chaos of inept lives and actions all about her) in spite of the laziness, carelessness, vanity, stupidity, indifference and faithlessness of the people with which she had to work—painters, actors, shifters, bankers, union bosses, lighters, tailors and costumers, producers and directors—the whole immense motley, and for the most part shabbily inept and tawdry crew which carried on the crazy and precarious affair that is known as "the show business."

No: the maid had seen enough of the hard world in which her mistress daily strove and conquered to convince herself that even if she had possessed any of the immense talent and knowledge that her mistress had to have, she did not have in all her lazy body as much energy, resolution, and power as the other woman carried in the tip of her little finger. And this knowledge, so far from arousing any feeling of resentment in her, only gave her a feeling of self-satisfaction, a gratified feeling that her mistress, not herself, was really the working woman and that, enjoying the same food, the same drink, the same shelter—yes! even the same clothing as her mistress—she would not swap places with her for any thing on earth.

Yes, the maid knew that she was fortunate, and had no cause for complaint: yet her grievance, ugly and perverse, glowered implacably in her inflamed and mutinous eye. And she could not have found a word or reason for that grievance, but as the two women stood there, it scarcely needed any word. The reason for it was printed into their flesh, legible in everything they did, in every act and move they made. It was not against the other woman's wealth, authority, and position that the maid's rancour was directed, but against something much more personal and indefinable—against the very tone and quality of the other woman's life. For there had come over the maid's life in the past year a distempered sense of failure, and frustration, an angry discontent, an obscure but powerful feeling that her life had somehow gone awry and dissonant, and was growing into a sterile and fruitless age without ever having come to any ripeness. And she was goaded, baffled, and tormented, as so many people have been, by a sense of having missed something splendid and magnificent in life, without knowing at all what it was. But whatever it was, the other woman seemed marvelously somehow to have found it and enjoyed it to the full, and this obvious fact, which she could plainly see, but could not define, goaded the maid almost past endurance.

Both women were about the same age, and so nearly the same size that the maid could wear any of her mistress' garments without alteration. But if they had been creatures from separate planetary systems, if each had been formed, filled and given life by a completely different protoplasm, the physical differences between them could not have been more extreme.

The maid was not an ill-favored woman. She had a mass of fairly abundant red-brown hair, coarsely woven and clean looking, brushed over from the side. Her face, had it not been for the distempered and choleric look which drink and her own baffled and incoherent fury had now given it, would have been a pleasant and attractive one. It had in it the warmth, and a trace of that wild fierceness, which belongs to something mad, red, and lawless in nature, at the same time coarse and delicate, murderous, tender, savagely ebullient like a lawless chemistry, which so many women of her race have had. Moreover, she still had a trim figure, which wore neatly the well-cut skirt of rough green plaid which her mistress had given her (for, because of her long service, her position in the household as a kind of unofficial captain to the other maids was recognized, and she was usually not required to wear maid's uniform).

But where the figure of the mistress was at once rich and delicate, small of bone and fine of line and yet lavishly opulent and seductive, packed as it was from top to toe with juice and sweetness (so that the woman when one looked at her jolly, glowing, marvelously delicate face and figure was not only "good enough to eat," but of such a maddening and appetizing succulence, such wholesome relish that it was with diffi-culty one restrained himself from leaping upon her and devouring her then and there), the figure of the maid was by contrast almost thick and clumsy-looking, no longer young, no longer living, and no longer fresh and fertile, but already heavied, thickened, dried and hardened by the shock, the wear, the weight, the slow inexorable accumulations of the intolerable days, the merciless years that take from people everything, and from which there is no escape. "No—no escape, except for *her*" the maid was thinking bitterly, with a dull and tongueless rancour, a feeling of inarticulate outrage, "—and for *her*, for *her*, there was never anything but triumph, there was never anything but an outrageous and constantly growing success. And why? Why?"

It was here upon this question that her spirit halted like a wild beast, baffled by a sheer and solid blank of wall. Had they not both drawn the nurture of their lives from the same earth? Had they not breathed the same air, eaten the same food, been clothed by the same garments, and sheltered by the same walls? Had she not had as much, as good, of everything as her mistress—yes! Even of love, she thought with a con-temptuous bitterness, for she had seen the other woman's lovers come and go for twenty years, and if that was what it took to keep a woman young she thought, she had had as many and as good herself.

Yet here she stood, baffled and confused, glowering sullenly with an ugly and truculent eye into the shining face of the other woman's glorious success—and she saw it, she knew it, she felt its outrage but she had no word to voice the sense that sweltered in her an intolerable wrong. Instead, she stood there stiffened and thickened by the same years that had given the other woman an added grace and suppleness, her skin dried and sallowed by the same lights and weathers that had added health and lustre to the radiant beauty of the other one, her body stunned and deadened of its youth and freshness by the merciless collisions of ten thousand furious days which had served only to pack the other woman to her red rose lip with health and sweetness, energy and joy—and the end of it all was that she was being devoured by the same qualities the other woman fed upon, that she was growing old on the same earth, beneath the same impartial sky, whereon the other woman grew more beautiful day by day, that time whose grey and cancerous tongs was feeding like an adder on her life had yielded to this woman all that it had of richness, strangeness, beauty, that there was pulsing in her constantly a wild and dissonant chemistry of ruin, hatred, and defeat, that fed the sullen flames of her distempered eye, while—in the other woman there coursed forever a music of health and joy, an exquisite balance of power and control, of ecstasy and temperance, a pulse, a flame, a star!—an exquisite confluence of all the forces of a rare and subtle beauty which was as vital as the omnipotent and everlasting earth, yet poised more sweetly than a bird in flight.

And all of this—the tidal flood of this all conquering ever growing beauty had found its well spring somehow in the hard and dismal rock of stony life from which her own ruined flesh and baffled soul had drawn no provender but an acrid and unwholesome dust. Oh, it was true, staring her in the face with an incontrovertible and overwhelming evidence, established by a literal and cruel comparison, so that the story of her ruin and the other woman's glory was written down in lip, cheek, eye, in every line and movement of the figure, and in the very chemistry of the blood which brought to one an ugly jungled dissonance, and to the other the singing and triumphant music of beauty and success, until the other woman's victory was evident with every breath she drew, and not only the color of her life, the health and radiance of her soul, seemed to shine out, with a charitable but merciless benignity upon the warped and blackened spirit of the maid, but the very texture of her flesh, the weave of her hair, the rose of her lip, the living satin of her skin, the spittle of her mouth, together with all combining sinews, nerves and tissues, juices, fibres, jellies, marrows, the whole warm integument of pulsing flesh that bound her life together seemed of a finer, rarer substance than the maid had ever known.

Yes, she saw it, she knew it, cruelly and terribly true past the last atom of hope and disbelief, and as she stood there before her mistress with the weary distemper of her mutinous eye, enforcing by a stern compulsion the qualities of obedience, and respect into her voice and into the composed humility of her face which betrayed her effect nakedly in the mottled and choleric color of her cheeks and jaws, she saw that the other woman read the secret of her envy and frustration plainly and pitied her because of it. And for this she hated her, because pity seemed to her the final and intolerable indignity.

And, in fact, although the kind, jolly and eager look on the other woman's lovely face had not changed a bit since she had greeted the maid, her eye had read instantly and with a merciless and deadly precision, every minute sign of fever, envy and inchoate mutiny, the unwholesome dissonant fury that was raging in the woman, mind and body, and at this moment, with a strong emotion of pity, wonder and regret, she was thinking:

"She's been at it again: this is the third time in a week that she's been drunk. I wonder what it is, I wonder what it is that happens to that kind of person," she thought, without knowing clearly what it was she understood by "that kind of person," but feeling the detached, momentary, and half-indifferent regret and curiosity that people of a powerful, rich and decisive character may feel when they pause for a moment from the brilliant and productive exercise of an energy and talent that has crowned their life with a triumphant ease and success almost every step of the way, and note suddenly, and with surprise, that most of the other people in the world are groping, reeling, fumbling, blindly and wretchedly about, eking out from day to day, the inept and wretched progress of grey lives, that are so utterly lacking in any individual distinction, character, or talent that each seems to be rather a small, grey and flabby particle of some immense and vicious life-substance than a living and beautiful creature who is able to feel and to inspire the whole intolerable music of love, beauty, joy, passion, pain and death, of wild regret, exultancy, desire and depthless sorrow, which men have felt and made immortal on the earth.

And now, the mistress, with a strong emotion of discovery and surprise, was feeling this as she looked at the servant who had lived with her familiarly for more than twenty years, and as she now for the first time reflected closely on the kind of life the other woman might have had:

"What is it?" she kept thinking. "What's gone wrong with her? She never used to be this way, it's all happened in the last six months. And Molly used to be so pretty, too," she thought. "Why—when she first came to us twenty years ago she was really a very handsome girl,"—and she started with a memory of surprise—"Isn't it a shame!" she thought indignantly, "That she should let herself go to seed like this—a girl who's had the chances that she's had! I wonder why she never married—she used to have a half dozen of those big policemen on the string, they were mad about her, she could have had her pick of them!"

And suddenly, as she stood there looking kindly at the servant, the woman's breath, foul, stale and sour with a rank whiskey stench was blown upon her, and she got suddenly a rank body smell, an old odor of pit and crotch, strong, hairy, female and unwashed. She frowned slightly with a feeling of revulsion that was almost like a physical pain, and her rosy and delicate face began to burn more deeply with a hot excited glow of shame, embarrassment, and acute distaste.

"God! But she stinks!" she thought, with a feeling of horror and disgust. "You could cut the smell around her with an axe! The nasty bitches!" she thought suddenly, now including all her servants in a feeling of indignant contempt. "I'll bet they never wash—and here they are all day long with nothing to do, and they could at least keep clean! My God! You'd think these people would be so damned glad to be here in this lovely place with the fine life that we've made for them, that they would be a little proud of it and try to show that they appreciate it—but no!—What trash they are—the lazy, lying, thieving sluts! They're just not good enough!" she thought scornfully, and for a moment her fine and delicate mouth was disfigured slightly at one corner by an expression, almost racial in its contempt and arrogance, and certainly common to people of her race.

It was an expression which had in it not only the qualities of contempt and scorn, but also a quality that was too bold and naked in its sneering arrogance, as if it was too eager to flaunt and brandish its insolent contempt into the face of any passer by. And although this ugly look, so full of pride and scorn, and a lewd and cynical materialism, rested only for a second, and almost imperceptibly, about the edges of the woman's mouth, it did not sit well on her lovely face, and for just a moment it gave her fine, strong and sensitive mouth a coarse touch of something ugly, loose and sensual. Then it was gone. But the maid had seen it, and that swift look, with all it carried of contempt and arrogance, had stung and whipped her frenzied spirit to the quick.

"Oh, yes, my fine lady!" she was thinking. "It's too good for the likes of us, you are, isn't it? Oh my, no, but we're very fine, aren't we? What with our fine clothes and our evening gowns, and our forty pairs of hand made shoes—Jesus! now! Ye'd think she was some kind of centipede to see the different pairs of shoes she's got—and our silk petticoats and step-ins that we have made in Par-is, now—yes!—that makes it very fine, doesn't it—it's not as if we ever did a little private [fucking] on the side, like ordinary people, is it?—Oh my, no! We are gathered together wit a friend fer a little elegant an' high-class entertainment durin' the course of the evenin'—What's this I heard her say to him?—'Yer face is so delicate,—it's like an angel's!' Jesus! now! But aint that nice!—His face!

God, it's the first time, that I ever knew of anyone to keep his face buttoned in his britches!—But maybe that's the way they do it now, in high society!—But if it's some poor girl without an extra pair of drawers to her name, it's different, now! It's 'Oh! you nasty thing! I'm disgusted wit you! I believe ye're no better than a common whore!' Yes! An' there's many a fine lady livin' on Park Avenoo right now who's no better, if the truth was told—That I know and could swear to—So just take care, my lady, not to give yerself too many airs, for it wouldn't take me long to pull ye down a peg or two when I got started," she thought with a rancourous triumph.

"Ah! If I told all that I know of you—wit yer angels and their faces and 'He's simply mad about me little Edith,' and 'Molly, if anyone calls when I'm not here I wish ye'd take the message yerself—Mr. Jack doesn't like to be disturbed'—Jesus! From what I've seen there's none of them who likes to be disturbed. It's live and let live wit them, no questions asked an' the devil take the hindmost, so long as ye do it in yer leisure hours, but if ye're twenty minutes late fer dinner, it's where the hell have ye been and what's to become of us when ye neglect yer family in this way? Sure," she thought, warming with a flush of humor and a more tolerant and liberal spirit, "It's a queer world, ain't it?—And these are the queerest of the lot! Thank God, I was brought up like a Christian in the Holy Church, and still have grace enough be ashamed when I have sinned! But, then—" and now, as often happens with people of strong but disordered feeling, she was already sorry for her flare of ugly temper, and her affections were running warmly in a different direction—

"But, then, God knows, there's not a better-hearted sort of people in the world—there's no one I'd rather work for, than Mrs. Jack, they'd give ye everything they have, if they like ye—I've been here twenty years next April and in all that time no one has ever been turned away from the door who needed food. Sure, there's far worse who go to Mass six days a week—yes, and would steal the pennies off a dead man's eyes if they got the chance. It's a good home we've been given here—as I keep tellin' all the rest of 'em," she thought with virtuous content, "and Molly Fogarty's not the one to turn and bite the hand that's feedin' her—no matter what the rest of them may do!"

*   *   *   *   *

All this had passed in the minds and hearts of the two women with the speed of light, the instancy of thought. Meanwhile, the maid, having set the tray down on a little table by the bedside, had gone to the windows, lowered one of them and raised the shades to admit more light, slightly adjusted the curtains, and was now in the bath room drawing the water for her mistress' bath, an activity signalized at first by the sound of thick tumbling waters, and later by a sound more quiet and sustained as she reduced the flow and tempered the boiling fluid to a moderate heat.

While this was going on, the other woman had seated herself on the edge of her bed, crossed her legs briskly in a strong, jaunty and yet graceful movement, poured out a cup of the black steaming coffee from the tall silver pot, opened the newspaper which lay folded on the tray, and now, as she drank her coffee, she was staring with a blank troubled frown at the headlines of the paper, meanwhile slipping one finger in and out of a curious and ancient ring which she wore on her right hand. It was an action which she performed unconsciously, but with great speed and deftness—a single swift and nervous movement of her hand which, when she was with people, always indicated in her a statement of impatience, nervousness, or strained attention and when she was alone, indicated the swift and troubled reflection of a mind that was rapidly collecting itself for a decisive action.

And now, her first emotions of regret, pity, and curiosity having passed, the more practical necessity of some vigorous and immediate action was pressing at her.

"He's been furious about it—That's where Fritz's liquor has been going," she thought. "She's got to stop it. If she keeps on at the rate she's going she'll be no good for anything in another month or two—God! I could kill her for being such a fool!" she thought furiously. "What gets into these people, anyway?"—Her small and lovely face now red with anger and determination, the space between her troubled eyes cleft deeply by a frown, she determined suddenly to speak plainly and sternly with the maid without any more delay.

And, this decision being made, the woman was conscious instantly of a feeling of great relief and certitude, almost of happiness. For indecision was alien to the temper of her soul, and the knowledge of the maid's delinquency had been nagging at her conscience for some time: now, with a feeling of surprise and relief, she wondered why she had ever hesitated. Yet, when the maid came back into the room again, and paused before going out for a moment as if waiting for further orders, and looking at her with a glance that now seemed affectionate and warm, she was conscious of a feeling of acute embarrassment and regret, as she began to speak to her and, to her surprise, she found herself beginning in a hesitant and almost apologetic tone,

"Oh, Molly!" she said rapidly in a sharp and somewhat excited tone, as she slipped the ring swiftly on and off her finger—"There's something I want to speak to you about—"

"Yes, Mrs. Jack," Molly answered humbly, and paused respectfully.

"It's something Miss Edith wanted me to ask you," she went on quickly, somewhat timidly, discovering to her amazement that she was beginning her stern warning and reproof in quite a different way from the way she had intended.

Molly waited in an attitude of studious and respectful attention.

"I wonder if you or any of the other girls remember seeing a dress Miss Edith had," she said and went on quickly—"One of those dresses she brought back last year from Paris. It had a funny grey-green kind of color and she used to wear it in the morning when she went to business. Do you remember?" she said sharply, clapping her hand to her ear, "Hah?"

"Yes, Ma'am," said Molly with a solemn wondering air. "I've seen it, Mrs. Jack."

"Well, Molly, she can't find it. It's gone."

"Gone?" said Molly, staring at her with a stupid and astonished look.

But even as she spoke the other woman saw a furtive ghost of a smile, thin, evil, Irish and corrupt, at the corner of the servant's mouth, in her sly and sullen humor, and a look of triumph in her eye, and she thought instantly:

"Yes! She knows where it is! Of course she knows! They've taken it!—Of course, they've taken it!—the lying sluts! It's perfectly disgraceful and I'm not going to stand it any longer!"—and a wave of angry indignation, hot, swift and choking boiled up in her, flushing the delicate rose color of her face a thick and angry red.

"Yes, gone! It's gone, I tell you!" she said angrily to the staring maid. "What's become of it? Where do you think it's gone to?" she asked bluntly.

"I don't know, Mrs. Jack," Molly answered in a slow, wondering tone. "Miss Edith must have lost it."

"Lost it! Oh, Molly, don't be stupid!" she cried furiously. "How could she lose it? She's been nowhere. She's been here all the time—and the dress was here, too, hanging in the closet, up to a week ago! How can you lose a dress?" she cried impatiently. "Is it just going to crawl off your back and walk away from you when you're not looking?" she said sarcastically. "You know she didn't lose it! Someone's taken it!"

"Yes, ma'am," Molly said with a dutiful acquiescence. "That's what I think, too. Someone must have sneaked in here when all of yez was out an' taken it. Ah, I tell ye," she remarked with a regretful movement of the head, "It's got so nowadays ye never know who to trust and who not to," she remarked sententiously. "A friend of mine who works fer some big people up at Rye was tellin' me just the other day about a man who came there wit some new kind of a floor-mop that he had to sell—ast to try it out an' show 'em how it worked upon their floors, ye know, an' a finer, cleaner lookin' boy, she says, ye wouldn't see again in yer whole life-time. 'And my God!' she says—I'm tellin' ye just the way she told it to me, Mrs. Jack—'I couldn't believe me own ears when they told me later what he'd done! If he'd been me own brother I couldn't have been more surprised,' she says.—Well, it just goes to show ye that—"

"Oh, Molly, for heaven's sake!"—the other woman cried with an angry and impatient gesture—"Don't talk such rot to me! Who could come in here without you knowing it? You girls are here all day long, there's only the elevator and the service entrance, and you see everyone who comes here—and besides, if anyone ever took the trouble to break in, you know he wouldn't stop with just one dress. He'd be after money or jewelry, or something valuable that he could sell."

"Well, now, I tell ye," Molly said, "that man was here last week to fix the frigidaire—I says to May at the time—'I don't like the look of him. There's something in his face that I don't like, you keep your eye on him,' I says, 'because—'"

"Molly!"—At the sharp, stern warning in her mistress's voice, the maid paused suddenly, looked sharply at her, and then was silent, with a dull, sullen flush of shame and truculence upon her face. For a moment the other woman stared at her with a burning and indignant look. Then she burst out on her plainly, with an open blazing anger before which the maid stood sullenly, hostile, silent and resentful.

"Look here!" the other woman broke out furiously. "I think it's a dirty shame the way you girls are acting! We've been fine to you! Molly, there are no girls in this town who've been treated better than you have."

"Don't I know it, Mrs. Jack," Molly cried in a lilting and earnest tone—"Haven't I always said the same? Wasn't I saying the same thing meself to Annie just the other day? 'Sure,' I says, 'but we're the lucky ones! There's no one in the world I'd rather work for than Mrs. Jack.

Twenty years,' I says, 'I've been here, and in all that time,' I says, 'I've never heard a cross word from her. They're the best people in the world,' I says, 'and any girl who gets a job wit them is lucky,'" she cried richly. "Sure, haven't I lived with ye all like ye was me own family? Don't I know ye all—Mister Jack an' Miss Edith and Miss Alma and Mr. Ernie—Wouldn't I get down on me knees right now an' scrub me fingers to the bone if it would help ye any—?"

"Oh, scrub your fingers to the bone!" the other woman cried impatiently. "Who's asking you to scrub your fingers to the bone? Lord, Molly, you girls have had it pretty soft. There's mighty little scrubbing that you've had to do!" she said. "It's the rest of us who *scrub*," she cried. "We go out of here every morning—six days in the week—and work like hell—"

"Don't I know it, Mrs. Jack?" Molly cried. "Wasn't I sayin' to May just the other day—"

"Oh, damn what you said to May!" the woman said. For a brief moment she looked at the servant with a straight, burning face of indignation. Then she spoke more quietly to her. "Molly, listen to me," she now said. "We've always given you girls everything you ever asked for. You've had the best wages anyone can get for what you do. And you've lived here with us just the same as the rest of us—you've had the same food, the same shelter—yes! even the same clothes—" she cried, "for you know very well that—"

"Sure," Molly interrupted in a richly sentimental tone. "It hasn't been like I was workin' here at all! Ye couldn't have treated me any better if I'd been one of the family!"

"Oh, one of the family my eye!" the other said impatiently. "Don't make me laugh! There's no one in the family—unless maybe it's my daughter Alma—who doesn't do more in a day than you girls do in a week! You've lived the life of Riley here!—The life of Riley!" she repeated, almost comically, and then stood there looking at the other woman for a moment, a formidable little dynamo trembling with her indignation, slowly clenching and unclenching her small hands at her sides. "Good heavens, Molly!" she burst out in a furious tone. "It's not as if we ever begrudged you anything! It's not as if we ever denied you anything you asked for! It's not the value of the dress—you know very well that Edith would have given it to you if you had gone to her and asked her for it. But—oh! It's intolerable! Intolerable!" She stormed out suddenly in a furious and uncontrollable anger. "That you should have no more sense or decency than to do a thing like that to people who have always been your friends!"

"Sure, and do you think I'd be the one who'd do a thing like that?" cried Molly in a trembling voice. "Is it me ye're accusin', Mrs. Jack, when I've lived here wit yez almost twenty years? Sure, they could take me right hand"—in her rush of feeling she raised and held the member up, "and drop it from me arm before I'd take a button that belonged to one of yez. And that's God's truth," she added solemnly. "I swear it to ye as I hope to live and be forgiven for me sins. Yes, I'll swear it to ye," she declared more passionately as the other woman started to speak—"that I never took a pin or penny that belonged to one of yez—and so help me God, that's true! And yes! I'll swear it to ye by everything that's holy!" she now cried, tranced in a kind of ecstasy of sacred vows.—"By the soul an' spirit of me blessed mother who is dead"—

"Ah! *Molly!*" the other woman cried with a furious and impatient exclamation, turning angrily away, and, in spite of her indignation, breaking into a short and angry laugh at the extravagance of the servant's oaths as she thought with a bitter, scornful and contemptuous humor: "God! There's not an honest bone in her whole body—yet she'll swear a thousand oaths and thinks that makes an honest woman out of her! Yes! And will stay stinking drunk all night and go to Mass next morning if she has to crawl to get there—and cross herself with holy water—and listen to the priest say words she cannot understand—and come out glorified—to steal from us all day! What strange and magic things these oaths and ceremonies are!" she thought. "They give a kind of life to people who have none of their own. They make a kind of truth for people who have found none for themselves. Love, beauty, everlasting truth, salvation— all that we hope and suffer for on earth is in them for these people, all that *we* have to do with our own blood and labor, and by the ambush of our soul, is done for *them*, somehow" she thought ironically, "if they can only swear to it 'by the soul an' spirit of me blessed mother who is dead!—'"

"—And, so help me God, by all the Blessed Saints, and by the Holy Virgin, too," she heard Molly's voice intoning, and instantly she turned upon her with a movement of furious and exasperated impatience.

"Molly, for God's sake, have a little sense!" she cried. "What is the use of all this swearing by the saints and virgins, and getting up and going out to Mass, when all you do is come back home to swill down Mr. Jack's whiskey? Yes, and to lie and steal from the people who have been the best friends that you ever had!" she cried out bitterly, and seeing the old and mutinous look which had returned now to the maid's sullen and distempered eye, she went on with an almost pleading earnestness: "Molly, for God's sake, try to have a little wisdom! Is this all you've been able to get from life?—To come in here and sneer and lie, and blow your stinking breath on me, when all we've ever done has been to help you?"—The woman's voice was trembling with her passionate and open anger, and yet one would instantly have known, had he heard her, that her anger was something more than personal, that she was speaking not so much because she felt the maid had lied to her and stolen from her sister, but because she felt that the maid had betrayed and insulted something decent and inviolable in life—a faith and integrity in human feeling that she felt should be kept and honored everywhere. And this fine, bold, passionate quality of indignation was so plainly and earnestly written down in every feature of her face, and in every line and member of her vital and determined little figure, that it somehow made the woman wonderful. For it was plain that she would have spoken out without fear or favor to anyone, and at any place and time, as she had spoken to the maid, if she had seen some cut of cruelty, injustice or dishonor; yet it was also evident that she was in no way a quarrelsome or officious woman, but as kind, happy, and liberal in her nature as anyone could be.

Finally, the very sight of her as she stood there would have been sufficient to evoke a whole human faith again, a belief in a high, rare, and wonderful value of human dignity—and with a strength and truth in her which was so much greater than anything in the maid that it soared triumphantly above the maid's sullen figure, establishing victoriously and forever above the servant's feeble sneer the reality of beauty, joy, and glorious and abundant living on the earth. And it was this quality, that sprang and flourished from the everlasting earth, that the maid had seen and hated dumbly in her rancourous and barren soul, and that made the woman wonderful.

This quality of exultancy, energy, and joy which this woman had is not only the most rare and wonderful thing in the world, it is also so familiar and living a possession that when people see it, even though they have never seen it before, they feel instantly not only its power and beauty, but they feel that they have known it forever, that it belongs to them, and that everyone should be a part of it. Yet not one person in ten thousand has it; when he has, it is scarcely too much to say that nothing else matters. People will want to be near him, to feel the power, joy, and beauty of his presence, to live in the world of ecstasy and magic that springs to life everywhere around him and that lives in everything he touches. What is this quality? From where does it come? Where does it go? In what kind of people does it live? It seems to be a power that is completely arbitrary and indifferent to human choice. It chooses, rather than is chosen, and one finds it as often in brutal, ignorant and indifferent men, as in people distinguished by their talent or intelligence.

One finds it sometimes in the heavy shambling figure of a man with the brutal and battered face of a vagabond: as he swings along at a shambling step he will carelessly thrust one hand into the pocket of his shapeless coat, draw forth a cigarette, light it briefly between a cupped palm and hard and twisted mouth, and then walk on, with a wire of acrid smoke expiring slowly from his nostrils. Yet this simple and familiar gesture will not only awaken in the beholder an overpowering desire to smoke, but that man has somehow discovered tobacco again: all the joy, the pungent fragrance, the relish and the deep content that the first man who ever smoked must have known has been revived in the wink of an eye by the gesture of a tramp.

In the same way a workman tearing the thick and glutinous halves of a meat sandwich between his blackened fingers may awaken an almost intolerable hunger in the spectator as the finest chef on earth could never do; an old man sitting at the throttle of a mighty locomotive as he steams slowly past, by his one gloved hand of curving, his lean and somewhat withered applecheeks, his glint of demon hawkeyes on the rail, may evoke in the beholder a sense of glory, power, and joy, a music of space and ecstasy, an instant vision of the whole vast structure of the earth, the sleeping woods, the great dark continent of night, and new lands, morning, and a shining city, as all the eightlocked driving wheels and flashing pistons in the world could never do.

And these examples, as bright as beings in a shining water, as literal as morning, as incontrovertible as the savage thirst and hunger with which we nailed them to the walls of our fierce memory could be multiplied, as everybody knows, indefinitely, but to no advantage, for everyone has seen them, everyone has known them for himself, and we all know this radiant and exultant power has struck like lightning everywhere on earth, and has been chosen as its rare agents the most obscure and humble people as often as the most renowned. Certainly it had never made its dwelling in a richer earth than in this woman, for it seemed to inhabit not only every atom of her flesh, but to be part of the whole radiance and energy of her spirit, so that it was in everything she did, everything she touched, everything she said, and if she had done, said, or touched nothing, it would have been with her, and around her, filling the very silence with the presence of its exultancy and joy: For this reason, she brought magic with her everywhere.

MORNING

. . .

JACK AND HIS WIFE

. . .

He rapped lightly at the door and waited. There was no answer. More faintly, listening, he rapped again.

"Are you there?" he said. He entered the room. She was sitting with her back to him at the other side of the room, seated at a small writing desk between the windows with a little stack of bills, business letters, and personal correspondence on her left hand, and an open check book on her right; she was vigorously and rapidly scrawling off a note. As he advanced toward her, she put the pen down, swiftly blotted the paper, and was preparing to fold and thrust it in an envelope when he spoke.

"Good morning," he said in the pleasant half ironic tone that people use when they address someone who is not aware of their presence.

She jumped, turned around quickly and then spoke to him in the jolly and eager but somewhat bewildered voice with which she usually responded to a greeting.

"Oh, hello, Fritz," she cried in a high, rather dazed tone. "How are you? Hah?" clapping her small hand swiftly to her ear.

He stopped in a somewhat formal and teutonic fashion, planted a brief, friendly and perfunctory kiss on her rosy cheek, and straightened, unconsciously shrugging his shoulders a little, and giving his sleeves and the bottom of his coat a brief tug to smooth out any wrinkle that might have appeared to disturb the faultless correctness of his costume. And although she continued to look at him with a jolly, eager, and innocent face, still seeming a little confused and bewildered, as deaf people are, she had missed not even the remotest detail of his costume for the day—shoes, socks, trousers, coat, and tie, together with the true perfection of a tailored line, and the neat gardenia in his buttonhole,—all this she observed in an instant together with his ruddy face and the small waxed points of his moustache, and she felt a swift secret and ironic amusement which did not tell even for a second upon her jolly and eager face. And as he straightened, her innocent and merciless eye swept briefly across the faultless smoothness of his buttoned coat, noting a just faintly perceptive disturbance in the smooth line of his coat at the place where his inside breast pocket was.

And remembering the small square envelope with the thin spidery writing which she had seen among the mail that morning, she thought with an ironic faintly bitter amusement: "Well, he's got it. Right over the heart—or, anyway, just underneath the pocket book." Yet, during all this time of merciless cognition, the somewhat confused and good-humored expression of her jolly face did not change a bit. Instead, as she sat there with her glowing face bent forward and her hand held firmly to one ear in an attitude of eager attentiveness, her jolly face had the puzzled and confused look of good-natured people—and particularly of good-natured people who are somewhat deaf—which seemed to say: "Now, I can see that you are laughing at me about something? What have I done now?"

As for Jack, he stood before her for a moment, feet apart, and hands akimbo on his hips, looking at her with an expression of mock gravity and sternness, in which, however, his good humor and elation were apparent.

"Hah?" she cried again, eagerly, bending forward with a cupped ear as if to hear what he had said, although he had said nothing.

In answer, Jack produced the newspaper which he had been holding folded back in one hand, and tapped it with his index finger, saying:

"Have you seen this?"

"No, who is it?" she cried eagerly. "Hah?"

"It's Elliot in the *Globe*. Like to hear it?"

"Yes. Read it. What does he say?"

And as he prepared to read, she bent forward, her rosy face glowing more deeply with excitement and attention, and one hand held firmly to her ear. Jack struck a pose, rattled the paper, frowned, and cleared his throat with mock pretentiousness, and then began in a slightly ironic and affected tone, in which however his own deep pleasure and satisfaction was manifest, to read the fancy and florid words of the review.

"Mr. Shulberg has brought to this, his latest production, the full artillery of his own distinguished gifts for suave direction. He has paced it brilliantly, timed it—word, scene, and gesture—with some of the most subtly nuanced, deftly restrained, and quietly persuasive acting that this too too jaded season has yet seen. He has a gift for silence that is eloquent—oh! devoutly eloquent—among all the loud but for the most part meaningless vociferation of the current stage. All this your diligent observer is privileged to repeat with more than customary elation. Moreover, Mr. Shulberg has revealed to us in the person of Montgomery Mortimer the finest youthful talent that this season has discovered. Finally"—Jack cleared his throat solemnly, "Ahem, Ahem"—flourished forward his short arms, and rattled the paper expressively, and for a moment stared drolly at her. "Finally, he has given us with the distinguished aid of Esther Jack a faultless and unobtrusive decor which warmed these ancient bones as they have not been warmed for many a Broadway moon. In these three acts, Miss Jack contributes three of the most effective settings she has yet done for the stage. Subtle, searching and hushed, with a slightly rueful humor that is all their own, there is apparent, in her elvishly sly design, a quiet talent that is growing constantly, and that need make obeisance to no one. She is, in fact, in the studious opinion of this humble but diligent observer, the first designer of her time."

Jack paused abruptly, looked at her drolly and gravely with a cocked head over the edges of the paper, and said:

"Did you say something!"

"God!" she yelled, her jolly face flushed with laughter and excitement. "Did you hear it! Vat is dees?" she said comically, making a Jewish gesture with the hands. "An ovation,—what else does he say?" she asked eagerly, clapping her hand to her ear and bending forward, "Hah?"

Jack proceeded:

" 'It is, therefore, a pity that Miss Jack's brilliant talent should not have better fare to feed as than was given it last evening at the Arlington. For the play itself, we must reluctantly admit, was neither—' "

"Well," said Jack, stopping suddenly and putting down the paper, "the rest of it is—*you* know," he shrugged slightly and made a gesture with his hands, "—a sort of so-so. Neither good nor bad! He sort of pans it.—But *say!*" he cried, with a kind of jocular indignation. "I like the nerve of that guy! Where does he get this *Miss* Esther Jack stuff? Where do *I* come in?" he said. "Don't I get any credit at all for being your husband? You know," he said, "I'd like to get in somewhere if it's only a seat in the second balcony. Of course"—and now he began to speak in the impersonal manner that people often use when they are being heavily sarcastic, addressing himself into the vacant air, as if some invisible auditor were there, and as if he himself were only an ironical observer—"Of course, he's nothing but her husband, anyway. What is he?—*Bah!*" he said in a scornful and contemptuous tone. "Nothing but a fat little stock broker who doesn't deserve to have such a brilliant woman for his wife. What does he know about art? Can he appreciate her? Can he understand anything she does? Can he say—What is it this fellow says?" Jack demanded, suddenly looking at the paper with an intent stare and then reading it in an affected and ironic tone—" 'subtle searching, and hushed with a slightly rueful humor'—a slightly rueful humor," Jack said ironically, "Not a *rueful* humor, but a *'slightly* rueful humor that is all their own.' "

"I know," she said in a tone of pitying contempt, as if the florid words of the reviewer aroused in her only a feeling of commiseration, although the pleasure and excitement which the words of praise had given her were still legible on her flushed face—"I know. Isn't it pathetic! They're all so fancy—these fellows, they make me tired.!"

" 'There is apparent in her elvishly sly design' " Jack continued—" '*Elvishly* sly'—now that's a good one! Not sly, but *elvishly* sly," he said, then with a droll and Jewish gesture of the palms he demanded of his unseen auditor—"Could her husband think of a thing like that? Nah-nah-nah!" he cried suddenly, in a curiously guttural accent, shaking his head with a scornful and angry laugh and waving a plump forefinger sideways before him. "Her husband is not smart enough!" he cried furiously. "He is not good enough! He's nothing but a common business man! He can't appreciate her!" he shouted in a furious and guttural tone,—and suddenly, to her amazement, she saw that his eyes were shot with tears, and that the lenses of his neat gold rimmed spectacles were being covered with a film of mist.

For a moment she stared at him in stupefaction, her warm and jolly little face bent towards him in an expression of startled and protesting concern, but even at the same moment she was thinking, as she had often thought: "What a strange man!" and feeling obscurely yet strangely, as everyone has felt, that there was something in life she had never been able to find out about, or to express. For she knew that in this sudden and reasonless display of strong feeling in this plump grey-haired, and faultlessly groomed man, there was no relation whatever to the review in the paper, which had praised her work so warmly. Neither was his chagrin because the reviewer had referred to her as "Miss," anything more than a playful and jocular pretense.

She knew that he was really bursting with pride and elation because of her success, and with a sudden poignant, and wordless pity—for whom, for what, she could not say—she had an instant and complete picture of the great chasmed downtown city, where he would spend his day, and where all day long, in the furious drive and turmoil of his business, excited prosperous looking men would pause suddenly to seize his arm, to grasp his hand, and to shout: "Say—have you seen today's *Globe?*—Did you see what it had to say about your wife?—Aren't you proud of her?—Congratulations!"

And she could see also his spruce plump figure, and his ruddy face beginning to blush and burn brick-red with pride and pleasure, as he received the tribute of prosperous men, and as he tried to answer them with an amused and tolerant smile, and a few casual and indifferent words of acknowledgment as if to say: "Yes, I think I did see some mention of it—but of course you can hardly expect me to be excited by a thing like that. That's an old story to us now. They've said that kind of thing so often that we're used to it."

And when he came home that night he would repeat what had been said to him—what Rosenthal and Straus, his two rich partners, had said to him, what Liliencron, the president of his luncheon club, had said, and what Clark and Stein, two of his richest customers, had said. And although he would repeat their words at dinner with an air of faintly cynical amusement, she knew that his satisfaction would be immense and solid, and that it would be enhanced by the knowledge that the wives of these rich men, handsome and splendid-looking Jewesses, as material-minded in their quest for what was fashionable and successful in the world of art, as were their husbands, for what was profitable in the world of business, would also read of her success, would straightway go to witness it themselves, and then would speak of it in brilliant chambers of the night; where even the heavy glowing air received an added menace of something cruel and erotic from the lavish bodies and the cruel faces of these handsome, scornful and sensual looking women.

All this she thought of instantly as she stared with an astounded face at this plump, ruddy, grey haired man, whose eyes had suddenly and for no reason that she knew, filled with tears, and whose firm scornful mouth now had the pouting, bitterly wounded look of a hurt child. "What a strange man!" she thought again, for she had seen these sudden and unexplainable surges of feeling come over him before, and had never known what they meant, but even as she thought all this, and as her heart was filled with a nameless and undefinable sense of pity, she was crying warmly in a protesting voice: "But, Fritz! You know I never felt like that! You know I never said a thing like that to you," she cried indignantly. "You know I love it when you like anything I do—I'd rather have your opinion ten times over than one of these fellows in the newspaper. What do they know anyway?" she muttered scornfully. "They make me tired, they're all so fancy."

And he, having taken off his glasses and polished them angrily, having blown his nose vigorously and put his glasses on again, now suddenly lowered his head, braced his thumb stiffly on his temple and put four plump fingers across his eyes in a shielding comical position, saying rapidly, in a muffled, guttural and apologetic tone:

"I know! I know! It's all right! I was only choking," he said with an absurd and pathetic smile, and then lowering his head abruptly, he blew his nose vigorously again, his face lost its ridiculous expression of wounded feeling, and he began to talk in a completely natural matter-of-fact tone, as if nothing he had done or said had seemed at all extraordinary:

"Well," he said, "How do you feel? Are you pleased with the way things went?"

"Oh, I suppose so," she answered in the dubious, vague and somewhat discontented tone she always used on these occasions, when her work was finished, and the fury, haste and almost hysterical tension of the last days before a theatrical production were at an end. Then she continued: "I think it went off pretty well—don't you? Hah? I thought my sets were sort of good—or did you think so" she demanded eagerly. "No," she went on in the comical and disparaging tone of a child talking to itself, shaking her head in a depressed fashion but hoping for the warm denial of the connotation of its elders. "I guess they were just ordinary—pretty bad—a long way from my best—hah?" she demanded, clapping her hand to her ear.

"You know what I think," he said angrily, "I've told you. There's no one who can touch you. The best thing in the show!" he said, strongly. "They were by far the best thing in the show!" (And, as always, in moments of strong feeling, his accent became guttural—and, instead of "show," he said "joe")—"By *far*! By *far*!" he said. Then, in a quiet tone, he said, "Well, I suppose you're glad it's over. That's the end of it for this year, isn't it."

"Yes," she said, "except for some costumes that I've promised Irene Morgenstein I'd do for one of her damned ballets. And I've got to meet some of the company for fittings again this morning," she concluded in a weary and dispirited tone.

"What, again! Weren't you satisfied with the way they looked last night? What's the trouble?"

"Oh," she said in a disgusted and impatient tone, "What do you think's the trouble, Fritz? There's only one trouble—it never changes: It's always the same! The trouble is that there are so many half-baked God-damned fools in the world who'll never do the thing you tell them to do! That's the trouble! God!" she said frankly, "I'm too good for it! I never should have given up my painting. The thing you do is so wonderful—the thing that happens when you design," she went on in an earnest but rather confused tone, wrinkling her low forehead in an almost animal-like expression of perplexity as if she knew exactly what she wished to say, but could not find the words to explain it, and as if that fault lay rather in the understanding of other people, and in the dimensions of language, rather than in herself. "Honestly! You don't *know* what goes on in me when I design!" she cried in an earnest half-accusing tone, as if, by not knowing, he were guilty of some fault: "No one ever asks me how it happens: No one seems to want to know," she said in an aggrieved and half resentful tone, "But it's the most wonderful thing you ever heard of! At first, it's all solid, like one thing. It's one solid mass up here," she went on tapping her head, and frowning again with the curiously bewildered and animal-like frown:—"Then, it all gets broken up somehow in little bits, like a picture," she went on vaguely, still frowning in the confused manner, "it all sort of swims around and arranges itself until—there it is! I've got it—all clear!" she cried triumphantly, "—The design!" She was silent, frowning in the perplexed and troubled fashion for a moment, then she burst out suddenly with her straight warm indignation, "Isn't it a shame!" she cried, "that a wonderful thing like that has got to be wasted on those people?"

"What people?" he said.

"Oh, you know," she muttered, "the kind of people that you get in the theatre. Of course there are some good ones—but God!" she said frankly, "Most of them are such trash! Did you see me in this and did you read what they said about me in that, and wasn't I a knockout in the other thing?" she muttered in a sullen and resentful tone. "God, Fritz, to listen to the way they talk you'd think the only reason a play ever gets produced is to give one of them a chance to strut around and show himself off upon a stage! When it ought to be the most wonderful thing in the world!—Oh! The magic you can make, the thing you can do with people if you want to—It's like nothing else on earth!" she cried. "Isn't it a shame no more is done with it!" She brooded for a moment with an angry almost sullen flash upon her face. Then, suddenly, her breast and warm full throat began to tremble, a burble of wild humor welled up in her throat, and finally she cast back her head and laughed, a wild full yell of woman's laughter, as she spoke: " 'As for me—as for me,' " she choked, " 'I am noted for muh torso' "—and rich wild helpless laughter rose from her and rang around the spacious room.

"Eh? What's that? What did you say? Who said that?" cried Jack eagerly, beginning to grin and scenting a good story to tell his business friends even before he understood the meaning of her reference.

"Oh, that fellow Atwater! That big bum!" she said in a disgusted tone.

"Reginald Atwater?—" Jack said eagerly. "The one who played the Older Man?"

"Yes, doesn't it sound like him?—God! I could have killed him!" she burst out furiously. "To think he'd have no more sense than to do a thing like that."

"What! What did he do?" said Jack.

"Why, coming on in the second act in that God-awful evening suit! I thought I'd have a fit when I looked at him!" she cried.

"Well, I did notice it!" Jack admitted. "It was pretty gay. I sort of wondered why you did it."

"I?" she cried indignantly. "Do you think I had anything to do with it? Do you think I'd have let him come on in a rig like that. No! Over my dead body!" she declared.

"Why, wasn't it the suit you'd picked out for him?"

"Of course not!" she cried furiously. "It was his own ham actor's outfit that he goes out shop-girl hunting with—or something," she muttered angrily. "Couldn't you tell it by looking at it—those fancy silk lapels about twice too wide, and that fancy actor's vest with rolled lapels, and about three acres of that God-damned shirt all bulged out in front like a pouter pigeon? Do you think I'd ever do a thing like that?" she said indignantly. "Not on your life."

"Then how did it happen?"

"—Oh, the way it always happens! If you're not there to watch over them every second of the time it will always happen. I had a beautiful quiet suit all picked out for him,—just the one he needed for the part—and got him fitted up in it—"

"Did he want to wear the other one—his own?"

"Oh, yes, of course! They always do!" she said impatiently. "That's what I'm always fighting with them for—trying to beat it into their heads that—'Look here, Atwater,' I said. 'It doesn't matter at all what *you* want to wear. What you think looks best on you! I'm not costuming you but the character in the play! You're not playing Atwater'—(which is a big lie, of course, he's always playing Atwater!) He couldn't play anything else but Atwater if he tried!" she said scornfully—"'You're playing the man in the play' I said. 'And you've simply got to get that into your head.' 'Yes, I know,' he said. 'I know.'—(God! Fritz, his face looks just exactly like a piece of cold sliced *ham*)—'I know,' he says, 'but then, you know we all have our points,'—Points!" she muttered resentfully. "That fellow has nothing else but points: He's one complete mass of sore thumbs as far as I'm concerned.—'We all have our points,' he said. 'And as for me'—sticking his chest out about a mile and hitting himself on it like a piece of ham—'As for me'"—her voice rose to a rich full yell of laughter. "'I am noted for muh Torso!'"

And their laughter joined and rang around the room.

"—But isn't it a shame," she went on presently in an indignant tone. "To give the words and thoughts of a great poet or anything that's any good to a fellow like that! You'd think they'd be so damned glad to make the most of the chance they have!—Really, you wouldn't believe it—some of the things they say. 'As for me I am noted for muh torso.'" she muttered. "God! I didn't believe I'd heard him right—'What did you say?' I cried. 'Oh what did you say, Mr. Atwater?'—It just didn't seem possible—I had to get off the stage as fast as I could! When I told Roberta I thought she'd have a fit!—'Torso!'" she muttered scornfully again. "I suppose he thought I should have dressed him up in a lion skin."

She was silent for a moment, then she said wearily, "Gee, I'm glad this season's at an end, I wish there was something else I could do.—If I only knew how to do something else, I'd do it. Really, I would," she said earnestly. "I'm tired of it. I'm too good for it," she said simply, and for a moment stared moodily ahead.

Then, still frowning in a sombre and perturbed manner, she fumbled nervously in a wooden box upon the desk, took from it a cigarette and lighted it. She got up nervously and began to walk about the room with short steps holding the cigarette in the rather clumsy charming and unaccustomed manner of a woman who rarely smokes, and frowning intently when she puffed at it.

"I wonder if I'll get some good shows to do next year," she muttered, as if scarcely aware of his presence. "I wonder if there'll be anything for me to do. No one's spoken to me yet," she said gloomily.

"Well if you're so tired of it, I shouldn't think you'd care," he said ironically, and he added, "Why worry about it till the time comes?"

MORNING

. . .

THE WORLD THAT JACK BUILT

. . .

Jack had, in fact, listened to her complaint and her account of her troubles in the recent production, with the serious attention, and the keen interest and amusement that her stories of her labors, trials and adventures in the theatre always aroused in him. For, in addition to the immense pride and satisfaction that he took in his wife's talent and success, he was like most rich men of his race, and particularly those who like himself were at that time living every day in a glamorous, unreal and fantastic world of speculation, strongly attracted by the glittering electric life of the theatre.

The progress of his life, indeed, for almost forty years when, as a boy, he had come to America from the little Rhineland town where his family lived, had been away from the quieter, more traditional, and as it now seemed to him, duller forms of social and domestic life, to those forms which were more brilliant and gay, filled with the constant excitement of new pleasures and sensations, and touched with a spice of uncertainty and menace. Thus, the life of his boyhood—the life of his family, who for a hundred years had carried on a private banking business in a little German town—now seemed to him impossibly dull and stodgy. Not only its domestic and social life, which went on as steadily and predictably as a clock from year to year, and which was marked at punctual intervals by a ritual of dutiful visits and counter-visits among dull and heavy-witted relatives, but its business life, also, with its small and cautious transactions, now seemed paltry and uninteresting.

His life, in fact, had for more than thirty years moved on from speed to speed and height to height—keeping time indeed, with all the most glittering and magnificent inclines of speed and height in the furious city that roared in constantly increasing crescendo about him. Now, even in the mad world in which he lived by day, and whose feverish air he breathed into his veins exultantly, there was a glittering, inflamed and feverish equality that was not unlike the night time world of the theatre in which the actors lived.

At nine o'clock in the morning of every working day, Jack was hurled southward to his employment in a great glittering projectile of machinery which was driven by a man who was himself as mad, inflamed, and unwholesome as any of the life around him. In fact, as the chauffeur prowled above his wheel, his dark and sallow face twisted bitterly by the thin and dry corruption of his mouth, his dark eyes glittering with the unnatural glitter of a man who is under the stimulation of a powerful drug, he seemed to be a creature which this new and furious city had created—whose dark and tallowy flesh seemed to have compacted, along with millions of other men who wore grey hats and had faces of the same lifeless and unutterable hue, out of a common city-substance— the stuff of pavement grey, as well as the stuff of buildings, towers, tunnels, bridges, streets. In his veins there seemed to pulse and flow, instead of blood, the feverish, unnatural, and electric energies to which the whole city moved, and which was legible in every act and gesture the man made, as his corrupt, toxic and sinister face prowled above the wheel, so that as his glittering eyes darted right and left as, with the coming of a maniac, the skill and precision of a sinister but faultless mechanism grazing, cutting, flanking, shifting, and insinuating, as he snaked and shot the great car through all but impossible channels and with a perilous and murderous recklessness, it was evident that the criminal and unwholesome chemistry that raced in him was consonant to a great energy that was pulsing everywhere about him in the city.

Yet, to be driven downtown by this sinister and toxic creature seemed to increase Jack's sense of pleasure, power and anticipation: as he sat behind his driver and saw his eyes now sly and cunning as a cat's, now hard and black as basalt, now glittering humidly with a drugged and feverish glitter, as his thin face now peered slyly and evilly right and left, now full of cunning and sly triumph as he snaked his car ahead around some cursing rival, now from the thin twisted corner of his convulsed, corrupt and obscene mouth snarling out his hate loudly at other drivers or at some careless pedestrian—"Guh-wan ya screwy bast-ed—guh-wan!"—more softly at the menacing figure of some hated policeman, or speaking to his master from the twisted corner of that bitter, sterile, and corrupted mouth a few constricted words of grudging praise for some policeman who would grant him privileges—"Some of dem are all right," he said. "*You* know," with a shining and a powerful and constricted accent of high strained voice. "Dey're not all basteds. Dis guy"—with a jerk of his head toward the policeman who had nodded and let him pass, "Dis guy's all right—I know him—Sure! Sure!—He's a brud-deh of me sisteh-in-law!"

And all of this—the sense of menace, conflict, cunning, stealth, and victory—above all else, the sense of privilege, added to Jack's pleasure and even gave him a heady tonic joy as he rode down to work. The unnatural and unwholesome energy of his driver, the man's drugged eyes and evil face evoked in Jack's mind, as well, a whole image of a phantasmal and theatrical world. Instead of seeing himself as one man among a million other men who were going to their work, in the homely, practical, immensely natural light of day, he saw himself and his driver as two cunning and powerful men pitted triumphantly against the world; and the monstrous and inhuman architecture of the city, the phantasmagoric chaos of the traffic, the web of the streets swarming with a million nameless people became a kind of tremendous, woven, chameleon backdrop for his own activities.

And just as that unreal and feverish world of gigantic speculation in which he lived by day and which had now come to have a theatrical cast and color was everywhere sustained by this great sense of privilege—the privilege of men, selected from the man-swarm of the earth because of some mysterious intuition or knowledge they were supposed to have, to live gloriously with labor or production in a world where their profits mounted incredibly with every ticking of the clock, or where their wealth was increased fabulously by a nod of the head, the lifting of a finger, so did it seem to Jack, not only entirely reasonable but even pleasant and desirable that the whole structure of society from top to bottom should be honeycombed with privilege and dishonesty.

He knew, for example, that this same driver, who was part Irish, part Italian, and whose name was Barney Dorgan, swindled and stole from him right and left, that every bill for fuel, oil, tires, repairs or overhauling was viciously padded, and that this same Dorgan was in collusion with the garage owner for this purpose, and received a handsome percentage from him as a reward. Yet this knowledge did not disturb or anger him. Instead, he actually got from it a feeling of pleasure and cynical amusement. The knowledge that his driver stole from him and that he could afford it, gave him somehow a sense of power and security. If he ever questioned his dishonesty at all, it was only to shrug his shoulders indifferently, and to smile cynically, as he thought: "Well, what of it? There's nothing to be done about it. They all do it. If it wasn't him, it would be someone else."

Similarly, he knew that the Irish maids in his household were stealing all the time, and that at least three members of the police force, and one red-necked Irish foreman spent most of their hours of ease in his kitchen and in the maid's sitting or bed rooms. He also knew all these guardians of the public peace and safety ate royally every night of the choicest dishes of his own table, and that their wants were cared for even before he, his family, and his guests were served, and that his best whiskey and his rarest wine was theirs for the asking.

But, beyond an occasional burst of temper and annoyance, when he discovered that a case of real Irish whiskey (with rusty sea-stain markings on the bottles to prove genuineness) had melted away almost overnight, a loss which roused his temper because of the rareness of the thing that was lost, he said very little. When his wife spoke to him about these thefts, as she occasionally did, in a tone of vague protest, saying: "Fritz, I'm sure those girls are stealing from us all the time. I think it's perfectly dreadful don't you? What do you think we ought to do about it?" His only answer was to shrug, smile cynically, and show his palms.

And although it had cost him more than seventy thousand dollars the year before to keep the five members of his family provided with shelter, clothing, service, food, and entertainment, the fact that a large part of this shocking amount had been uselessly squandered or actually stolen from him caused him no distress whatever. Rather, the extravagance, waste, and theft in his own household expense seemed to give authority and justification to that unbelievable madness which he was witnessing every day in the business world which was at that time mounting to its crest. Neither was the indifferent and tolerant acquiescence he gave to this shameful waste the fact of a man who feels his world is trembling on a volcanic crust that certain ruin and collapse is before him, and that he will make merry with all his might and spend riotously until the crash comes.

No. He gave consent to the theft, extravagance, and privilege which he saw everywhere about him not because he doubted but because he felt secure, convinced that this rotten fabric was woven from an iron thread, not because he felt that ruin was impending, but because he was so convinced that ruin would never come—that the tottering, corrupt, and fictitious edifice of speculation was hewn from an everlasting granite, and would not only endure, *but* would grow constantly greater.

It was an ironic fact that this man who now lived in a world in which every value was false and theatrical should see himself, not as a creature tranced by a fatal and illusionary hypnosis, but rather as one of the most practical, hardheaded, and knowing men alive. Just as he saw himself, not as a theatrical and feverishly stimulated gambler, obsessed and fascinated by his belief in the monstrous fictions of speculation, but rather as the brilliant and assured executive of great affairs, who at every moment of the day had his "finger on the pulse" of the nation, so when he looked about him and saw everywhere in the world from top to toe, nothing but the million shapes of privilege, dishonesty and self-interest, he was convinced that this was inevitably "the way things are."

Moreover, he was so far from understanding that his own vision was distorted, false, and theatrically easy that he flattered himself on his "hardness," fortitude, and intelligence for being able to swallow this black picture of the earth with such an easy and tolerant cynicism. The real substance of this "hardness," fortitude, and intelligence was to be painfully demonstrated in another year or two when, the gaudy bubble of his world having been exploded overnight before his eyes, this plump, ruddy, and assured man would shrink and wither visibly in three days' time into a withered and palsied senility. But now nothing could exceed his satisfaction and assurance. He looked about him in the world, and, like an actor, found that all was false and evil, and this brilliant discovery only enhanced the joy and pleasure which he took in life.

In fact, at this time, the choicest stories which Jack and his associates told each other, all had to do with some facet of human chicanery, treachery, or dishonesty. They delighted in matching stories concerning the delightful knaveries of their chauffeurs, maids, cooks, and bootleggers, describing the way in which these people had cheated them as one would describe the antics of a household pet, and they found that these stories usually had a great success at the dinner table, and were characterized by the ladies as: "I—think—that—is—simply—price-less!" (Spoken slowly and deliberately as if the enormity of the tale has simply stunned and duped the listener into a state of stupefaction), or, "Isn't it in-credi-i-bul!" (Spoken with a faint rising scream of laughter), or, "Stop! You *know* he didn't," delivered with a lady-like shriek—all the fashionable and stereotyped phrases of people who are listening to an "amusing" story, and whose lives have become so sterile and savorless that laughter has gone dead in them.

One of the stories which Jack told with considerable success, was this: A year or two before (when he was still living in the brown-stone house on Seventy-Fourth Street which he had occupied for more than twenty years), his wife was giving one of the jolly open-house parties which she gave every year to the members of a "group" theatre for which she worked. At the height of the gaiety when the party was in full swing and the actors were swarming through the rooms, gorging themselves to their heart's content on the food and drink with which the tables were groaning, there was a great screaming of police sirens on Riverside Drive, which was only a few yards away, and the sound of motors driven to their limit, and approaching at top speed. Suddenly the entourage turned into the street, and to the alarm and stupefaction of Jack and his guests who now came crowding to the windows, a high powered motor truck flanked by two motor cycle policemen pulled up before the house, and stopped. Immediately, two burly policemen, whom Jack instantly recognized as friends of his Irish maids, sprang to the ground from the body of the truck and, in a moment more, with the assistance of their fellows, they had lifted a great barrel from the truck and were solemnly rolling it across the sidewalk and up the stone steps into the house. This enormous barrel, it turned out, was filled with beer which the police were contributing to the party to which they had also been invited (for when Jack's wife, Esther, gave a party to the actors and actresses, the maids and cook were also allowed to give a party to the policemen and firemen in the kitchen).

Then when Jack, moved and gratified by this act of friendship and generosity on the part of the police, had desired to pay them for the trouble and expense the beer had cost them, one of the policeman had said to him: "Forget about it, boss. It's O.K. I tell you how it is," the man then said lowering his voice in a tone of quiet and confidential intimacy. "Dis stuff don't cost us nuttin', see? Nah!" he vigorously declared. "It's given to us. Sure! It's a commission dey give us," he added delicately, "for seein' dat dere stuff goes troo O.K. See?"

Jack saw, and told the story many times to his delighted guests. For

Jack was really a good and generous little man and an act like this, even when it came from men who had eaten and drunk royally and at his expense for years the value of a hundred barrels of beer, warmed and delighted him.

As is invariably the case with the cynic, cynicism and sentiment were woven indissolubly together, and his black picture of the earth, false and theatrical as it was, was saved from monstrousness by his own character, which had in it so much that was liberal, kind, and tolerant. Of this there was constant and repeated evidence. Jack would act instantly and materially to help people who were in distress, and he did this again and again—for actors down on their luck, for elderly spinsters with schemes for the renovation of the stage which were never profitable,—he even pensioned off every month one of his wife's aunts, a dyed and varnished old hag of eighty-two, who had cheated his wife and her sister out of the little nest egg which their father had left to them, and whom Jack detested not only for this but for all other reasons.

"Oh," the old witch would croak at him, as she wagged a vindictive varnished claw in his face on one of her frequent visits to his house, "— Oh, you don't like me now," she croaked, but I'll bet you, Fritz!" she cackled vindictively, "I'll bet you, if I had a million dollars that you'd treat me different then—Heh! Heh! Heh! Heh!" At which Jack, red in the face from anger and exasperation would fling down his paper, jump to his feet, shout angrily—"You can bet your sweet life I would!" and stamp out of the room. Yet, he not only sent this old harpy an allowance of one hundred dollars on the first of every month, which she rarely found adequate to her own extravagances (the chief of which was a passion for shoes with high red heels which she wore by day and night and in all times and weathers) but he also invariably yielded to her begging cries for additional help, the chief of which the old hag craftily embodied in a plea for new false teeth—(a plea she used so often and so forgetfully that it was found she had desired money for eleven sets within eight months' time).

Thus, as often happens, there was housed in the compact well-groomed figure of this plump ruddy grey haired Jew with the waxed moustache ends a vision of the earth which was false and black as hell, together with as kind, liberal and tolerant a spirit as one is likely to meet in the course of a day's journey. If this had not been true, the man would have been a monster. For not only, in his belief, was the dishonesty of his servants, the corruption of the police, and the complete tyranny of privilege everywhere on earth, from the greatest to the most trifling affairs, a condition to be accepted without even the most casual and languid feeling of surprise, but the total corruption of humanity everywhere was also to be understood and accepted in this same matter-of-fact way.

Thus, in his view of the world, every man had certainly his price, as every woman had hers, and if, in any discussion of conduct, it was suggested to him that people had acted as they had for motives other than those of total self-interest and calculating desire—had acted as they had because they loved each other, or because they would rather endure pain themselves than cause it to other people that they loved, or were loyal because of loyalty, or could not be bought or sold for no other reason than the integrity of their own characters—Jack's answer to this was to smile politely but cynically, make a brief motion with his arms and hands, and say: "All Right. But I thought you were going to be intelligent. Let's talk of something else that we both understand."

And that was all.

Such a man, then, was this ruddy, smartly groomed, and faultlessly tailored little fellow of fifty-four who was hurled southward to his business every morning in a powerful projectile of glittering steel that was driven by a maniac and who, as immense and cruel architectures beetled all about him, and he saw the man-swarm passing in its million-footed weft, found nothing strange therein.

Such a man was Frederick Jack—a spruce, assured, and very prosperous looking figure, who had in his bearing, dress, and feature something of the "distinguished" manner of the great banker, together with that little extra and indefinable cut to everything—a somewhat heightened color, cut, and vividness, an added knowingness and swagger, a kind of sporty dash and tone and recklessness, that was like a dash of paprika, and that somehow related him with others who live constantly among the theatrical and feverish excitement of a life which is disturbed, out of focus, and unnaturally stimulated—in other words, with politicians, gamblers, quack joint-and-gland and lay-the-hand-on specialists, and all other quacks whatever fashionable psycho-analysts, hit-the-trail evangelists, suave racketeers—and actors!

Such a man was Frederick Jack: a little man forever certain and forever wrong, a resident in a world which accepted the fabrications of its own distorted and intoxicated fury as the very heart and care of harsh reality, and which rejected reality itself with an impatient and dismissing gesture and a cynic's smile. Frederick Jack was a man who daily lived, breathed, and believed in all the acts and passions of a fantastic, theatrical and incredible world, and who subscribed to a vision of life that was as black, as vile, as viciously false and ineptly, uselessly sinister as any on this earth could be—and yet he was a man with as much grace, kindliness, and charity as anyone could wish for the most liberal and tolerant spirit.

He was a loving and indulgent father, who lavished gifts and luxuries upon his two children with prodigal hand, and he had on countless occasions responded with the instant and liberal help of his purse not only to the needs of friends but also to the troubles of many people whom he scarcely knew—to all the improvident, drunken, haphazard, or futile people whom his wife had met in her experience in the theatre, and who, in time of distress inevitably clustered about her strong, clear and victorious personality as slaves of steel cluster about a powerful magnet—as well as to a great motley regiment of others—to a raw-boned half-demented old nurse who had been in attendance at the birth of his two children, and had subsisted largely on his bounty ever since, to his wife's childhood and schoolgirl friends who had made poor marriages, to decrepit or impoverished relatives of his own and his wife's family, no matter how distant the relationship or how heartily he detested them, and finally, and always, to members of his own family living in Germany, and to his own begotten blood and seed.

For strangely, curiously, and pathetically, this little man who lived among all the furious and constantly shifting visages of a feverish and unstable world, had always held with a desperate and tenacious devotion to one of the ancient traditions of his race and youth—a belief in the sacred and inviolable stability of the family. And through this devotion, in spite of the sensational tempo and its furious constantly mounting instability of the city life, in spite of the unwholesome life of the theatre in which each member of his family was somehow involved, and which constantly menaced the security of the family life, he had managed to keep his family together. And this was really the only bond which now connected him with his wife. They had never loved each other, they had long since ceased to care what separate loves and ardours each might have, but they had joined together in a material effort to maintain the unity of a family life, as distinct from the lives of each individual in it. And through this effort, and by this compromise—which avoided deliberately and almost studiously, a close inspection of the individual life—they had succeeded in keeping the unity of the family group, and for this reason, and on this ground, Jack respected and had a real affection for his wife.

Such was the well-groomed little man who was delivered at his business every morning by a maniac. And if such dissonance between his own belief and practice, between his sinister view of men's acts and motives, and the charity and generosity of his own character, seems remarkable, or if his skill and cunning in the acts of balance seems remarkable, where his sole remaining anchor to an older and more traditional form of life was his belief in the permanence of the family, it was by no means so. For every morning, within a hundred yards of the place where his maniac delivered him, ten thousand other men, in dress, style, form and feature much the same as he, in their fantastic and sinister beliefs, and even in kindness, mercy, love and tolerance, much the same as this portly little Jew, were even as he descending from their gleaming thunderbolts and moving towards another day of legend, smoke and fury.

*   *   *   *   *

At length, having been delivered at his business with a murderous haste by this furious automation, Jack was shot up to his office where all day long men in whom this same unnatural and feverish energy seemed to be at work, bought, sold, and traded in an atmosphere which was not so openly, obviously and frantically alive, as it was quietly, murderously alert, with madness.

This madness was everywhere about him all day long, and Jack was himself aware of it. Yet he said nothing. For it was one of the qualities of this time that men should see and feel and know the madness all about them, and never mention it. Jack had known for several months, for example, that Rosenthal, the senior partner of his firm, was mad. Everyone else knew it as well, yet no one spoke of it until two years later when Rosenthal had to be confined in an asylum. Then, to be sure, they all said, with wise nods: "Sure, we knew it, all the time!"

But often in the morning Rosenthal would ride up in the same elevator with Jack, and not only would he fail to respond to his junior partner's morning greeting, but he would stare at Jack with a gloomy Napoleonic look, seeming to stare right through the other man who was not a foot away from him. Moreover, when Rosenthal entered his office he would enter through a certain door, and give orders that an office boy and his secretary must always be there in the room to greet him, stand-

The World That Jack Built   ᴁ   89

ing at attention and facing the door when he would enter, even when there was no real reason for their being there.

Having seated himself at his magnificent desk—for everything he had as we shall see, pens, paper, desks, inkwells, chairs, and so forth, now had to be the most magnificent and expensive that money could buy— having seated himself at his magnificent desk Rosenthal would at once go into a gloomy Napoleonic attitude of deep meditation from which he would presently start up and rouse himself to say in a harsh tone of voice to his secretary who still was standing dutifully at attention: "Who is waiting?" The girl would answer that Mr. Clark—or whoever it was—was waiting, whereupon Rosenthal would wave his hand in a furious and gloomy gesture of dismissal saying: "Tell him I cannot see him today," although he had himself made the appointment just the day before.

Then he would lapse into his moody soliloquy again, from which he would presently rouse himself to mutter gloomily: "And who comes next?"

"Mr. Seligman, sir—at nine-thirty."

There would be a portentous darkening pause, and finally Rosenthal would whisper hoarsely: "Tell him—tell Mr. Seligman—that I shall see him—at ten-fif-teen," although there was no reason whatsoever for the delay.

Again, when about to sign a letter, he would start to dip his pen in the inkwell, and suddenly stop, drawing back from the inkwell and shudder- ing as if it were a viper and had stung him.

"This—this—" he would say in a choked and trembling tone, throw- ing down his pen and pointing to the inkwell with a palsied finger. "Where did *this* come from?" he would scream, although it had been there on his desk all the time. Then he would seize the inkwell and hurl it against the wall or smash it on the floor, yelling that it was a disgrace that such a man as he should have to use such an inkwell. Then he would shout out orders, and demand the finest inkwell for himself and his secretary "that money could buy." And they would finally arrive, as his awed secretary would tell her fascinated auditors when she went home to Brooklyn—"made of saw-lid silveh—Duh one on *his* desk costs sixteh-*seven* dollehs—an'duh one on *my* desk costs fawty-*six* dollehs! O-O-oh! Ya know, I think that's *aw-w-ful*! I think that's *ter-ri-bul*!"

But this frightened little stenographer was the only one who did. As for the others—Rosenthal's business partners, and his clients, although they saw the man was mad they considered his madness as being an- other evidence of his financial genius.

Thus, when he would suddenly emerge from his office and come out into the great room where the stock-board was, casting wild and gloomy glances all about him, peering intensely into the faces of men he had known for twenty years without speaking to them or giving any indication that he recognized them, the while he muttered and mumbled cunningly to himself words that no one understood, rubbing his white plump hands softly and greedily together, and from time to time chuckling craftily as he peered about him, his associates accepted this strange conduct as evidence that deep and cunning projects were being contrived in his brain, and that presently he would startle the entire market with a series of brilliant financial manipulations.

Among all these people, only the frightened little stenographer read in the man's conduct the omens of ruin and collapse, not only for Rosenthal himself but for the whole structure that supported him, and gave to such a madman its final utter faith. Day by day, this poor girl would go home to the great jungle of obscure and nameless people from which she came and tell her stories, which grew constantly more extravagant and incredible to an awed circle of shop girls, fellow stenographers, and bewildered elders.

"Gee! D'ya know what he says to me this mawnin?" she would begin, as they all crowded forward eagerly. "D'ya know what he asts me? He says ta me, he says, 'Who is dat man, Miss Feinboig? Who is dat man dat just came in here?' 'Wah-h-, *Misteh* Rosenthal!' I says. 'Dontcha remembeh—gee!' I thought he was kiddin' me or somethin'—*you* know!" she cried. "'Dontcha remembeh Misteh Mahtin? Wah *he's* been comin' in heah to see ya faw *yeahs*!' 'Who's dat?' he says. '*Wah* Misteh Mahtin—gee!' I thought he maht be kiddin' me or somethin'—*you* know!" she cried painfully. "So I says, 'You been doin' business with Misteh Mahtin all yoeh life.' 'Neveh hoid of 'im before,' he says, 'Wah-h, *Misteh* Rosenthal!' I says. He don't remembeh any moeh," she now cried earnestly. "Honest, he don't know what he's *doo*-in," she said with comical solemnity. "'Ya gotta 'n engagement, Misteh Rosenthal. Ya gotta 'n engagement to have lunch mit Misteh Huddlem' an' ah says, An' honest! He don't know what I'm tawkin' about—He acts as if he's neveh hoid of 'im—He don't remembeh 'im at all! Gee! Ya know that's *ter*-ri-bul! Ya know that's aw-w-ful!"—But this shocked and frightened little typist was the only one who did.

THE GREAT BUILDING
· · ·
(APRIL, 1930)
· · ·

From the outside the building was—just a building. True it was a very impressive one. It was not beautiful, certainly, but it impressed one by its bulk, its weight, its squareness, its sheer massivity. In the course of a day's journey on that fabled rock one would see a hundred buildings that one could remember more sharply for some startling or sensational quality. There were sky-soaring spires and splintered helves of steel and stone, and dizzy vertices, cliff-like facades, stupendous architectures that seemed themselves a part of the cold atmosphere of the high air. They were an aether of imperial stone and steel that framed the sky in etchings of immortal masonry, that caught the breath of man, appalled his eye, put a cold numbness in his flesh, and gave to that sea-girt isle a portion of its own fabulous and special weather, its time-sense that was so strange, so peculiarly thrilling, so different from the time of any other place on earth.

Yes, there were more special shapes that gave the swarming rock its startling quality, its fabulous uniqueness, its distinctive place among the super-cities of the world. These were the shapes the European thought about when he thought about "New York," about "America," the thing that caught the breath of travelers spell-bound, looking from a liner's deck, as that appalling and inhuman loveliness sustained there lightly on the water like a congeries of fabled smoke first went home to their seafilled eyes, and stilled their tongues.

This building, then, was none of these. In this great brede of appalling and man-daring shapes, the frame of this insolent and tormented loveliness, this square and massive building would have gone unnoticed, and had one seen it in his questing of the tortured rock he might not later have remembered it.

And yet the building in its way was memorable. In all that scheme of splintered jaggedness, the transient landscape of these tormented, ever-changing skies, the building stood for permanence, for enduring substance in the midst of ceaseless change.

It had, where so much else was temporal and ethereal, a monumental quality. The splintered helves would go and be replaced by madder stalactites of steel and stone, the spire-pierced skies would alter to new shapes of jaggedness—but this, one felt, was changeless and would still endure.

A mighty shape, twelve stories high, with basal ramparts of enduring stone, above huge planes of rather grimy, city-weathered brick, spaced evenly by the interstices of a thousand square and solid windows, the great building filled a city block, and went through squarely to another city block, and fronted on both sides. It was so grand, so huge, so solid, and so square-dimensioned that it seemed to grow out of the very earth, to be hewn from the everlasting rock itself, to be built there for eternity, and to endure there while the rock itself endured.

And yet this really was not true at all. That mighty building, so solid-seeming to the eye, was really tubed and hollowed like a giant honey-comb. It was sustained on curving arches, pillared below on riddled vacancy. It was really a structure upon monstrous stilts, its nerves and tubes and bones and sinews went down depth below depth among the channeled rock: below these basal ramparts of enduring stone, there was its underworld of storied basements. Below all these, far in the tortured rock, there was the tunnel's depth.

Therefore, it happened sometimes that dwellers in this imperial tenement would feel a tremor at their feet as something faint and instant passed below them, and perhaps remember that there were trains there, there were trains, far, far below them in these tunneled depths.

Then all would pass, recede, and fade away into the riddled distances of the tormented rock. The great building would grow solidly to stone and everlastingness again, and people would smile faintly, knowing that it was enduring, solid, and unshaken, now and forever, as it had always been.

A little before seven o'clock, just outside the building, as he was going in for the night's work, old John was accosted by a man of perhaps thirty years who was obviously in a state of vinous and unkempt dilapidation.

"Say, Mac—" At the familiar words, uttered in a tone of fawning and yet rather menacing ingratiation, the face of the old man reddened with anger, he quickened his step, and tried to move away. But the creature in its greasy clothes kept after him, plucked at his sleeve with unclean fingers, and said in a low tone—"I was just wonderin' if you could spare a guy a—"

"Nah-h!" the old man snapped angrily before the other one could finish the familiar plea. "I can't spare you anything! I'm twice your age and I always had to work for everything I had. If you was any good you'd do the same!"

"Oh, yeah?" the other jeered, looking at the old man with eyes that had suddenly gone hard and ugly.

"Yeah!" old John snapped back in the same tone, and then went on, feeling that this ironic repartee was perhaps a little inadequate but the best he could do on the spur of the moment.

He was still muttering to himself as he entered the great arched entrance of the building and started along the colonnade that led to the South wing.

"What's the matter, Pop?"—It was Ed, the day elevator man who spoke to him—"Who got your goat?"

"Ah-h!" John muttered, still fuming with resentment, and the unsatisfied inadequacy of his own retort—"It's these panhandling bums! One of 'em just stopped me outside the building and asked me if I could spare a dime! A young fellow no older than you are tryin' to panhandle from an old man like me! He ought to be ashamed of himself! I told him so, too!—I said, 'If you was any good you'd work for it!'"

"Yeah?" said Ed, in a tone of mild interest.

"Yeah," said John, feeling a little more satisfied this time with his answer—"'If you was any good,' I says, 'you'd work for it—the way I always had to do.'" He seemed to derive a little comfort from the repetition, for in a moment he went on forcefully but in a less bitter tone. "They ought to keep these fellows away from here," he said. "They got no right to bother the people in this building. The kind of people we got here oughtn't to have to stand for it." There was just a faint trace of mollification in his voice as he spoke the words, "the kind of people we got here": One felt that on this side reverence lay—"The kind of people we got here" were, at all odds, to be protected and preserved.

"That's the only reason they hang around this place," the old man said. "They know they can work on the kind of people we got here and get it out of 'em. Only the other day I saw one of 'em panhandle Mrs. Lewis for a dollar. A big fellow, as well and strong as you are! I'd a good notion to tell her not to give him anything! If he wanted work, he could go and get him a job the same as you and I! But of course they know how to play on the sympathy of the kind of people we got here. It's got so it's not safe for a woman in the house to take the dog around the block. Some greasy bum will be after her before she gets back. If I was the management I'd put a stop to it. A house of this kind can't afford it. The kind of people we got here don't have to stand for it!"

And having made these pronouncements, so redolent of convention, outraged propriety, and his desire to protect "the kind of people we got here" from further invasions of their trusting sanctity by these cadging frauds, old John, somewhat appeased, went on around the colonnade, went in at the service entrance of the south wing, and in a few moments was at his post, ready for the night's work.

THE ELEVATOR MEN

. . .

John Enborg was an American of first-generation stock. He had been born in Brooklyn more than sixty years before, the son of a Norwegian seaman and an Irish serving-girl. In spite of this mixed parentage, it would have been hard to find anyone whose appearance was more decisively "old stock" American than the old man's. One would have said without hesitation that he was sparely, dryly, American—New England Yankee. Even his physical structure had in one brief generation taken on those national characteristics which are perhaps partly the result of weather and of time, partly the result of tempo, speech, and local custom, a kind of special pattern of the nerves and vital energies wrought out and engraved upon the features, upon the whole framework of flesh and bone, so that, whatever they may be or from whatever complex source they are derived, they are still instantly and unmistakably "American"—so to be recognized, so unmistakably defined wherever they are found, at whatever place on earth.

Old John was "American" in all these ways. He had the dry neck of the American—the lean, sinewy, furrowed neck that is engraved so lankily and so harshly, with so much weather. He had the dry face, too, also seamed and lank and squeezed dry of its moisture, the dry mouth, not brutal certainly but a little harsh and stiff and woodenly inflexible, the lower jaw out-cropping slightly, the whole mouth a little sunken in above this bleak prognathousness as if the very tension of the nerves, some harsh and jarring conflict in the life around him had hardened the very formations of the jaw into this sinewy tenacity. In stature, he was not very tall, somewhat above the average height, but suggesting tallness by this same stringy, nervous and hard-sinewed leanness which was apparent in his neck and face. The old man's hands were large and bony, corded with heavy veins, as if he had done much work with them. Even in speech he was distinctively "American." His speech was spare, dry, nasal, and semi-articulate. It could have passed with most people for New England Yankee speech, though it did not have pronounceably the New England twang. What one noticed about it especially was its Yankee spareness, a kind of tartness, a dry humor, that was really not at all truculent, but that at times seemed so. He was very far from being a sour-tempered or ill-natured old man, but at times he may have seemed to be. It was just his way. He really loved the exchange of banter, the rough and ready interplay of wit that went on among the younger elevator men around him. But his humor concealed itself dryly, tartly, behind a mask of almost truculent denial. This was apparent now as Herbert Anderson came in. Herbert was the night elevator man for the south entrance. He was a young, chunky, good-natured fellow of twenty-eight or thirty years, with two pink, modelled, absurdly fresh spots in his plump cheeks, lively and good-humored eyes, and a mask of crinkly, curly brownish hair of which one somehow felt he was rather proud. He was really John's especial favorite of the whole building, although one might not have instantly gathered this from the exchange that now took place between them.

"Well, what do you say, Pop?" cried Herbert as he entered the service elevator. "You haven't seen anything of two blondes yet, have you?"

The faint, dry grin about John Enborg's mouth deepened a little, almost to a stubborn line, as he swung the door to and pulled the lever.

"Ah-h," he said sourly, almost in a disgusted tone, "I don't know what you're talkin' about!"

He said nothing more, but stopped the machine and pulled the door open at the basement floor.

"Sure you do!" Herbert said vigorously as he walked over to the line of lockers, peeled off his coat, and began to take off his collar and tie. "You know those two blondes I been talkin' to you about, doncha Pop?"

By this time he was peeling his shirt off his plump, muscular-looking shoulders, and supporting himself with one hand against the locker he had stopped to take off his shoe.

"Ah-h," said the old man, sour as before. "You're always tellin' me about something. I don't even pay no attention to it. It goes in one ear and comes out the other."

"Oh yeah?" said Herbert with a rising, ironical inflection on the last word. He bent to unlace his other shoe.

"Yeah," said John in the same tone.

The old man's tone had from the beginning been touched with this dry and even sour note of disgusted and disinterested unbelief. And yet, somehow indefinably, there was the unmistakable suggestion that he was enjoying himself. For one thing, he had made no move to depart. Instead he had propped himself against the side of the open elevator door, and, his old arms folded loosely into the sleeves of the worn grey alpaca coat which was his "uniform," he was waiting there with the dry, fixed stubborn little grin around his mouth as if against his own admission he was enjoying the debate and was willing to prolong it indefinitely.

"So that's the kind of a guy you are?" said Herbert, taking his neat coat and disposing it carefully on one of the hangers which he had taken from the open locker door. "Here I go and get you all fixed up and you run out on me. O.K., Pop,"—his voice now shaded with resignation, Herbert was stepping out of his neatly pressed trousers and arranging them also with crease-like precision on a hanger. "I thought you was a real guy, but if you're goin' to walk out on a party after I've gone to all the trouble, I'll have to look for someone else."

"Oh yeah?" said old John dryly as before.

"Yeah," said Herbert in the accent proper to this type of repartee. "I had you all doped out for a live number, but I see I've picked a dead one."

Herbert said nothing for a moment, and grunted a little as he bent to unlace his other shoe.

"Where's old Organizin' Pete?" he said presently. "Seen him to-night?"

"Who?" said John, looking at him with a somewhat bewildered expression.

"Henry."

"Oh!" The word was small but the accent of disgust was sufficient. "Say!" the old man waved a gnarled hand stiffly in a downward gesture of dismissal. "That guy's a pain in the neck!"—He spoke the words with the kind of dry precision old men have when they speak slang and when they are trying to "keep up with" a younger man, a little stiffly and awkwardly and not quite accustomed. "A pain in the neck!" he repeated. "No, I ain't seen him to-night."

"Oh, Hank's all right when you get to know him," said Herbert cheerfully. "You know how a guy gets when he gets all burned up about somethin' he gets too serious about it—he thinks everybody else in the world ought to be like he is. But he's O.K. He's not a bad guy when you get him to talkin' about somethin' else."

"Yeah!" cried John suddenly and excitedly, not by way of agreement, but as if he was suddenly remembering something—"And you know what he says to me the other day? 'I wonder what all the rich mugs in this house would do if they had to get down and do a hard day's work for a livin' once in a while—And these old bitches'—Yeah!" cried John in a dry excited voice, as he nodded his head in angry affirmation—"'that I got to help in and out of cars all night long, and couldn't walk up a flight of stairs by themselves—what if they had to get down on their hands and knees and scrub floors like your mother and my mother did?'—That's the way he goes on all the time!" cried John indignantly—"and him a-gettin' his livin' from the people in this house, and takin' tips from them—and talkin' about them like he does!—Hah-h!" John muttered to himself and rapped his fingers on the walls—"I don't like that way of talkin'! If he feels that way, let him get out! I don't like that fellow."

"Oh," said Herbert easily and indifferently, "Hank's not a bad guy, Pop. He don't mean half of it—-He's just a grouch." By this time, with the speed and deftness born of long experience, he was putting on the stiff, starched shirt-front which was a part of his uniform on duty, and buttoning the studs.

"Ah-h," said old John surlily, "you don't know what you're talkin' about. I had more girls in my day than you ever thought about."

"Yeah?" said Herbert.

"Yeah," said John, "I had blondes and brunettes and every other kind."

"Never had any red-heads, did you, Pop?" said Herbert grinning.

"Yeah, I had red-heads too," said John sourly. "More than you had, anyway."

"Just a rounder, hunh?" said Herbert, "Just an old petticoat-chaser."

"Nah-h, I ain't no rounder or no petticoat-chaser," said John sourly. "Hm!" he grunted contemptuously, "I've been a married man for forty years. I got grown-up children, oldr'n you are!"

"Why, you old—!" Herbert exclaimed and turned on him indignantly. "Braggin' to me about your blondes and red-heads, and then boastin' that you're a family man! Why, you—"

"Nah-h," said John, "I never did no such thing. Wasn't talkin' about *now*—but *then*! That's when I had 'em—forty years ago."

"Who?" said Herbert innocently, "Your wife and children?"

"Ah-h," said John disgustedly, "get along with you. You ain't goin' to get *my* goat. I've forgotten more about life than you ever heard about, so don't think you're goin' to make a monkey out of me with your cute talk."

"Well, you're makin' a big mistake this time, Pop," said Herbert with an accent of regret. He had drawn on the neat grey trousers of his uniform, adjusted his broad white stock, and now, facing the small mirror on the wall, he was engaged in carefully adjusting the coat about his well-set shoulders.

"Wait till you see 'em—these two blondes. I picked one of 'em out just for you."

"Well, you needn't pick any out for me," said John sourly. "I've got no time for no such foolishness."

A moment later, stooping and squinting in the mirror, he said half-absently: "So you're goin' to run out on me and the two blondes. You can't take it, hunh? O.K. O.K.," said Herbert with resigned regret as he buttoned up his coat. "If that's the way you feel about it—only, you may change your mind when you get a look at them."

"What do you say, pal?" he cried boisterously to Henry, the night doorman, who had just come in, and was rattling his key in the locker door. "Here I get Pop all dated up with a couple of hot blondes and he runs out on me. Is that treatin' a guy right or not?"

Henry did not answer. His face was hard and white and narrow, his eyes had the look and color of blue agate, and he never smiled. He took off his coat and hung it in the locker.

"Where were you?" he said.

Herbert looked at him startled.

"Where was I *when*?" he said.

"Last night."

"That was my night off," said Herbert.

"It wasn't *our* night off," said Henry. "We had a meetin'. They was askin' about you." He turned and directed his hard look toward the old man, "And you too," he said in a hard tone, "You didn't show up either."

Old John's face had hardened too. He had shifted his position, and began to drum nervously and impatiently with his old fingers upon the side of the elevator, a quick, annoyed tapping that was characteristic of him in moments of annoyance or exacerbated tension. Now his own eyes were hard and flinty as he returned the other's look, and there was no mistaking the dislike of his glance, the hostility instinctive and inherent to two types of personality that must always clash.

"Oh yeah?" he said again in a hard voice.

And Henry answered briefly: "Yeah. You'll come to the meetin's like everyone else, see? Or you'll get bounced out. You may be an old man but that goes for you like it does for everyone."

"Yeah?" said John.

"Yeah."

"Jesus!" Herbert's face was red with crestfallen embarrassment and he stammered out an excuse. "I forgot all about it—honest I did! I was just goin'—"

"Well, you're not supposed to forget," said Henry harshly, and for a moment he looked at Herbert with a hard accusing eye. "Where the hell do you suppose we'll be if everybody forgets?"

"I—I'm all up on my dues," said Herbert feebly.

"That ain't the question. We ain't talkin' about dues." For the first time a tone of indignant passion was evident in the hard voice as he went on earnestly. "Where the hell do you suppose we'd be if everyone ran out on us every time we hold a meetin'? What's the use of anything if we ain't goin' to stick together? No, you're supposed to be there like anyone else. And that goes for you too," he said harshly looking briefly at the old man.

He was silent for a moment, looking almost sullenly at Herbert whose red face really now did suggest the hang-dog appearance of a guilty schoolboy. But when Henry spoke again, his tone was gentler and more casual, and somehow suggestive that there was buried underneath the hard exterior in the secret sources of the man's life, a genuine affection for his errant comrade. "I guess it's OK this time," he said quietly. "I spoke to O'Neil. I told him you'd been out with a cold and I'd get you there next time."

He said nothing more, and began swiftly to take off his clothes.

Herbert looked flustered but relieved. For a moment he seemed about to speak, but changed his mind. He stooped swiftly, took a final appraising look at his appearance in the small mirror, and then, turning toward the elevator with a simulation of fine regret, he said: "Well, O.K. O.K. If that's the way you feel, Pop, about the blondes—only you may change your mind when you get a look at them."

"No, I won't change my mind, neither," said John with sour implacability. "About them, or about you."

"Oh yeah?" he looked at the old man for the first time now, laughing, the pink spots in his fresh cheeks flushed with good-humor, his lively eyes dancing as he slammed the locker door shut and came back, fully uniformed now for the evening's work, and took his place upon the elevator. "So that's the kind of guy you think I am?" he said menacingly, and gently poked the old fellow in the ribs with closed fist. "So you don't believe me, huh?"

"Ah-h," said John, grouchily, as he slammed the door, "I wouldn't believe you on a stack of bibles." He pulled the lever and the elevator started up. "You're a lot of talk—that's what you are. I don't listen to anything you say." He pulled the lever back and stopped the elevator and opened the heavy green-sheet door of the service car.

"So that's the kind of a friend you are?" said Herbert, stepping out into the corridor. Full of himself, full of delight with his own humor, he winked swiftly at two pretty, rosey Irish maids who were waiting to go up, and jerking his thumb toward the old man, he said, "What are you goin' to do with a guy like this anyway? I go and get him all dated up with a blonde and he won't believe me when I tell him so. He calls me a big wind."

"Yeah, that's what he is," said the old man grimly to the smiling girls. "He's a lot of wind. He's always talkin' about his girls and I bet he never had a girl in his life. If he saw a blonde he'd run like a rabbit."

"Oh yeah?" said Herbert.

"Yeah," said John. His manner had not changed an atom in its tone of unyielding belligerence, but it was somehow evident that the old man was enjoying himself hugely.

"Just a pal!" said Herbert with mock bitterness, appealing to the smiling maids. "O.K., then. When they get here, keep 'em here till I get back?"

"Well, you'd better not be bringin' any of 'em around here," said John pugnaciously. He shook his white head shortly with a movement of dogged inflexibility. "I don't want any of 'em comin' around here— blondes or brunettes or red-heads or any of 'em," he muttered. "If they do, you won't find 'em when you come back."

"My friend," said Herbert bitterly, to the two girls and jerked his thumb toward the old man again. "A pal of mine!" he said and started to depart. "Yeah, pals!" the old man muttered. "And I don't believe you anyway—" he called out as a happy after-thought after Herbert's plump retreating figure. "You ain't got no blondes. You never did have—You're a momma's boy!" John cried almost triumphantly, as if he had now had the happiest inspiration of the evening. "That's what you are!"

Herbert paused at the door and looked back menacingly at the old man, a look that was belied by the exuberant sparkle of his eyes. "Oh yeah?" he said, dangerously.

"Yeah!" said John implacably. Herbert stared fiercely at him a moment, then winked swiftly at the two girls and departed.

"That fellow's just a lot of talk," said John sourly as the two girls stepped into the car and he closed the door. "Always talkin' about his girls and the blondes he's goin' to bring around. I'll betcha he never had a girl in his life. Yeah!" he muttered scornfully, almost to himself as he pulled on the lever and the car started up. "He lives with his mother up in the Bronx, and he'd be scared stiff if a girl ever looked at him."

"Still, John, Herbert ought to have a girl," one of the girls said practically, in a thick Irish brogue. "Herbert's a nice boy, John,"

"Oh he's all right, I guess," the old man muttered, in a dry and unwilling tone that nevertheless somehow indicated the genuine, though submerged affection for the younger man.

"And a nice looking boy, too," the other maid now said.

"Oh, he'll do, I guess," said John; and then abruptly: "What are you folks doin' to-night anyway? There are a whole lot of packages waitin' to come up."

"Mrs. Jack is having a big party," one of the girls said. "And, John, will you bring everything up as soon as you can? There may be something we need right away."

"Well," he said in that half-belligerent, half-unwilling tone that seemed to be a kind of inverted attribute to his real good-nature, "I'll do the best I can. If all of them are giving their big parties to-night—" he grumbled, "It goes on some time here till two or three o'clock in the morning. You'd think all some people had to do was give parties all the time. It would take a whole regiment of men just to carry up packages to them. Yeah!" he muttered angrily to himself. "And what do you get? If you ever got so much as a word of thanks—"

"Oh, John," one of the girls now said reproachfully, "you know that Mrs. Jack is not like that—You know yourself—"

"Oh, she's all right, I guess," said John unwillingly as before, and yet his tone had softened imperceptibly, in his voice there was now the same indefinable note of affection as when he had spoken of Herbert, just a moment before. "If all of them was like her," he began—but then, as the memory of that night's experience with the pan-handler came back to him, he muttered angrily: "She's too good-hearted for her own good. Them pan-handling bums—they swarm around her like flies every time she leaves the building. I saw one the other day get a dollar out of her before she'd gone twenty feet. A big strapping fellow not over thirty, looked like he'd never done a day's work in his life. She's crazy to put up with it—I'm goin' to tell her so, too, when I see her!"

The old man's face had flushed with anger at the memory. He had opened the door on the service landing, and now, as the girls stepped out, he muttered to himself again: "The kind of people we got in this building oughtn't to have to put up with it. Well then, I'll see—" he said concedingly, as one of the maids unlocked the service door and went in. "I'll get it up to you."

And for a moment, after the door had closed behind the maids—just a blank dull sheet of painted tin with the numerals 9C on it—the old man stood there looking at it with a glance in which somehow affectionate and friendly regard was evident. Then he closed the elevator door, pulled the lever and started down.

Henry was just coming up from the basement as the old man reached the ground floor. The doorman, uniformed, ready for his night's work, passed morosely without speaking. John called to him.

"If they try to deliver any packages out front," he said, "You send 'em around here."

Henry turned and looked at the old man unsmilingly a moment, and then said curtly: "What?"

"I say," said John, raising his voice a trifle shrilly, and speaking more rapidly and excitedly, for he did not like Henry and the man's habitual air of sullen curtness angered him, "—If they try to make any deliveries out front, send them back to the service entrance."

Henry continued to look at him without speaking, and the old man added: "The Jacks are giving a party to-night. If there are any deliveries, send them back here."

Henry stared at him a moment longer and then, without inflection, said: "Why?"

The question, with its insolent suggestion of defied authority—*someone's* authority, his own, the management's, or the authority of "the kind of people that live here"—infuriated the old man, affronted his authority-loving soul. His face, beneath its fine shock of silvery silk-white hair, flamed crimson. A wave of anger, hot, choking, insubordinate, welled up in him, and before he could control himself, he rasped harshly: "Because that's where they ought to come—that's why. You ought to know enough for that. Haven't you been working around places of this kind long enough to know the way to do? Don't you know the kind of people we got here don't want every Tom, Dick and Harry with a package to deliver running up in the front elevator all the time, mixing in with all the other people, annoying all the people in the house? You ought to have sense enough to have learned that much by now!" he muttered angrily.

"Why?" said Henry with deliberate insolence. "Why should I?"

"Because," old John shouted, his face now crimson with anger at the effrontery of this insolence—"if you haven't got sense enough to know it, you ought to quit and get a job diggin' ditches somewhere. You got no business in a job like this. You're bein' paid to know it. That's part of your job as doorman in a house like this. If you ain't got sense enough now to know what a doorman's supposed to do, to where delivery people are supposed to go in a place like this, you'd better quit and give your job to someone who knows what it's all about."

Henry did not answer him for a moment. He just looked at him with an expressionless face and with eyes which were just as hard and emotionless as two chunks of agate.

"Listen," he said in a moment in a quiet and toneless voice. "You know what's going to happen to you if you don't watch out? You're gettin' old, Pop, and you'd better watch your step. You're goin' to be caught in the street some day worryin' about what's goin' to happen to people in this place if they have to ride up in the same elevator with a delivery boy. You're goin' to worry about their gettin' contaminated—about them catchin' all sorts of diseases because they got to ride up in the same car with some guy who carries a package. And you know what's goin' to happen to you, Pop? I'll tell you what's goin' to happen to you. You're goin' to worry about it so much that you ain't goin' to notice where you're goin. And you're goin' to get hit. See?"

The tone was so hard, so inflexible, so unyielding in its toneless savagery that for a moment—just for a moment—the old man felt something in him tremble at the unutterable passion of that flinty monotone.

"You're goin' to get hit, Pop. That's what's goin' to happen to you. And it ain't goin' to be by nothing small or cheap. It ain't goin' to be by no Ford truck or by no taxi-cab. You're goin' to get hit by somethin' large and shiny that cost a lot of money. You're goin' to die happy. You'll get hit by at least a Rolls Royce. And I hope it belongs to one of the people in this house. Because I want you to be happy, Pop, I want you to push off knowin' that it wasn't done by nothin' cheap. You'll die like any other worm, but I want you to know that it was done expensive—by a big Rolls Royce—by one of the people in this house. I just want you to be happy, Pop."

Old John's face was purple. The veins in his forehead stood out like corded ropes. For a moment, he glared at the hard and flint-like face of the younger man with such murderous fury that it seemed as if apoplectic strangulation was inevitable. He tried to speak but no words came, and at length, all else having failed him, he managed to choke out, but this time with no vestige of even submerged good-nature, only the implacable dryness of unforgiving hate, the familiar phrase: "Oh yeah?"

Just for a moment more the agate eye, the flint-like face surveyed him with their granite hostility.

"Yeah!" said Henry tonelessly, and departed.

BEFORE THE PARTY

· · ·

Mrs. Jack came from her room a little after eight o'clock and walked along the broad hallway that traversed her big apartment from front to rear. Her party would begin at half past eight: Her guests had been invited for that hour, but long experience in these matters told her that the affair would not be going at full swing until after nine. Nevertheless, as she walked along the corridor at a brisk and rapid little step, she felt sharply, as she always felt on these occasions, a tension of excitement, not unpleasurable, even though it was now sharpened, as it always was, but the tincture of an apprehensive doubt.

Would all be ready? Had she forgotten anything? Had the girls followed her instructions? Or had they slipped up somewhere, failed or blundered in some way—would something now be lacking?

The wrinkled line between her eyes grew deeper as she thought about these things. Her firm, short step grew brisker and unconsciously she began rapidly to slip the old jade ring on and off her finger with a quick movement of her small, strong hand. It was a familiar and unconscious gesture, a gesture nervous and impatient that defined her state exactly at a time like this. It was the gesture of an alert, resourceful, highly able person who, through reliance on her own superior powers, her own abilities to make, and act, and do, had come to have a certain instinctive mistrust in the abilities of other people less gifted than herself. So understood, it was a gesture of impatience and some scorn, a scorn not born of arrogance, a scorn assuredly not born of wilful pride or any lack of warm humanity, but one that was inclined to say—at least to *feel*—a trifle sharply: "Yes, yes, I know! I understand all that. There's no need telling me all that. Let's get to the point: What can you do? What have you done? Can I depend on you to do what must be done?"

Such thoughts as these, too swift for utterance, too sharp and quick for definition, like water flicks of light upon a pool, were darting across the surface of her mind as she walked briskly down the hall.

"I wonder if I have forgotten anything?" she was thinking. "And have the girls remembered to do everything I told them? Oh, Lord! If only Molly hasn't started drinking! What has happened to her anyway? She used to be so clean, so sweet, and so reliable—and now! If she's begun again I'll!—And Annie! Oh, she's as good as gold, of course—But, God! She *is* a fool! And Cookie!—Well, Cookie, she can cook, but after that she doesn't know April from July! And if you try to tell her anything she gets flustered and begins to gargle German at you! And then it's worse than if you never spoke to her at all! As for the rest—well, all you can do is to hope and pray! My God, you'd think they'd be so happy to be here!"

The line between her troubled vision deepened. The ring slipped on and off her finger like a flash and for a moment her flowerlike and fresh-colored face burnt deeper with a glow of righteous indignation!

"You'd think they'd be so happy to be here! You'd think they'd realize how well off they are!—How good a life they lead! The life of Riley! The life of Riley!—that's what it is!"—she thought indignantly, and then the volutes of her nostrils curved just slightly with the dilation of commiserating scorn: "Oh, well, poor things! I suppose they do the best they can. I suppose all you can do is to reconcile yourself to it—realize that the only way you can be sure that everything will be all right is to do it all yourself!" By this, of course, she meant *herself*.

By this time she had reached the entrance to the living room and still with the worried tension in her eyes, still slipping the jade ring on and off her nervous little hand, she was looking quickly about the room, taking everything in in a dozen splintered little glances, assuring herself by a moment's swift inspection that everything was in its proper place.

Her examination pleased her. The worried look about her eyes began to disappear. The little wrinkle went away. She slipped the ring back on her hand and let it stay there, and her earnest little face began to undergo a subtle transformation: in fact, it actually began to bloom, to bloom gently, softly, impalpably, to be suffused by a look of peace and of relief, to take on imperceptibly somehow the look of satisfaction of a child when it regards in silence some object of its love and art and self-creation and finds it good.

The big room was ready for the party. It was just quietly the way that she would have it always, perfectly itself. It was a room of grand dimensions, high ceilinged, so nobly proportioned as hardly to escape a regal massiveness, and yet so subtly toned by the labor of her faultless taste that whatever forbidding coldness its essential grandeur may have had was utterly subdued. To a stranger the room would have seemed not only homelike in its comfortable simplicity, but even, on a closer inspection, a trifle shabby. Almost everything in it was somewhat worn. The coverings of some of the chairs and couches had become in places threadbare. On three sides of the room were bookshelves extending a third of the way up. And these bookshelves were crowded with a friendly and somewhat dog-eared company of worn-looking books. Obviously the books had been read and read again. The stiff sets of tooled and costly bindings that ornament the bookshelves of the rich with unread awe were lacking here. Neither was there any evidence of the greedy and revolting mania of the professional collector. If there were "first editions" on these friendly shelves, they were here because their owner liked them and had bought them in the first place to be read. They were here because they had been read, because their covers were well thumbed, dog-eared, warm and worn and homely looking, like all the other books up on the shelves.

The warm light of the room, the crackling dance of the pine logs on the great marble hearth all cast their radiance warmly on the three thousand covers of these worn books. Her eyes warmed and glowed with comfort as she looked at the rich and homely compact of their colors; with pride and satisfaction as she looked at the great books of decoration and design, of painting, drawing, architecture, which she had collected in a dozen countries, upon a dozen voyages, throughout a crowded lifetime of work, of travel and of living. She saw the old worn backs of her favorite books, the novels and the histories, the plays, the poems, the biographies. She took the joy and pride in them that she took in all good things which had been born for use and joy and comfort and the growth of man's estate. And the good books glowed there in warm light as if the knowledge of their use and comfort was written in their very hue.

Everything else in the great room had this same air of homeliness and use. The very carpet that covered the floor with its pattern of old faded green was somewhat threadbare by long use. The gatelegged table with its pleasant shaded lamp and the stacks of books and magazines upon it had the air of waiting to be used. Upon the creamy slab of marble mantle which was itself a little stained and worn, there was spread out, as always, a green, old, faded strip of Chinese silk. And on top of it there was a little figure of green jade. It was one of those lovely figures of compassionating mercy with carved lifted fingers that the Chinese made. There were a few drawings on the high, cream-colored walls, a few of her own designs, a portrait of herself in her young loveliness at twenty-five which a painter now dead and famous had made long ago.

And everywhere there was the strange fused miracle of the woman's life. For, all these objects of a thousand different kinds, these chairs and tables, these jades and silks, all the drawings, and the paintings, and the books, themselves acquired on a hundred several occasions, themselves the product of a dozen periods, were brought together in this room into its magic and its harmony from the instinctive sources of the woman's life.

It is no wonder, therefore, that the eye of Mrs. Jack should soften and her flower face take on an added glow of loveliness as she looked at her fine room. The like of it indeed, as she well knew, could no where else be found for "Here"—she thought—"Ah, here it is, and it is living like a part of me. And God! How beautiful it is"—she thought—"How living and how warm—how true—It's—it's not as if it was a place that we have rented—just another room in an apartment house. No—the whole place—" she glanced swiftly down the long and spacious width of the big hall—"It's really more like some grand and noble house than like an apartment on Park Avenue. If it weren't for the elevator there you'd think it was some grand old house. I don't know—but—" a little furrow, this time of reflectiveness and of effort, came between her eyes as she tried to shape her meaning—"there's something sort of grand—and simple—about it all."

And indeed there was: the amount of simplicity which could be purchased even in those times for a yearly rental of fifteen thousand dollars was quite considerable. And as if this very thought had found in the phrasing of *her* mind an echo, she went on: "I mean—when you compare it with some of these places that you see nowadays—some of these godawful places that all these rich people live—I mean, there's simply no comparison. I don't care how rich they are, there's—there's just something here that money cannot buy."

And really, as her mind phrased the accusatory words "all these rich people nowadays," the volutes of her nostrils twitched again and her rosy little face glowed deeper in instinctive feeling of sharp scorn. For Mrs. Jack had always had great scorn of wealth: it was, curiously one of her unshakable and dogmatic convictions that she, herself, and none of her family could ever possibly be described as "rich."

She was not "rich." One thing was certain: she could never be called "rich"—"Oh, not *really*—not the way people are who really *are*—not the way—" and her mind now embattled to defensive consciousness, her spirit stubbornly aroused to feminine denial, she would curiously have looked for confirmation not at the hundred million people there impossibly below her in this world's hard groove, but at that fabulous ten thousand who perhaps were there above her on the moneyed heights—and who, therefore, by the comparison, were "really rich."

Besides, there really was no need for spurious confirmation. She was "a worker." She had always been "a worker." The evidence of her life of work, her love of work, her grand accomplishment of work was all about her—in those great books and folios of costume and design, thumb-worn and marked by such devoted ardours of study and of labor, upon the shelves; by the lovely grace, the human vitality of the costume drawings on the walls—costumes that had adorned the figures of some of the most celebrated and beautiful women of the time, and that even here, without the figure, had in their vital lines all the life, the movement and the character, of human personality, here in these designs as wonderfully present as if the voice, the eye, the living flesh and blood were also here. No, she was not "rich." She had no need of riches—she had *worked*. One look at the strength, the grace, the swiftness of those small, sure hands—and with the thought, she lifted them before her, turned them, flexed them, and regarded them with a little smile—could tell the story of their owner's life, of talent, energy and creative fashioning—a life of work. In that accomplishment lay deep pride, the last integrity of this indomitable person who now stood there looking at the wing-like strength and grace of those strong hands. "Is not my help within me?" Well, hers *was*. She had needed no man's help, the benefits of no man's purse, the succor of no man's shielding strength. The wife of a rich man, the economic necessity for work had long been lacking in her life. But she had made her way. She had supported herself. She had gone on working. She had known insecurity in youth, hard toil in youth, doubt, perplexity, and sorrow in youth, but she had gone on working. And now in her forties, the wife of a wealthy man, secure from every need, and surrounded by every luxury that wealth could buy, she had made for herself a name that asked support from nothing. She loved clothes. She had always loved clothes, she had been born with a kind of poetry of clothes inside her. Clothes had a life for her, a philosophy, a meaning that translated the whole meaning of personality and character. As a result, she had for twenty years or more created for the theatre and for the purposes of art a gallery of costume that was touched with genius, and for fifteen years or more, she had been the chief designer for the most fashionable and expensive woman's store in the country. For this reason there was ample justification for the look of quiet pride with which she now surveyed those small, strong hands. She had been born with a genuine and useful talent, and she had used it well, with energy, with intelligence and with a deep and grand integrity, a reverent respect for good work and for high achievement. She had created beautiful and enduring things—things that would endure because their quality was unforgettable. There had never been a lazy bone in her whole body. Therefore it is no wonder that she never thought of herself as being "rich." She was a worker: she had worked.

But now, her inspection of the big room satisfied and ended, she turned quickly to investigation into other things. The living room gave on the dining room through glass doors opening from the right. These were now closed and curtained filmily. Mrs. Jack moved toward them at her quick and certain little step and threw them open. Then she stopped short, her small strong hand flew quickly to her bosom. She gasped out an involuntary little "Oh!" of wonder and delight. It was too beautiful! It was quite too beautiful! But really it was just the way she expected it to look—the *way* all of her parties looked—the "way" that made her parties memorable to fame and history. None the less, every time she saw it, it filled her with the emotion of a grand and new discovery, a wonder of new joy.

Everything had been carried out beautifully—to perfection—and— well, it was just too grand and lovely! All she could do was gasp and stare at it. Before her the great slab of the dining table glowed faultlessly, a single sheet of walnut light. The great chairs, old Italian chairs with stamped backs of ancient leather, had been drawn back and placed against the walls. This was to be a buffet supper—the guests could come and help themselves according to their taste and whim and—well, the materials of the banquet were there before her on that noble table.

That mighty table simply groaned with food. The mind and memory of man could scarcely contemplate the lavish total of its victualling. Upon an enormous silver trencher at one end there was a mighty roast of beef done to a turn and crisply browned all over. It had just been "begun on" at one end, for a few succulent slices had been carved away to leave the sound rare body of the roast open to the inspection or hunger of anyone who might be tempted by its juicy succulence.

At the opposite end, upon another enormous trencher, and similarly carved, was a whole Virginia ham, sugar cured and baked and stuck all over with a pungent myriad of cloves. Just to look at it was enough to make one's mouth water, and to smell it brought tears of happiness into one's eyes.

And in between and all around that massive board was a staggering variety of mouth-watering reliefs. There were great bowls of mixed green salads, bowls of chicken salad, platters containing golden slabs of smoked salmon, the most rare and delicate that money could buy or the market could provide. There were dishes piled with caviar and countless other dishes loaded with a staggering assortment of hors d'oeuvres, with mushrooms, herring, sardines and small, toothsome artichokes, with pickled onions and with pickled beets, with sliced tomatoes and with deviled eggs, with walnuts, almonds, and pecans, with olives and with celery—in short with almost everything that could tempt the tongue or tickle the palate of jaded man.

It was a gargantuan banquet. It was like some great vision of a feast that has been made immortal on the page of history and of legendry. It was like something that you read about. In these thin modern times where even the board of wealth is for the most part tainted with a touch of meagreness, where there is in general and so curiously, in especial, in the houses of the great, a blight of not-enoughness, there was here a quite triumphant staggering excess, an overwhelming too-muchness out of everything. And yet, the whole thing was miraculously right.

It was, perhaps, an even greater triumph for the genius of a woman's taste that it could provide a herculean banquet of this sort and yet control and govern it with the same faultless and instinctive rightness with which it governed everything it touched—a shelf of old worn books, a piece of old worn silk, a little idol on the mantle, or a simple drawing on the wall. There was, indeed, in the vision thus provided by that lavish table a concept of abundance, a breadth of imagination and a boldness of execution on which few other people in the world, and no one in the city, would have dared to venture. Certainly, in those pyramided vertices of wealth that now blazed all around her in the nocturnal magic of their skyflung faery, there were other purses that could have so provided, but there were no other spirits that could so have dared.

Few "rich" people would have dared venture on a banquet such as this of Mrs. Jack's and in this fear of venturing they would have been right. Only Mrs. Jack could do a thing like this; only Mrs. Jack could do it right. And that was why her parties were such very famous things, why everyone who could, and was invited, would always come when there was going to be a party at the Jacks'. For, wonderful to tell, there was no where on the surface of that lavish board a suggestion of disorder or obscene excess. That groaning table was a miracle of noble planning and of right design. Just as no one looking here could possibly have wanted anything to be added, so could no one here have felt that there was any need.

And everywhere, from the centre of the great, rich board where on a carpet of thick lace a great bowl blossomed with a fragrant harvest of cut flowers, to the four edges of the table where stood in orderly array big stacks of the grand plates which she had bought in Dresden years before, and gleaming rows of old and heavy silver, the knives and forks and spoons so strong in weight and beauty, which she had brought from England—everywhere, even in the arrangement of the countless dishes —there was evident this same instinctive faultlessness of taste, this same style that never seemed to be contrived, that was so casual and so gracious and so right.

To the right the polished service of the great buffet glittered with an array of flasks, decanters, bottles, syphons, and tall glasses, thin as shells, which covered it. Elsewhere, two tall delicately lovely cupboards of the Colonial period stood like graces with their splendid wares of china and of porcelain, of cut glass and of silverware, of grand old plates and cups and saucers, tureens, and bowls, and jars, and pitchers, as smooth as velvet and as rich as cream. The great room with its simplicity and strength, its delicacy and massivity, had also been touched everywhere with the same spirit of casualness and grace, of power and beauty that one felt everywhere.

Here, too, all was in readiness and the mistress, after a moment's long inspection, in which delight and wonder were again commingled with a satisfied appraisal, walked rapidly across the room and through the swinging door that separated it from the pantries and the kitchen and the servants' quarters. As she walked through the narrow hallway that led past the pantry to the kitchen she heard the rich excited voices of the maids, their lilty brogue, and laughter broken by the gutturally mixed phrases of the cook.

Here, too, the mistress found a scene of busy order and of readiness. The big kitchen glittered like a sheet of tile—it was a joy to see. You could have eaten your dinner off the floor. The great range with its marvelous hood, itself as large as those one sees in a big restaurant, seemed to have been freshly scrubbed and oiled and polished till it glittered like a jewel. The vast company of copper cooking vessels, the skillets, kettles, pots and pans, the frying pans of every size and shape, from those just large enough to hold a fair sized egg to those so huge it seemed that one might cook in them the rations of a regiment, had been scrubbed and rubbed and polished until Mrs. Jack could see her face in them.

The big kitchen table in the centre of the room was so startlingly clean and white that for a moment one had a shocked illusion that the table really belonged in a surgeon's office. Even the very pantry shelves, the drawers and cupboards and the bins looked as if they had just been freshly scrubbed and gone over with sand-paper and above the voices of the girls there brooded the curiously quiet, intent, dynamic hum of the great electric ice box which was itself, in its white splendor, like another perfect jewel.

"Oh this!" thought Mrs. Jack, "Oh this—" Her small clenched hand flew up against her breast again, her breath came quickly, and her eyes grew bright as stars. "This is quite the most perfect, lovely thing of all!" she thought. "This is the best room in the house. I love the others—but is there anything in the world as grand and beautiful as a fine kitchen! How wonderful! How strong and clean and beautiful!—and God!"—as her eye caught the gleaming rows of copper pots and pans—"How grand they are, how thrilling and how beautiful! And how Cookie keeps the place! She is a queer old thing but my God! She can cook and she can keep a kitchen! If I could only paint it! If only I had never given up my painting! I'd like to have a try at it—but no! It would take a Brueghel to do it! There's no one nowadays to do it justice—and God! Oh, Cookie!"

And now, at last, she spoke these words aloud: "What a lovely cake!"

Cook looked up from the great layer cake on the table to which she had been adding the last prayerful tracery of frosted icing and for a moment a faint smile illuminated the gaunt, blunt surface of her germanic face. "You like him, yes?" said Cook. "You think he is nice?"

"Oh, Cook!"—cried Mrs. Jack, with a face flushed with excitement and in a tone of such eager childlike earnestness that Cook smiled this time a little more broadly than before—"It is the most *beautiful*—the most wonderful—" she turned away with a comical shrug of despair as if words failed her and then said humorously: "Well, all I can say is, you can't beat Gilbert and Sullivan, can you?"

The literary significance of this remark was probably lost on Cook and the smiling maids, but no one, not even a Chinaman, could have missed the intent of the emotion it conveyed. Cook laughed gutturally with satisfaction, and Molly, smiling, and in a brogue that could have been cut with a knife said: "No'm, Mrs. Jack, that you can't!"

Mrs. Jack looked happily about her. Everything had turned out perfectly, better than she could possibly have hoped for. Nothing had been forgotten, everything was in readiness. Janie and Lily in their trim, crisp uniforms, and with their smiling, rosy faces, were really awfully pretty and Molly—she looked swiftly at Molly with relief—Molly, although much older than the other girls, looked indeed the middle aged woman that she was, but looked also clean and plain and sober as Molly used to look. Thank heaven! She had pulled herself together, she hadn't had a drink: drink worked on her like poison, you could tell the moment that she'd had a single one. But everything had turned out perfectly: it ought to be a glorious party.

PIGGY LOGAN

. . .

At this moment the buzzer of the bell rang sharply. Mrs. Jack clapped her little hand up sharply to her deaf right ear, looked rosily, inquiring around her as she always did when she was not certain whether she had heard, and said quickly: "Hah? Did the bell ring, Janie? Is there someone at the door?"

"Yes'm," said Janie, coming to the door of the maids' sitting room. "I'll go, Mrs. Jack."

"Yes, you'd better, Janie, I wonder who—" she cast a puzzled look up at the clock up on the wall, and then at the little shell of platinum on her wrist. "It's only 8:15! I don't think any of them would be this early. Oh!—" as illumination came—"I think, perhaps, it's Mr. Logan. If it's Mr. Logan, Janie, show him in. I'll be right out."

"Yes, Mrs. Jack," said Janie, and departed. And Mrs. Jack, after another quick look about the kitchen, another smile of thanks and approbation for Cookie and her arts, followed her.

It was Mr. Logan. Mrs. Jack encountered him right away in the entrance hall where he had just paused to set down two enormous black suit cases each of which, from the bulging look of them, carried enough weight to make strong muscles ache. This impression was justified by Mr. Logan's own appearance at the moment. He had seized the biceps of one muscular looking arm with the fingers of another, and with a rueful look upon his face was engaged in flexing and bending the aching member up and down. As Mrs. Jack approached he turned, a thickset, rather burly looking young man of about thirty years, with bushy eyebrows of coarse black, a round and heavy face smudged darkly with the shaven grain of a heavy beard, a low corrugated forehead and close cropped hair of stiff black bristles mounting to a little brush-like pompadour in front.

"Gosh!" said Mr. Piggy Logan, for by such affectionate title was he known to his more intimate acquaintance—"Gosh!"—the expletive came out somewhat windily, a steamy expiration of relief. At the same moment he released his aching arm and shook hands firmly with his hostess with a muscular and stubby hand, haired thickly on the back up to the very fingertips with fuzzy black.

"You must be simply dead!" cried Mrs. Jack. "Why didn't you let me know you had so much to carry? I'd have sent our driver—he could have handled everything for you."

"Oh, it's quite all right," said Piggy Logan. "I always handle everything myself. You see, I carry everything right here—my whole equipment—" he indicated the two ponderous cases. "That's it," said Piggy Logan, "everything I use—the whole show. That's all there is, so naturally,"—he smiled at her quickly and quite boyishly—"I don't like to take any chances. It's all I've got. If anything went wrong—well, I'd just rather do it for myself and then I know where I am!"

"I know!" said Mrs. Jack, nodding her head with a look of quick understanding—"I feel the same way about everything I do. You simply can't depend on people. If anything went wrong—and after all the years you must have put in making them! People who've seen it said it's simply marvelous," she went on, "Everyone is so thrilled to know you're going to be here and that at last they're going to have a chance to see it. We've heard so much about it—really, all you hear around New York these days is—"

"Now—," said Mr. Logan abruptly, in a manner that was perfectly courteous but that indicated he was no longer paying any attention to her, as indeed he wasn't: he had become all business and while she talked had been making a quick appraisal of the place. He walked over to the entrance of the living room, was looking all about the room with thoughtful speculation. "Now—," he continued, "I suppose it's going to be in here, isn't it?"

"Yes—that is, if you like it here. If you prefer, we'll use another room —but this is the largest one we have—"

"No, thank you," crisply, absently. "This is quite all right. This will do very nicely. Hm!" meditatively, as he pressed his full lower lip between two hairy fingers—"best place, I should think, would be over there—" briefly he indicated the opposite wall, "facing the door here, the people all around on the other three sides. Hm! Yes—just about the centre there, I should think posters on the book shelves—we can clear all this stuff away, of course—" he made a quick but spacious gesture with his thick hand which seemed to dispose of a large part of the furnishings with a single movement. "Yes! That ought to do it very well! Now, if you don't mind"—All business now, he turned to her rather peremptorily and said: "Have you got a place where I can change my clothes? I'll have to change to costume—if you have a room—"

"Oh, yes," she answered quickly, "here, just down the hall, the first room on the right. But won't you have a drink and something to eat before you start—You must be terribly—"

"No thank you," said Mr. Logan crisply. "It's very nice of you but—" He smiled swiftly, winningly at her under the beetling collectivism of his bushy brows—"I never take anything before a performance. Now,—" he crouched, gripped the handles of the big cases with his hairy fingers and heaved mightily—"if you'll just excuse me—," he grunted.

"If there is anything we can do—" Mrs. Jack began helpfully.

"No, thank you—nothing—" Mr. Logan somewhat gruntingly replied and began to stagger down the hall with his tremendous freight. "I can get along—quite—nicely—thank you," he groaned as he staggered through the door of the room to which she had directed him. "Nothing —at—all—" his grunts came back more faintly now. She heard the two ponderous baggages hit the floor with a leaden thump and then Mr. Logan's long expiring "whush" of exhausted relief.

For a moment after the young man's lurching departure from the scene his hostess continued to look after him with somewhat over-whelmed expression touched faintly with alarm. She felt a little dazed. His businesslike dispatch and the rather spacious nonchalance with which he had suggested indefinite but widespread alterations in her beloved room touched her with vague apprehension. But—she shook her head and reassured herself on the sharp decision—it was bound to be all right! She had heard so many people speak of him: he was really all the rage this year, everyone was talking of his show, there had been write-ups of him everywhere. He was the darling of all the smart society crowd—of all those "rich" Long Island and Park Avenue people—here the lady's nostrils curved again in a faint dilation of patronizing scorn. Nevertheless, she could not help feeling a pleasurable sense of triumph, a kind of satisfying glow that she had landed him.

Mr. Piggy Logan *was* the rage that year. He was the owner and creator of a kind of puppet circus of wire dolls, and the enthusiasm, the excitement, the applause with which this curious entertainment had been greeted was astonishing. In fact, it was not enough to say that Mr. Piggy Logan *had* a vogue: he *was* one. Not to have read about him, not to know about him, not to be able to discuss him and his little wire dolls with some show of intelligence was, in smart circles, akin to never having heard of Jean Cocteau, to never having heard of Surrealisme, to being completely at a loss when such names as those of Picasso and Brancusi, of Utrillo and of Gertrude Stein were mentioned. Mr. Piggy Logan and his art was spoken of with the same animated reverence that the knowing used when they spoke of one of these.

And, like all of these, Mr. Piggy Logan and his art demanded their own special vocabulary. To speak of him correctly one must know a kind of special language, a language whose delicate phrasings whose subtle nuances were becoming more highly specialized month by month, as each succeeding critic outdid his predecessor, as each succeeding critic delved deeper in the bewildering complexities, the infinite shadings and associations of Mr. Piggy Logan and his circus of wire dolls.

It is not too much to say that an entire literature in the higher aesthetics had by this time been created by Mr. Logan and his puppet dolls. It is by no means too much to say that entire critical reputations had that season been made or ruined by Mr. Logan and his dolls. It is furthermore a certainty that the last criteria of fashionable knowingness that year was an expert knowledge of Mr. Logan and his dolls and that if one lacked this knowledge he was lower than the dust, and if one had it his connoisseurship in the arts was definitely established, his eligibility for any society of the higher sensibilities was instantly confirmed.

One could, in fact, in that sweet year of grace and in that great and chosen citadel of this earth's fashion and its art, admit with utter nonchalance that the late John Milton bored him and was in fact a large "stuffed shirt." "Stuffed shirts" indeed were numerous in the findings of the critical gentry of the time. The chemises of such inflated personalities as Goethe, Ibsen, Byron, Tolstoy, Whitman, Dickens, and Balzac had been ruthlessly investigated by some of the most fearless intellects of the time and found to be largely composed of straw wadding. Almost everything in fact was in a process of debunking. Almost everyone was being fearlessly debunked except debunkers and Mr. Piggy Logan and his dolls.

And life had recently become "too short" for many things that people once found time for. One could blithely admit that "life was simply too short" for the perusal of any book longer than two hundred pages, and that, as for *War and Peace*—no doubt all that "they" said of it was true—and all of that—but as for one's self—well, one had tried, and really it was quite too—too—Oh, well, life simply was too short.

And life that year was far too short to be bothered by Browning and by Arnold; by Whitman, Dickens, Mr. Dreiser or Dean Swift. But life was not too short that year to be passionately concerned with Mr. Piggy Logan and his circus of wire dolls.

To a future world, no doubt, a less acute and understanding race of men all this may seem to be a trifle strange. To the future historians of that year of grace it may seem somewhat strange that the subtle-souled psychologists and aesthetes of that period, the privileged flower of the time should have been bored by quite so much and passionately concerned with so curiously little. And yet it was indubitably a fact: the highest intelligence of the time—the very subtlest of a chosen few—were bored by many things. They tilled the waste land, and erosion had grown fashionable. They were bored with love; and they were bored with hate. They were bored with men who worked, and with men who loafed. They were bored with people who created something and with people who created nothing. They were bored with marriage and with single blessedness; they were bored with chastity and they were bored with adultery. They were bored with going abroad and they were bored with staying at home. They were bored with most of the great poets of the world who had lived and died and about whom they knew nothing. They were even bored with the great poems which had been written and which they had never read.

They were bored with hunger in the streets, with the injustice, cruelty and oppression all around them, with the men who were killed, with the children who starved, with justice, freedom and man's right to live. Finally, they were bored with living, they were bored with dying but!— they were *not* bored that year with Mr. Piggy Logan and his circus of wire dolls.

War, death and famine, the surge of chaos, all of the grief, the sweat, the labor, anguish and defeat that left their scar upon the suffering and tormented soul of man could only fill the minds and spirits of these gentry with the languors of unuttered boredom. They had heard about it all so often. It was old stuff now. Life was "too short." They simply could not be bored. And so they turned their spirited and enthusiastic interest to a contemplation of Mr. Piggy Logan and his works.

There had been those at first among the cognoscenti—those happy pioneers who had got in at the very start of Mr. Logan's vogue—who had characterized his performance as "frightfully amusing." But that too was old stuff now and anyone who now dared to qualify Mr. Logan's art with such a paltry adjective as "amusing" was instantly dismissed as a person of no cultural importance. He was annihilated with the contempt that such insensitive appraisal richly warranted. Mr. Logan and his circus had long since ceased to be "amusing." He had ceased to be "amusing" when one of the more sophisticated columnists of the daily press had discovered that "not since the early Chaplin has the art of tragic humor through the use of pantomime reached such a faultless elevation."

This, in more modern phrase, was the "payoff." After this, the procession formed upon the right, and each newcomer paid his tribute with a new and glittering coin. The articles in the daily press were followed by others in the smarter publications. There was a whole page of pictures in *Vanity Fair*, a Profile in *The New Yorker*. The dramatic critics took it up, the offerings of the current stage were held up to barbed shafts of ridicule, the withering fire of admonitory criticism. Unfortunate actresses enjoying a long run were admonished to view Mr. Logan and his dolls and take seriously to heart the miming of the barebacked rider. Young actors were solemnly enjoined to observe the conduct of the dashing young doll on the flying trapeze, and to learn something from him in the arts of balance. The leading tragedians of the theatre were instructed to pay special attention to Mr. Logan's clown before they next essayed the role of Hamlet.

The solemn discussions broke out everywhere. There were articles about Mr. Logan and his dolls in every publication of any standing. Two eminent critics engaged in a rapier-like duel which reached a culmination of such adaptive subtlety that in the end it was said there were not over seven people in the modern world who could understand the final passages at arms. The central issue of this battle was to establish whether Logan in his development had been influenced more by the geometric cubism of the early Picasso or by the geometric abstractions of Brancusi. Both schools of thought had their impassioned followers, but in the end it was generally conceded that the Picassos had somewhat the best of it.

And the Centre of the storm? The Cause of all this tumult? The generating Force behind this mighty revolution in the world of art—

which, as one critic had so aptly put it, was a great deal more than just another "movement," a great deal more than just a new "development," the expression of a new and individual talent in modern art: it was rather a whole new universe of creation, a whirling planet which in its fiery revolution may throw off the generation of its own sidereal system—and It!—The colossal Talent which had done all this—What was It doing now? It (under the care of her gracious hospitality) was now enjoying the privacy of one of the lovely rooms in Mrs. Jack's apartment, and, as if It was utterly unaware of the huge disturbance It had made or the towering position It now enjoyed in the great world—It was calmly, quietly, mod-estly prosaically and matter-of-factly occupied in pulling off Its own trousers and pulling on a pair of canvas pants.

What did *It* think and say and feel about the cataclysmic commotion It had thus occasioned? Well,—*It*, from all that one could see and tell, said and thought and felt and did very little about it. Indeed, as more than one critic significantly pointed out—*It* had "the essential simplicity of the great artist: an almost childlike naiveté of speech and gesture that pierces straight to the heart of reality." Essentially, *It*—in critic phrase—had an "intelligence that sees things in large masses. Its vision is univer-sal, hence elliptical—It sees life and the universe simply in essences of Mass Matter. Its creations thus are whole and instant, the fusion of planetary substances."

Even the life of *It*, Its previous history, resisted investigations of the biographers with the impenetrability of the same baffling simplicity. Or, as one critic clearly phrased it: "As in the life of almost all great men of art there is little in Logan's early years to indicate his future achieve-ment. Like almost all supremely great men his development was slow—it might almost be said, unheeded—up to the time he burst suddenly, like a blazing light, upon the public consciousness."

This states it very fairly. To state the facts, however, a trifle more concretely, the naked biography of It was as follows: It had come from quite an old, distinguished family in New England. It had been sent to St. Paul's School where It had been generally known among Its fellows by the name of Piggy. It had then gone to Harvard and It had left Harvard at the end of two years when It had handsomely failed to qualify for Its succeeding year. It had then gone to Yale and remained a year with no greater progress than It had known before. Then It had gone to Paris where It had stayed for the next five years and—save for Its final burst of glory—the rest was almost silence.

It had been seen regularly and constantly about the cafes of the Left Bank for the next five years. It had been well known and a great favorite there. It had made the acquaintance of Mr. Ezra Pound and during the last year of Its sojourn in the capital of Art it had given first performance of Its wire dolls. The performance had been largely attended by Its friends and by Its enemies, by Its partisans and by Its opponents, by Its two schools of thought of which there were in those days almost thirty-seven in this fair city by the Seine.

And during the course of Its famous first performance, while Its enemies were loudly united in booing It and all Its works into oblivion, Its fiery champion, Mr. Pound, had leaped to his feet, brandished his fist and screamed: "Assassins!"—after which, of course, the affair broke up in a general brawl, and the career and fame of It were thus gloriously established.

Since then Its career had been a chain of unbroken constantly growing triumphs. When It had returned to Its native shores the autumn before, the adepts of the arts were already ripened for idolatry. And now, at this very moment, in this very place, on this very spot, in the month of April of this year of grace, It Itself was here in Mrs. Jack's apartment, under the care of her gracious hospitality, was now enjoying the privacy of one of the lovely rooms in Mrs. Jack's apartment, and, as if It was utterly unaware of the huge disturbance It had made or the towering position It now enjoyed in the great world—It was calmly, quietly, modestly, and matter-of-factly pulling off its own trousers prosaically and pulling on a pair of canvas pants.

THE FAMILY

. . .

Meanwhile, while this momentous happening was taking place, events were moving smoothly to their consummation in other quarters of the house. The swing door between the kitchen and the dining room kept slatting back and forth as the maids came in and out to make the final preparations for the feast. Janie came through the dining room bearing a great silver tray filled with bottles, decanters, a bowl of ice, and tall lovely glasses crystal thin.

As she sat the tray down upon a table in the living room the shell-thin glasses chimed together musically, there was a pleasant clink of bottles, the cold, clean rattle of cracked ice. Then the girl came over toward the hearth, removed the big brass screen and knelt before the dancing flames. She poked the logs with a long brass poker and a pair of tongs. For a moment there was a shower of fiery sparks, the fire blazed and crackled with new life. The girl restored the tongs and poker to their place and for a moment stayed there on her knees in a gesture of sweet maiden grace. The fire danced and cast its radiance across her glowing face and Mrs. Jack looked at her for a moment with a softened glance, thinking how sweet and clean and pretty the girl was.

Then the maid arose and restored the screen to its former position. And Mrs. Jack, after arranging anew a vase of long-stemmed roses on a small table in the hall and glancing at herself for a brief moment in the mirror above, turned and walked briskly and happily down the broad, deep-carpeted hallway towards her own room at the other end.

Her son was just coming from his room as she passed his door. He was fully dressed for the evening. She looked at him with an expert eye that missed no detail of his costume. And she saw how well his clothes fit him and how he wore them as if they had grown on him. He was a young man, only twenty-six or seven. But, compared to his mother's fresh and jolly face, her quick and nervous movements, her habitual expression of almost bewildered innocence and surprise, of childlike innocence—a manner and expression so naive and ingenuous that it made everyone smile affectionately when they saw her, although it did not always take everyone in—his own face, his own voice and manner and expression were by the contrast curiously tainted and sophisticated.

It was not that he was in any way a dissipated man. He was, on the contrary, a very wise and knowing one. He took excellent care of himself. He was certainly by no means inexperienced in the pleasures and temptations of the flesh but he knew how far to go. He knew very well beyond what point lay danger, beyond what point lay chaos, shipwreck and the reef. Looking at him quickly, in one of those swift and comprehensive glances that missed nothing, despite the deceptive and half bewildered innocence of her jolly little face, she was amazed to see how much he knew, a little troubled, perhaps, to find he knew so much, that he knew even more, perhaps, than she could see or fathom.

The young man's face was heavy, white, blue jowled and thick jawed. It was a curiously sleepy, almost stupid looking kind of face. The eyes also were dull and sleepy looking. But it was the eyes that gave him away. The face was a bland and heavy mask, but the eyes had something jeering in their sleepy depths that he could not wholly hide. It was not something that jeered bitterly. It was not something that had ever been fierce and young and wounded sorrowfully. It was not the bitter jeering hurt of anguish that came from the young soul's torment, the anguish of a ruined innocence, the bitter desolation and despair of youth's lost dream, its shattered world.

No, it was none of this and for this reason it was more terrible. It was something that had never had a youth or known innocence. It was something that had sprung full-born and full-begotten, old and dark and weary and corrupt as hell out of its race and womb. It was something that had never looked upon this earth and on the strange and bitter miracle of living with a child's fierce eyes of love and hope and terror and fierce passion, with horror, pity or with desperate pride. It was something that had been born with ancient eyes and with an ancient soul, with all the weary visions of ten thousand years of pain, of fear, of craft, of stealth and of perverse contrivings and that had come here from the cradle, can-opied with the full armor of all its sorrowful and ill-starred wisdoms, with all the guilt and caution of its unhappy findings, with all the faithlessness of its lost faith, the hopelessness of its lost hope, the bitter damnations of its own security—which was to live, to breathe, to flourish and grow sleek, to profit and to prosper, somehow not to die—to survive, just to survive by any means.

So lost, it was no longer to be lost or desperate, or drawn in, wisely to know where peril lay, and to avoid it. A barren gain! To be so knowing and so wrong, to see so clearly and to be so blind to be betrayed at last by its own knowingness, duped out of wisdom by its own ancient and remediless unrighteousness: to look for ever on all the pain, the ruin, the victory and defeat, the error, the frustration, the despair of the tormented race of man as if it were a barren comedy, the provender of a mirthless laugh, with the sleepy and unfathomed cynicism of those jeering eyes—ah, comfortless! Profitless comfort! Comfortless gain! He bent smoothly over her small figure as she approached. He said: "Oh, hello," in a tone in which suave courtesy was curiously commingled with a kind of heavy insolence. He kissed her lightly and perfunctorily on one rosy cheek. It was the kiss of an ambassador, the heavy smoothness of the whole man-ner, the entire gesture of greeting and of welcome was really one of old and polished sophistry, instead of youth. His manner and his tone, the perfect bland assurance of everything he did, were more like the ges-tures of an old and jaded diplomat—an automaton of faultless conduct, perfect courtesy, from whom all the warmth and sincerity of life had gone.

He was growing bald, his short, silky hair was getting very thin on top and on the sides it crinkled in unpleasant little scrolls. She was con-scious of a moment's distaste and repugnance as she looked at him, but then she remembered what a perfect son he was, how thoughtful and how good and how devoted and how, no matter what the unfathomed implications of those jeering eyes might be he had said nothing—for all that anyone could prove, saw nothing.

"He's a sweet boy," she was thinking as she responded brightly to his greeting: "Oh, hello, darling. You're all ready, aren't you? Listen,"—she spoke rapidly—"Will you look out for the bell and take care of anyone who comes? Mr. Logan is changing his costume in the guest room—won't you look out for him if he needs anything? And see if Edith's ready. And when the guests begin to come you can send the women to her room to take off their wraps—oh, just tell Molly—she'll attend to it! And you'll take care of the men yourself—won't you, dear? You can take them back into your father's room—is he ready yet? You'd better go and tell him that it's time. I'll be out in a few minutes. If only everything!—" she began in a worried tone, slipped the jade ring quickly from her finger and slipped it back again. "I do hope that everything's all right!" She spoke rapidly, nervously, with a little line of tension between her eyes.

"But *isn't* it?" he said in his heavy, smooth and blandly jeering tone. "Have you looked?"

"Oh, everything looks perfect!" she cried. "It's really just too beautiful! The girls behaved wonderfully—only—" the little furrow came between her eyes again—"Do keep an eye on them, won't you, Ernie? You know how they are if you're not around. Something's so likely to go wrong. And of course I can't hear everything that's going on any longer. It's such a nuisance getting deaf this way!—" she said impatiently—"So please do listen and look out for me, won't you, dear? And look out for Mr. Logan. I do hope—" she paused, with a look of worried abstraction in her eyes. She began to snap the ring on and off her finger again.

"You do hope what?" said Ernie pointedly, with just the suggestion of an ironic grin around the corners of his heavy mouth.

"I do hope he won't—" she began in a troubled tone, then went on rapidly—"He said something about—about clearing away some of the things in the living room for his show—"

She looked at him rather helplessly, then, catching the irony of his faint grin, she colored quickly and laughed, shortly richly: "God! I don't know what he's going to do. He brought enough stuff with him to sink a battleship! Still, I suppose it's going to be all right. Everyone's been after him you know—everyone's thrilled at the chance of seeing him—Oh, I'm sure it'll be all right. Don't you think so? Hah?" She looked eagerly, earnestly at him with her flushed and rosy little face with a look of such droll, beseeching inquiry as she clapped a small hand to her ear that, unmasked for a moment, he laughed abruptly, coarsely, as he turned away, saying:

"Oh, I suppose so, I'll look after it."

Mrs. Jack went on down the hall, pausing just perceptibly as she passed her daughter's door, cupping her hand swiftly to her ear and listening for a moment. She could hear just faintly the girl's voice clear, cool, and young, humming the jaunty strains of a tune that was popular at the moment:

"You're the cream in my coffee—You're the salt in my stew-w-"

The woman listened eagerly, a little smile of love and tenderness suffusing her face as she did so. Then she went on down the hall and entered her room, leaving her door slightly ajar behind her.

It was a very simple, lovely room. It was a room that had a kind of haunting chastity, a moving austerity. At first glance the room seemed almost needlessly severe: There was, in the centre of one wall, a little narrow wooden bed, so small, and plain, and old, that it seemed it might almost have served as the bed of a medieval nun, as perhaps it had. Beside this bed there was a little table with a few books, a telephone, a glass and a silver pitcher and in a silver frame a photograph of a girl in her early twenties. This was Mrs. Jack's daughter.

In the centre of the wall at the left as one entered there was an enormous old wooden wardrobe, which she had brought from Italy and which was a product of the Italian renaissance. On the opposite wall, two high broad windows looked out on the street and between these windows there was a small writing table, with some ink, some paper and a pen.

Along the wall that faced the bed and near the door of the big closet were all her beautiful dresses, gowns and suits and the wonderful collection of wing-like little shoes which had been made by hand to house her perfect little feet, and which were one of her special and most proud extravagances. There was a gay old painted wooden chest, a product of the Pennsylvania Dutch, carved and colored in quaint and cheerful patterns. Here she kept her fine old silks and laces and the wonderful and noble Indian saris which she loved so well and which adorned her small but lovely figure with such gracious dignity.

Facing this old chest, along the opposite wall, between the bed and window, there was a small drawing table. It was a single sheet of white perfect wood on which were arranged with faultless precision a dozen sharpened pencils, a few feathery brushes, some crisp sheets of tracing papers on which the geometric figures of design were legible, a pot of paste, a ruler, and a little jar of golden paint. Exactly above this table hanging from the wall in all the clean perfection and beauty of their strength and accuracy were a triangle and a square. At the foot of the little bed there was a chaise longue covered with a flowered design of old faded silk.

There were a few simple drawings on the wall and a single painting of a strange, exotic flower. It was such a flower as never was, a kind of dream flower of the brain which this woman had painted long ago. There was an old chest of drawers with a few silver toilet articles and a small square mirror on its top, and these were the sole adornments of the room.

Mrs. Jack regarded herself for a moment in the mirror. She had a very lovely face, her brown and pleasant eyes were a little tired and there were webbings of fine wrinkles about them. But the healthy, jolly freshness of her rosy cheeks and lips needed the redemptive aid of no artifice of rouge. She never used it. Her hair was brown, a little dull and coarse, just touched a little by filaments of grey. The hair itself was not distinguished by its beauty, but it was clean and healthy looking. The forehead was low, not an impressive one, certainly not showing signs of intellectual grandeur. But the wise eyes were kind and shrewd and sharp and lively and missed nothing. The quality of the whole face had an expression of serious and acute intelligence a little worn by time, by care, by experience and the responsibilities of life and work. The face itself was a fine one: it was almost perfectly heartshaped. The glowing rosy features sloped firmly, perfectly, to a rounded but most determined chin. The chin was slightly cleft. The nose was somewhat too large and fleshy for the contours of the face, which were characterized not only by the strength, the decision, the firmness of the features, but also by a quality of delicacy and loveliness that can only be described as flowerlike.

It was a strange and moving congruence of age and youth, of innocence and maturity, of an almost childlike eagerness, surprise and wonder, with the shrewd intelligence, the driving will and energy of an extremely resourceful, able and experienced child of Eve.

She looked at herself for a moment. She regarded and admired herself. She found herself good.

And, as the woman continued to look at herself in the privacy of her mirror, her face and manner betrayed a childlike vanity that would have been ludicrously comical if anyone had seen her. First she bent forward a little and looked at herself long and earnestly with an expression of a childlike innocence, an air of surprised wonder which was one of her characteristic expressions when she faced and met the world.

Apparently she found the contemplation of her own rosy guilelessness quite pleasing, for in a moment she began to regard herself from first one angle, then another. She put her hand up to her temple and smoothed her brow, and regarded herself with rapt complacency again.

Her expression now, indeed, barely escaped a smirk of satisfaction and for the first time, now, there was a sense of looseness about the mouth and nostril, a kind of cynic smirk not wholly good to see.

Then slowly, raptly, she lifted the small, strong hand and looked at it. She flexed the firm and slender fingers and turned her wrist, meanwhile regarding the miracle with a fascinated stare. And now, the look upon her face was truly childlike in its vanity. She admired the old Jade ring upon her finger. She brooded with a kind of dark and smouldering fascination on the thick bracelet around her arm—a rich and sombre chain of ancient India, studded with dull and curious gems.

She looked at her slender fingers, at her warm, slightly worn neck, and traced out with her fingertips the strange and opulent design of the old necklace, also a work of India, that she wore. She surveyed her smooth and naked arms, her smooth, bare back, her breast and gleaming shoulders and the outlines of her small and lovely figure and arranged half consciously with practiced touches of an expert hand the folds of her simple, splendid gown.

She looked demurely at her small feet, shod beautifully in golden wings. Then she lifted arm and hand again and half-turning with the other hand upon her hip she ogled herself absurdly in the friendly mirror.

But even while this ritual of adoring self was taking place, its spellbound abbess was discovered in the act. As the elder woman turned and worshipped at the shrine of her own beauty a girl, young, slender, faultless, cold and lovely—with the hard perfection, the perfect convention of Egyptian Nefratete, whose likeness she so strikingly suggested—had entered through the bathroom that connected two rooms and, standing in the door, paused in a moment of cold irony as she caught the other woman in the act.

Slowly the mother turned, arm raised and hand extended in the orbit of her own self worship. Slowly she turned, still rapt in contemplation of her loveliness, gasped suddenly with surprise and fright, and uttered a little scream. Her hand flew to her throat in a gesture of alarm and realizing now that she was not alone she looked up and saw the girl. Her face went crimson as a beet. For a moment longer the two women continued to look at each other, the mother utterly confused and crimson with her guilt, the daughter coolly and appraisingly with the irony of sophisticated mirth.

Then, as they continued to look at each other and full consciousness of the moment dawned upon the older woman, something quick and instant passed between them in their glance. Like one who has been discovered and who knows that there is nothing more to say, the woman suddenly cast up her head and laughed, a rich, full-throated, woman's yell of free acknowledgment, unknown to the race of man.

As for the girl, now grinning faintly, she approached and kissed her mother, saying, "Well, Mother, was it good?" And again the woman was shaken with a rich hysteria of helpless mirth; then both freed from all argument by that all-taking moment, were calm again.

Thus passed there in a flash the whole tremendous comedy of womankind. No words were needed, there was nothing left to say. All had been said there in that voiceless instant of complete and utter understanding, of mutual recognition and conspiracy. The whole universe of sex had been nakedly revealed for just a moment in all its horror, guile, deception and its overwhelming humor.

And the great city, the unceasing city, the unnumbered temporal city, with its seven million lives roared on unwittingly around that secret cell and never knew that here for a moment had been revealed a buried force more strong than cities and as old as earth.

THE PARTY BEGINNING
. . .

But now the guests were beginning to arrive. The electric *thring* of the doorbell broke sharply and persistently on accustomed quietness. People began to come in and fill the place with the ease and familiarity of old friends. In the hallway and in the rooms at the front there arose now the confused but crescent medley of a dozen voices—the rippling laughter and quick excited voices of the women with the deeper and more vibrant sonorities of the men. One could listen and without looking sense and feel and hear the growing momentum of the party.

It was a mixture smooth as oil, the ingredients of a liquor which mixed, and fused, and grew, and mounted steadily with each arrival. There were, with every sharp electric ringing of the bell, with every opening and closing of the door, new voices and new laughter, a babel of new greeting, new gaiety and new welcome. There was the tinkle of ice in shell-thin glasses, voices and people coming closer, voices and people moving down the hall, voices and people moving in and out of rooms, weaving back and forth, circulating everywhere in beautiful and spontaneous patterns as natural and as fluent as all life until the whole place was invaded, filled, completely inhabited with the flashing iridescent gaiety of all these voices, all these people.

Already the party, like all the parties Mrs. Jack had ever given, seemed to run itself. Without any sense of strain or supervision it was mounting swiftly, easily, naturally to full swing. People were coming down the hall now, women were coming in to Mrs. Jack's room, greeting and embracing her with the affectionate tenderness of old friendship. And outside, the voices of the men could be heard engaged in solemn discussion or in jesting interplay of wit, going in and out of Mr. Jack's apartment, moving back and forth from one end of the place to the other.

The whole place, and all its rooms from front to back, was now thrown open to the party. Mrs. Jack, her face glowing and excited, her eyes sparkling with the joy and happiness that giving parties, meeting people, welcoming old friends, the whole warm and brilliant flux and interplay of life, of movement, beauty, color, conversation and design around her always gave to her, had now left her room and was moving up the hall greeting people everywhere, stopping to talk to everyone with a voice and manner and a rosy, beaming face, that showed plainly her state of eager and somewhat surprised delight.

This quality of surprise and wonder was now indubitably real—somewhat akin, no doubt, to her own deafness—the effect of which was not to give her the expression of a person who feels that delighted wonders will never cease. Although she had invited all these people, although she had known most of them for years, although she must have known that all of them were coming, her manner now as each greeted her in turn in her triumphant progress through the throng was the manner of one who is really taken aback, a little bewildered and stunned by the happiness of an unexpected and unhoped-for encounter with an old friend that one has not seen for a long time. And this was really true, the woman had great goodness in her, and her feeling towards her friends was deep and warm.

Her voice, as she talked, grew a trifle higher with its excitement, even at times a little shrill, her rosy, glowing little face was seen everywhere, blooming like a flower, one could see her bend forward eagerly and clap her hand to her ear as she strove to catch every word of what people were saying to her. And people smiled at her; almost as people smile who look at a happy and excited child, they looked after her and smiled.

And when new people would come up and speak to her she would turn with her rosy face fairly burning with excitement and earnestness. Her whole face would light up with a kind of bewildered and delighted surprise as she saw who her new guest was. One could hear her voice saying excitedly and in an almost confused tone:—"Oh, Steve! I didn't see you! I didn't know that you were here! I am so glad that you could come! And Mary—Did you bring her with you? Is she here too? Hah?—" And she would clap her hand up to her ear and bend forward with her rosy beaming face eagerly focused to hear all that was being said.

The whole party was in full blast now, moving wonderfully, miraculously, beautifully, in full swing, with a wonderful harmony, with spontaneous rhythm; people were moving in and out of rooms with glasses in their hands, people were leaning against walls talking to each other, splendid, distinguished looking men were leaning on the mantle engaged in the casual earnestness of debate, the seriousness of mutual interests, the informal conversation of old acquaintanceship and chance meeting, beautiful women with satiny backs were moving through the crowd with velvet undulance, the young people had gathered together in little parties of their own, spontaneously attracted by the crystalline magic of their youth.

Everywhere people were talking, laughing, debating, chattering, bending to fill glasses with long frosty drinks, moving around the loaded temptations of the dining table and the great buffet with that "choosey," somewhat perturbed and doubtful look of people who would like to taste it all but know they can't. And the clean, sweet, rosily and smiling maids were there to do their bidding, help them, urge them *just* to have a little more. It was wonderful, greeting one another, weaving back and forth in a celebrated pattern of white and black and gold and power and wealth and loveliness and food and drink.

And through it all, like the magnetic star, through it all like the thread of gold, the line of life, through all the wonder of this wealth of life, warmth, joy and gaiety together, through it all like some strange and lovely flower, bending and welcoming on its gracious stem, moved the flushed and rosy face, the dancing eye, the warm heart and the wise, the subtle, childlike, magic spirit that was Mrs. Jack.

She seemed to give a tongue to loveliness: to weave a magic thread into the labyrinth of movement and of sound. And to the pattern of this swarming web she seemed to give the combining purpose of her presence, the unifying magic of her one and single self. Here, in these rooms, between these walls, was now collected a good part of all the best in strength, in power, in talent and in beauty that the city could produce or that life could know. And all of it had been miraculously resumed, fused to a flower of life by the unique genius of a single spirit. And the result of that great fusion was—as it had always been solely and inimitably itself:—a party at Jack's.

THE GUESTS ARRIVING

· · ·

Mrs. Jack glanced happily through the crowded rooms. It was, she well knew, a notable assemblage of the best, the highest, and the fairest that the city had to offer. And others were arriving all the time. At this moment, in fact, Miss Lily Mandell arrived upon the arm of Mr. Lawrence Hirsch: the tall smoldering beauty swung undulant away along the hall to dispose of her wraps and schooled in power, close clipped hair groomed and faultless, the banker came into the room, wove greetings through the throng toward the focal centre of his rosy hostess, shook hands with her and kissed her lightly on one cheek saying with that cool irony of friendly humor that was a portion of the city style: "You haven't looked so lovely, darling, since the days we used to dance the cancan together."

The guests were now arriving in full force. Sometimes the elevator was so crowded with new arrivals that one group had hardly time to finish with greetings before the door would open and a new group would come in. Miss Roberta Heilprinn arrived with Mr. Robert Ahrens and made their greetings to their hostess: they were old friends of hers "in the theatre" and her greetings to them, while not more cordial or affectionate than to her other guests, were indefinably yet plainly more direct and casual: it was as if one of those masks—not of pretending, but of formal custom—which life imposes upon so many of the human relations, had been here sloughed off. It was here simply; "Oh, hello, Bertie—hello Bob:" the shade indefinable told everything: they were "show people": they had "worked together."

There were a good many "show people." Roy Farley had now arrived accompanied by two young men from the Art Theatre where he was employed and by the Misses Hattie Warren and Bessie Lane, two grey-haired spinsters who were also directors of the theatre. Mr. Farley and his two young companions divested themselves of their light overcoats with graceful movements, gave them to the waiting maid and made their way into the crowded room to pay their duties to the hostess.

Old Jake Abramson came in with his sister, Irita; Stephen Hook, the novelist, arrived with his sister Mary. A moment later, Amy Van Leer, her beautiful head all sunning over with golden curls, arrived with a young Japanese, the sculptor, Nokamura, who had enjoyed a fashionable success the year before and had been for the nonce her lover, and with an immensely wealthy young Jew with a talent for music, who had written two of the songs of a current revue, and was her present one.

Many other people had filtered in, the place was crowded: there was Helen Reagan, a very beautiful woman with a Gibson face, touched by Irish freckles: she was the business manager of a repertory theatre, but it was rumored that her greatest talent lay in wangling large sums of money from infatuated millionaires for the support of her organization. One of these enamored Maecenases, a middle-aged plutocrat named Pendleton, was now with her. With proud and graceful carriage, and straight shoulders, slender, naked, hued like ivory, this beautiful woman moved along a miracle of cold seductiveness, in all the fragile cool intoxication of her beauty.

Saul Levenson came in with his wife, Virginia. He was one of the leaders of the modern theatre and one of its most eminent designers. He had been a friend of Mrs. Jack's since childhood.

In addition to all these other more or less gifted, beautiful or distinguished people, most of whom had some connection with the arts, there were a number of the lesser fry—that is, people who had no great worldly renown, or any particular claim to distinction save that they were friends of Mrs. Jack.

There was her friend Agnes Wheeler and her husband. They were people who lived quietly in the country. Agnes Wheeler had been a girlhood friend of Mrs. Jack's, had gone to school with her in childhood, had married a man who had died tragically and horribly after an agony of years of a cancer of the face which had finally eaten into his brain, and was now married again to a man who was dull and drab and unremarkable in every way. They had a small income and they lived modestly upon it.

There was also a lawyer named Roderick Hale and his wife. Hale wrote little verses which occasionally were published in newspaper columns and he had a wife who was interested in social service work. And there was also a young girl, a dancer at Irita Abramson's Repertory Theatre, another girl who was the seamstress and the wardrobe woman there, and another girl of twenty, who was Mrs. Jack's assistant in her own work.

It was a wholesome and admirable quality of her character that, as she had gone on in her profession and "up" in her career, as success, wealth, and renown had come to her and members of her family, she had not lost the sane and healthy practicality that was one of the essential elements of her life. She had not, as do so many people who achieve success or fame, lost her touch with life—with everyday life, the life about her, the life of the people with whom she worked, whom she worked for, who worked for her, or whom she had known in her youth.

As a result, she was always in touch with the common heart of life—not only with the lives and interests of the wealthy or celebrated people that she knew, but with the lives and interests of her maids, her cook, the man who drove her car, the stage-hands at the theatre, the seamstresses and helpers, the painters and carpenters who built her sets for her, the electricians who lighted them, as well as with all the actors, actresses, directors and producers whose names were current in the daily press.

It was a wonderful, a saving quality. A celebrity herself, she had escaped the banal and stereotyped existence that so many celebrities achieve—a life that is no life at all, made up no more of life, but of just a kind of barren parliament of famous names, a compendium of famous stories, a collection of jokes and anecdotes and stories about famous people, eagerly to be lapped up at secondhand and passed about among the popular—but really just a counterfeit of life, empty dead and stale as hell.

She had escaped this. The line of life ran like a golden thread through this woman's years from first to last. She remembered every living thing that she had touched. And nearly everything that she had touched had lived. She had known sorrow in her youth, insecurity and hardship in her youth, heart break, disillusion and poor people in her youth. And she remembered all of them. She had not forgotten her old friends; she had a talent rare in modern life for loyal and abiding friendships and most of the people that were here tonight, even the most celebrated ones, were people that she had known for many years, and her friendship with some of them went back to childhood.

Another childhood friend of Mrs. Jack's was present. This was Margaret Ettinger: she had married a bad painter, and tonight she had brought her husband. And her husband, who was not only a bad painter but a bad man, too, had brought his mistress, a young buxom, and full-blown whore, with him. This group provided the most bizarre and unpleasantly disturbing touch to an otherwise distinguished gathering.

THE LOVER
. . .

And yet, someone was still lacking.

"Long, long into the night I lay," thought Mrs. Jack. "Thinking about you all the time."

For someone was still absent and she kept thinking of him—well, *almost* all the time. At least, so she would phrase it next day in her mind with that kind of temporal infatuation which a woman feels when she is thinking of her lover: "I keep thinking of you all the time. I do nothing but think of you all the time. When I wake up in the morning the first thing I think about is you. And then I think about my little Alma: the two people that I love the best in all the world. Did you ever try to tell a story? Once when I was a child I felt sure I had to tell a story. It kept growing in me, it was like an immense and golden dream. I thought it was the most wonderful story that anyone had ever told. I was sure that it would make me rich and famous. I felt I had the whole thing in me, it kept swelling up in me and seemed to fill me, soak me through and through with all its gold. And yet, when I began it all that I could think of was 'Long, long into the night I lay thinking of how to tell my story.' Wasn't that wonderful? It seemed to me to be the most beautiful and perfect way to begin a story—but I could go no further. And now I know the end. 'Long, long into the night I lay—thinking of you.' I think about you all the time. You fill my life, my heart, my spirit and my being. I have an image that I go around with you inside me—*here*. I have you inside of me—and I keep thinking of you all the time. And that's the story, 'Long, long into the night I lay—thinking about you all the time.' And that's the story. Ah, dearest, that's the story."

And so this lovely and successful woman really felt—or thought she felt. Really, when she thought of him, she kept *thinking* she was "thinking of him all the time." And on this crowded and this brilliant evening, he kept flashing through her mind. Or maybe he was really *there*, as someone we have known and loved is *there*—and really can't be lost, no matter what we're doing, what we're thinking of—and so, in such a wise, we keep "thinking of them all the time."

"I wonder where he is," she thought. "Why doesn't he come? If only he hasn't been—" she looked quickly over the brilliant gathering with a troubled eye and thought impatiently—"If only he liked parties more! If only he enjoyed meeting people—going out in the evening—Oh well! He's the way he is. It's no use to change him. I wouldn't have him any different. I think about him all the time!"

And then he arrived; a hurried but relieved survey told her that he was "all right." He was a little too quick and a trifle more feverish than was his wont. Just the same, he was, as Esther had phrased it to herself, "all right."

"If only my people—my friends—everyone I know—didn't affect him so," she thought. "Why is it, I wonder. Last night when he telephoned me he talked so strange! Nothing he said made any sense! What could have been wrong with him? Oh, well—it doesn't matter now. He's here. I love him!"

Her face warmed and softened, her pulse beat quicker, and she went to meet him. He greeted her half fondly and half truculently, with a mixture of diffidence and pugnacity, of arrogance and humility, of pride, of hope, of love, of suspicion, of eagerness, of doubt.

"Oh, hello, darling," she said fondly. "I'm so glad you're here at last. I was beginning to be afraid you were going to fail me after all."

He had not really wanted to come to the party. From the moment she had first invited him he had objected. They had argued it back and forth for days, and at last she had beaten down his reasons and had exacted his promise. But last night he had paced the floor for hours in an agony of self-recrimination and indecision, and at last with desperate resolve he had telephoned her and had blunderingly awakened the whole household before he got her. But he had told her then that he had decided not to come and had repeated all his reasons. He only half-understood them himself, but they had to do with her world and his world, and his belief, which was more a matter of feeling than of clear thought, that he must keep his independence of the world she belonged to if he was to do his work. He was almost desperate as he tried to explain it all to her, because he couldn't make her understand what he was driving at. She became a little desperate, too, in the end. First she was annoyed and told him for God's sake to stop being such a fool about things that didn't matter. Then she became hurt and angry, and reminded him of his promise.

"We've been over all of this a dozen times!" she said angrily, and there was also a tearful note in her voice. "You promised, George! And now everything's arranged. It's too late to change anything now. You can't let me down like this!"

This appeal was too much for him. He knew, of course, that the party had not been planned for him and that no arrangements would be upset if he failed to appear. No one but Esther would even be aware of his absence. But he *had* given his promise to come, however reluctantly, and he saw that the only issue his arguments had raised in Esther's mind was the simple one of whether he would keep his word. So once more, and finally, he had yielded. And now he was here, full of confusion, and wishing with all his heart that he was somewhere else—anywhere but here.

"I'm sure you're going to have a good time," Esther was saying to him in her eager way. "You'll see!"—and she squeezed his hand. "There are lots of people I want you to meet. But you must be hungry. Better get yourself something to eat first. You'll find lots of things you like. I planned them especially for you. Go in the dining room and help yourself. I'll have to stay here a little while to welcome all these people."

Mrs. Jack looked happily about her. Now they were all together— even to the one she loved.

George stood for a moment, scowling a little as he glanced about the room at the brilliant assemblage. In that attitude he cut a rather grotesque figure. The low brow with its frame of short black hair, the burning eyes, the small, packed features, the long arms dangling to the knees, and the curved paws gave him an appearance more simian than usual in his not-too-well-fitting dinner jacket. People looked at him and stared, then turned away indifferently and resumed their conversations.

"So," he thought with somewhat truculent self-consciousness, "these are her fine friends that she's been telling me about! I might have known it!" he muttered to himself, without knowing at all what it was he might have known. The very poise and assurance of all these sleek and wealthy faces made him fear a fancied slight where none was offered or intended. "Well, here they are! I'll show them!" he growled,—but God knows what he meant by that.

It was, he knew, a distinguished gathering. It included brilliant men and beautiful women. But as he looked them over, he saw unmistakably that it also included some who wore another hue. That fellow there, for instance, with his pasty face and rolling eyes and mincing ways and hips that he wiggled as he walked—could there be any doubt at all that he was a member of nature's other sex? And that woman, with her mannish haircut and angular lines and hard enameled face, holding hands over there in the corner with that rather pretty young girl—a nymphomaniac, surely. His eye took in Krock, standing a little apart there with his wife and his mistress. He saw Mr. Jack moving among his guests, and suddenly with a rush of shame he thought of himself. Who was *he* to feel so superior to these others? Did they not all know who he was and why he was here?

Yes, all these people looked at one another with untelling eyes. Their speech was casual, quick, and witty. But they did not say the things they knew. And they knew everything. They had seen everything. They had accepted everything. And they received every new intelligence now with a cynical and amused look in their untelling eyes. Nothing shocked them any more. It was the way things were. It was what they had come to expect of life.

Just the same, they were an honored group. They had stolen no man's ox or ass. Their gifts were valuable and many, and had won for them the world's grateful applause.

Was not the great captain of finance and industry, Lawrence Hirsch, a patron of the arts as well, and a leader and advanced supporter of *The Federalist*, the nation's leading "journal of ideas," the leader everywhere of advanced—nay! *radical* opinion? And this gentlemen's own opinions on child labor, share cropping, the trial of Sacco and Vanzetti, and other questions that had stirred the indignation of the intellectual world— were they not well known everywhere, and was there any flaw in them? Were they not celebrated for their liberality, the advanced and leftward trend of their enlightenment?

Of what then to utter the blunt truth?—which was that Lawrence Hirsch derived a portion of his enormous income from the work of children in the textile factories of the South?—that another part of it was derived from the labor of share-croppers in the tobacco fields of North

Carolina?—that another came from steel mills in the Middle West where armed thugs had been employed and used to shoot into the ranks of striking workers?—and that this man's enormous combining and financing and directing cunning was being called into use everywhere by great corporations of which he was a member, to betray the rights of labor, and to protect the powers of wealth?

Of what use, then, to criticize in ways like these? What useful purpose could it serve? Had Mr. Hirsch's life and work, the sources of his mighty wealth, been seriously called to an accounting, there was scarcely a skilled young liberal—hardly a well trained revolutionary on the staff of Mr. Hirsch's *Federalist*—who could not have leaped to the defense of his employer, who could not have pointed out at once that criticism of this sort was childish—elementary, Watson! Elementary!—That the sources of Mr. Hirsch's wealth and power and income were quite accidental and beside the point—and that his position as an enlightened liberal, "a friend of Russia," a leader in advanced social thought, a scathing critic of—God save the mark!—the Capitalist class!—was so well known as to place him in the very brain and forehead of enlightened thought, secure beyond the reach of envious and incondite carping of this sort.

And, as for the others of that brilliant and that celebrated company— did one cry "privilege?" Privilege? Which one of these had ever said, "Let them eat cake?" When the poor had starved, had these not suffered? When the children toiled, had these not bled? When the oppressed, the weak, the stricken and betrayed of men had been falsely accused and put to death, had these tongues not lifted in indignant protest—if only the issue had been fashionable? Had these not written letters to the press? Carried placards upon Beacon Hill? Joined parades, made contributions, gave the prestige of their names to form committees of defense?

Had they not done all these things? Were they not well known for these acts? Was their position in all questions that demanded an enlightened stand not known in advance? And were their names not known with honor everywhere among enlightened men?

Of what use then to say that such as these might lift their voices and parade their placards to the crack of doom, but in the secret and entrenched resources of their life they had all battened on the blood of common man, and wrung their profits from the sweat of slaves, like any common overseer of money and of privilege that ever lived?

Of what use to point out that the whole issue of these princely lives, the dense and costly web of all these lesbic, all these pederastic loves, and these adulterous intrigues, the perverse and evil pattern of this magic fabric, hung there athwart the beetling ramparts of the city, and spun like gossamer across the sky-flung faery of the night, had been spun from man's common dust of sweating clay, derived out of the exploitation of his life, and sustained in midair now, floating on the face of night like a starred veil, had, none the less, been unwound out of the entrails of man's agony.

Such thoughts as these came from the baffled and inchoate bitterness of youth. And youth? A thorny paradox, to be so stretched out on the rack of this tough world and here to ache with so much beauty, so much pain. To see the starred face of the night with a high soul of exaltation and of noble aspiration, to dream great dreams, to think great thoughts. And in that instant have the selfless grandeur turn to dust, and to see great night itself, a reptile coiled and waiting in the nocturnal blood of life.

And these! And these! Great God! To know such love, such longing, and such hatred all together—and to find no ear or utterance anywhere for all the blazing baffled certitudes of youth! To find man's faith betrayed and his betrayers throned in honor, themselves the idols of his bartered faith. To find truth false and falsehood truth, good evil, evil good, and the swarming web of life so changing, so mercurial. To find even love suspect of whoredom, even whoredom touched with love!

A thorny paradox, to find it all so changing, so unfixed, so baffling to our certain judgments and our hard necessity for certitude; so different from the way we thought that it would be. Was there no other end than this hard road, for all the anguish, sorrow, disappointment of man's baffled innocence then the resigned dejection of the Russian's summing up: "Prince Andrey turned away—His heart was heavy and full of melancholy. It was all so strange, so different than what he had anticipated."

Well, there they were then, anyway. And, paradox or not, it would be hard to find another group of people comparable to this one in achievement, beauty, or in talent, in any other place save here, where it had assembled to such brilliant consummation as it had to-night—at Jack's.

The party was now moving in a magic inter-flux. Lawrence Hirsch, having made his greetings to his hostess, now turned away and took his place among the crowd. Polished, imperturbable, his face just like his moustache and his hair, close cropped and packed and perfectly contained, a little worn but assured, vested with huge authorities of wealth, in its unconscious arrogance, it was a perfect visage of great Croesus and

Maecenas, both conjoined with all the complex fusions of the modern world. He moved, this weary, able son of man, among the crowd and took his place assuming, without knowing he assumed, his full authorities.

Meanwhile, Lily Mandell, who had gone away to take off her wraps, returned to the big room. The tall smouldering beauty swung sensually along the hall and entering wove her way along towards Mrs. Jack with a languid naked undulance.

The heir of Midas wealth, child of a merchant emperor and a hoard amassed by nameless myriads of slave sweat, this voluptuous absentee of bargain basements in huge department stores which she had never visited, was a voluptuary of esthetics arts as well. She was an adept of obscurities, William Beckford's *Vathek*, T. S. Eliot, and the works of Marcel Proust.

She was a tall, dark beauty, shockingly arrayed, a woman of great height and of sensual and yet delicate massivity. She had a shock of wild dark hair, a face too eloquent in its sleepy arrogance, and heavy lidded eyes whose most naked living qualities were the qualities of her insolence and pride.

Everything about this tall and stunning woman was sensational and startling. In the sleepy insolence of her dark smouldering face, in the languorous arrogance of her rich and throaty voice, even in the lazy undulance of her voluptuous figure there was a quality of naked indifference and contempt for life that barely escaped brutality.

Moreover, in the sensational way in which she exhibited and displayed herself there was an insolent immodesty that was so shameless that it left people dazed and gasping. The dress she wore was a magnificent gown made from a single piece of some dull old golden cloth. But that gown had been so made and so contrived to display her charms that her tall voluptuous figure seemed literally to have been poured into it. It was a miracle of sheer carnality, a masterpiece of insolent sensuality. If she had walked into that room stark naked the impact of her sex, the deliberate emphasis of physical allure could not have been so arrogantly and shamelessly signified as it was now as she wove her way through the crowd with sleepy undulance, bent over the smaller figure of her hostess, kissed her and in a yolky voice in which affection and arrogance were curiously commingled, said: "Darling, how are you?"

The guests were now moving freely around, greeting one another and talking together. Groups were already forming here and there. Stephen

Hook had come in with his sister Mary, and greeted his hostess by holding out to her a frail limp hand. At the same time he turned half away from her with an air of exaggerated boredom and indifference, an almost weary disdain, as he murmured: "Oh, hello, Esther. . . . Look—" he half turned toward her again, almost as if this were an after thought— "I brought this to you." He handed her a book and turned away again. "I thought it was rather interesting," he said in a bored tone. "You might like to look at it."

What he had given her was a magnificent book of Peter Brueghel's drawings—a book that she knew well of, whose costliness had frightened even her. She looked quickly at the flyleaf and saw that in his fine hand, he had written there primly: "For Esther—from Stephen Hook." And suddenly she remembered that she had mentioned to him casually, a week or two before, her interest in this book, and she understood now that this act, which in a characteristic way he was trying to conceal under a mask of labored boredom and indifference, had come swift and shining as a beam of light out of the depths of the man's fine and generous spirit. Her little face turned crimson, something choked her in the throat, and for a moment, she could not say why, her eyes were hot with tears.

"Oh, Steve!" she gasped—"This is simply the most beautiful—the most wonderful—"

He seemed fairly to shrink away from her in horror, fairly to shrink away into the fat envelope of his unhealthy body. His white, flabby face took on a gesture of disdainful boredom and aloof indifference that was so exaggerated it would have seemed comical if it had not been for the look of naked pleading terror in his hazel eyes—a look swift, frightened, lacerated–the look of a proud, noble, strangely twisted and tormented man—the look really almost of a frightened child, which, even while it shrank away from the life, the companionship, the security, it so desperately needed and wanted, was also pleading pitifully for help—which almost said: "For God's sake—help me if you can! I am afraid!"

She saw that look of naked pleading terror in his eyes as he turned pompously away from her with a look of such exaggerated boredom on his pursed face as would have made Pooh Bah look like an exuberant sophomore by the comparison. And the look went through her like a knife and in a moment's flash of stabbing pity she felt also the wonder, the strangeness and the miracle of living. "Oh, you poor tormented creature," she was thinking—"What is wrong with you? What are you afraid of? What's eating on you anyway? What a strange man he is," she thought more tranquilly. "And How fine and good and high."

At this moment, as if reading her own thoughts, her daughter, Alma, came to the rescue. Cool, poised, lovely, perfectly chiseled and rather cold, the girl came across the room, moved up to Hook, and said coolly:

"Oh, Hello, Steve. Can I get you a drink?"

The question was a godsend. He was extremely fond of the girl—He liked her polished style, her faultless elegance, her cool, hard, friendly, yet perfectly impenetrable manner. It gave him just the foil, the kind of protection that he so desperately needed. He answered her at once hiding his enormous relief in turning away from her disdainfully with an air of elaborately mannered boredom. "You," he said. "What you have to say quite fascinates me—" he murmured in a bored tone and moved over to the mantle, where he leaned as spectator and turned his face three-quarters away from the room as if the sight of so many appallingly dull and stupid people was something more than he could endure.

All this was not only completely characteristic of Hook, it was really almost the man's whole history. Even the elaborately mannered indirection of his answer when the girl had asked him if he wanted a drink was completely characteristic of Stephen Hook, and provided a key to his literary style. "What you have to say really fascinates me"—contained the kernel of Hook's literary style and the books he wrote. He was the author of a great many stories which he sold mostly to magazines and from which he derived the income with which he supported himself and his family. And in addition he was the author of two or three very fine distinguished books on which his considerable reputation had been established but which had had almost no sale. And yet he was famous not for his stories but for these books: As he himself had ironically pointed out, almost everyone, apparently, had read his books and no one had bought them. In these books, also the curious complex of Hook's strange, frightened, desperately shy personality were fully revealed. And here also, in these books he tried to mask this shyness and timidity by an air of boredom and disdain, by the intricate artifice and circumlocution of an elaborately mannered style. In other words, what Hook was always saying in his books when someone asked him if he'd have a drink was half turning away and looking passionately bored—"What you have to say quite fascinates me."

Mrs. Jack, after staring rather helplessly at this paunchy image of disdain turned to his sister, a red-haired spinsteress with twinkling eyes and an infectious laugh who shared her brother's charm, but lacked his tormented spirit, and whispered: "What's wrong with Steve tonight, anyway? He looks as if he's been seeing ghosts."

"No—just another monster," Mary Hook replied, and laughed. "He had a pimple on his nose last week and he stared at it so much in the mirror that he became convinced it was a tumor. Mother was almost crazy. He locked himself in his room and refused to come out or talk to anyone for days and days. Four days ago he sent her a note leaving minute instructions for his funeral and burial: he has a horror of being cremated. Three days ago he came out in his pajamas and said good-bye to all of us. He said life was over—all was ended. Tonight he thought better of it and decided to dress and come to your party."

Then laughing, with the twinkle of wise infectious humor in her blue eyes, Mary Hook glanced shrewdly in the direction of her brother, whose paunchy figure was now leaning on the mantle, turned indifferently away, like some plump Mandarin, with a pursy and disdainful face, and answered Mrs. Jack's perturbed glance with a humorous shrug of the shoulders. Mrs. Jack's rosy face colored richly, and suddenly she laughed an involuntary and astounded laugh, crying:

"God! Isn't it the most!—" while she continued to stare helplessly at Mary Hook. Mary Hook, laughing good naturedly with a humorous shrug and a shake of her head, moved away into the crowd. And Mrs. Jack, still with an earnest and rather troubled little face, turned to talk to old Jake Abramson, who had been holding her hand and gently stroking it during this whole puzzled interlude.

The mark of the fleshpots was plain upon Jake Abramson. He was an old, subtle, sensual, weary Jew and he had the face of a vulture. Curiously enough, for all its vulturesque quality, his face was a strangely attractive one. It had so much weariness and patience, and a kind of wise cynicism, and a weary humor. There was something kind and understanding about him. Even his evening clothes sat on him with a kind of casual weariness as if he were a kind of immensely old and tired ambassador of life who had lived so long, who had seen so much, who had been so many places, and who had worn evening clothes so many times that the garments themselves were as habitual as his breath and hung on him with a kind of weary and accustomed grace as if he had been born in them.

He had taken off his heavy coat and his silk hat and given them to the maid, and then had come wearily into the room and greeted Mrs. Jack.

He was evidently very fond of her. While she had been talking to Mary Hook he remained silent and he brooded above her like a benevolent vulture. He smiled beneath his great nose and kept his eyes intently on her face; then he took her small strong hand in his weary old clasp and, as he continued to gaze at her intently, and to talk, he stroked her smooth arm. It was a gesture frankly old and sensual, jaded, and yet strangely fatherly and gentle. It was the gesture of a man who had known and possessed many pretty women and who still knew how to admire and appreciate them, but whose strong lust had passed over into a kind of paternal benevolence.

And in the same way he now spoke to her, continuing to talk to her all the time with a weary, coarse, old humor which also had in it a quality that was fatherly and kind.

"Momma," he said as he kept stroking her arm with his old hand and looking intently at her with his weary eyes—

"You're looking nice! You're looking pretty!" He kept smiling vulturesquely at her and stroking her arm—"Just like a rose she is!" the old man said, and never took his old, beady stare from her.

"Oh! Jake!" she cried excitedly and in a surprised tone, as if she had not known before that he was there. "How nice of you to come! I never knew you were back! I thought you were still in Europe!—"

"Momma," the old man said, still smiling fixedly at her and stroking her smooth arm,—"I've been and went. I've gone and come. I was away but now I've come back already yet," he declared humorously.

"You're looking awfully well, Jake," she declared earnestly. "The trip did you lots of good. You've lost a lot of flesh. You took the cure at Carlsbad, didn't you?"

"Momma," the old man solemnly declared, "I didn't take the cure. I took the diet—" Deliberately he mispronounced the word to "die-ett." And instantly Mrs. Jack's rosy face was suffused with crimson; her shoulders began to shake hysterically. At the same moment she turned to Roberta Heilprinn, seized her helplessly by the arm, and clung to her, and shrieked faintly: "Did you hear him? He's been on a diet! God! I bet it almost killed him! The way he loves to eat!"

Miss Heilprinn chuckled fruitily and her oil-smooth features widened in a grin of such proportions that her eyes contracted to closed slits.

"Momma," said old Jake solemnly as he continued gently to stroke the bare smooth arm of Mrs. Jack, "I've been die-et-ting—"

The way he said this with all the connotations it evoked drew from her shaking figure another hysterical little shriek.

"I've been die-etting ever since I went away," said Jake. "I was sick when I went away—and I came back on an English boat," the old man said with a kind of melancholy and significant leer that drew a scream of laughter from the two women.

"Oh, Jake!" cried Mrs. Jack hilariously. "How you must have suffered! I know what you used to think of English food!"

"Momma," the old man said with a resigned sadness—

"I think the same as I always did—only ten times more!"

She faintly shrieked again, then gasped out, "Brussels sprouts?"

"They still got 'em," said old Jake solemnly. "They still got the same ones they had ten years ago. I saw Brussels sprouts this last trip that ought to be sent to the British Museum—And they still got that good fish—" he went on with a suggestive leer and Mrs. Jack shrieked faintly again and Roberta Heilprinn, her bland features grinning like a Buddha, gurgled fruitily: "The Dead Sea fruit?"

"No," said old Jake sadly, "not the Dead Sea fruit—that ain't dead enough. They got boiled flannel now," said Jake, "and that *good* sauce, Momma, they used to make?"—He leered at Mrs. Jack with an air of such insinuation that she was again set off in a fit of shuddering hysteria:

"You mean that awful—tasteless—pasty—*goo*—about the color of a dead lemon?"

"You got it," the old man nodded his wise and tired old head in weary agreement. "You got it—That's it—They still make it. . . . So I've been die-etting all the way back!" For the first time his tired old voice showed a trace of energetic animation. "Carlsbad wasn't in it compared to the die-etting I had to do on the English boat!" He paused, then with a glint of old cynic humor in his weary eyes, he said: "It was fit for nothing but a bunch of goys!"

This reference to unchosen tribes, with the complete evocation of the humorous contempt, now really snapped a connection between these three people that nothing else had done. And suddenly one saw these three able and resourceful people in a new way. The old man smiling thinly, vulturesquely, with a cynical intelligence, the two women shaken suddenly and utterly by a helpless paroxysm of understanding mirth. And now one saw they really were *together*, able, ancient, and immensely knowing, and outside the world, regardant, tribal, communitied in derision and contempt for the unhallowed, unsuspecting tribes of lesser men who were not party to their knowing, who were not folded to their seal. It passed—the instant showing of their ancient sign. The women smiled more quietly, they were citizens once again.

"But Jake! You poor fellow!" Mrs. Jack said sympathetically. "You must have hated it! But oh Jake!" she cried suddenly and enthusiastically as she remembered—"Isn't Carlsbad just *too* beautiful? . . . Did you know that Bert and I were there one time?" she cried rapidly and eagerly with the animation that was characteristic of her when she was remembering something or telling someone a story—and as she uttered these words she slipped her hand affectionately through the arm of her blandly smiling friend, then went on vigorously, with a jolly laugh and a merry face: "Didn't I ever tell you about that time?—Really, it was the most wonderful experience!—But God!" she laughed suddenly and almost explosively and her face flushed almost crimson—"Will you ever forget the first three or four days, Bert?" she appealed rosily to her smiling friend—"Do you remember how hungry we got? How we thought we couldn't possibly hold out?—Wasn't it dreadful?" she said frankly and then went on with a serious rather puzzled air as she tried to explain it:—"But then—I don't know—it's funny—but somehow you get used to it, don't you, Bert? The first few days are pretty awful, but after that you didn't seem to mind. I don't know." Again her low brow furrowed with a puzzled air, and she spoke with a shade of difficulty—"I guess you get too weak, or something—I know Bert and I stayed in bed three weeks—and really it wasn't bad after the first few days." She laughed suddenly, richly. "We used to try to torture each other by making up enormous menus of the most delicious food we could think of— We had it all planned out to go to a swell restaurant the moment our cure was over and order the biggest meal we could think of!—Well!" she laughed. "Would you believe it—the day the cure was finished and the doctor told us it would be all right for us to get up and eat—I know we both lay there for hours thinking of all the things we were going to have. It was simply wonderful!" she said, flushing with laughter and making a fine little movement with her finger and her thumb to indicate great delicacy, her voice squeaking like a child's and her eyes wrinkling up to dancing points—"In all your life you never heard of such delicious food as Bert and I were going to devour. We resolved to do everything in the greatest style!—Well, all I can tell you is," she went on humorously, "the *very best* of everything was just about half good enough for us—that's the way we felt! . . . Well, at last we got up and dressed. And God!" she cried with her jolly crimson face and twinkling eyes, "you'd have thought we'd been invited to meet the King and Queen at Buckingham Palace. We were so weak we could hardly stand up but we wore the prettiest clothes we had and we had chartered a Rolls Royce for the occasion and a chauffeur in livery.—In all your *days*," she cried with her twinkling little face,—"you've never seen such swank. We got into the car and were driven away like a couple of queens. We told the man to drive us to the swellest, most expensive restaurant he knew. He drove us to a beautiful place outside of town. It looked like a chateau!"—she beamed rosily around her—"and when they saw us coming they must have thought that we were royalty from the way they acted. The flunkies were lined up, bowing and scraping for half a block—Oh, it was thrilling! Everything we'd gone through and endured in taking the cure seemed worth it—Well!" she looked around her and the breath left her body audibly in a sigh of complete frustration—"would you believe it? When we got in there and tried to eat we could hardly swallow a bite! We had looked forward to it so long—we had planned it all so carefully—and well! all I can say is, it was a bitter disappointment—" she said humorously. "Would you believe it—all we could eat was a soft boiled egg—and we couldn't even finish that! It filled us up right to here—" she put a small hand level with her chin—"It was so tragic that we almost wept!—I don't know," she went on turning her eyes away in a glance of serious and rather puzzled reflection—"but isn't it a strange thing? I guess it must be that your stomach shrinks up and gets little while you're on the diet. You lie there day after day and think of the enormous meal you are going to devour just as soon as you get up—and then when you try it you're not even able to finish a soft boiled egg—but is that life, or isn't it? I ask you—" She shrugged her shoulders, and lifted her hands questioningly, with such a comical look on her face that everybody laughed.

Even the weary jaded old man, Jake Abramson, who had been regarding her fixedly with a vulpine smile during the whole course of her animated monologue, now smiled a little more warmly as he turned away to speak to other friends. He had really paid no attention to what she was saying, but Mrs. Jack's way of telling a story was so pleasant, her rosy face and twinkling eyes were so full of life and eagerness, she spoke with such excitement, with such gusto, with such ready humor, that everything she said was interesting. And, in a tired and jaded world, people could just look at her animated little face and figure, her eager and excited voice for hours at a time, without growing tired.

The two women—Miss Heilprinn and Mrs. Jack who were now left standing together in the centre of the big room, offered a remarkable and instructive comparison in the capacities of their sex. Miss Heilprinn was in appearance as in face a very distinguished woman. The thing that one noticed about her immediately was her bland and smiling pallor. She suggested oil—smooth oil, oil of tremendous driving power and generating force. And although no one would ever have called her a beautiful woman, no discerning eye could fail to see instantly that she was a very handsome one.

She was a woman perhaps of middling height, perhaps a little under it: at any rate she was a little taller than Mrs. Jack. Her smooth and smiling face, her plump figure, hips and ankles, were inclined to heaviness and corpulence. Her face was almost impossibly bland. It was a blandness without unction, a blandness without hypocrisy. On first sight the smooth, plump, smiling features had a look of almost Buddhistic quality and the fruity tones, the infectious chuckle, the eyes that narrowed into jolly slits whenever the lady laughed or even smiled, contributed to a first impression of imperturbable and unquenchable good nature.

But let the ingenuous spirit be not too easily deceived: a closer examination of this lady would have revealed a pair of twinkling eyes that missed nothing and that were as hard as agate. Her distinguished looking grey hair was combed back in a pompadour and she was splendidly gowned with a suavity that was perfectly adapted to the bland and imperturbable assurance of her worldliness. She would, and could, if occasion or necessity had demanded it, have taken the gold fillings out of her best friend's teeth and never for a moment lost the oily blandness of her smiling face, the infectious chuckle of her throaty voice, as she did so.

To say merely that she was "as hard as nails" would be to put an unfair strain upon the durability of common iron. In the theatrical profession, and along Broadway, where she had reigned for years as the governing brain and directive force behind a celebrated art theatre she was known familiarly as "the Duchess." And the business acuity which had wrung this homage from the hard lips of that milling street was fully deserving of all the tributes, all the oaths, that had been heaped upon it.

As the two ladies, both of whom were warm old friends, stood looking at each other affectionately in the act of greeting, a very instructive performance in worldly shrewdness was being quietly unfolded between them for the enlightenment or amusement of one privileged to see. Each woman was perfectly cast in her own role. Each had found the perfect adaptive means by which she could utilize her full talents with the least waste and friction and with the greatest smooth persuasiveness.

Miss Heilprinn's role in life had been essentially a practical and not a romantic one. It had been her function to promote, to direct, to govern, and in the tenuous and uncertain speculations of the theatre to take care not to be fleeced by the wolves of Broadway. The brilliance of her success, the power of her will, and the superior quality of her mettle, was written plain upon her. It took no very experienced observer to see instantly that in the unequal contest between the Duchess and the wolves of Broadway it had been the wolves who had been fleeced. Lucky, indeed, was the wolf who could escape an encounter with the Duchess with a portion of his native hide intact.

And in that savage unremitting warfare, when bitter passions had been aroused, when undying hatreds had been awakened, when eyes had been jaundiced and when lips had been so bitterly twisted that they had never regained their rosy pristine innocence and now lay written on haggard faces like a yellowed scar, had the face of the Duchess grown hard and bitter? Had her mouth contracted to a grim and bitter line? Had her jaw out-jutted like a granite crag? Were the marks of the wars visible anywhere upon her? By no means.

The more murderous the fight, the blander her face. The more treacherous and guileful the strategy in its snaky intrigues, the more cheerful and good-natured the fruity lilt of her good-humored chuckle. She had actually thriven on it. She seemed to blossom like a flower beneath the dead and barren glare of Broadway lights. And she never seemed to be so happily and unconsciously herself as when playing about ingenuously in a nest of rattlesnakes.

The other lady presented a tactical problem of quite another sort. Mrs. Jack's career had been romantic rather than executive. Yet, in a strange, hard way, each woman was completely worldly, each woman was wholly practical, each woman was fundamentally concerned with her own interests, her own success.

In a curious way, Mrs. Jack's strategy was more guileful and complex than that of her smooth companion. Mrs. Jack's strategy was that of the child: she had early learned the advantages of possessing the rosy, jolly little face of flowerlike loveliness. She had early learned the advantages of a manner of slightly bewildered surprise, naive innocence, of smiling doubtfully and inquiringly yet good-naturedly at her laughing friends, as if to say: "Now, I know you're laughing at me, aren't you? I don't know what it is. I don't know what I've done or said now. Of course, I know I'm not clever the way you are—all of you are so frightfully smart—but anyway I have a good time, and I like you all—Hah?"

She had even learned in recent years that deafness itself might have its compensations in furthering this illusion of her happy, somewhat bewildered innocence. She had early learned as well the value of tears in a woman's life and what an effective weapon tears may be. She had learned the supreme value of romantic emotion as a triumphant answer-all to reasoned thought or to the objections of fair play and a sense of justice. She knew better than most women that if any act of hers was ever called in question, if any act of hers which she was trying to conceal was ever discovered, and she was confronted with it, there was no answer so effective, so annihilating as tempestuous tears—romantic and irrational declaration:

"All right. All right—I'm through!—She's finished!—She's no good anymore!—Throw her out—Let her go!—She's tried to do the best she could but you've thrown her out now—You've told her she wasn't any good anymore—All right, then—" Here she would smile a pathetic twisted smile as she squeaked these touching little words, move aimlessly toward the door in a pathetic gesture of departure, smile a pathetic twisted little smile again and wave her hand childishly in farewell as she squeaked pathetically—"All over—Finished—Done for—She's no good —Goodbye, Goodbye—" After which, of course, there was nothing but embarrassed, half amused, half angry, half disgusted surrender.

She had her faults, no doubt—she was "romantic." Most people, even those who knew her well considered her affectionately to be a "most romantic person—" "a very romantic woman." For this reason she had triumphantly escaped censure for many acts that would have brought down upon many another less privileged, less gifted and less favored person a heavy punishment. She was essentially not less shrewd, not less accomplished, not less subtle and not less hardly determined to have her own way, to secure her own ends in the hard world than was the blandly, suavely smiling Roberta Heilprinn—But oh! As her friends said she was "so beautiful," she was "such a child," she was so "good"—and everybody loved her!

Not everyone, however, was so easily deceived by Mrs. Jack's deceptive innocence. The bland lady who now confronted her in greeting was one of these: hence the instructive quality of the moment. Miss Roberta Heilprinn's hard and merry eye, indeed, missed no artifice of that rosy, innocently surprised, small person. And hence perhaps the twinkle in her eye as she greeted her old friend was a little harder, brighter and more lively than it usually was, the bland, Buddhistic smile, a little smoother in its oily suavity, and the fruity tones, the engaging yolky chuckle, a trifle more infectious, and on all of these accounts, perhaps more full of genuine affection as she bent and kissed the rosy, glowing little cheek.

And she, the blooming object of this affectionate caress, although she never changed the expression of surprised delighted innocence on her rosy face, knew full well all that was going on in the other woman's mind. For a moment, so quickly imperceptibly, that no one save Olympian Mercury could have followed that swift glance, the eyes of the two women, stripped bare of all concealing artifice, met each other nakedly. And in that moment there was matter for Olympian laughter. But no one of these gifted worldlings saw it.

✳   ✳   ✳   ✳   ✳

"I *mean!*—You *know!*—" At the words, eager, rapid, uttered in a rather hoarse, yet strangely seductive tone of voice, Mrs. Jack smiled and turned: "There's Amy!"

Then, as she saw the angelic head, with its unbelievable harvest of golden curls, the snub nose and the little freckles, and the lovely face so radiant with an almost boyish quality of eagerness, of animation, of enthusiasm, she thought; "Isn't she beautiful! And—and—there is something so sweet, so lovely, so—so good about her!"

She did not know why or how this was true. Indeed, as she well knew, from any worldly point of view it would have been hard to prove. If Amy Van Leer was not "a notorious woman" the reason was that she had surpassed the ultimate limit of notoriety, even for New York, years before. She had a reputation that stank even in the more decadent groups of the great capitols on the Continent.

By the time she was nineteen years old she had been married and divorced and had a child. And even at that time her conduct had been so scandalous that her first husband, a member of one of the most powerful of the American plutocracies, had had no difficulty in getting a divorce and in demonstrating her unfitness for the custody of her own child. There had been a sensational case which fairly reeked. Since that time, seven years before, it would have been impossible to define or chronicle her career in any terms measurable to time or to chronology. Although the girl was now only twenty-six years old, her life seemed to go back through aeons of iniquity, through centuries of vice and dissipation, through a Sargassic seadepth of depravity.

Thus, one might remember one of the innumerable scandals connected to her name and that it had happened only three short years before, and then check oneself suddenly with a feeling of stunned disbelief, a feeling that time had suddenly turned phantom, that one had dreamed it all, that it had happened in a kind of outrageous night-mare. "Oh no! It can't be!—That happened only three short years ago and since then she's—why she's—"

And one would turn to stare in stupefaction at that angelic head, that snub nose, that boyish eager face—as one who, in this bewildering guise, might know that he was looking at the dread Medusa, or that, couched here in this pleasant counterfeit of youthful eagerness and naiveté, he was really looking at some ageless creature, some enchantress of Circean cunning whose life was older than the ages and whose heart was old as Hell.

What was the truth of it or what the true image of that sun-headed, golden counterfeit of youth and joy no one could say. It baffled time, it turned reality to phantasmal shapes. One could, and had, as here and now, beheld this golden head, this tilted nose, this freckled, laughing, eager face, here at its very noon of happy innocence. And before ten days had made their round, one had come on it again in the corruptest gatherings of Paris, drugged fathoms deep in opium, foul bodied and filth spattered, cloying to the embraces of a gutter rat, so deeply rooted in the cesspool that it seemed its very life was nothing but a tainted plant, whose roots had grown out of sewage and who had never known any life but that.

And then one would remember the laughing boyish, eager, and hoarse-throated girl with the snub nose, the freckles and the golden head that one had seen four-thousand miles away just seven days before. And time would turn into a dusty ash, the whole substantial structure of the world would reel in witches' dance, and melt away before one's eyes like fumes of smoke.

And she?—the cause, or agent of this evil miracle—Medusa, Circe or unhappy child—whatever was the truth—to tell her story!—Oh, it was impossible! That story could be told no more than one could chronicle the wind, put halters on a hurricane, saddle Mercury, or harness with a breded skein of words the mapless raging of tempestuous seas.

Chronology?—Well, for birth, she had the golden spoon; she was a child of Pittsburgh steel, the heiress of enfabled wealth, of parentage half—perhaps the fatal half—of Irish blood; she had been born O'Neill.

And youth? It was the youth and childhood of a dollar princess, kept, costly, cabined, pruned, confined; a daughter of "Society":—and of a woman, twice divorced and three times married. Her girlhood had been spent in travel and rich schools, in Europe, Newport, New York and Palm Beach. By eighteen she was "out"—a famous beauty; by nineteen she was married. And by twenty her name was tainted and divorced.

And, since then? There were not words to tell the story, and although there were warm apologists who tried to find the reason for it, or to make for it excuse, there was not enough logic in the Universe to find a reason or to shape a plan, to phrase an argument for that maelstrom of a life.

"The facts speak for themselves"? The very facts were unspeakable; could one have spoken them there would not be space enough for a full record, and no one credulous enough for their belief; one could not quote the simple and accepted truths, which were that she had been three times married and that one marriage had been annulled and had lasted only twenty hours; and that a third had ended tragically when her husband, a young French writer of great talent, but a hopeless addict of cocaine, had shot himself.

And before and after that, and in between, and in and out, and during it and later on, and now and then, and here and there, and at home and abroad, and on the seven seas, and across the length and breadth of the five continents, and yesterday and tomorrow and forever—could it be said of her that she had been "promiscuous"? No, that could not be said of her. For she had been as free as air, and one does not qualify the general atmosphere of the sidereal universe with such a paltry adjective as "promiscuous."

She had just slept with everybody, with white, black, yellow, pink or green or purple—but she had never been promiscuous.

It was, in romantic letters, a period that celebrated the lady who was lost, the lovely creature in the green hat who was "never let off anything." The story of this poor lady was a familiar one: she was the ill-starred heroine of fate, a kind of martyr to calamitous mischance, whose ruin had been brought about through tragic circumstance which she could not control, and for which she was not responsible.

Amy had her own apologists who tried to cast her in this martyred role. The stories told about her ruin—her "start upon the downward path" were numerous: there was even one touching *conte* which dated the beginning of the end from the moment when, an innocent, happy and fun-loving girl of nineteen years, she had, in a moment of desperation, in an effort to enliven the gloom, inject a flash of youth, of daring, or of happy spontaneity into the dismal scene, *lighted a cigarette* at a dinner party in Newport, attended by a large number of eminent Society Dowagers; the girl's downfall, according to this moving tale, had been brought about by this thoughtless and harmless little act. From this moment on—so the story went—the verdict of the dowagers was "thumbs down" on the unhappy Amy: the evil tongues began to wag, scandal began to grow, her reputation was torn to shreds, then, in desperation, the unhappy child did go astray; she took to drink, from drink to lovers, from lovers to opium, from opium to—everything.

And all because a happy laughter-loving girl had smoked a cigarette! All because an innocent child had flaunted prejudice, defied convention! All because the evil tongues had wagged, because the old and evil minds had whispered! All of this of course, was just romantic foolishness. She was the ill-starred child of fate indeed, but the fate was in her, not outside of her. She was the victim of a tragic doom, but she herself had fashioned it: with her the fault, as with dear Brutus, lay not in her stars but in herself—for having been endowed with so many rare and precious things that most men lack—wealth, beauty, charm, intelligence and vital energy—she lacked the will to do, the toughness to resist, the power to shape her life to mastery: so, having almost all, she was the slave to her own wealth—an underling.

It is true, she was the child of her own time, the unhappy incarnation of a sickness of her time. She let her own time kill her. Her life expressed itself in terms of speed, sensational change and violent movement, in a feverish tempo that never drew from its own energies exhaustion or surcease, and that mounted constantly to insane excess. The only end of this could be destruction. Her life then was already sealed with doom. The mark of her destruction was already apparent upon her.

People had once said, "What on earth is Amy going to do next?" But now they said, "What on earth is there left for her to do?" And really if life is to be expressed solely in terms of velocity and sensation, it seemed that there was very little left for her to do. She had been everywhere, she had "seen everything" in the way in which such a person sees things, as one might see them from the windows of an express train traveling eighty miles an hour.

And having so quickly exhausted the conventional kaleidoscope of things to be seen in the usual itineraries of travel she had long since turned to an investigation of things much more bizarre and sinister and hidden, which her great wealth, her powerful connections, and her own driving energies opened to her, but which were closed to other people.

She had possessed for years an intimate and extensive acquaintance among the most sophisticated and decadent groups in society, in the great cities of the world. And this intimacy matured swiftly into familiarity with even more sinister border lines of life. She had an acquaintanceship among the underworld of New York, London, Paris and Berlin which the police might have envied and which few criminals achieve. It was rumored that she had taken part in a holdup "just for the fun of the thing." And the police and some of her friends knew that she had been present at a drinking party at which one of the chieftains of the underworld had been killed.

But even with the police her wealth and power had secured for her dangerous privileges. Although she was nearsighted—in fact her eye sight was myopic, seriously affected—she drove a yellow racing car through city traffic at murderous speed. This great yellow car was well known in the seething highways of Manhattan and always brought the courtesy of a police salute. In some way, known only to persons of wealth, privilege, or political influence she possessed a police card and was privileged to a reckless license in violation of the laws in the operation of her car. Although, a year or two before, she had demolished this car, and killed a young dramatist who had been driving with her, this privilege had never been revoked.

And it was the same everywhere she went. It seemed that her wealth and power and feverish energy could get her anything she wanted in any country in the world. And the answer to it all? Well, speed, change, violence and sensation was the only answer—and then more speed, more change, more violence, and more sensation—until the end. And the end? The end was already in sight; it was written in her eyes—in her tormented splintered, and exploded vision. She had sowed the wind and now there was nothing left for her to reap except the whirlwind.

People now said: "What on earth is there left for her to do?" Nothing. There was nothing. She had tried everything in life—except living. And she could never try that now because she had so long ago, so irrecoverably lost the way. And having tried everything in life save living, and having lost the way to live, there was nothing left for her to do except to die.

And yet that golden, that angelic head; the snubbed nose and the freckled face—"I *mean!*—You *know!*"—the quick excited laugh, the hoarse and thrilling tones, the eager animation of a boy—were all so beautiful, so appealing, and somehow, one felt in this hard mystery, so good,—"If only—" people would think regretfully as Mrs. Jack now thought as she looked at that sunny head—"Oh, if only things had turned out differently for her!—" and then would seek back desperately through the labyrinthine scheme to find the clue to her disorder—saying, "Here—or here—or here—it happened here, you see—if only!—If only men were so much clay, as they are blood, bone, marrow, passion, feeling!—if they only were!"

"I *mean*!—You *know*!—" at these familiar words, so indicative of her inchoate thought, her splintered energies, her undefined enthusiasm, Amy jerked the cigarette away from her lips with a quick and feverish movement, laughed hoarsely and eagerly, and turned to her companions as if fairly burning with an excited desire to communicate something to them that filled her with a conviction of exuberant elation—"I *mean*!" she cried hoarsely again,—"When you compare it with the stuff they're doing nowadays!—I *mean*! There's simply no comparison!"—and laughing jubilantly as if the meaning of these splintered phrases was perfectly clear to everyone, she drew furiously upon her cigarette again and jerked it from her lips.

During the course of this exuberant and feverish monologue, the group of young people, of which Amy was the golden centre and which included besides Alma and Ernest Jack, Roy Farley and his two young male companions, the young Japanese sculptor and the rich young Jew who had accompanied Amy to the party, had moved over toward the portrait of Mrs. Jack above the mantle, and were looking up at it.

The famous portrait, which was now the subject of Amy's jubilant admiration, was deserving of its reputation and of the enthusiastic praise that was now being heaped upon it. It was one of the best examples of Henry Mallows' early work and it had also been created with the passion, the tenderness, the simplicity of a man in love.

"I *mean*!" cried Amy jubilantly again, pausing below the portrait, and gesturing at it with rapid movement of her impatient cigarette, "When you look at it and *think* how long ago that was!—and how beautiful she was then!—and how beautiful she is now!" cried Amy exultantly, laughed hoarsely, then cast her lovely grey green eyes so full of splintered torment around her in a glance of almost feverish exasperation—"I *mean*!" she cried again and drew impatiently on her cigarette—"There's *simply* no comparison!"—without saying what it was there was simply no comparison to or for or with, and certainly not saying what she wanted to say—"Oh, I mean!" she cried with a tone and gesture of desperate impatience, jerked her golden head and tossed her cigarette angrily and impatiently away into the blazing fire—"The whole thing's obvious," she muttered leaving everyone more bewildered than ever. Then, turning toward Hook with a sudden and impulsive movement, she demanded; "How long has it been, Steve? It's been twenty years ago, hasn't it?"

"Oh, quite all of that," Hook answered in a cold bored tone. In his agitation and embarrassment he turned still farther away from her with an air of fatigued indifference, until he almost had his fat back turned upon the whole group. "It's been nearer thirty, I should think," he tossed back indifferently over his fat shoulder and then with an air of bored casualness, he gave them the exact date which he knew precisely as he knew all such dates, "I should think it was done in nineteen one or two,—wasn't it, Esther?"—he drawled in a bored tone, turning to Mrs. Jack, who, rosily beaming, and with a jolly and rather bewildered look upon her face, had now approached the group, "Around nineteen one, wasn't it?"—he said more loudly in answer to her sharply lifted little hand cupped at the ear and her eager and inquiring "Hah?"

"Hah? What?" cried Mrs. Jack in an eager rather bewildered tone, then went on immediately, "Oh, the picture! No, Steve—it was done in nineteen—" She checked herself so swiftly that it was not apparent to anyone but Hook that she was not telling the truth—"In nineteen-four." She saw just the momentary trace of a smile upon the pale bored features as he turned away and gave him a quick warning little look, but he just murmured in a casual and disinterested tone: "Oh . . . I had forgotten it was as late as that."

As a matter of fact, he knew the exact date, even to the month and day it had been finished—which had been October, 1902. And still musing on the vagaries of the sex, he thought: "Why will they be so stupid! She must know that to anyone who knows the least thing about Mallows' life, the date is as familiar as the Fourth of July—"

"Of course," Mrs. Jack was saying rapidly, "I was just a child when it was made, I couldn't have been more than eighteen at the time—if I was that—"

"Which would make you not more than forty-three at the present time," thought Hook cynically—"if you are that! Well, my dear, you were twenty when he painted you—and you had been married for two years and had a child and you had been Henry Mallows' mistress for a year. . . .

Why do they do it!"—he thought impatiently, and turned away with a feeling of sharp annoyance—"Does she take me for a fool!"

He turned toward her almost impatiently and looked at her and saw her quick glance, an expression startled, almost pleading in her eye. He followed it, and saw the hot eye, the fierce packed features of ungainly youth: he caught it in a flash: "Ah! It's this boy! She's told him then that—" and suddenly remembering the startled pleading of that look—so much of child, of folly, even in their guile—was touched with pity: "Oh! I see!"

Aloud, however, he merely turned away and murmured indifferently, with no expression in his heavy eyes: "Oh, yes, you couldn't have been very old."

"And God!" cried Mrs. Jack. "But I was beautiful!" She spoke these words with such gleeful conviction, with such a jolly and good-humored face, with such innocent delight that they lost any trace of objectionable vanity they might have had, and people smiled at her affectionately, as one might smile at a child, and Amy Van Leer, with a quick hasty little laugh, said impulsively,

"Oh, Esther! Honestly you're the most—But I *mean*!" She cried impatiently, with a quick toss of her golden head, as if answering some invisible antagonist—"She *is*!"

"In all your days," cried Mrs. Jack, her tender little face suffusing with laughter and good-humor like a flower, "You never saw the like of me! I was just like peaches and cream," she said; then with her rich plain humor, simply "I'd have knocked your eye out!"

"But *darling*! You do now!" cried Amy—"What I mean to say is, darling you're the *most*—isn't she, Steve?" She laughed hoarsely, uncertainly, turning to Hook with a kind of feverish eagerness in her tone.

And he, seeing the ruin, the loss, the desperation in her splintered eyes was sick with horror and with pity. He looked at her disdainfully, with weary lidded eyes, and a haughtily pursy face, like a gentleman who has just been accosted in his club by a drunken sot who has clutched him by the sleeve, and after looking at her for a moment in this way, with this disdainful hauteur, he said, "What?" quite freezingly, and then turned pompously away, saying in a bored and weary tone: "Oh . . ."

He saw the rosy smiling face of Mrs. Jack beside him, and above, the portrait of the lovely girl that she had been. And the anguish and the majesty of time stabbed through him like a knife.

"My God, here she is!" he thought. "Still featured like a child, still beautiful, still loving someone—another boy!—Almost as lovely now as she was then when Mallows was a boy, and she had just begun to sleep with him in—in—"

1902! Ah! Time! The figures reeled in drunken dance before his eyes. He rubbed his hand before his eyes, and turned wearily away. No figures these—but symbols in a witches' dance, a dance of evil and enchanted time. In 1902!—How many centuries ago was that?—How many lives and deaths and floods, how many million days and nights of love, of hate, of anguish and of fear, of guilt, of hope, of disillusion and defeat here in the geologic aeons of this monstrous catacomb, this riddled isle!—in 1902! Good God! It was the very Prehistoric Age of man!—the Neolithic Era of this swarming Rock! Why, all *that* had happened several million years ago—so much had happened after that, so much had begun and ended, been forgotten, so many, many million lives of truth, of youth, of old age, death, and new beginning, so much blood and sweat and agony had gone below the bridge—why he himself had lived through at least ten million years of it! Had lived and died a million births and lives and deaths and dark oblivions of it, had striven, fought, and hoped and been destroyed through so many centuries of it that even memory had failed—the sense of time had been wiped out—and all of it had seemed to happen in a timeless dream; a kind of Grand Canyon of the human nerves and bones and blood and brain and flesh and words and thought, all timeless now, all congealed, all there solidified in a kind of timeless and unchanging stratum, there impossibly below, mixed into a general geologic layer with all the bonnets, bustles and old songs, the straw hats and the derbies, the clatter of forgotten hooves, the thunder of forgotten wheels upon forgotten cobbles, together with lost words, lost music and lost songs, the skeletons of lost thought and lost ideas— merged together now there in a geologic stratum of the sunken world— while *she*

—She! Why surely she had been a part of it with him—with Mallows —with all these times, these places—what?—

She had turned to listen to another group with Lawrence Hirsch, and he could see her rosy little face serious and attentive now, and saying earnestly:—

"Oh, yes, I knew Jack Reed. He used to come to Mabel Dodge's place; we were great friends—That was when Alfred Stieglitz had started his salon—"

Ah, all these names! Had he not been with these as well? Or, was it but another shape—a seeming!—in this phantasmal and traumatic shadow-show of time! Had he not been beside her at the launching of the ship?—When they were captive among Thracian faces?—Or lighted tapers to the tent when she had come to charm remission from the lord of Macedon?—All these were ghosts—save she! And she—Circean she, this time-devouring child of time—had of this whole huge company of ghosts alone remained immortal and herself, had shed off the chrysalis of all these her former selves, as if each life that she had loved was nothing but an out-worn garment—and now stood here—*here*! Good God! Upon the burnt out candle-ends of time—with her jolly face of noon, as if she had just heard of this brave new world on Saturday—and would see if *all* of it was really true tomorrow!

Mrs. Jack had turned again at the sound of Amy's eager and throat-husky tone and now beaming rosily, she had bent forward to listen to the girl's disjointed monologue, one hand cupped to her ear, and an eager, childlike little smile upon her lips.

"I *mean*! You *know*! But Esther! What I mean to say is!—Darling, you're the most!—It's the most!—I *mean*, when I look at both of you, I simply can't—I mean, there's simply no comparison, that's all!" cried Amy, with hoarse elation, her lovely face and head all sunning over with light, with eagerness, with generous enthusiasm and boyish animation. "Oh, what I mean to say is!" Amy cried, then shook her head with a short strong movement, tossed her cigarette away impatiently and cried with the expiration of a long sigh—"Gosh!"

Poor child! Poor Child!—Hook turned pompously and indifferently away to hide the naked anguish in his eyes—So soon to grow, to go, to be consumed and die like all of us—beyond this timeless breed, unlike them so unschooled, incautious, and so prone to peril and to go too far. Like him she was, he knew, unused to breathe the dangerous vapors of this most uncertain place; unlike these children of the furious street, so soon to feel unhoused, unhomed, unhearted, strangers and alone!

Never to walk as they, with certitude and hope, the stoney canyons of these cruel vertices, to speak with joy the babel of its strident tongues—like him, to deafen to strong steel,—alas! To want the nightingale, and to shrink beneath these monstrous and inhuman pyramids of Asiatic pride! She was, like him, too prone to die the death upon a single death; to live the life upon the single life; to love the love upon the single love—never to save out of anything, life, death, or love—a prudent remnant for the hour of peril or the day of ruin; but to use it all, to give it all, to be consumed, burnt out like last night's moths upon a cluster of hard light!

Poor child! Poor child!—thought Hook—So quick and short and temporal, both you and I, the children of a younger kind! While she!—just for a moment, briefly, seeming-cold, he surveyed the innocence enrosed of Mrs. Jack. And these!—the sensual volutes of strong nostrils curved with scornful mirth: he looked at them—These others of this ancient chemistry—unmothed, reborn, and venturesome, yet wisely mindful of the flame—these others shall endure! Ah time!—Poor Child!

MR. HIRSCH WAS
• • •
WOUNDED SORROWFULLY
• • •

Mr. Lawrence Hirsch was wounded sorrowfully, but he could wait.

He did not seem to follow her. It was just that one always knew he was there. She wove through the complications of that brilliant crowd the lavish undulation of her opulent behind. And Mr. Lawrence Hirsch—he did not follow her. But he was always there:

"Oh absolutely!"—the tone was matter-of-fact and undisturbed: It carried the authority of calm conviction—"We have positive proof of their innocence—evidence that was never allowed to come to light. The *Federalist* is publishing it in the next issue. It proves beyond the shadow of a doubt that Vanzetti could not have been within fifty miles of the crime—"

Mr. Lawrence Hirsch spoke quietly, and did not look at her.

"But how horrible!" cried Mrs. Jack with a flushed, indignant little face. "Isn't it dreadful to know that things like that could happen in a country like this?"

She turned to Lawrence Hirsch with a flaming face and with round righteous anger blazing up in her: "I think the whole thing's the most damnable—the most dastardly—the most disgraceful thing I ever heard!" she cried. "These—these miserable people who could be guilty of such a thing!—These despicable horrible rich people!—It's enough to make you want a Revolution!" cried Mrs. Jack—

"Well, my dear," said Mr. Hirsch with a cool irony—"you may have your wishes gratified—It's not beyond the realm of possibility—and it if comes *that* case may still return to plague them yet. The trials, of course, were perfectly outrageous and the judge should have been instantly dismissed. The men were put to death without a fair trial."

"But these terrible old men!" cried Mrs. Jack. "To know that there are people living who could do a thing like that!" At the bottom of her heart she had always been convinced that she was a "radical"—a revolutionary! As she now said, turning to another member of the group and speaking earnestly, and with a quiet pride: "You know I have always been a Socialist. I vote for Norman Thomas every time he runs—You see," she spoke very simply and with honest self-respect, "I've always been a worker. All my sympathy is on their side."

Suddenly she held her small strong hands out before her, looked at them and their firm swift shape with pride, turned them over with palms upward, turned them back again, and said quietly: "Look at those hands. You can see that they have worked. How strong and deft and sure they are!"

Mr. Hirsch did not seem to be following anybody. Not really. However, there was now a very strong sense—a *feeling* that he knew someone was there. His manner had become a trifle vague, detached, as if he were no longer paying strict attention.

"It is a *cause célèbre*," said Mr. Lawrence Hirsch, and, as if rather liking the sound of the words he repeated them portentously: "A *cause célèbre*." And, distinguished, polished, and contained, he moved away towards the next group and in the general direction of that lavish undulance, those weaving buttocks. And yet he did not seem to follow her.

For Mr. Lawrence Hirsch was wounded sorrowfully. But he could wait.

*   *   *   *   *

"Oh Beddoes! *Beddoes!*"

Miss Mandell had woven her undulant voluptuous charms toward Robert Ahrens, and his exultant words had been uttered in response to some remark of hers.

Mr. Ahrens was a connoisseur of books, a collector of editions, an aesthete of rare letters. Almost his whole time since he had entered the room with Miss Roberta Heilprinn and paid his cheerful duties to his hostess, Mrs. Jack, had been spent in a cherubic investigation of that lady's books. And never before or since Erasmus' time, was there a more cheerful, a more mellow investigator. Just to look at him as he browsed around—yes, that was the word for it!—Mr. Ahrens was a *browser*, if there ever was one—was enough to make one's mouth water for a good book, a cheerful nook or corner by the blazing fire, a pipe—oh, by all means, a pipe! A pipe!—And a bottle of old port—or, a crusty flagon, say, of Nut Brown Ale. This was the effect Mr. Ahrens had on people when they saw him with a book. He made one think of bowered cottages in the English country-side—of the one we heard about last week in Sussex, which could be had for sixteen bob a week—(our informant was completely English)—and which was simply charming.

Mr. Ahrens revived man's wistful yearnings for such a life, his desires to "get away from all of this," to spend the remainder of his days in charming rustication, in peaceful gossip with the cook, the maid, the vicar, and the old men at the pub, and his evenings in his cottage by the fire with a pipe, a bottle of old port, a shaggy dog, and a volume of Charles Lamb. Mr. Robert Ahrens thus became in the maelstrom of the vexed tormented city, a kind of living wish-fulfillment—if not the answer to a maiden's prayer, at least a kind of embodiment of many a jaded mortal's secret hope.

Miraculously, Mr. Robert Ahrens, in the feverish torment of the city's life seemed to have achieved somehow for himself the things that other men think they will have to go to Sussex for—the pipe, the port, a collie, the charming cottage, and the book. Mr. Robert Ahrens seemed to carry these things around with him. Here, in the strident and uncertain life of this great city, among the brilliant glitter, the fine nerves, the compli-cated lives of this sophisticated gathering, Mr. Ahrens alone seemed to carry about with him the furniture of his own content. He *was* his pipe, his port, his collie, and his cheerful hearth, his English cottage and his volume of Charles Lamb. He didn't need to travel anywhere to find them because he had them there inside him all the time.

He was a cheerful, pleasant, and distinguished looking man in his mid-forties, an engaging combination of gentleness and happy exuber-ance, of energy and gay good humor, of fastidiousness and of casual ease. Unlike the remainder of the gathering he was not in evening dress. He wore grey English flannels—"Oxford bags" as they were called by the more knowing kind—a shaggy coat of grey-brown tweed, thick English shoes with heavy soles, woollen socks, a soft white shirt and a red tie.

In appearance, he was fairly tall, something over middling height, in figure rather slight and graceful. He had fine hands and his face was very healthy looking. He was somewhat bald and his high forehead and bald head were pleasantly browned and freckled as if he had spent much time out of doors in the wind and sun. His face also was healthy, ruddy, and pleasant looking. His blue eyes twinkled with gaiety and good humor, and his pleasant face really did have a cherubic look, especially when his elated spirits would rise up in him and he would cry out exuberantly as he now did: "Oh Beddoes! *Beddoes!* By all means, you must read *Beddoes!*"

He had been looking at a book as Miss Mandell approached him, thumbing the pages with loving fingers, pausing from time to time to take a puff at an immensely long, fastidious, and very costly amber cigarette holder. His features suffused with a cherubic glow, he was as completely absorbed in his pleasant investigation, even in the midst of this brilliant and sophisticated throng, as if he had been in his study in an Oxford College. He seemed in fact to have just come in from a long walk across the country-side, or on the moors, and now to be quietly looking forward to an evening with his books—and with a pipe. As Miss Mandell approached him, he looked up, and in response to her question, "Have you ever read anything by a man named Beddoes?"—he but answered in the way, and in the tone, described.

It was, by the way, a habit of Miss Mandell's always to preface a man's name no matter how famous that name might be, by the qualifying phrase "a man named." Why she did this is hard to say, unless she felt instinctively it was another sop to arrogance—a kind of concession to her own snobbishness and pride, a way of saying that if she was bending her stiff neck a little, she was doing it indifferently.

Thus, if she were discussing her literary acquaintanceship, particularly among the rarer coteries of precocity, which was large, she might say: "Did you ever read a book called *'To the Lighthouse'* by a woman named Virginia Woolf. I know her rather well. I just wondered if you had read anything of hers and what you thought of it."

Or, "I wonder if you've read a poem called 'The Waste Land' by a man named T. S. Eliot. I used to see a good deal of him in London. I just wondered if you had never heard of him and what you thought of his work."

Or, "I wonder if you ever read a piece called *'Tender Buttons'* by a woman named Gertrude Stein. She lives in Paris. I used to see a lot of her while I was there. She's quite a fascinating person—a good deal of a charlatan, but enormous charm. I just wondered if you'd ever read anything she'd written and what you thought of it."

Or, more simply, sleepily, with a smouldering look of her dark face: "Have you read anything by a man named Proust?" This simpler method was even more effective. By not admitting anything herself, simply by asking such a question with a kind of casual indirection, and a smouldering look on her dark untelling face she managed to convey an impression not only of enormous erudition but of very superior critical reserve. It was as if she were accustomed to hold conversations with Mr. T. S. Eliot in which the greater part of knowledge—what the common cry of letterly mankind: the professors, Ph.D's, book reviewers, and average critics spend a life-time in laboriously gathering and expanding—was a matter of such tedious commonplace, as to be regarded entirely in conversations of such succinct allusiveness and such connotative subtlety that the results were distillations of the rarest gold, to be revealed only at intervals of ten years in volumes of no more than forty pages at a time.

When she was in this vein there was an air of "more to this than meets the eye" to everything she said. And the impressed and flattered questionee would not only hastily blurt out that he not only had heard of a man named Proust but had actually read something that he had written, and would then proceed to lay out with great eloquence his critical opinion.

The manner in which this ill-timed outburst was received was decidedly depressing to the unhappy victim. For, at the conclusion of his harangue, Miss Mandell would just look at him searchingly for a moment with a kind of lingering contempt, murmur "um-m," non-committally and then turn arrogantly away, weaving her way through the crowd with lavish undulance as if in search of some likelier material for her deep searchingness.

So stranded, the unfortunate person who had been duped into these critical loquacities would not only feel that he had made a fool of himself, but also that what he had to say must seem to be the most infantile and driveling stuff to an intelligence which, after he had done his best, could only look at him a long moment with a smouldering stare, murmur "Um," and undulate away.

Mr. Robert Ahrens, however, was made of different stuff—if not of sterner stuff, at least of stuff too exuberantly assured, too cherubically concerned with its own interests to be very seriously perturbed by any look that Miss Mandell might give him, whether smouldering or not, or by anything she might or might not say. Besides, they had known each other for years; and they were both theatrical people, he in his actual practice and profession, she in the conduct of her life.

So when the lady approached and smouldered at him, and then said, "Have you ever read anything by a man named Beddoes?"—Mr. Ahrens immediately took the long amber holder from his mouth, looked up at her with a face fairly glowing with cherubic warmth, and elatedly cried: "Oh Beddoes! *Beddoes!*"—The name seemed to give him such exuberant satisfaction that he actually shook his head a little and chortled— "Ah, ha-ha-ha! Beddoes! Oh by all means, *Beddoes!*" cried Mr. Ahrens. "Everyone should be compelled to read him! I *love* Beddoes!"

And, with these words, he lifted his cherubic face which by this time was positively glowing with delight as if he had just consumed a whole quart bottle of port wine, put the enormously long amber holder in his mouth again and drew on it a long fastidious inhalation, let it trickle out in a long luxurious exhalation, and then shook his head again with a short strong movement and cried exultantly: "Oh *Beddoes*, by all means!"

"He *was* mad, wasn't he?" inquired Mr. Lawrence Hirsch at this moment. He had just casually seemed to wander up, as if attracted by the noises of these cultural enthusiasms, and without appearing to follow anyone:—"I mean, didn't he die in an asylum?—in Switzerland, I believe. Really a fascinating case of misplaced identity, wasn't it?" Polished, casual, imperturbable, he turned for the first time toward Miss Mandell in an explanatory manner—"I mean, the man was really born out of his time. He should have been an Elizabethan, shouldn't he?"

Miss Mandell said nothing for a moment. She just looked at Mr. Lawrence Hirsch with a long smouldering stare of lingering contempt. Then she murmured "Um-m," in a non-committal tone, and moved undulantly away. And Mr. Hirsch did not follow her.

For Mr. Lawrence Hirsch was wounded sorrowfully—but he could wait.

He never seemed to follow her. Instead, he stayed there for some moments talking about—Beddoes! He was informed and imperturbable, authoritatively assured, on his aesthetic toes—the very model of what a distinguished leader of enlightened thought—a modern Federalist—should be. There was a little Sacco and Vanzetti here, a little first hand secrecy from Washington there, a sophisticated jest or so, an amusing anecdote of what happened only last week to the President, a little about Russia with a shrewd observation culled from the latest cry in Marxian economy and a little Beddoes now and then. And it was all so perfectly informed, all so suavely contained, all so alertly modern that it never for a moment slipped into a cliché, always represented the very latest mode in everything—art, letters, politics, and economics—and Beddoes!

It was a remarkable accomplishment!—An inspiring example of what the busy modern man of affairs, the great captain of finance, can really accomplish if he only applies himself—not for fifteen *minutes*, but for fifteen *hours*, a day.

And in addition to all this there was Miss Mandell. He never seemed to follow her.

Mr. Lawrence Hirsch was wounded sorrowfully. But he could wait.

He did not beat his breast, or tear his hair, or cry out "Woe is me!" If he had, he might have found some easement of his agony, some merciful release for his swart pain. But instead, Mr. Hirsch remained himself, the captain of his soul, the man of many interests, the master of immense authorities. And he could wait.

And so he did not follow her by so much as a glance. And yet one always knew that he was there. He did not speak to her in any way, nor say to her, "Beloved, thou art fair, beloved, thou art fair: thou hast dove eyes," nor did he say, "Tell me, O thou whom my soul loveth, where thou feedest," nor did he compare her to a company of horses in Pharaoh's chariots, nor say to her, "Also our bed is green." He did not remark to her that she was beautiful as Tirzah or comely as Jerusalem or terrible as an army with banners, nor that her teeth were as a flock of sheep which go up from the washing, nor that her navel was like a round goblet which wanteth nor liquor, nor that her belly was like a bag of wheat set about with lilies.

In fact he did not even speak to her in any way, nor ask anyone to stay him with flagon or comfort him with wine, or confess that he was sick of love. And as for confessing to anyone that his beloved put her hand in at the hole of the door and that his bowels were moved by her, the idea probably never occurred to him.

For Mr. Lawrence Hirsch was wounded sorrowfully. But he could wait.

He did not cry out to her in his agony: "Flaunt me with your mockery and scorn, spurn me with your foot, lash me with your tongue, trample upon me like the worm I am, spit upon me like the dust of which I am composed—revile me to your friends and ridicule me to your lovers, make me crawl far and humbly, if you like, to pimp for you, to act as your procurer, to act as willing cuckold and as pander to the systems of your transient and adulterous lovers—do anything you like, I can endure it— but oh, for God sake, notice me! Look at me for just a moment—if just with scorn! Speak to me with just a word—if just with hate! Be near me for just a moment, make me happy with just a touch—even if the near- ness is but loathing, and the touch a blow! Do anything you like! Treat me in any way you will!—But, in the name of God, I beg you, I implore you—oh beloved as thou art—" Out of the corner of his steady but tormented eye he followed for a moment the lavish undulations of that opulent behind—"In God's name, let me see you know that I am here!"

And yet he did not seem to follow—anyone. For Mr. Lawrence Hirsch was wounded sorrowfully. But he could wait.

"Hm! Interesting!" Mr. Hirsch murmured politely. He craned a little at the collar and ran attentive fingers underneath the collar's rim. The eyeballs of his weary eyes were shot with red.—"I had not realized the real facts were so interesting—Oh absolutely! I agree with you entirely— He was an Elizabethan out of place, if ever there was one."

And distinguished and assured he moved on, following the weaving undulations of that lavish form, without ever seeming so to follow it. It was grotesquely, in that brilliant gathering of fashion, talent, and of wit, a brutal comedy: a hunt that dogs could follow even in these best of men. But though the eye might burn and redden, yet the tongue was cool— "Oh really?—Absolutely—You're looking awfully well." And Beddoes! *Beddoes!*—But the hunt was on.

For Mr. Lawrence Hirsch was wounded sorrowfully. But he could wait.

*   *   *   *   *

There was a sound of music in one corner of the room. Teddy Sam- uels, Amy Van Leer's most recent lover, had been playing some of the songs he had written for his last revue: he was seated at the grand piano in the corner, running through the scores, playing a few bars of the deft, neat music lightly, then changing swiftly into something else. Mean- while, the young people gathered around him—Amy, Ernest, Jack, and Alvin, the gay Japanese, and two or three of the young people from the repertory theatre leaned on the polished leaf of the great piano humming the catchy airs and in a graceful and engaging group keeping time to their brisk rhythm with tapping feet, light drumming fingers, and moving shoulders.

At this moment there was a burst of laughter from the group: someone had looked up and espied Roy Farley who had gone out and returned and was now standing in the door, looking languorously over the crowd, with deep violet-lidded eyes and the drowsy arrogance of a prima donna. Samuels stopped playing suddenly, and looked up laughing, and Amy's hoarse excited voice could be heard, laughing, saying quickly: "There's Roy!—But look at him! Isn't he the most!—I mean!—you know!" Thus encouraged, Roy Farley took full advantage of the moment: It was, he knew, "Good theatre" and he "played it up" for all that it was worth. The drowsy arrogance of his prima donna manner deepened perceptibly: he burlesqued the role absurdly, slowly looking around the room with eyes that were now so heavy-lidded that they were almost closed. He had to hold his head far back even to see out of them at all. Finally, pretending to see someone in the crowd he knew, he waved his hand with a kittenish gesture, at the same time saying, "Oh, hello," in a tone half-way between a greeting and a croon, and then, lidding his eyes still further, and making his voice yield the last atom of lewd suggestiveness he could put into the words, he said: "You *must* come over."

With these words, simpering like an ancient whore, he advanced into the room, now closing his eyes and lifting his head with a tragic mien, at the same time saying in the husky and melodramatic monotone of a famous actress: "That's all there is. There isn't any more."

The gathering apparently found this curious performance hilariously amusing: there were little shrieks of laughter from the women, coarser guffaws from the men, as Mr. Farley made his calculated entrance.

The comedian was a frail young man with lank reddish hair, a thin face of unnatural whiteness—it looked indeed, as if it had been coated with white powder—and a thin, ruined mouth. He was by profession an actor but his greatest celebrity had come from his impersonation of female parts in which at the moment he enjoyed a considerable minor reputation, and he was also on occasions of this sort in considerable demand as a kind of court jester.

It was the spirit of the time. People of Mr. Farley's type and gender enjoyed a perverse celebrity. There was scarcely a fashionable hostess of the period or a smart gathering which did not have their own accredited Mr. Farley as an essential functionary of the feast. He was a kind of privileged comic personality, a cross between a lapdog and a clown.

The homosexual had in fact usurped the place and privilege of the hunchback jester of an old king's court. It was a curious analogy: his own deformity had become, like the crooked backs of royal clowns, a thing of open jest and ribaldry. And his mincing airs and graces, his antics and his gibes, the spicy sting of his feminine and envenomed wit, were like the malicious quips, the forked tongues of the clowns of ancientry, approved and privileged by the spirit of the time and given license that is given only to a clown—or a king. It was, perhaps, an aspect of those times that the great, full throat of laughter, the huge side-shaking humor of the belly, the full, free, commonality of hearty mirth, wise, simple, deep, affectionate and all-embracing, were so rarely heard.

These were more piping times: the world had grown older, subtler, more aware—such ribaldry as made their fathers laugh, or as enlivened coarse breeds of human clay were not for gentry such as these. Their palates now were more adept and jaded, it took a subtler sauce, a more cunning chef to stir the appetites of these sophisticates.

Therefore, in that great citadel of wealth and power and loveliness and sky-flung faery to which the lowly of the earth so yearningly aspire, there was small laughter in those years of grace that did not have the serpent's fangs behind it, and little mirth that was not omened by the rattles of the snake. And for such splendid folk as these, such jests as shook the ribs of Rabelais and filled the taverns of Elizabeth with lusty mirth were not enough. These gentle folk had grown wise and fine beyond all reckoning in their wits' demand. They could no longer be prodded into laughter by the coarser thumbs of Fielding, Dickens, or of Swift—apparently their risible refinements could only be aroused by the humors of a mincing whore.

The subtlety of this celebrated performance was now being graciously unveiled by Mr. Farley in its full and finest flower for the benefit of the admiring host. He made his entrance opportunely, with all eyes fixed upon him and faces already half upon the grin as they waited for the latest flowering of his genius. So encouraged, so inspired—for Mr. Farley like all his precious tribe and others of the Thespian cult—could do nothing unless the eyes and ears of men were fixed upon him—made an impressive entrance. His wit apparently depended largely upon the arts of mimicry—and the art of mimicry where Mr. Farley was concerned depended solely upon impersonation of the female sex.

And this impersonation, to judge from the effect it immediately produced upon the audience, was—in common phrase—"simply killing."

Mr. Farley minced forward delicately with a languorous and exaggerated movement of the hips. As he did so he kept one frail and slender hand arched gracefully upon his thigh as with the other he pawed daintily at the air with plucking fingers as if reaching timidly for an unseen flower.

Meanwhile, he kept his head, the powdered whiteness of his parchment face, held languidly to one side, the weary eyes half closed and heavy-lidded—with an expression of simpering coyness at the lewd confines of his ruined and sunken mouth. And, as he minced along in this position he paused from time to time to wave maidenly at various people of his acquaintance in different parts of the big room saying, as he did so, "Oh, hello!—There you are!—How are you?—You *must* come over!"—in such an irresistibly mincing and ladylike manner that the effect upon that distinguished gathering was convulsing.

The ladies shrieked with laughter, the gentlemen spluttered and guffawed. As for Mrs. Jack, her rosy face grew almost purple. She was fairly overcome, she shrieked faintly: "Honestly!—isn't he the most killing—" and was unable to continue.

The celebrated wit now came mincing up to her, took her hand and kissed it, and taking full advantage of the expectant silence that had fallen, he said, quite loudly in a throaty, languid and effeminate tone that could be heard in every corner of the room: "Oh, Esther, darling! I have news for you! . . ."

He paused and waited, and thus forewarned she clapped her little hand up to her deaf ear, turned her jolly little face half away from him with the expression and manner of a child listening eagerly and gleefully for the first time to the music coming from a gramophone, and said quickly: "Hah? Yes? What is it—What did you hear, Roy?"

"Well," he said languidly in a voice, however, of great carrying power, "you know the Hotel Manger there on Broadway?"

"Yes? What about it, Roy?"

"They're going to change its name," he said.

"Hah?"—eagerly, almost gleefully—"Why? Why are they going to change its name, Roy?"—with her own theatrical training she was the good trouper now and played right into his hands to give full point and flavor to his jest.

"Because of what people have to say," said Mr. Farley.

"Hah? What have they begun to say, Roy?"

"Why," said he with lewd insinuation, "*you* know?—If it's good enough for Jesus it's good enough for me?"

In the roar of laughter that followed this splendid sally he sauntered mincingly away as one adept in the "timing" of the stage, waving his hand girlishly at various guests and speaking to them as if he were completely, nonchalantly unaware of the humorous sensation he had created.

But now the doorbell rang again. Mrs. Jack looked around doubtfully, inquiringly, a little startled, as if she were not certain whether she had heard its sharp ring. Then she saw Molly going towards the door: she looked quickly at the little watch upon her wrist. It was after ten o'clock. In a moment the door from the centre vestibule was opened, and a woman and a man came into the hall. It was Saul Levenson and his wife, Virginia. He had been a true and devoted friend of Mrs. Jack's since childhood, but one would never have suspected it from the sneering arrogance of the look which he now gave her. Even as he stood there in the hall waiting for his wife to return, and arrogantly surveying the crowd within the room, the tragic fact of an incurable distemper in the man was instantly apparent. It stuck out all over him. He was a mass of sore thumbs. He had gnawed his own liver for so long a time that it had colored his whole life. Even his flesh seemed to have been soaked in bile; he was dyed through with the pigments of his own distemper, a kind of tragic stain of his own torment that could never be got out. And yet—and this was also apparent—he was a richly talented man. Just lacking genius, he had many shining gifts. He wrote brilliantly, he was a subtle and a penetrating critic, he was deep in the history of the arts, and an authority on modern painting, and he had a true and just appreciation of literature. Furthermore, he was one of the leaders of the modern theatre and one of its most eminent designers.

With gifts like these, with talents of such extraordinary variety, and with an accomplishment of work that had crowned his career with recognition and success for many years, it might be inferred that Levenson was a very happy man. Such, unhappily, was not the case. He was a very extraordinary man, he was often, where appreciation of true merit, or recognition of the good work of other people was concerned, a very generous and fine spirited man. But he was not a happy man. He was a tormented, wretchedly inverted, complicated man.

The result was grotesque but it was also terrible. The man's face was simply unbelievable. One's first and involuntary impulse on seeing him for the first time was to burst out in an explosive and uncontrollable laugh in which incredulity was mixed with amusement. But such a laugh was swiftly checked when one saw what inconceivable anguish of the mind and spirit it must have taken to wreak such anguish on the features of a high and sensitive man.

His face was a kind of living crazy-quilt of obnoxious and distressful colors. Or, rather, with its naturally oriental and Hebraic swarthiness, it was now a kind of Turkish rug into which every color of distemper and spiritual distress had been ruthlessly and grotesquely poured.

It was purple, it was green, it was dingy yellow, it was crimson, it was black. It seemed to have in it, in about equal proportions, the mixtures of jaundice and of apoplectic strangulation. It was, as Mrs. Jack thought instantly and with a momentary tendency toward explosive mirth, "the damnedest face you ever saw"—and then, with the instant repercussion of overwhelming sympathy: "Poor thing! Poor thing!"

To say that Levenson carried this grotesque patchquilt of a visage proudly like a flaming banner would be a modest understatement of the truth. He not only carried it, he brandished it. And as if those gargoyle features were not in their unhappy state of nature enough to do him vengeful service had he wished—to frighten little children with, had he so willed, to startle strangers and to shock his friends—he made it do a double duty in repulsion by conforming it to every eloquent expression that contempt and scorn can know.

It was an outrageously arrogant face. The quality of its arrogance was so exaggerated, so extravagant, so insultingly enlarged and emphasized that by comparison the expression of the celebrated Pooh Bah was ingenuous in its sweet democracy.

Even before Levenson spoke to anyone, even before he greeted a stranger, those jaundiced eyes and that chromatic gargoyle of a face looked his unhappy victim up and down with such hyperbole of sneering contempt and disdain that if he had at the same time emitted a mocking laugh and snarled: "Really, who is this low fellow anyway? Do I have to be bored by such a clodhopper or will not some good Samaritan come and rescue me from having to endure any more of the drivel of this bourgeois num-skull"—his arrogance and scorn could not have been more plainly uttered.

And this really was the way he often felt. His was a tragic paradox of the gifted intellectual of his race. He wanted to have his cake and eat it too. Gifted by nature and by inheritance not only with an artist's talent, but with an artist's love and appreciation of beauty, and of the gifts and talents of other people, no one could be more quick and warm and selfless in his generous and intelligent recognition of the work of other men. And yet he could also be torn by feelings of envy. He could writhe with a torment of jealousy and scorn.

Likewise, endowed by nature with a brilliant mind, a fine intelligence and with a critical faculty that sought and loved the truth for its own sake, these high intellects were being constantly twisted and perverted from their clear purposes, their grand detachments, and their nobler impersonality, by the corrosive vanities of the intellectual. As a result, he was constantly getting embroiled in picayune and acrid arguments with other people of this sort, the total effect of which too often was that both sides failed to see the woods because there were so many trees. "What *precisely* I said in my last letter to your columns and what *precisely* Mr. Katzstein said in his reply is now a matter of record—" etc., etc.,—and so on back and forth until all that was left of the original issue, had there been one, was the sordid spectacle of two embittered egotisms crossing useless t's and dotting worthless i's.

All these unhappy and conflicting qualities in this tormented and yet exceptional and distinguished spirit were now evident as he made his entrance at the party at Jack's. While his wife, a plain featured, and rather ugly little New Englander whom he loved devotedly and for whom he had felt such a consuming passion that he had turned all colors of the rainbow until his face positively resembled an outbreak of the plague, and for whom he had left a beautiful and voluptuous spouse of his own race, had undergone a complete physical collapse and an eight months' period of reconstruction at Zurich under the enlightened eye of Dr. Jung—while this quiet little lady, who had been the cause of so much shipwreck and so many rainbow hues was divesting herself of her wraps in the room that had been given over to the women, Levenson remained in the outer corridor, removed his hat, took off his light spring overcoat and slowly and disdainfully unwound from his collar an outrageous scarf which was a confusion of so many violent and distempered colors that it seemed almost that he must have chosen it in a deliberate effort to outdo his face.

He waited until his wife came back before entering the crowded living room. She entered first and for a moment Levenson remained standing in the door, slowly and insolently turning upon the combined assemblage the small-pox battery of his bubonic face. The look of scorn and revulsion upon his astounding features was now so eloquent in its violence that people turned and stared at him appalled. If he had chosen that moment to break into a loud and sneering laugh and say: "So! It has come to this, hey? I have taken all this trouble to get here— and this—ha, ha, ha,—is what I find."—His contempt could not have been more explicit than it now seemed to be, and few people would have been surprised.

In a moment, however, his wife, feeling his absence and sensing from the lull that had descended upon the gathering that something was amiss, turned quickly, saw him, and gave him a quiet, quick, and warning look. This swift warning glance of his small guardian angel toned him down at once. He immediately composed himself, came into the room, and began to greet people in a natural tone of voice. Then he spoke to Mrs. Jack with the quiet affection of an old and valued friend.

"Esther, I'm sorry that we're late," he said, "We stopped in to look at your new show. I wanted to see your set."

"Oh, did you see it, Saul?" she cried, clapping her hand to her ear and bending forward a little to hear better as her rosy face flushed deeper with excitement and interest: "Did you like it? Hah?"

For a moment his face was again distempered by its old look of arrogance and scorn:

"Oh, I suppose it will pass very well as an example of La Jack in one of her better moments. Of course, nothing anyone could do could hurt a piece of tripe like *that* play anyway. So I suppose it doesn't matter much what the set is like. If they haven't got sense enough to come to me in the first place it doesn't matter who designs it."

She was not annoyed. She had known him too long. She knew too much about him. She laughed and said: "God! You hate yourself don't you?"—At the same time taking him in—the whole discolored pamphlet of his face—in one swift glance, thinking a trifle cynically, but good-humoredly and utterly without rancour:

"That fellow thinks he's hell, doesn't he? And, my God!"—for a moment as she looked at the polychromia of his astounding face the old swift impulse to explosive and incredulous mirth rose up in her and almost choked her—"What a face! Would anyone believe it! It's—it's—it's like something out of Grimm's Fairy Tale!"—she thought, and then immediately, with a swift and overwhelming sense of pity: "Poor Saul! Poor thing!"

More quietly now, her face still flushed with laughter, her wise eyes twinkling shrewdly and good-naturedly, she looked at him and said: "Well, Saul, I'll tell you something. No one's ever going to get a swelled head from staying around you."

"Don't listen to him, Esther," Levenson's wife said quietly. "He's crazy about your set—he told me so. And I thought it was beautiful," she added simply.

Levenson's voice, when he spoke again, was also quiet, his face and manner had lost all their former arrogance and there was now no doubt whatever about his complete and utter seriousness.

"Esther," he said, "you are one of the best designers in the world! The set tonight was lovely. At your best," he said. "There's no one else who can touch you."

Mrs. Jack's face now really did flush deeply with happiness and joy. A wave of warm swift feeling, of gratefulness and affection, filled her being: "How generous and good!" she thought. "What a fine high man he really is!"

When she answered him her voice too was quiet, the voice of a person talking to an old friend at such a moment, stripped free of mirth or any playful pleasantry, when there is nothing but plain speech to say:

"Well, Saul," she said. "You know the saying: 'Praise from Sir Topas is praise indeed.' That's the way I feel now."

He turned away from her, having resumed his former manner, saying arrogantly and disdainfully as he did so: "Not that there's not room for a lot of improvement! And when I think you're lousy—as you frequently are—I'll tell you so!"

She laughed richly: "I'll bet you will."—And then her rosy little face, twinkling with good humor, she raised her hands, palms upward, Jewishly, shrugged her shoulders, and said plaintively: "I vont even have to esk"—a comicality that so delighted her by its quick spontaneity that she shook hysterically with helpless appreciation of her own humor, putting a handkerchief to her mouth and saying quickly: "I know—but it was funny, wasn't it!"—although no one said it wasn't.

Levenson grinned a little, then moved away and joined the crowd. He could be seen moving from group to group, his amazing patchwork of a face arrogantly contorted in the full and swarthy volutes of dark oriental scorn.

Anyone who might have been present on this famous evening, would undoubtedly have noted, among the crowd of brilliant and distinguished people, most of whom seemed to know one another with the familiarity of long acquaintanceship, a weird little group, which seemed to be marooned, to be sorrowfully enisled there in the crowd in the lonely isolation of a lepers' colony, and which provided the most bizarre and disturbing touch to an otherwise distinguished gathering.

Mr. Hirsch Was Wounded Sorrowfully ☙ 183

This was a man named Krock, a sculptor, his wife, who had been a girlhood friend of Mrs. Jack's, and who was the reason for their being present, and his mistress, a young, buxom, and fullblown whore.

It was an astounding and unhappy little party. Krock was a Germanic kind of man with a carnal face, a little blond goatee that tufted out of the deep hollow below his sensual mouth and an unpleasant habit of moistening his full red lips and rubbing his hands, tenderly along his heavy thighs, at the same time, murmuring intimately as he did so that he had varicose veins and that his legs were very tired, and couldn't "they" go off quietly somewhere to another room away from all this noise and sit down—this last remark being made invariably to any attractive woman that he met as he eased gently toward her with a straddling movement.

His wife looked like someone who had been struck by lightning. She was a blown shell of a woman with a fragile face—a wisp of life with sunken, brightly staring eyes. And the mistress, whom he introduced as his "model," was like something out of one of the drawings of Felician Rops. She had carnal lips, eyes and lashes that had been weirdly stained with some nocturnal dye, and blondish hair combed down and cut in a straight bang across her forehead. She was a bold featured and bold figured girl with full outstanding breasts, and although she was dressed in a street costume, her blouse was low. It was a shocking little group, strange mixture of flaunting carnality and frail surrender, of Madonna and of Mary Magdalene, of the Twentieth Century and the Moulin Rouge.

And although such liaisons were certainly not unknown to this gathering, although such carnal triangles were familiar to them all, and the forms even present here tonight, of conventional concealment had been here so ruthlessly violated, the naked fact was here so ruthlessly revealed, that the other people at the party evidently felt the circumstance a little shocking and perhaps, like sinners gone to church, enjoyed the luxury of feeling virtuous.

The little group was somewhat isolated—a fact which seemed to trouble the painter and his mistress not at all—and from time to time people would glance at them with speculative looks—at the wife with wonder and commiseration, at the man and the young woman with distaste and a kind of cynical amusement.

The carnal history of the whole group was written with such brutal nakedness that men would stare at them for a moment heavily, then turn away with a short ejaculative laugh that summed up everything, and women, after staring at them with a curiosity mixed of wonder and repulsion, would turn away, saying with a kind of helpless and astounded laugh: "Isn't it the most?—" It was only when people looked at the frail and tragic-looking wife that their expressions would soften into kindly interest. Men looked at her with quiet sympathy, and women with a more active and aroused compassion would say involuntarily:

"The poor thing!"

Well, here they were then, three dozen of the highest and the best, with shimmer of silk, and ripple of laughter, with the tumultuous babel of fine voices, with tinkle of ice in shell-thin glasses, and with silvern clatter, in thronging webs of beauty, wit and loveliness—as much passion, joy, and hope, and fear, as much triumph and defeat, as much anguish and despair and victory, as much sin, viciousness, cruelty and pride, as much base intrigue and ignoble striving, as much unnoble aspiration as flesh and blood can know, or as a room can hold—enough, God knows, to people hell, inhabit heaven, or fill out the universe— were all here, now, miraculously composed, in magic interweft—at Jack's!

PIGGY LOGAN'S CIRCUS
. . .

The hour had now arrived for Mr. Piggy Logan and his celebrated circus of wire dolls. As he made his appearance there was a flurry of excited interest in the brilliant throng. People in the dining room crowded to the door, holding tinkling glasses or plates loaded with tempting victuals in their hands, even old Jake Abramson deserted for the moment his painstaking circuit of the loaded table, and appeared in the doorway gnawing coarsely at a chicken leg: an old man with loose teeth patiently worrying a bone.

Mr. Piggy Logan was now attired for the performance. His costume was a simple yet an extraordinary one. He wore a thick blue sweater with a turtle roll neck of the kind in favor with college heroes thirty years ago. And on this sweater—God knows why—was sewn an enormous "Y." He wore an old white pair of canvas trousers, a pair of tennis sneakers, and a pair of battered knee pads which were formerly in favor with professional wrestlers. On his head he wore a battered football helmet, the straps securely fastened underneath his round and heavy jowls. And thus arrayed, he now made his appearance, staggering between his two enormous cases.

The crowd scattered, made way for him, and regarded him with awe. Mr. Logan grunted forward with his two enormous valises, which at length he dropped with a floorshaking thump, and breathed an audible sigh of relief. He immediately pushed back the big sofa which obstructed his view of the premises, began to push back all chairs and tables and any other objects of furniture which might obstruct his free view, pushed back the carpet and then ruthlessly began to take books from the shelves and dump them on the floor. He looted a half dozen shelves in various parts of the room and then fastened up in the vacant spaces big circus posters which he had procured somewhere and which in addition to the familiar paraphernalia of tigers, lions, elephants, clowns, and trapeze performers, bore such descriptive legends as "Barnum & Bailey—May 7th and 8th," "Ringling Brothers—July 31st," and so on.

The gathering watched him curiously as he went about this labor of methodical destruction. When he had finished he came back to his valises, and began to take out a great variety of objects. There were little miniature circus rings made of rounded strips of tin or copper which fitted neatly together. There were trapezes and flying swings made of wire. And in addition there were a great variety of figures made of wire designed to represent the animals and performers of a circus. There were clowns and trapeze performers, acrobats and tumblers, bareback lady riders and wire horses. There was almost everything, in fact, that one could think of, or that a circus would need. And all of it was made of wire, and Mr. Logan's celebrated dolls.

It took him a good time to set all this up for he was evidently of a patient turn of mind, and although his little figures were constructed of wire only, he would not be content until he had fairly represented the paraphernalia of a good sized circus. He got down upon his kneepads and for some time he was extremely busy with his work. He set up his wire trapezes and his wire rings. He set up his little wire figures of elephants, lions, tigers, horses, camels, and the other personnel of the circus menagerie. He set out his little wire figures of the circus per-formers, and he even set up a little sign that said "Main Entrance."

It was some time before he had finished his patient labors. Mean-while, the people who had been invited regarded him curiously for a time, then resumed the rapid clatter of their talk with one another.

At length Mr. Logan was ready and signified his willingness to begin by a gesture to his hostess. She made a sign to her guests that asked for silence and attention. At the same moment, the doorbell rang and a host of new and uninvited guests were ushered in by Molly. Mrs. Jack looked somewhat bewildered. The new arrivals, who had not been invited were, for the most part, young people and obviously they belonged to Mr. Piggy Logan's "social set." The young women had that subtle yet unmistakable appearance of having gone to Miss Spence's School for Girls and the young men, by the same token, seemed to have gone to

Yale and Harvard and one was also sure that some of them were members of the Racquet Club and were now connected with a firm of "investment brokers" in downtown New York.

In addition, there was with them a large well-kept somewhat decayed looking lady of advanced middle age. She had evidently been a society beauty in her palmy days, but now she was a picture of corrupted elegance: everything about her, arms, shoulders, neck, and face, and throat were somewhat blown, full and loose, like something that has been elegantly kept but is decayed. In addition, she had large bright eyes and a throaty and indifferent voice: it was a picture of corrupted wealth—what Amy Van Leer *might* look like twenty years from now, if she were careful and survived. One felt unpleasantly that she had lived too long in Europe, and preferred the Riviera, and that there was somewhere in the offing something with dark liquid eyes, a little moustache, and pomaded hair—something quite young and private and obscene—and kept.

This lady was accompanied by a gentleman past sixty, faultlessly attired in evening dress, as were all the others, and with a cropped moustache and artificial teeth, which were revealed occasionally when the clipped cachinnation of his speech was broken and he paused to lick his thin lips lecherously, and to stutter out—"What—what." Both of these people looked remarkably like some of the characters portrayed by Mr. Henry James, if Mr. Henry James had written of them in a slightly later period of decay.

All these people streamed in noisily and vociferously, headed by an elegant young gentleman in a white tie and tails whose name, curiously, was Hen Walters, and who was evidently Mr. Logan's bosom friend.

Mrs. Jack looked rather overwhelmed at this invasion, but was dutifully murmuring greetings and welcome when all the new people swarmed right past her ignoring her completely, and stormed into the room shouting vociferous gaieties at Mr. Logan. He greeted them from his kneepads with a fond and foolish grin, waved at them and beckoned them to a position along one wall with a spacious gesture of his thick hand. They swarmed in and took the place. They paid absolutely no attention to any of the other invited guests, except for a greeting here and there to Amy Van Leer who apparently they considered one of them, even though a fallen angel.

There was even an interlude of contact here. Amy came over and joined her people for a moment. Her golden head could be seen sunning out of the chattering group; she seemed to know them all: the debutantes and the young men were polite but crisply detached. One could see that they had all heard of her, and had been warned. Some of the young people drew away after the formalities of greeting and eyed her curiously as one would look, and rather furtively, at a famous scarlet woman who was once a member of the flock. It was a look that said as plain as words could do: "So this is she?—the Dread Medusa or the Fallen Angel we have heard so much about?"

One or two of the other people were more unreserved and natural. Hen Walters greeted her quite cordially: he said, "Oh, hello, Amy," in a voice that constantly suggested he was burbling with suppressed fun, and was just about to break into a burbling laugh. Some of his friends professed to like it, and thought his laugh a quite infectious and engaging one. But it was really not a pleasant voice: it was too moist and yolky and it seemed to circulate around a nodule of fat phlegm. He was, to use a phrase by which Mrs. Jack had already mentally described him, "A lowdy-dow-young man." As such, in his own "set," he was a privileged character, an Original.

He was one of the impoverished young men of the high plutocracy, whose family, however, is a "good" one and whose social standing high. His friends described it in this way: "Of course he's frightfully poor! He has nothing."—In Mr. Walters' case "nothing" was seven thousand dollars every year.—"But he's *most* amusing. You've simply got to meet Hen Walters: you'll adore him."

Cast in this role, Mr. Walters was the generating force of much hilariousness:—the list of his accomplishments was a most impressive one. He was, for example, the first one to organize a party on roller skates around Central Park; he was the originator of the famous "busman's dinner"—a gustatory expedition that began in Greenwich Village and that then *jumped* course by course—by taxi, trolley, or by bus—all over town. And although this repast was calculated to wreak havoc with the nervous system and the digestive tract, it was carried out from soup to nuts, and was the great sensation of the year.

In addition to all these other contributions to sophisticated gaiety, Mr. Walters owned a Ford of such ancient vintage that it threatened to fall to pieces every time it hit a bump. The Ford was famous everywhere through "Society": Mr. Walters drove it everywhere hilariously, and it was his custom to appear at the most grandiose receptions—the coming-out of a famous deb, a dinner or a dance—clad in full evening dress, with "tails" and a silk hat, in his decrepit Ford, insinuating this rusty rattletrap among the purring lanes of sleek Rolls Royces with as much aplomb as if it were the President's car.

All of these facts were in themselves enough to establish Mr. Walters as the pet of fashion and the spur of wit.

But there was more—much more. In addition to all these other claims to eminence, he was the chosen crony of the idol of the hour:—of Mr. Piggy Logan and his circus of wire dolls.

It was small wonder then that he was Privileged—chosen to do and dare what others could not dare to do, to walk with crowds, nor lose his virtue, to talk to kings, nor lose the common touch, to rush in blithely where the most experienced angels fear to tread, even to greet the most notorious Fallen Angel of the upper crust, with the cordial assurance of familiarity—only Mr. Hen Walters was privileged to do these things.

So he greeted her now with all the gleeful elations of his burbling voice:

"Oh, hello, Amy! I haven't seen you for an age. What brings *you* here?"—in a tone that somehow indicated, with all the unconscious arrogance of his kind, that the scene and company was amusingly bizarre and beyond the pale of things accepted and confirmed,—that to find anyone of his own group in such a place was an astounding experience.

The tone and implication stung her sharply, "got her Irish up." As for herself, she had received the slings and arrows of outrageous fortune, the vicious scandal and the slander of her name, with beautiful good nature. But an affront to someone that she loved was more than she could endure. And she loved Mrs. Jack.

Almost before she was aware of what she was saying, she was repeating quickly:

"What brings *me* here—of *all* places! Well, first of all it's a very good place to be—the best I know—And I *mean*! You know!—" She laughed hoarsely, quickly, jerked the cigarette from her mouth and tossed her head with a movement of almost furious impatience and said: "I *mean*! After *all*, I *was* invited, you know—which is more than I can say—" She checked herself and turned away with a short laugh. Her green gold eyes were flashing dangerously, and for the first time there was a flush of color on her golden face: the freckled pugnacity of her snub-nosed visage was more apparent than it had ever been.

Unconsciously, instinctively, with a gesture of protective warmth, she had slipped her arm around Mrs. Jack who, still rather over-whelmed by this tumultuous and unexpected invasion, had been standing by her, with her hand held to her ear, her rosy little face beaming with trustful confidence, as if still a little doubtful what was happening, but blissfully assured it was all right.

"Esther, darling," Amy said. "This is Mr. Walters—and some of his friends"—but for a moment she looked at the cluster of young debutantes and their escorts, and then turned away, saying frankly, to no one in particular, but with no effort to subdue her tone: "God, aren't they simply dreadful!—I *mean*!—You know!" She addressed herself now to the elderly man with the clipped stammer and the artificial teeth— "Charley—In the name of God, what are you trying to do?—You old cradle-snatcher, you—I *mean*! You *know*! After all, it's not *that* bad, is it?" She surveyed the group of girls again with a short glance, then turned away with a brief, hoarse laugh: "My God! How do you stand it! I *mean*! After *all*!" She laughed suddenly hoarsely. "Six little vaginas standing in a row and not a grain of difference between them. Chapin's School last year. Harvard and their first—this! All these little Junior League bitches," she muttered. "How do you stand it, anyway! You old bastard!" She said quickly, and not at all awkwardly, and looking at him for a moment, laughed her short hoarse laugh. "Why don't you come to see me any more?"

Before he answered her he licked his lips nervously and bared his artificial teeth.

"Wanted to see you, Amy, for ever so long—What?—Intended to stop in—Matter of fact, did stop by some time ago but you'd just sailed— What—You've been away, haven't you—What—"

As he spoke these words in a kind of clipped staccato stammer, he kept licking his thin lips with nervous lechery, and at the same time he scratched himself, rooting rather obscenely into the inner thigh of his right leg in a way that suggested he was wearing woollen underwear, or was being bitten by a flea. The result of this operation was that his trouser leg was pulled up and stayed there, revealing the tops of his socks, and a portion of white meat.

Meanwhile, Hen Walters, still smiling his bright wet smile, was burbling on to Mrs. Jack:

"—So nice of you to let us all come in." Although she, poor lady, had had nothing at all to do with it. "Piggy told us it would be all right. I hope you don't mind."

"But no-o—not at all!" she protested earnestly, still with a somewhat puzzled and bewildered look. "Any friends of Mr. Logan's—But won't you all have a drink or something to eat? There's loads to eat—"

"Oh, *heavens*, no!" cried Mr. Walters, in a tone of such burblesome glee that it seemed he really could not keep his little secret any longer— that the joke which he had been harboring all evening, jubilantly suppressing in his moist throat now simply had to *out*—could be contained no longer, just *had* to be shared with the attendant universe. "We've all been to Tony's and we simply *gorged* ourselves!"—he burbled gleefully. "If we took another mouthful, I'm absolutely positive we should explode!"

He uttered these words with such ecstatic jubilation that it really seemed for a moment that explosion was imminent—that he was likely to evaporate at any moment in a large moist bubble.

"Well, then, if you're sure," she began.

"Oh, *absolutely*!" cried Mr. Walters rapturously. "But we're holding up the show!" he cried. "And, after all, that's what we're here to see. It would simply be a tragedy to miss it. Oh, Piggy," he cried to his friend, who now had all his materials assembled and, cheerfully grinning, was crawling on his kneepads on the floor. "Do *begin*! Everyone's simply dying to see it! I've seen it a dozen times myself," he announced gleefully to the general public, "and it becomes more fascinating every time. So if you're ready, please begin!"

Mr. Logan was ready and began.

The new arrivals took up their positions along the wall to the left and as he prepared to start his show carried on a vociferous and curious conversation with one another of which they themselves apparently had the key or understood the vocabulary. The other people, after looking at the newcomers with a somewhat puzzled and troubled expression, remained to themselves and made no further effort at contact. In fact, they withdrew a little to the other three corners of the room, leaving the assemblage now cleanly divided in two parts as if a knife had been drawn between them and cut them apart—the people of wealth, of talent, and of mixed abilities upon one side and those of fashion or "Society" upon the other.

On a signal from Mr. Logan, Mr. Walters detached himself from his group, came over, arranged the tails of his coat, and knelt down gracefully beside his friend. Then, in answer to instruction, he read a sheet of typewritten paper which Mr. Logan handed to him. It was a whimsical document of sorts, the effect of which was that to understand and enjoy the circus one must make an effort to recover his lost youth and have the spirit of a child again. Mr. Walters read this document with great gusto in a cultivated tone of voice which burbled with happy laughter. When he had finished, he got up and resumed his former position among his friends against the wall and Mr. Logan then began the performance of his circus.

It began, as all good circuses should, with a grand procession of the animals in the menagerie. Mr. Logan accomplished this by taking the wire figures of the various animals in his thick hands and walking them around the circus ring and then solemnly out again. This took some time, but was greeted at its conclusion with vociferous applause.

Then Mr. Logan had the grand procession of the performers. He marched them around in the same way with manipulations of his hairy paws. This also was carried out in full detail and was greeted with applause.

Then came the great performance. The circus started first with an exhibition of the bareback riders. Mr. Logan galloped his wire horses into the ring and round and round with movements of his hand. Then he put his bareback riders on top of the wire horses, and holding them firmly in place, he galloped these around too. Then he brought in an interlude of clowns and made these wire figures tumble around by working and manipulating them with his hands. After this there was a procession of the wire elephants, etc. This performance gained particular applause because of the clever way in which Mr. Logan made the figures imitate the swaying ponderous lurch of elephants.

People were not always sure what each act meant, but when they were able to identify an act, a pleasant little laugh of recognition would sweep the crowd and they would applaud the act vigorously. There was now an act by the trapeze performers. This occupied a long time, because Mr. Logan first, with his punctilious fidelity to actuality, had to put up a little net below the trapeze, just as nets are put up in circuses. The trapeze act began and it was unconscionably long, largely because Mr. Logan was not able to make it work. First of all the little wire figures swung and dangled from their flying trapezes. Then Mr. Logan tried to make one little figure swing through the air, leave its trapeze and catch the other figure by its downswept hands. This wouldn't work. Again and again the little wire figure soared through the air, caught at the outstretched hands of the other doll—and missed ingloriously.

It became painful: people craned their necks and looked embarrassed—all, indeed, except Mr. Logan who did not look at all embarrassed, but giggled happily with each new failure and tried again. It went on and on. It must have taken twenty minutes while Mr. Logan tried to make his trapeze figures catch and hang. But nothing happened. At length, when it was obvious that nothing was going to happen, Mr. Logan settled the whole matter himself by taking one of the little figures firmly between two thick fingers conveying it to the other and carefully hanging it to the other's arms. When he had finished he looked up at his audience and giggled with cheerful idiocy. And the gathering, after a brief and somewhat puzzled pause, broke into applause.

Mr. Logan was now ready for what might be called the *pièce de résistance* of the entire occasion. This was the celebrated sword swallowing act on which he obviously prided himself a great deal. He picked up a small rag doll, stuffed with wadding and with crudely painted features, and with the other hand he took a long hairpin and began patiently and methodically to work it down the throat of the rag doll.

People looked on with amazement and then, as the meaning of Mr. Logan's operation was conveyed to them, they smiled at one another in a puzzled and rather doubting way. And then, after another pause, they began to applaud decorously but half-heartedly.

It was a horrible exhibition. Mr. Logan kept working the hairpin down with thick, probing fingers and when some impediment of wadding got in his way he looked up and giggled foolishly. Half way down he struck an obstacle, and it seemed indeed he would not be able to go any farther. But he persisted—persisted horribly.

He kept working, and pressing with his hairpin while people looked at one another with distressed faces, and suddenly a gap appeared in the side of the bulging doll and some of the stuffing began to ooze out shockingly. At this manifestation some people gave up utterly. A few of the men looked at one another with an expression of disgust and loathing and quietly filtered out into the hall, or in the restorative direction of the dining room.

Miss Lily Mandell looked on with an expression of undisguised horror and, as the stuffing began to ooze out of the doll, she placed one hand against her stomach in a gesture of undisguised nausea, said "ugh," and made her hasty exit in the direction of a nearby room.

The young "society people," however, looked on with a simulation of eager interest and applauded everything enthusiastically. In fact, as Mr. Logan began to probe with his hairpin and the stuffing in the doll began to ooze out, one of the young women, with the pure, cleanly chiseled face that is so frequent in her class, turned to the young man who was standing beside her, who also had the lean head, the cropped shining hair, the small-boned and decisive features that are so familiar in his type, and said: "I think it's *frightfully* interesting—the way he does that. Don't you?"

To which the young man, also in what was evidently an approved accent, said briefly, "Eh," an ejaculation that might have been indicative of almost anything but which here obviously was taken for assent.

This conversation had taken place in a curiously muffled clipped speech which apparently was the fashion among these people: when the girl had spoken she had barely opened her mouth and her words seemed to come out between almost motionless lips. The young man had answered her in the same way, the conversations of the other people in this group were likewise characterized by this formula or fashion of clipped and somewhat muffled speech, so that it was sometimes difficult to follow what they said.

It was a curious spectacle and would have furnished interesting material for the speculations of a thoughtful historian of life and customs of this golden age. It was astounding to see so many able and intelligent men and women, people with quick minds, tense nerves, high abilities, who could and had enjoyed almost every high and rare entertainment of travel, reading, music, and aesthetic taste, and who were for the most part so impatient of the dull, the boring, the trivial, patiently assembled here to give their respectful attention to an exhibition of this sort.

But even respect for the accepted mode was wearing thin. Save for this audience of the devoted young, people were beginning to get a trifle restless and impatient. The performance had already lasted a wearily unreasonable time, and it was evident that the main trouble with Mr. Logan's dolls was that they wouldn't work. His clowns, his trapeze performers, and his bareback riders, if they performed at all, performed only by the muscular assistance of their creator's aiding fingers. He showed the persistence of a cheerful idiot and when he had tried something for twenty minutes or more, and had it fail, he would then make it work by using his own hands.

People had now begun to go out into the halls, and a few of the more cynical and less believing could be seen and heard talking to each other ironically with little laughs.

Even Mrs. Jack, who had slipped on a wonderful jacket of gold thread and seated herself cross-legged on the floor, like a dutiful child, squarely before the maestro and his puppets, had got up and gone out into the hall, where a number of her guests were now assembled. Here she found Lily Mandell, and approaching her with a bright affectionate little smile, she queried, hopefully:

"Are you enjoying it, Lily? And you, darling?" she now turned fondly to her young lover—"Do you like it?—Hah?—Are you having a good time?—Hah?"

Lily Mandell answered in a tone of throaty protest and disgust:

"When he started pushing that long pin into the doll, and all its insides began oozing out—ugh!"—She made a nauseous face and put a hand upon her stomach—"I simply couldn't stand it any longer! It was horrible! Had to get out!—I thought that I was going to puke!"

Mrs. Jack's shoulders shook, her face reddened, and she gasped in a hysterical whisper:

"I know! Wasn't it awful?"

"But what is it, anyway?" said the attorney Roderick Hale, as he came up and joined the group.

"Oh, hello, Rod!" said Mrs. Jack—"What do you think of it?—Hah?" and held her hand up to her eager and attentive ear.

"I can't make it out," he said, and took another disgusted look into the living room where Piggy Logan was still patiently probing out the entrails of his rag doll, oozing insides out upon the floor—"What is it all supposed to be about, anyway? . . . And who is this fellow?" he said in an irritated tone as if his legal and fact-finding mind had been annoyed by some phenomenon he could not fathom. "It's like some puny form of decadence," he muttered in a discontented tone, and after another disgusted look into the room, he turned away.

At this moment, Mr. Jack came from the living room, approached his wife, and lifting his shoulders in a bewildered shrug, and with an alarmed face and accent, thickened Germanically by his perturbation, he said:

"What is this? My Gott, perhaps *I'm* crazy!"

His bewildered protest was irresistibly comical.

Mrs. Jack shuddered, her face flamed, and she chuckled faintly, helplessly, as she put her handkerchief to her mouth:

"Poor Fritz!"

Jack turned, with the same bewildered face and gesture to his son, who had also now come out into the hall:

"What is it?" he said. "Can you find out?" He cast another bewildered look into the living room, surveyed the wreckage there, then turned away suddenly with a short explosive laugh:

"Gott! Tell me if he leaves the furniture! I'm going to my room!" he said decidedly, and Mrs. Jack chuckled faintly again, and said, "Poor Fritz!"

He looked at her a moment, then at the weird performance in the living room, then at his son, shrugged his shoulders helplessly again, shook his head with a gesture of defeat, and then, with a short laugh said:

"Mein Gott!—Your Mother!"

Mrs. Jack chuckled faintly, and with a crimsoned face, she leaned forward eagerly, clapped her small hand to her ear, and still trembling with laughter, said, "Hah?"

He looked at her cynically a moment, then shook his head and said:

"Nah-h!—Nah, Esther—"

"What?" she gasped in a feeble little squeak. "What?"

"Nah-h," said Jack as before, turning to the smiling company in an explanatory way:

"The trouble with her iss not that she iss deaf. She iss dumb!"

Then, with another helpless shrug, a bewildered look into the living room, a defeated, baffled, "Gott!" he departed in the direction of his own room, followed by his wife's hysterical little shriek, his son's short heavy laugh, and the general amusement of the other people.

Mrs. Jack and Lily Mandell bent together shuddering helplessly in the way women have when they communicate whispered laughter to each other:

"Isn't it the most *horrible*—" Miss Mandell whispered: the word, as she pronounced it slowly and with laughing emphasis, sounded almost like "how-w-rible." She had lived in England for a year or two, and she had acquired, or affected, a thick British accent.—"The most awful!"— Mrs. Jack faintly chuckled, then taking another look into the wreckage of the living room, and the creature on his kneepads still fondly forcing entrails from the insides of his doll, with a smile of idiot pertinacity, she was overcome again, pressed her handkerchief to her trembling mouth, and squeaked hysterically: "God!"

At this moment, the sculptor, Krock, who from the beginning had paid no attention to the circus, but had devoted himself exclusively to a methodical effort at seduction of every attractive woman in the gathering, approaching each in turn, and rubbing his legs, while he whispered intimate details concerning the condition of his varicose veins, now came up to Mrs. Jack, and whispered softly:

"I'm a great admirer of your work. . . . I should so much like to see you sometime and talk it over with you." During all this time while he whispered to her in this silly and repulsive whisper, he had been coming closer to her, meanwhile tenderly rubbing the insides of his heavy thigh, and now saying plaintively:

"I am very tired of standing up. I have varicose veins, and when I stand it hurts me—I wish we could go off to a quiet place and sit and talk!"

She had not caught the exact meaning of his whispered words, but their purport was plain because he had sidled up to her all the time until he was now almost straddling her. She looked around quickly with an alarmed glance and saw the face of her young lover, saw that it had now grown fierce and dark with passion, and that his fist had closed tightly in a menacing knot, and moving hastily away, she murmured: "Oh, yes, thank you Mr. Krock"—although she had not heard what he had said.

She put one hand quickly, warmly, upon the arm of the young man, and another upon the arm of Lily Mandell, and smiling, said in a soft and gentle tone, that had an almost rapt and brooding quality, as if she were speaking hypnotically to herself:

"These are the best! The best. The two I love, and both of them the best."

As she uttered these words, she drew them together and closed their hands in a gesture of friendship. Lily Mandell responded timidly, with an almost frightened look, and the young man flushed deeply, awkwardly and with uneasy constraint. Just for a moment he had looked up and caught the eyes of Hale, of Ernie, and of several other people fixed on him in a hard attentive stare, in which curiosity was mixed with cynical amusement. And so caught, so revealed, in all the anguish of his youth, his passion, and his jealousy, he suddenly felt naked and ashamed. It was the old look of the city that he knew so well. It was not wholly unaffectionate, but it was jaded, worn, and wearily experienced. It had in it also a touch of quick and eager curiosity, such as an old worn-out man might display in the hot passions, the quick and sensual heats, of hasty youth, but it was also wearily amused and jaded as if it knew that such ardours as love, or hate, or scalding jealousy were youthful follies which the years would cure.

He turned away, his face deeply, darkly flushed, clumsily holding Lily

Mandell's hand. And she, too, awkwardly self-conscious, ill at ease, looked at him helplessly with an expression that, in contrast to her customary arrogance, was timid, frightened, almost child-like.

Even as they stood there, holding hands with this awkward constraint, Lawrence Hirsch came up and joined them, saying in a tone of casual puzzlement:

"A curious performance, isn't it? I mean, I really can't quite make out—"

She turned on him almost furiously, so quickly and fiercely that he recoiled. His eyes had the look of a whipped dog.

"Esther" she cried, turning to her friend in a tone of yolky complaint, "If I don't get away from this—"

She did not say what "this" was, but her meaning was so evident that Hirsch winced involuntarily, then turned away with a look of naked anguish in his eye, at the same time saying casually:

"Oh, these are some of your latest designs, aren't they, Esther?" He strolled over to the wall and bending, examined them with professional curiosity:

"How interesting! Hm! I hadn't seen these. I wish you'd—"

Miss Mandell regarded him with a look of loathing, then turned toward her friend:

"Honestly, if I don't get some place! . . . These awful worms!" she muttered; then, kindly, in a tone of yolky protest she murmured vaguely, and to no one in particular:

"Why can't they go off and *die*—or something!—Oh, *darling!*" She turned impulsively to Mrs. Jack—"When you're so lovely!—Why do they have to bother you?" she said.

Mrs. Jack received this indefinite commiseration with a rapt and tender smile. Surveying both her lover and her friend with a soft and tender look, she took their hands in hers again, and said gently:

"These two! My two! The best. The best." She turned to the young man and said: "Lily is one of the finest and most beautiful people I have ever known." And turning to Miss Mandell, holding her lover by the hand and patting it as she spoke, she said in a low voice that glowed and rose with an exultant pride: "And *he*—he is the best! The highest and the best!" she said, in a kind of chant, "He is my music and my joy—my great angel—my great George!—the one I love the most in all the world!—Oh, Lily, he is meat, drink, bread, and wine to me—he fills my life until without him there is nothing in it—my demon, my great genius, my child!—Oh, Lily, if you knew him as I do!—You two," she murmured now softly as before, "If only you each knew the other better—Oh, you must!"

They stared at each other for a moment helplessly—the lover and his love's voluptuous friend: they stared at each other almost with strong terror, the woman with a frightened and yet wildly eager look, he fiercely, with all the anguish, all the repulsion of desire: he broke from her almost desperately, turned furiously upon his mistress and cried bitterly:

"Oh, you! In the name of God what are you trying to"—and then was baffled, maddened, and defeated, as he always was by the rose-sweet innocence of that trusting face, enigma of that guileless guile, that dew-fresh flower of baleful night and dark sophistries, so hued with innocence and morning—Oh thorny paradox! By that whole complex of this ancient and chameleon world, so much too old, too wise, too subtle, too mercurially woven of deceptive lights, of all the ancient troubling weathers of man's soul, to be here fathomed, here defined, by youth's harsh light, its fierce antitheses of light and shade, of truth and evil, good and bad—too hard, too complex, and too subtle for the fierce hurt, the anguish, madness, hope, and pride and faith and desperate love of youth.

"My two! The two I love," said Mrs. Jack raptly as before. "Now you must talk together—get to know each other as I know you both—I want to share my love for both of you with both."

"Oh, Esther," Mr. Hirsch, who had been examining the drawings on the wall, now called out in a tone of aroused excitement, "—I think this one here is *simply*"—

"Oh, *where*?" cried Lily desperately. "Can we never get away from him?" she muttered. "Is there nowhere we can go?"—

"Darling, why don't you two go in Edith's room. You can talk there: You'll be quiet."

Miss Mandell looked at the young man with desperate frightened eyes: at the door of the room they stood awkwardly for a moment, regarding each other helplessly. Then, instinctively they turned and looked in the direction of Mrs. Jack, as if seeking there some confirmation or some aid. And she, still following them with her rosy smiling little face, nodded her head affirmatively and happily, and again said softly, raptly, like a child: "My two."

"Oh, Esther," said Mr. Hirsch again, who had moved down nearer in his inspection of the drawings on the wall—just for a moment his naked look, full of terror, pain, and anguished pleading, met Miss Mandell—"I wonder if you could tell me—"

"Oh, that fool!" Miss Mandell muttered furiously, and went into the room. "Why can't these awful people—these—these *worms*—Why don't they *die*, or something?"—she murmured yolkily, with brooding disinterest, as before.

"He's after you, I guess," the young man said. "He doesn't seem to follow you, but he's always there."

"Oh—the *worm*!" she muttered. "I'd like to step on him!"

"I guess he wants you pretty bad," the young man said.

"It's—it's—" For a moment he paused, then grinned—"It's like a hot hound after a—"

"Stop!" she shrieked faintly. "You're terrible!"

"But is it." And, after a brief pause: "Are you going to marry him?"

"Him?" A whole lexicon of scorn was packed into that little word. "That—that worm." Then slowly, painfully she muttered:

"That greasy Kike"—

"No, Lawrence."—Mrs. Jack's voice, explanatory, sweetly patient, was nearer now: Mr. Hirsch was coming down the hall—"I did these last year:—You remember when the League was doing a show? They were going to follow it with Hedda—"

"Oh, but Esther! She's so lovely!" Lily Mandell said. They were facing each other now, close together—

"She's—she's the most beautiful!—the most glorious!—Oh, she loves you so!"—Her voice broke yolkily, half hysterically, as she spoke the words, and her hand came out instinctively upon his arm. Still standing apart, they were holding each other now clumsily, their hands resting on each other's arms, regarding each other with a desperate, searching, and half-frightened look—"If anything should happen to her!"—she whispered, breathing quickly now—"I mean, she is too beautiful!—If anything should hurt her!"

Her wheaten belly was against him now, they were holding to each other tightly: his own breath was coming hoarse and hard, he spoke thickly, furiously, caught there in a trap of lust and loathing, of sweltering desire and his own self-shame. He fairly grated through his teeth: "Oh she!—she!—" Then bitterly, desperately—"She sent us here! She put us here!"—Then furiously, as every torturing doubt of the whole tormenting complex returned to catch him in the web, and baffle him, he cried:

"—Oh, she must have known!—She's not so innocent as that!—She's planning something!—You—You *people*!" This in a strangling gasp, then savagely: "Oh damn you! Damn you!—Now, by God!—" They were locked together now in a fierce clasp, devouring each other with passionate kisses; they seemed to grow together, to become a single animal: locked lip to lip, and tongue to tongue, they consumed each other, her amorous belly passionately undulant into the hard thrusting cradle of his loins.

"You bitch!" he panted. "—You lovely bitch!—By God!" His grip about her tightened savagely. "—*I'll*"—

"—Don't hurt me!" she whimpered like a frightened child. "Oh darling, I'm so little. I'm afraid—don't hurt me. Oh, darling, darling, darling, darling—Not here!" she panted, widening to his knee—"Not here! —Oh darling, darling, darling." They fell over on the bed, locked together in the fierce undulations of the embrace, her breast, round, melon-heavy, nippled like a bud, was in his hand, her dress came up above her knees, his fierce fingers were gripped bruisingly in the sensual opulence of her creamy, slightly yellow thighs, and all the while her wild dark head rolled on the pillow, tossed like storm, she cried out weeping bitterly—"Oh God! God!—All that beauty—All that pain—That loveliness inside me—God! God! God!—"

Mr. Lawrence Hirsch was wounded sorrowfully, but he could wait.

*　　*　　*　　*　　*

"—Oh, Esther!—What is this?—How very interesting—" The voice was very close now, casual, anguish-laden, they could fairly hear him sweating blood. The voice came close: panting, they scrambled to their feet—"Oh, Esther"—breathing heavily, wildeyed, disarranged, they stood erect, reeling, stupidly staring at the door—

"What have you here?"—The casual tone was cracking underneath the strain as Mr. Hirsch approached that fatal door. His gloom cropped face of agony peered in, the eyeballs shot with lacings of bright red, the whole glance pleading like a beaten dog's—"Oh a room. Hm, now— Yes—Oh, hello, Lily—I didn't know you were in here—"

Panting, she regarded him with a black look of smouldering contempt.

"But how very interesting, Esther!"—More himself again, he turned to her, and she looked at him, at *them*, at everyone with that rosy smile of trustful innocence. "I had no idea there were so many of them—"

And the climax of that grotesque comedy—so mixed of loathing, anguish, broken faith, the hot lust of animals so obscenely fuming underneath its undeceptive mash of skilled urbanity—was over. And the chase was on: the actors in the play were on their way again.

THE GUESTS DEPARTING

· · ·

THE FIRE

· · ·

But now there was the sound of voices in the living room. The performance had ended and there was a ripple of perfunctory applause when
Mr. Logan finished. The fashionable young people of his own group
clustered around him, chattering congratulations, and then, without
paying attention to any of the other guests, or without a word of thanks to
their hostess, they began to leave.

Other people now gathered around Mrs. Jack and made their fare-
wells. Meanwhile, Mr. Logan was busy with his enormous valises, his
wire dolls, the general wreckage he had created. People began to leave
singly and in pairs and groups until presently there was no one left
except those intimates and friends who are usually the last to leave a big
party, Mrs. Jack and her family, her lover, Miss Mandell, Amy Van Leer
and Mr. Logan. Already a curious and rather troubling change was
apparent in the atmosphere of the whole place. It was an atmosphere of
completion, of absence, of departure: it was the atmosphere one feels in
a house the day after Christmas, or the hour after a wedding or when
most of the passengers have disembarked from a great liner at one of the
channel ports, leaving only a small, and rather sorrowful remnant who
know the voyage is really over, and who are now just marking time for a
few hours until their own destination is reached.

Mrs. Jack looked at Piggy Logan and at the wreckage he had made of a large part of her fine room with an air of bewilderment, then turned doubtfully and with a questioning look to Lily Mandell. The two women looked at each other for a moment, then Mrs. Jack shrugged her shoulders in a protesting, helpless way as if to say: "Can you understand all this? What has happened?"—

And then, catching her friend's expression of drowsy arrogance, her own face suddenly flushed crimson, she cast her head back and laughed helplessly, hysterically, saying: "God!"

Meanwhile the others looked at Mr. Logan, who seemed absorbed with the litter that surrounded him, utterly and happily oblivious of their presence, with varied expressions of bewilderment, and amusement, and irony. Mr. Jack, who had been unable to stand the full protraction of the performance now appeared again, stared in at the kneeling figure of Mr. Logan and at all the wreckage of which he was the author then turning to his wife and son with a protesting gesture he said: "What is it?" Then he retired again, leaving everybody helplessly convulsed with hysterical laughter.

Amy Van Leer stretched herself out flat on the carpet beside Ernie with her hands beneath her head and began to talk to him in her rapid, eager, excited, curiously husky voice. Miss Mandell surveyed Mr. Logan with looks of undisguised distaste. Meanwhile the maids were busily clearing up the debris of the party—glasses, bottles, bowls of ice, and so on, and Molly was quietly and busily engaged putting the books back on their shelves. The other people looked on rather helplessly at Mr. Logan and his work, obviously at a loss what to do, and waiting evidently for the young man's departure.

The happy confusion, the thronging tumult of the party had now ended. The guests had departed, the place had grown back into its wonted quiet, and the unceasing city, like an engine of immortal life and movement which had been for the moment forgotten and shut out, now closed in upon these lives again, pervaded these great walls: the noises of the street were heard again.

Outside, below them, there was the sound of a fire truck, the rapid clanging of a bell. It turned the corner into Madison and thundered excitingly past the big building. Mrs. Jack went to the window and looked out. Other trucks now appeared from various directions until four or five had gone by.

"I wonder where the fire can be," she remarked presently in a tone of detached curiosity. Another truck roared down and thundered into

Madison. "It must be quite a big one, too—six trucks have driven past: I wonder where it is. It must be somewhere in this neighborhood."

For a moment the location of the fire absorbed the idle speculation of the group, but presently they began to look again at Mr. Logan. His labors were now, apparently, at long last, almost over. He began to close his big valises and adjust the straps.

At this moment Lily Mandell turned her head with an air of wakened curiosity in the direction of the hall, sniffed sharply, and suddenly said: "Does anyone smell smoke?"

"Hah? What?"—said Mrs. Jack with a puzzled air. And then, suddenly and sniffing sharply, she cried excitedly: "But yes! There is quite a strong smell of smoke out here. I think it would be just as well if we got out of the building until we find out what is wrong."

Mrs. Jack's rosy face was now burning with excitement. "But isn't it queer?" she appealed to everyone, in a protesting and excited tone—"I mean, it is so strange after the party and—to think that it should be in this building—I mean—" She was evidently not quite certain what she meant and looked around her rather helplessly. "Well, then—" she said indefinitely, "I suppose we'd better, until we find out what it is. Oh, Mr. Logan!—" She lifted her voice as she spoke to him, and in a moment he lifted his round and heavy face with an expression of inquiring and cherubic innocence—"I say—I think perhaps we'd all better get out, Mr. Logan, until we find out where the fire is. Are you ready?"

"Yes, of course," said Mr. Logan cheerfully, "but fire?" he said, in a puzzled tone, "What fire? Is there a fire?"

"I think the building is on fire," said Ernie smoothly, but with an edge of heavy irony, "so perhaps we'd better all get out—that is, unless you prefer to stay."

"On no," said Mr. Logan cheerfully, and clumsily getting to his feet, "I am quite ready, thank you, except for changing to my clothes—"

"I think that had better wait," said Ernie.

"Oh those girls!" cried Mrs. Jack suddenly, and snapping the ring on and off her finger, she walked quickly toward the dining room. "Molly—Janie—Lily! Girls! We're going to have to get out—there's a fire somewhere in the building. You'll have to get out until we find out where it is!"

"Fire, Mrs. Jack?" said Molly rather stupidly, staring at her mistress, and Mrs. Jack, glancing quickly at her, saw her dull eye, and her flushed face, and thought: "Oh, she's been at it again!"

"Yes, Molly, fire" she said, and impatiently, "Get all the girls together and tell them they'll have to come along with us—and Oh! Cook!—" she cried quickly—"Where is Cookie? Go get her someone. Tell her she'll have to come too!"

The news obviously confused and upset the girls. They looked helplessly at one another then they began to move aimlessly around, as if no longer certain what to do.

"Shall we take our things, Mrs. Jack?" said Molly, looking at her stupidly. "Will we have time to pack?"

"Oh, of course not, Molly!" cried Mrs. Jack impatiently. "We're not going anywhere! No one is moving out! We're simply getting out till we find out where the fire is and how bad it is!—And Molly, please get Cook and bring her with you! You know how rattled and confused she gets!"

"Yes'm," said Molly, and staring at her helplessly, "and is that all?"

"Yes, Molly, of course, and do please hurry! We'll be waiting for you here!"

"Yes'm," said Molly as before, hesitated a little, then said—"And will that be all, mum?—I mean," and gulped, "will we need anything?"

"Oh, Molly, no, in heaven's name!" cried Mrs. Jack, beginning to slip the ring on and off her nervous hand. "Nothing except your coats. Tell all the girls and Cook to wear their coats!"

"Yes'm," said Molly, dumbly, hesitated, and in a moment, looking fuddled and confused, she went uncertainly through the dining room to the kitchen.

Ernie meanwhile had gone out into the hall and was ringing the elevator bell. The others joined him there. He rang persistently and presently the voice of John, the elevator man, was heard shouting up the shaft from a floor or two below: "All right! All right! I'll be right up, folks, as soon as I take down this load!"

The sound of people's voices, excited, chattering, could be heard down the shaft on the floor below, and presently the elevator door closed and the elevator went away.

Meanwhile, Mrs. Jack, her family and her guests, waited in the hall. The smell of smoke in the hallway was now quite pronounced and although no one was seriously alarmed all of them were conscious of the nervous tension. Presently the sound of the elevator could be heard again as it came up. It mounted and then suddenly paused somewhere half a flight or two below them. The elevator man could be heard working his lever and fooling with the door. There was no response.

Ernie rang again impatiently and hammered on the door, and in a moment more the man shouted up so clearly that all of them could hear him very plainly: "Mr. Jack, will you all please use the service entrance? The elevator's out of order: I can't go any farther."

The people gathered in the hall now looked at one another with an air of bewildered and rather troubled surprise. In a moment, Ernie said: "Well, that's that. I suppose that means we'll have to walk down."

He and his father put on derby hats, donned overcoats, and without another word started down the hall.

At this moment all the lights went out. The place was plunged in inky blackness. There was just a brief, a rather terrifying moment, when the women caught their breaths sharply. In the darkness the smell of the smoke was perceptively stronger, more acrid and biting than it had ever been. Molly moaned a little and the maids began to mill around like stricken cattle. But they quieted down when they heard the comforting assurance of Ernie's quiet voice speaking in the dark: "Mother, we'll have to light candles. Can you tell me where they are?"

She told him. He reached into a table drawer, pulled out a flashlight, and went back through the dining room into the kitchen. In a few moments he reappeared with a box of tallow candles. He gave everyone a candle and lighted them. The procession was really now a somewhat ghostly one. The women lifted their candles and looked at each other with an air of bewildered surmise. Mrs. Jack, deeply excited, but still retaining her customary interest in events, held up her candle and turned questioningly to the young man who was her lover. "Isn't it strange?" she whispered—"Isn't it the strangest thing? I mean the party— all the people—and then this"—And holding up her candle she looked about her at that ghostly company and suddenly he was filled with love and tenderness for her, because he knew the woman like himself had the mystery and strangeness of all life, all love in her heart.

In the steady flame of their upheld candles the faces of the maids and Cookie showed dazed, bewildered, and somewhat frightened. Cookie grinned confusedly and muttered jargon to herself. Mr. Jack and Ernie, their derby hats fixed firmly now on top of their well-kept heads, raised their candles and led the way. The women followed after, and the young man came last of all. Mrs. Jack, just in front of her young lover, was bringing up the end of the procession behind her guests and had reached the door that opened out to the service landing when she noticed a confusion in the line and glanced back along the hallway, and saw two teetering candles disappearing in the general direction of the kitchen. It was Cook and Molly.

"Oh Lord!" cried Mrs. Jack with an accent of exasperation and despair. "What on earth are they trying to do? Oh, Molly!" She raised her voice sharply. Cook had already disappeared but Molly heard her and turned in a bewildered way. "Oh, Molly, in God's name, where *are* you going?" cried Mrs. Jack impatiently.

"Why—why, mum,—I just thought I'd go back here and get some things," said Molly in a confused and thickened tone.

"No, you're *not* either!" cried Mrs. Jack furiously thinking bitterly at the same moment, "she probably thought she'd sneak back there and get a drink." "You don't need any things." She lifted her voice sharply again. "You come right along with us! And where is Cook?" she cried in an exasperated tone, then seeing the two bewildered looking girls, Lily and Janie, milling around her helplessly, she seized them impatiently and gave them a little push towards the door: "Oh, you girls get out!" she cried. "What are you gawking at?"

Then she came fuming back along the hall in the direction of her lover, who had gone after the bewildered Molly, herded her down the hall, and was now going into the kitchen to find Cook. Mrs. Jack followed him into the kitchen with her candle in her hand, said anxiously, "Are you there, darling?" And then raising her voice sharply: "Oh, Cook! Cook! Where are you?"

Suddenly, like a spectral visitant, still holding her candle, and flitting from room to room down the narrow hallway of the servant's quarters Cook appeared. Mrs. Jack cried out angrily: "Oh, Cookie! What in the name of God are you doing!" At the same time she thought to herself again, as she had thought so many times before, "She's probably an old miser, I suppose she's got her wad hoarded away back there somewhere. That's why she hates to leave."

"Cook!" she cried again sharply with peremptory command. "You've simply got to come on now? We're waiting on you." Cook glided away down the hallway with spectral stealth and disappeared into her room. After another fuming silence Mrs. Jack turned to the young man, they regarded each other for a moment in that strange light and circumstance with perplexed and troubled faces and suddenly both laughed explosively.

"My God!" cried Mrs. Jack. "Isn't it the damnedest—"

At this moment Cook, flitting like a phantom, appeared again; they

yelled at her as she flitted away and followed her into one of the maids'
bedrooms and caught her in the act of locking herself away into a
bathroom. "Cook!" cried Mrs. Jack, angrily.

"You've simply got to come on now!"

Cook goggled at her and sneered infuriatingly, and then muttered
some incomprehensible jargon, in an ingratiating tone.

"Do you hear, Cook?" Mrs. Jack cried furiously. "You've got to come
now! You can't stay here any longer."

"Augenblick! Augenblick!" muttered Cook cajolingly—In a moment
she reappeared again, thrusting something into her bosom, and still
looking unwillingly behind her, she was still obviously unwilling to
leave, but allowed herself to be prodded, herded, pushed, and propelled
down the servants' hallway and out into the main part of the apartment.

When Mrs. Jack got out into the broad front corridor again she found
to her consternation that although the others had gone out, Molly had
not yet made her departure and that the other two maids had sidled back
into the hallway and were huddled together talking in dazed whispers.
When they saw Mrs. Jack and Cook they began to sidle toward their
mistress as if attracted by a magnet.

"Oh, no, you're not either!" she cried furiously. "You girls are not
coming back in here! You get out now—this instant!"

And herding Cook before her, and shooing the others along as if she
were mothering a flock of silly chickens, she drove them down the hall
and through the door on to the service landing.

The others were now gathered here, waiting while Ernie tested the
bell of the service elevator. There was no response in reply to his repeated efforts and in a few moments he remarked: "Well, I suppose
there's nothing for us to do now except to walk down."

Mr. Jack had apparently reached this conclusion on his own account
and had started down the nine flights of concrete stairs that led to the
ground floor and safety. In a moment all the others followed him.

THE FIRE

. . .

THE OUTPOURING OF THE HONEYCOMB

. . .

The electric lights in the service hallways were still burning dimly. But the smell of smoke had noticeably increased. The smoke, in fact, had now become quite dense and filled the air with floating filaments and shifting plumes that made breathing acrid and uncomfortable.

And the service stairs from top to bottom was providing an astounding spectacle. Doors were opening now on every floor and other tenants of the building, and their servants and their guests, were coming out to swell the tide of refugees which now marched steadily downstairs.

It was an extraordinary and bizarre conglomeration—a parade of such fantastic quality as had never been witnessed in the world before. And it was a composite of classes, types, and characters that could have been found no where else in the world at the time save in such a building as this. It is probable that most of these people had never seen their neighbors before now. But now, because excitement and their need for communication had broken through the walls of their reserve, they all showed a spirit of fellowship, of friendliness, and of help which that enormous honeycomb of life had never seen before.

It was an astounding aggregation. There were people fully attired for the evening in splendid evening dress, and beautiful women blazing with jewels and wearing costly wraps. There were other people who had apparently gone to bed when the fire alarm had sounded, and who were now attired in pajamas, slippers, dressing gowns, kimonos, or whatever easy and convenient garment they could snatch up in the stress and excitement of the moment. There were young people and there were old people. There were people of every kind and quality and age and physical variation.

And in addition to these there was a babel of strange tongues, the excited jargons of a dozen races. There were German cooks and there were French maids. There were English chauffeurs and there were Irish serving girls. There were Swedes and Danes and Italians and Norwegians, with a sprinkling of white Russians. There were Poles and Czechs and Austrians, Negroes, and Hungarians; and all of these poured out on the landing stages of the service stairway helter-skelter, were poured out in a noisy, chattering gesticulating tide to join in with their lords and masters, united now in seeking refuge, their interests all united now in their common pursuit of safety.

As the refugees neared the ground floor, helmeted and coated firemen began to come up the stairs. A few policemen came up after them and these men tried in various ways to allay any panic or alarm that anyone may have felt.

"It's all right, folks! Everything's okay!" one glib policeman cried cheerfully as he came up past the members of Mrs. Jack's party. "The fire's over now."

These words, spoken really for the sake of quieting confusion and alarm and of expediting the orderly progress of the tenants in the building, had an opposite effect from the one which the big policeman wanted to produce. One of the male members of Mrs. Jack's party, the young man, who was bringing up the end of the procession, paused upon hearing the policeman's reassuring words, spoke to the others and turned, about to retrace his way upstairs again.

As he did so, he saw that the effect upon the policeman had been alarming. The man was stationed half a flight above him on the landing, and as he started to mount the stairs again, he saw the policeman was making frantic gestures to him and looking at him with an agonized face, the whole effect of which was silently and desperately to entreat him not to come back any further or to encourage any of the others to come back, but to leave the building as quickly as possible.

So warned and so exhorted, the refugee turned again and hastened down the stairs. As he did so, he could hear some tapping and hammering noises from the service elevator shaft. He paused and listened for a moment: the tapping began, then stopped—began again—and stopped again.

The space outside the great apartment building, or rather *between* it—for the tremendous building was constructed in the shape of a hollow square—was now a wonderful spectacle. No more imposing stage for the amazing scene could have been provided. This great central court or hollow was covered for the most part with loose gravel and there was also two or three terraces or earthy beds of flowers and plants built up above the general level, and surrounded by low walls.

The sides of the tremendous building the whole way around were flanked by a broad brick pavement on which opened at evenly spaced intervals the entrances into the big apartment house and by arches which also ran the whole way around and flanked the walk. The effect of this arrangement was to give the whole place, court and all, something of the appearance of an enormous cloister—a cloister different, vaster, and more modern than any other one which had been seen, a cloister whose mighty walls soared fourteen flights into the air, and whose beetling sides were still blazing with all the thrilling evocation of night lights, one thousand radiant squares of warmth, of wealth, of passion, beauty, and of love, one thousand cells still burning with all the huge deposit of their still-recent, just-departed life, with a whole universe of flesh, and blood, a world incarnate with all the ecstasy, anguish, hatred, joy, and vexed intrigue that life could know, or that the heat and hunger of man's high enfamished soul could ever compass—with all the magic, all the loveliness and grace, the whole sky-flung faery of the marvelous, the nocturnal, the unceasing everlasting city.

And this great cloistered space was now filled surely with one of the strangest companies of the devout which any cloister had ever seen—a company of all sizes, kinds, and ages, dressed variously in costumes that went all the way from full evening dress to simply pajamas, from the bare back and sleeveless arms of a lady's splendid gown to the modest uniform of a maid, and from white ties and full tails to a chauffeur's livery. Here, around the four sides of their great cloister, pouring out of two dozen entry ways in a milling and gesticulating stream, adding constantly to the shuffling, bewildered, motley crowd that packed the gravel court, the babel of their own tumultuous tongues, a horde of people were now constantly flooding out of the huge honeycomb and adding their numbers to the assembled crowd.

Seen so, the tremendous pageantry of the scene was overwhelming in the range, the power, the variety, and the miraculous *compression* of its reality and beauty, and, like every high and ultimate reality, the scene had in it something of the nearness, the intensity of a vision, a nearness and intensity that was so wonderful, so *real*, that it attained an almost supernatural, unbelievable quality. Anyone looking at that scene would feel instantly, and with a still wonder in the heart, that he would never see such a thing again—that here, miraculously compressed, was assembled before him the whole theatre of human life—a universe such as few people ever see in a whole life time, and which can be brought before them only by the tremendous vision, the combining genius of a Shakespeare or a Brueghel.

It was really like the scene of an appalling shipwreck—one of those great shipwrecks of modern times, where a great liner, still ablaze with lights along the whole stern's sweep of her superhuman length, her life gored out upon an iceberg, keeling slowly to the racing slant of her proud funnels with her whole great company of people—the crew, the passengers, the rich, the poor, the mighty and the lowly—all the huge honeycomb of life that goes down to the bottom of a great ship's hollowed depths—assembled now, at this last hour of peril, in a living fellowship—the whole family of earth, and all its classes, at length united on these slanting decks.

This scene here now in this great cloister was like this—except that the ship was this enfabled rock beneath their feet, the ship's company the whole company of life, of earth, and of the swarming and unceasing city.

As yet few people seemed fully to have comprehended the full significance of the event which had thus unceremoniously dumped them out of their sleek nest into the open weather. The only people, indeed, who did now seem to be aware of peril or an immediacy of danger which touched their own lives and fortunes were isolated individuals here and there whose own welfare and interest had in some way been touched.

At this moment, in fact, a window on the first floor on the opposite side of the building flew up and a man with a bald head and a pink, excited face appeared at the window. It was instantly apparent from his tone and manner that under the pressure of these events the man was on the verge of emotional collapse. He immediately cried out loudly in a high, rather fat tone that already was being shaken by incipient hysteria: "Mary!—Mary!—" his voice rose almost to a scream as he sought for her below and a woman in the crowd coming forward below the window looked up and said quietly, "Yes, Charles."

"I can't find the key!" he cried in a trembling voice. ". . . and the door's locked! I can't get out!" he almost screamed.

"Oh, Charles," the woman said in a quieter tone in which perhaps some sorrow was evident, "don't get so excited, dear. You're in no danger —and the key is bound to be there somewhere. I'm sure you'll find it if you look."

"But I tell you it isn't here," he babbled in a high trembling tone. "I've looked, and it's not here. I can't find it!—Here, you fellows!" he shouted at a group of firemen who were dragging a heavy hose across the gravel court, "I'm locked in here!—I want out of here!—"

Most of the firemen paid no attention to him at all, but one of them raised his head for a moment, looked at him, and then saying briefly: "Okay, chief!" resumed his work and paid no further attention to the man.

"Do you hear me?—" the man screamed, "You fireman you!—I tell you—"

"Dad. Dad—" a young man beside the woman on the ground now spoke quietly to the flushed, excited man in the open window above. "Don't get excited—You're in no danger there. All the fire is on the other side—They'll let you out in a moment when they can get to you."

Elsewhere—from the very entrance, indeed, from which the Jacks had issued, a man in evening clothes had been staggering in and out accompanied by two other men, one of whom was a chauffeur and one his butler, with great loads of ponderous ledgers. He had already accumulated a staggering pile of them, which he was stacking up on the gravel and leaving in the guardianship of the butler. This man's activities from the beginning had been as furiously self-absorbed, as completely buried in his own work, as if he was completely unconscious of every one around him and cared nothing for anyone's activity except his own. Now, as he again prepared to rush into the smoke-filled corridor with his chauffeur, he was stopped by the police.

"I'm sorry, sir," the policeman said, "but you can't go in there again. We've got orders not to let anyone else in."

"But I tell you!" the man shouted, "I've got to. I'm Henry J. Baer!"— he mentioned the name of a man who was at that time famous in the motion picture industry, and whose accounts and earnings had only recently been called into investigation by a board of Governmental inquiry. "There are seventy-five million dollars worth of records in my apartment," the man shouted, "and I've got to get them out! They've got to be saved!" He tried to thrust by again but the policeman blocked the way, barred his entrance, and thrust him back.

"I'm sorry, Mr. Baer," he said obdurately, "but we have our orders. You can't come in."

The effect of this refusal upon the man was instantaneous and shocking. If he had been King Croesus, forced to stand by idly while he saw all of his huge treasures go up in flame and smoke, he could not have been more maddened. He became like a wild animal, he lost any vestige of dignity or self-respect which he might heretofore have had. The whole principle of his life, which was that money is the only thing in life that counts and that people will do anything for money—the naked philosophy of tooth and claw which, in moments of security and in comfort, was veiled beneath a velvet sheath—now became ragingly insistent to the exclusion of every other value.

A tall, dark man, with a rapacious beak-nosed face, he became now like a beast of prey. He went charging in among the people, offering everyone, any stranger that he saw, fabulous sums of money if they would go with him to help in the salvation of his cherished records. He saw a group of firemen dragging a great hose into position and he rushed up to them, seizing one of them by the arm in his frantic eagerness and shaking him, crying: "I'm Henry J. Baer—I live in there! You've got to help me! I'll give any man here ten thousand dollars if he'll help me get my records out!"

The man whom he had thus addressed and interrupted, a burly fireman with a weathered face, turned now and spoke: "On your way, Mac!" he said.

"But I tell you!" the man shouted, "You don't know who I am. I'm—"

"I don't care who you are!" the fireman said. "On your way now! We've got work to do!" and roughly, he pushed the Croesus back.

Most of the crowd, however, was quieter, more bewildered. For some time the people shifted and moved about, taking curious side looks at one another out of the corners of their eyes. For most of them it was undoubtedly an illuminating experience—for all of them, certainly, the first time that they had had the opportunity of appraising at first hand and, so to speak, unprepared, the full personnel of the great building.

People who would never, under any ordinary circumstances, mingle with one another were now seen laughing and talking together with the familiarity of long acquaintanceship. A famous courtesan, wearing a chinchilla coat which her aged but fabulously wealthy lover had given

her, and which must have cost a king's ransom, now took off this magnificent garment and, walking over to an elderly woman with a delicate
and patrician face, she threw the coat over this woman's thinly covered
shoulders, at the same time, saying in a tough but somehow kindly little
voice:

"You wear this, darling. You look cold."

And the woman, after a startled expression had for a moment crossed
her proud and sensitive face, smiled graciously and thanked her tarnished sister in a sweet tone; then the two women stood talking together
like old friends.

Elsewhere, a group of eager idol-worshipping girls had gathered
around a famous comedienne of the revue and musical comedy stage.
And this woman, an Englishwoman with a beautiful small head, and the
instinctive elegance, the fine features and the figure of an aristocrat was
delighting these adoring children by spontaneously carrying on for
them in the comic vein for which she was famous.

"Tell me, my lambs," she was saying in her cool clipped tones, "Do
you like me with—or without—my face?"—As she uttered these words,
she threw her lovely features out of shape in a rubbery grimace that was
irresistibly comical, and instantly was herself again, cool, clipped,
poised, and elegant, going from one hilarity to another with a comic
inventiveness that was wonderful, and that gained in effectiveness because its essentially bawdy quality was always conveyed with the imperturbable elegance, the exquisite refinement of a great lady.

Meanwhile, her companion, another tall and beautiful Englishwoman with a lovely voice, who was also a famous actress of the comic
stage, was listening to the fervent adorations of an earnest little woman
who looked as if she might have been a school teacher, as if she were
enchanted with these banal platitudes and had never listened to such
understanding and delightful comment on her act in her whole life.

Elsewhere, a haughty old Bourbon of the Knickerbocker type was
seen engaged in earnest conversation with a Tammany politician whose
corrupt plunderings were notorious, and whose companionship, in any
social sense, the Bourbon would have spurned indignantly an hour
before.

Proud aristocrats of patrician lineage, whose names appeared but
rarely in the most exclusive gatherings of the aristocracy could be seen
chatting familiarly with the plebeian parvenus of the new rich who had
got their name and money both together, only yesterday.

And so it went, everywhere one looked:—one saw haughty gentiles with rich Jews; stately ladies with musical comedy actresses; a woman famous for her charities with a celebrated whore.

Curiously, the appraisal was an increasingly friendly one. It was as if the stress of danger, the shock of surprise, the informality of their attire had created the feeling of mutual interest and affection which no amount of formal meeting could have brought about. People who had never seen one another before, people who had never spoken to one another, now began to move about, to greet one another with friendly smiles and to engage familiarly with other people who up to that time had been complete strangers to them.

Even the servants—the French chauffeurs, the Irish maids, the German cooks, and so on—under these informal circumstances, were now beginning to fraternize and to talk to one another as they had never done before.

In one place a group of liveried chauffeurs had gathered together and were furiously discussing politics and the problem of international economy, the chief disputants being a plump Frenchman with a waxed moustache, whose sentiments were decidedly revolutionary, and an American, a little man with corky legs, a tough seamed face, a birdy eye, and the quick impatient movements of the city.

The scene, the situation, and the contrast between these two men was absurdly funny. The plump Frenchman, his cheeks pink with excitement, was talking and gesticulating volubly: he would get so excited that he would lean forward with the fingers of one plump hand closed daintily in a descriptive circle that meant—everything! The air about him fairly screeched with objurgations, expletives, impassioned cries of *"Mais oui!—Mais oui! Absolument!—C'est le vérité!"*—or with laughs of maddened exasperation as if the knowledge that such stupidity could exist was more than he could endure:

"—Mais non!—Mais non!—Vous avez tort—Mais c'est stupide!" he would cry, throwing his plump arms up in a gesture of defeat, and turning away with an exasperated laugh as if he could endure it no longer, and was departing—only to return immediately, talking and gesticulating more furiously than ever.

Meanwhile, the target of this deluge, the little American with the corky legs and the birdy eye was listening with a look of cynical impassivity, leaning against the wall of a terrace, taking an occasional puff at a cigarette, and with an air that seemed to say: "O.K.—O.K.—Frenchy —When you get through spouting, maybe *I'll* have something to say."

"*Seulement un mot!*" the Frenchman finally declared, when he had exhausted his vocabulary and his breath. "One vord!" he cried impressively, drawing himself up to his full five feet three, and holding one plump finger in the air, as if he were about to deliver Holy Writ—"I'ave to say one vord more!"

"O.K.! O.K.!" said the corky little American with an air of cynical weariness—"Only don't take more than an hour and a half to say it! . . . The trouble with you guys," he went on in a moment, after a preliminary puff upon his cigarette, "is that you have been over there all your life where you ain't been used to nothing—and the moment you get over here where you can live like a human being you want to tear it all down—"

"*Mais non!*" the Frenchman cried in a tone of impassioned protest. ". . . *Mais c'est stupide!*" he turned to the whole company in a gesture of exasperated appeal—"*C'est—*"

"Noos! I got noos for you!"—another chauffeur, obviously of Germanic origin, with bright blue eyes, and a nut-cracker face somewhat reminiscent of a vulture's, at this moment rejoined the group with an air of elated discovery—"I haf been mit a drifer who has liffed in Rooshia and he says that conditions there far *worser* are—"

"Non! Non!" the Frenchman shouted, red in the face with anger and protest "*Ce n'est pas—*"

"Oh, for Christ's sake!" the American said, tossing his cigarette away, with a gesture of impatience and disgust—"Why don't you guys wake up? This ain't Russia! You're in America!"—And the heated and confused dialog would become more spirited than ever.

Meanwhile, the crowd continued to watch curiously the labors of the firemen. The firemen had dragged in across the court from all directions a network of great white hose. Squadrons of helmeted men would dash into the smoky corridors from time to time, some would go upstairs, others would emerge from the lower regions of the basements and confer intimately with their chiefs and leaders.

As for the crowd itself, save for the unmistakable presence of smoke in the halls and corridors, it was in ignorance concerning the cause and extent of the fire. There was, indeed, at first, save for this mist of acrid smoke in the hallways, little evidence of fire.

But now the indications became much plainer. For some time now upon the very top floor of the south wing—just three floors indeed above Mrs. Jack's apartment and in the vicinity of her husband's bedroom,

infrequent wisps of smoke had been curling through the open window of a room in which a light now somewhat somberly had been left
burning.

Now the amount of smoke began to increase in volume and in density and suddenly a great billowing puff of oily black smoke accompanied by a dancing fire of sparks burst through the open window. And,
as it did, the whole crowd drew in its single and collected breath in a
sharp intake of excitement in which a curious and disturbing eagerness—the strange wild joy that people feel when they see fire, even if fire
means ruin or peril to them or their neighbors—was evident.

Steadily the amount of smoke increased in density and volume.
Nothing apparently was as yet affected except that single room on top,
but the black and oily looking smoke was now billowing out in belching
folds and the smoke itself in the room within was colored luridly by the
sinister and unmistakable glow of fire.

Mrs. Jack gazed upward with a rapt, a fascinated gaze. "How terrible!"
she thought, "How terrible!—but God! How beautiful it is."

Mrs. Jack turned to Hook with one hand raised and lightly clenched
against her breast, and whispered slowly: "Steve—isn't it the strangest—I
mean isn't it the most—" She did not finish, but with her face deeply
flushed, her eyes quietly, deeply concerned with the sense of wonder
that she felt and that she was trying to convey, she just stood there with
her hand loosely clenched and looked at him.

He understood her perfectly—too, too well. His heart was sick with
fear, with hunger and with fascinated wonder. For him it was too hard,
too strong, too full of terror, of wonder, awe, and overwhelming beauty
to be endured. He was sick with terror, fainting with it, he wanted to be
borne away, to be sealed hermetically somewhere, in some dead and
easeful air where free for ever more of violence and terror, of this consuming and heart-sickening fear that wracked his flesh, he could live in
everlasting peace and security, could live a life in death, if such it was—
but at least could live, live, live. And yet he could not leave it. He looked
at it with sick but fascinated eyes like some man mad with thirst who
drinks the waters of the sea and sickens with each drop he drinks, yet
cannot leave the wetness and the coolness, the unsated hungers of his
unslaked thirst. He looked at it and loved it with all the desperate ardour
of his sick hate. The wonder of it, the strangeness of it, the beauty and
the magic and the nearness of it, the richness of its overwhelming reality—a reality so near, so close, so overpowering in its impact that it had,

as all moments of supreme reality have, the quality of a vision or a dream, the concentrated omnipresence of a ship-wreck when the sloping decks of a tremendous liner, or of a gigantic catastrophe when a fabulous city such as this—a reality that is all the more overwhelming and unbelievable because one knows that it is so, one knows he has always foreseen it, has always imagined it, and now that it is here in its sheer texture, in its complex substance, now that it is here not a hand's breadth away, to be seen, felt, smelled, touched, visioned and experienced in a design that is if anything more overpowering than anything mind or imagination could contrive, becomes therefore more incredible. "It can't be true," thought Hook, "but here it is. It is not true—it's just a dream—it's unbelievable—but, here it is!"

And there it was. He didn't miss a thing. And yet he stood there, ridiculously, a derby hat upon his head, his pale, plump hands thrust into the pockets of his overcoat, the velvet collar turned up around his pale, plump neck, his butty figure turned as usual three-quarters away from the whole world, his heart simply sick with fear, and his haughty, pursey face, his heavy-lidded, wearily indifferent eyes, surveying the scene with a glance of mandarin contempt, as if to say: "Really, what is this curious assembly? Who are these extraordinary creatures that go milling about me? And why is everyone so frightfully eager, so terribly earnest about everything?"

A group of firemen thrust past him coarsely, dripping the powerful brass-nozzled end of a great hose. The hose slid coarsely through the gravel like the heavy tough-scaled hide of a giant boa-constrictor, and as the firemen passed him, Hook heard their booted and unconscious feet strike gravel and he saw the crude strength, the simple driving purpose of their coarse strong faces. And his life shrank back within him as he looked at them with butty heavy-eyed indifference. But his heart was sick. Sick with fear, with wonder, with hunger and with love of the unconscious strength, the joy, the energy and the violence of life itself.

A coarse voice, drunken, boisterous and too-near, cut the air about him. It jarred his ears, angered him, and made him timorously hope it would not come closer, invade him with its brutal and insensitive intrusion. Turning slightly toward Mrs. Jack, in answer to her whispered question, he murmured in a bored tone: "Um—yes. An interesting revelation of the native moeurs."

Amy Van Leer seemed really happy. It was not that her manner had changed. It was really as if, for the first time that evening, she had achieved, had found something that she was looking for. Really, it was now as if, for her, the party had just begun. Nothing had changed really very much in her manner or appearance. The quick impetuous speech —the broken interrupted semi-coherent phrases—the hoarse short laugh —the exuberant expletives—the lovely, golden, crisp-curled head, snub nose and freckled face were just the same. But it was as if all these explosive fragments had now been gathered into a kind of harmony. It was as if she had, so to speak, now been able to articulate herself. It was as if all the dissonance had been brought together to a congruent whole. It was as if all the splintered elements of her personality had now, under the strong and marvelous chemistry of the fire, been brought together into crystalline union. She was, in short, as she had been before except the torment was left out and wholeness was let in.

Poor child! For it would have been now instantly apparent to anyone who knew her and with half an idle look that, as were so many of the "lost" people that we know, she was not lost at all—if only there can be a fire all the time. The girl could not accept getting up in the morning or going to bed at night, or doing accustomed things in their accustomed order. But she could and did accept the fire. It did not seem to her at all strange. It seemed to her to be wonderful, the most natural thing in the world, instantly to be accepted and understood when it occurred. She was delighted with everything that happened: the movements of the firemen with the hose, the action of the police, the conduct of the crowd—all fascinated her, all aroused at once her eager and excited interest, her perfect understanding. She threw herself into the whole thing not as a spectator but as a vital and inspired participant. It was apparent at once that she knew people everywhere—she could be seen moving about from group to group, her gold head bobbing through the crowd, her voice eager, hoarse, short, abrupt, elated, infusing everyone somehow, wherever she went, with the energy and exuberance of her own ebullient spirit.

She returned to her own group: "I mean!—You know!—These firemen here!—" she gestured hurriedly. "When you think of what they have to know!—Of what they have to do!—I went to a big fire once!—" she shot out quickly in explanatory fashion "—a guy in the department was a friend of mine!—I mean."—She laughed hoarsely, elatedly, gesturing toward a group of helmeted men who dashed into a smoke-filled corridor with a tube of chemicals—"When you think of what they have to—" At this point there was a splintering crash within: Amy laughed hoarsely, jubilantly and made a quick and sudden little gesture as if this answered all: "After *all*, I mean!" she cried.

While this was going on, a young girl, fashionably attired in evening dress, and wearing a cloak had wandered casually up to the group and with that free democracy of speech which the collision of the fire seemed in some amazing way to have induced among all these people, now addressed herself, without a word of preliminary introduction, in the somewhat flat, nasal and almost toneless accents of the middle west, to Stephen Hook: "You don't think it's very bad, do you?" she said, looking up at the billowing puffs of oily smoke and flame that now really were belching formidably from one of the windows of the top floor. "I mean," she went on, before anyone had a chance to answer, "I *hope* it's not bad—"

Hook, who was simply terrified at her raw and unexpected intrusion, had turned three-quarters away from her and was looking at her side-ways with eyes that were almost closed and with a face of such mandarin-like aloofness and haughty contempt that it seemed it would have abashed a monkey. But it didn't phase the young girl a bit. Getting no answer from him, she turned in an explanatory fashion to Mrs. Jack: "I mean," she said again, "It will be just too bad if anything was wrong up there, wouldn't it?—"

Mrs. Jack answered quickly, her face full of friendly and earnest reassurance, in a gentle, quiet and comforting voice: "No, dear," she said. "I don't think it's bad at all." At the same moment, instinctively, she looked up quickly with trouble in her eyes at the billowing mass of smoke and flame which now, to tell the truth, not only looked "bad" but distinctly threatening. Then lowering her perturbed gaze quickly, she turned to the girl again and said encouragingly: "I'm sure everything is going to be all right."

"Well," said the girl, "I hope you're right—Because," she added, apparently as a kind of after-thought as she turned away. "That's Mama's room, and she's up there, it will be just too bad, won't it?—I mean, if it *is* too bad," she remarked casually in a flat and nasal tone that betrayed no more emotion than if she were asking for a glass of ice-water.

There was dead silence for a moment. Then Mrs. Jack turned to Hook with an earnest and even alarmed face as if she were not certain she had heard aright. Hook returned her glance with a sideways look of bored indifference. "But did you hear—" Mrs. Jack began in a bewildered and protesting tone.

"But I mean!" cried Amy at this moment, with a short, hoarse, even exultant laugh. "There you are! What I mean to say is—the whole thing's there!" she cried exultantly.

Mrs. Jack continued to look at Hook for a moment with her alarmed, questioning and deeply concerned face.

"Hah?" she cried eagerly and demanding, and getting no answer, suddenly her shoulders began to shake hysterically: "God!" she screamed faintly, "Isn't it the most—in all your life, did you ever hear—?"

"Um," he murmured noncommittally, as he turned completely away from her. For a moment she was shaken with wild laughter, and Hook, so sick, so frightened, so full of terror and of fear as he was, was yet pierced instantly with strong, incredible humor. His lips twitched slightly, just for the fraction of a second his plump shoulders quivered.

THE FIRE

. . .

THE TUNNELED ROCK

. . .

The lights around the cloistered sides of the building now flashed off, plunging the court in darkness save for such light as was provided by the billowing bursts of fiery smoke on the top floor. There was a restless stir in the crowd. In a few moments two or three young men, attired in evening dress, began to move back and forth among the dark mass of people, rather arrogantly flashing electric flashlights into the faces of various people they passed as if they now suspected everyone of being a jewel thief and of being determined, in this hour of crisis, to protect the vested accumulations of property and wealth.

The police now also began to move upon the crowd and good-naturedly but firmly, with outstretched arms, started to herd them back, out of the court, through the arches and out across the street. The streets surrounding the great building were laced and criss-crossed everywhere with a bewildering skein of hose, and the powerful throbbing of the fire machines could everywhere be heard. The residents of the great building were forced back across the street to take their place among the humbler following of the general public.

A number of the ladies finding themselves too thinly clad in the cool night air sought refuge in neighboring hotels or in the apartments of friends who lived in the neighborhood. Some people tired of waiting went to hotels to spend the night. Others hung on curiously, eager to see what the outcome might be: Mr. Jack, Ernie, Alma, Amy, and two or

225

three smart-looking young people of their acquaintance repaired to the Ritz, which was nearby. Mrs. Jack, her maids and servants, Miss Mandell and Logan, and a few of the other guests who still remained, looked on curiously for a while, but presently went into a small drug store near at hand, seated themselves at the counter, ordered coffee or sandwiches and engaged in eager chatter with many other people of their acquaintance who now filled the store.

The conversation of these people was friendly, casual, and pleasant: some were even gay. But in their talk it would have been possible to detect a note of perturbation, something troubled, puzzled, and uncertain, as if something was now happening which they could no longer fathom or control. And in this feeling they were right. They were the lords and masters of the earth, the proprietors of vast establishments, those vested with the high authorities and accustomed to command. And now they felt curiously helpless, no longer able to command anything, no longer even able to find out what was happening.

They had been firmly but unceremoniously herded out of their regal appointments, and now there was nothing for them to do except to wait, herded together in a drug store, or standing on the corner, huddled together in their wraps like shipwrecked voyagers, looking at one another with helpless eyes. They felt somehow that they had been caught up by some mysterious and relentless force, that they were being borne on helplessly by the momentum of some tremendous machine, that they were caught up and enmeshed in the ramifications of some tremendous web, some design so vast and complicated that they had not the faintest notion where it had its roots or what its pattern was, and that there was nothing for them to do except to be caught up and borne onwards, as unwitting of the power that ruled them as blind flies fastened to the revolutions of a wheel.

And in this feeling they were right.

* * * * *

For, in ways remote and far from the blind and troubled kennings of this helpless group, the giant web was at its mighty spinning: deep in the bowelled earth, the threads were being spun.

* * * * *

Not far from them, indeed, in one of the smoking corridors of that enormous hive, two men in helmets and in boots had met and now were talking quietly together.

"Did you find it?"

"Yes."

"Where is it?"

"It's in the basement, chief. It's not on the roof at all: the draft is taking it up a vent—but it's down here"—he pointed thumb-wise down below.

"Well, then, go get it: you know what to do."

"It looks bad, Chief. It's going to be hard to get."

"What's the trouble?"

"If we flood the basement we will flood the tracks, too. You know what that means."

The other man looked at him: for a moment their troubled glances met and held each other steadily.

Then the older man jerked his head, spoke shortly, started down the stairs:

"Come on," he said. "We're going down."

*   *   *   *   *

Far from the troubled kennings of these helpless folk also, deep in the tunnel's depth there in the bowelled earth, there was a room where lights were burning, and where it was always night.

There, now, a phone rang, and a man with a green eyeshade seated at the desk was there to answer it:

"Hello—oh, hello, Mike"—he listened carefully for a moment, suddenly jerked forward taut with interest, and pulled the cigarette out of his mouth: "The hell you say!—Where? On number thirty two!—They're going to flood it!—Oh, the hell!—"

*   *   *   *   *

Far from the kennings of these helpless folk, in these enormous congeries of dark, deep in the marvelous honeycombs of that bowelled rock, things began to happen with the speed of light, the beautiful complication of a vast design: lights changed and flashed, the marvelous lights, green, red, and yellow, silent, lovely, poignant as remembered grief, burned there upon the checkerboard of the eternal dark: all happened smoothly, there was no delay.

*   *   *   *   *

Six blocks away just where the mighty network of that amazing underworld begins its mighty flare, lights shifted, changed, and flared immortally: the Overland halted swiftly, but so smoothly that the passengers, already standing to debark, felt only a slight jar, were unaware that anything had happened.

Ahead, however, in the cab of the powerful electric locomotive which had pulled the great train the last miles of its continental span along the Hudson River, the engineer peered out and read the signs: He saw these shifting patterns of hard light against the dark, and swore:

"Now what the hell." Turning, he spoke quietly across the darkness to another man:

"We're going in on Twenty-One—I wonder what the hell has happened."

Smoothly, swiftly, the train slid forward again, the enormous network of cold rail flared out around it. And there, unknowing of these other lives, there in the tunnel's depths, five hundred men and women who had been hauled across the continent in one of the crack trains of the nation were sliding smoothly in now to their destination, each to his own end, his own goal, and his own desire in this immortal and unceasing web—which to a better end, a better goal, what man can say?

*   *   *   *   *

On the seventh landing of the service stairs, the foremen were working ruthlessly with axes. The place was dense with smoke: the sweaty men were wearing masks, and the only light they had to work by was that provided by a torchlight and a flare.

They had battered open the doorway of the elevator shaft, and one of them had lowered himself down on to the roof of the imprisoned elevator half a floor below, and was cutting in the roof with his sharp axe.

"Have you got it, Ed?"

"—O.K.—I'm almost through—Here it is."

The axe smashed through; there was a splintering crash, and then:

"O.K.—Wait a minute—Hand me down that flashlight, Tom—"

"See anything?"

And in a moment, quietly: "Yeah—I'm going in—Jim, you better come down too: I'll need you—"

There was a silence for a moment, then the man's quiet voice again:

"O.K.—I've got it—Here, Jim, reach down and get underneath the arms—Got it?—O.K. Tom, you'd better reach down and help, Jim—Good."

In such a way they lifted it from its imprisoned trap, looked at it for a

moment by the flare of their flashlight, and laid it down, not ungently—
something old and tired and dead and very pitiful—upon the floor.

* * * * *

At this moment Mrs. Jack went to the window of the drug store and
peered out at the great building across the street.

"I wonder if anything's happening over there," she said, and turning
to her friends with a puzzled and earnest look on her rosy little face, she
said: "Do you suppose it's over? Have they got it out?"

* * * * *

The cold immensity of those towering walls told nothing. But there
were other signs that it was really "out." The lines of hose that had
threaded the street in a thick skein were noticeably fewer, one could see
firemen pulling in the hose, and putting it back again into the wagon,
and now and then there was the heavy beating roar of a great engine as a
fire-truck thundered away. Firemen were coming from the building
putting their tools and apparatus back into their trucks: At the corner a
great engine throbbed quietly with a suggestion of departure, and although the police still held the line, and would not yet permit the
tenants to return to their apartments, there was every indication now that
the fire was over.

Meanwhile, the newspapermen, who had arrived upon the scene,
were beginning to come into the drug store to phone their stories to the
papers. They were a motley crew, a little shabby and threadbare, with
battered hats in which their press cards had been stuck, and occasionally
with the red noses of the speakeasy period.

It is hard to say why or how one knew that all these men were
members of the press. Yet anyone would have known it at once. The
signs were indefinable but unmistakable. There was something jaded in
the eye, something a little battered, worn, tarnished about the whole
man, something that got into his face, his tone, the way he walked, the
way he smoked a cigarette, even into the hang of his trousers, and
especially into his battered hat that told one that these were gentlemen
of the press.

It was something wearily receptive, wearily cynical, something that
said wearily: "*I* know, *I* know. But what's the story? What's the racket?"

And yet it was something that one liked, too, something corrupted
but still good, something that had once blazed with hope and fired with

The Tunneled Rock ⚘ 229

aspiration, something that said, "Sure. I used to think I had it in me too, and I'd have given my life to do something good. Now I'm just a whore. I'd sell my best friend out to get a story. I'd steal the glass eye out of an orphan's head to get a story. I'd betray your trust, your faith, your friendliness, twist everything you say around until all the sincerity, sense and honesty of what you say is made to sound like the meanderings of a buffoon or a clown—if I thought that it would make a better story. I don't give a damn for truth, for accuracy, for facts, for telling anything about you people here, your lives, your speech, the way you look, the way you really are, the special quality, tone and weather of this moment—of this fire—except insofar as it will help to make a story. I don't care for what is true, for what is right, for what is really important if I can get a special 'angle' on my story. There has been grief and love and ecstasy and pain and life and death tonight: a whole universe of living has been here enacted—but all of it doesn't matter a damn to me if I can only pick up something that will make the customers sit up tomorrow and rub their eyes—tell them that in the excitement last night Miss Lena Ginster's pet boa constrictor escaped from its cage and that the police and fire departments are still looking for it while Members of Fashionable Apartment House Dwell In Terror—So there I am, folks, with yellow fingers, weary eyeballs, a ginny breath, and what is left of last night's hangover, and I wish to God I could get to that telephone to send this story in, and the boss would tell me to go home, I'd like to go around to Eddy's place for sixteen or twenty highballs before I call it another day—but don't be too hard on me. Sure, I'd sell you out, of course. No man's name or any woman's reputation is safe with me—if I can make a story out of it—but at the bottom, I'm not such a bad guy, after all. I have violated the standards of decency again and again, but in my heart I've always wanted to be decent. I don't tell the truth, or I've twisted the truth around a thousand times until it has a different meaning, but there's a kind of bitter honesty in me for all of that. I'm able to look myself in the face at times, and tell the truth about myself and see just what I am. And I hate sham and hypocrisy and pretense and fraud and crookedness and if I could only be sure that tomorrow was *really* going to be the last day in the world—oh, Christ! What a paper we'd get out tomorrow! And, in addition, I have wit, a sense of humor, a love of gaiety, of the whole flashing interweft, the thrilling and unceasing pageantry of life, of food, of drink, of good talk, and of good companionship—So don't be too severe on me. I'm really not as bad as some of the things I have to do!"

Such, indefinably and yet plainly, were the markings of these men—the legend written on their persons that spoke so clearly that it did not need to speak. It was as if the world's coarse thumb which had so soiled them with its grimy touch, had also left upon them some of its warm earthiness, the redeeming virtues of its rich experience, its humor, wit, and understanding, the homely fellowship of all its pungent speech. Seen so, their presence here was an engaging one: people looked at them, and smiled, and felt a strange familiarity as if they had known all of them for years, and so knowing them, and what they were, were not afraid of them.

Two or three of them now approached the soda counter where Mrs. Jack and various other people were seated and began to interview some of the people there. The questions of these men seemed ludicrously inappropriate. They approached some of the younger, more attractive girls, found out if they lived in the building and immediately asked them—with a kind of naive eagerness, for, strangely, naiveté was also a characteristic of this cynical breed—if they were "in the Social Register." If any of the girls admitted that she was in the Social Register, the Press would immediately demand her name and address, details of her parentage, and so on.

Many of the younger girls, excited at the prospect of having their names and pictures in the tabloid press, readily admitted, when asked, that they were in the Social Register, even though it was almost ludicrously apparent, from their beak-nosed physiognomies, that they could not have been. Meanwhile, one of the representatives of the Press, a rather battered looking gentleman with a bulbous red nose and infrequent teeth, had called the City Desk on the telephone, and was now engaged in reporting his findings to the man at the other end:

"—Sure, that's what I'm tellin' yuh—The police have arrived," he went on in a rather important tone of voice that showed he was probably as much fascinated by his own journalese as any reader could be—"the police have arrived and thrown a cordon round the building—"

There was a moment's pause at the conclusion of this item, but in a moment more the red nosed man rasped out irritably. "No—No—No!—Not a *squadron*! A *cordon*!—What's'at? *Cordon*—I say!—C-o-r-d-o-n—cordon—For pete's sake!" he went on presently, in a somewhat aggrieved tone of voice, "How long have you been workin' on a newspaper, anyway?—Didn't you ever hear of a cordon before?—Now, get this: Lissen—" he went on in a careful voice, glancing at some scrawled notes upon a piece of paper in his hand, "—Among the residents are included the names of many Social Registerites and others prominent among the younger set—What?—How's that?" he said abruptly, rather puzzled—"Oh!—" He looked around briefly to see if he was being overheard, then lowered his voice and he spoke again: "Oh, sure!—*Two*!—Nah, there was only two—that other story was all wrong—Yeh—both of them were elevator men—" He lowered his voice a little more, then looking at the notes upon his piece of dirty paper, he read carefully, in lowered voice: "John Enborg- -age 64—married—three children—Lives in Jamaica, Queens—You got that?" he said quietly in a moment, then proceeded, "—and Herbert Anderson—aged 25, unmarried, lives with his mother, 841 Southern Boulevard, the Bronx—Have yuh got it?—Sure. Oh, sure!" Quietly after a moment's pause, he looked around briefly again, then lowered his voice before he spoke again, "—No, they couldn't get them out—They were on the elevators and they were goin' up to get the tenants when the current was shut off—Sure: That's the idea—They got caught between the floors—They just got Enborg out," his voice sank lower, "They had to use axes to get in through the top—Sure—Sure." He nodded quietly into the mouthpiece, "That's it—smoke: Too late when they got to him—no, that's all—just those two—no, they don't know about it yet—the management wants to keep it quiet if they can—no, none of the tenants know it—what's that? Heh? Speak louder, can't yuh—you're mumblin' at me!—" He spoke sharply, irritably, then listened attentively for a moment—"Oh!—Yes, it's almost over—Sure, it was tough—They had trouble gettin' at it—It started in the basement, then it went up a flue and out at top—Sure, I know," he nodded—"That's what made it so tough!—The tracks are right below it—they were afraid to flood the basement, if they did, they'd flood two tunnels and four sets of tracks—They were afraid to risk it—Sure, they tried to get at it with chemicals—It's going down now, but it's been tough—Okay, Mac—Shall I hang around?—Okay," he said at length, and hung up.

*   *   *   *   *

Mr. Jack and Ernie came back presently and rejoined the people in the drug store. They had met some old friends at the Ritz and had left Alma and two or three of her companions with them. The two men looked cheerful and were in good spirits: Their manner showed mildly and pleasantly that they had partaken of some refreshment on the way. Ernie greeted his mother with his customary bland and heavy "Oh

Hello." He was carrying a woman's coat upon his arm and he now slipped it around her shoulders, saying: "Mrs. Feldman sent this to you, Mother. She said you could send it back tomorrow."

"But how sweet of her!" cried Mrs. Jack, her little face beginning to glow and sparkle again with friendly warmth as she felt how good and kind and thoughtful everyone was in a time of hardship and of stress. "Aren't people just the most—" she began very earnestly, but failed to finish, feeling a little inadequate—feeling hospitably, anyway, that people were "the most"—well, "the most *something*," anyway.

They went out on to the street again. People were beginning to straggle out of the store, watching and waiting on the corner. They were still held back by the police, but there were already unmistakable signs that the fire was under control, was, in fact, almost extinguished. The firemen had hauled in the great lines of hose and packed them away in the trucks. Most of the big fire machines had already gone and two or three more were now throbbing powerfully and in a moment more roared away with a sense of finality in their departure. In a very short time the street was clear. The remaining firemen were coming out of all sides of the building, packing up their equipment, and one by one the great trucks were thundering away. Presently the police on duty got the signal to allow the tenants to go back into the house again.

AFTER THE FIRE
· · ·
THESE TWO TOGETHER
· · ·

The fire was over. The people began to stream back across the street and through the arch-like entrances into the court, collecting servants, maids, cooks, chauffeurs, the scattered personnel of their establishments, as they did so. An air of authority and order had already been re-established. One could hear masters and mistresses giving orders to their servants, the cloister-like arcades were again filled with streams of shuffling people going back into their entrances.

But now the people were more orderly and assured. The confusion, bewilderment and excitement that had marked their first pell mell outpouring from the building had now disappeared. Indeed, the informality and friendliness of their first appearance seemed now to have vanished. A kind of ordered formality, a sense of cold restraint even, had come upon them. It was almost as if they were now a little ashamed of the emotions of excitement and danger which had betrayed them into injudicious cordialities, unwonted neighborliness. Each little group, master and mistress, servants and members of the family, had now collected somewhat frigidly into their own separate entity and were filing back to their cells in the enormous hive.

Mrs. Jack collected her own maids and Cook around her and gave them some instructions. Then, accompanied by her husband, Ernie, Miss Mandell, and the young man, she went in at her entrance. There

234

was still a faint smell of smoke, slightly stale and acrid, but the power had been restored, the elevator was running again. She noticed with casual surprise that the doorman, Henry, took them up, and she asked him if Herbert had gone. He paused just perceptibly, and then said quietly: "Yes, Mrs. Jack."

"You all must be simply worn out!" she said quickly, warmly, with her instant sympathy. "Hasn't it been a thrilling evening?" she went on quickly, eagerly: "In all your life did you even know of such excitement, such confusion as we had tonight?"

Again, the man said: "Yes, Ma'am" in a tone so curiously unyielding, formal, that she felt stopped and baffled by it, as she had many times before. "What a strange man he is!" she thought. "And what a difference between people! How different he is from Herbert. Herbert is so warm, so jolly, so—so—human. You can talk to him. And this one—he's—he's so stiff, so formal: you can never get inside of him. And if you try to speak to him he snubs you—puts you in your place as if he doesn't want to have to talk to you. How unfriendly!"

And for a moment she felt almost angry, wounded and rebuffed: She was herself a friendly person, and she liked people around her, even servants, to be friendly, too. But already her active and constantly inquiring mind was working loosely on the curious enigma of the doorman's personality: "I wonder what is wrong with him," she thought. "He seems always so unhappy, so disgruntled, nursing some secret grievance all the time. I wonder what has done it to him—how he got this way—Oh, well, poor thing, I suppose the life he leads is enough to turn anyone sour:— opening doors and calling cabs and helping people in and out of cars and answering questions all day long—But then Herbert has to do these things also, and he's always so sweet and so obliging about everything!—"

And, giving partial utterance to her thoughts, she said: "I suppose Herbert will be back upon the job tomorrow?"

He made no answer whatever. He simply seemed not to have heard her. He had halted the elevator and opened the door at her own landing, and after a moment he said quietly: "This is your floor, Mrs. Jack."

She was so annoyed for a moment after he had gone, that she halted in the little vestibule, turned to her family and guests with flaming cheeks, and said angrily:

"Honestly, that fellow makes me tired! He's such a grouch. And he's getting worse every day. It's got so now he won't even answer when you speak to him."

After the Fire ⚘ 235

"Well, Mother, maybe he's tired out tonight with all the excitement of the fire," suggested Ernie, more pacifically.

"Maybe it's all our fault?" said Mrs. Jack ironically, then with a sudden flare of her quick and jolly humor, she shrugged comically and said: "Vell, ve should have a fire sale!"—which restored her to good humor, and a full-throated appreciation of her own wit.

They opened the door then and went in. Everything was curiously unchanged—curiously, because it seemed to Mrs. Jack so much had happened since their excited departure. The place smelled close and stale and there was still an acrid scent of smoke. But by this time the maids were streaming in from the service entrance at the back and Mrs. Jack directed them to throw up the windows.

The big living room also now had a curiously stale, disordered look: the chaos of Mr. Logan's performance had never been cleared away, and now it rather startled her. So much had happened, it seemed, since Mr. Logan and his celebrated circus of wire dolls. Mrs. Jack stopped short and bit her lip, then turned away with a sharp feeling of vexation and distaste.

She called out sharply to the girls and ordered them to clean up the mess; then feeling rather angry with herself and Mr. Logan and with the general state of the living room—she could not quite say why—she turned and walked rapidly away toward her own room.

There things were better. Her pleasant room had not changed a bit. It still had its customary appearance of chaste austerity. The windows, according to her instructions, had been thrown up and the stale smoke-acrid air, with its unpleasant reminders of an extinguished fire, was becoming cool and sweet again. She took off her coat and hung it up in the closet, and carefully brushed and adjusted her somewhat disordered hair. When she walked out into the hall again everything was looking better. The air was clearing out: it seemed fresher and more clean. The girls had tidied up the living room and were now, in the full process of interrupted routine, busy cleaning up the dining room. Lily Mandell who had gone into the guest room for her wraps, now came out wearing her splendid cape and said goodbye.

"Darling, it has been too marvelous," she said throatily, with weary arrogance. "Fire, smoke, Piggy Logan, everything—I've simply adored it!" she said while Mrs. Jack shook with laughter. "Your parties are too wonderful!" she said. "You never know what's going to happen next." Turning to the young man, she extended a limp hand, and murmured:

"So nice to have seen you again—I'm staying at the Chatham. Couldn't you come in sometime for a drink: I should so like to talk to you."

Then she turned and said good-bye to Mr. Jack and Ernie, who were still attentively awake but obviously ready for their beds.

There was an air of finality about everything. The party was over, the fire was over, the remaining guests were ready to depart, and the men were waiting to go to bed. Miss Mandell kissed Mrs. Jack goodbye affectionately and in a moment more was taken down in the elevator.

Ernie kissed his mother goodnight and went off to bed. In a moment Mr. Jack, also kissing his wife formally and lightly upon her rosy cheek, said goodnight casually to her lover, and departed. Lovers could come, and lovers could go, but Mr. Jack was going to get his sleep. The young man was also going now, but she, taking him by the hand, said quickly, coaxingly, "Don't go yet. Stay a few minutes, dear, and talk to me."

For a moment she looked around her with an air of thoughtful appraisal. Everything was just the same. The place looked just the same as it had looked when she had first examined it that evening before the people came, before Mr. Logan and his horrible performance, before the fire, all the excitement, all the confusion. Now, it was just the same. If anyone came in here now he would never dream that anything had happened.

And wasn't everything so strange? Wasn't everything so strange—and yet so—so—kind of simple? And wasn't that what made everything in life so thrilling?

Well!—This thought was uppermost in her mind when she turned to him again:

"Wasn't it all so strange?—And wonderful?" she said. "Don't you think it was a wonderful party? And that everybody had a good time?— And the fire! Wasn't the fire the strangest thing!—I mean, the *way* it happened"—again her tone had grown a little vague and puzzled as if there was something she could not quite express—"I don't know, but the way we were all sitting here, after Mr. Logan's performance—Then all of a sudden the fire alarms, and then the big trucks going past in the street—I don't know," again her tone was vague and puzzled. "There was something so—sort of strange—about it—The fire was right here in our building—And for a long time we didn't know about it—We thought the trucks were going somewhere else—I mean it's all so strange—It shows!" Her low brow furrowed with a look of difficulty and again her tone was vague and puzzled as if she were trying to find words to express the emotion she had defined as "strange"—"I don't know—but it sort of frightens you, doesn't it?—No, not the fire!" she spoke quickly—"That didn't amount to anything. No one got hurt—it was terribly exciting, really—I think everyone was thrilled!—What I mean," again her brow was furrowed with a look of vagueness and of puzzled difficulty as she sought for words—"When you think of how sort of *big*—things have got—I mean the way people live nowadays—these big buildings where they live—And how a fire can break out in the same building where you live and you won't even know about it—I mean, there's something sort of *terrible* about it, isn't there?—And God!" she burst out suddenly with a kind of sudden exclamatory eagerness that was so warmly, naturally a part of her—"In all your life, did you ever see the likes of them? I mean the people in this house!—The kind of people who live here—The way they all looked—The way they looked, pouring out into the court—Have you ever *dreamed*—" Her excitement and eagerness as she spoke these words were almost comical, she actually gesticulated with her hand in order to give her meaning emphasis—"Well, it was the most astonish-ing—the queerest—I mean, in all your days you'd never dream that there were people like this—I mean," she said confusedly—"it's—it's—"

She paused, holding his hand, and looking at him tenderly, then, with a rapt look on her face, like an enchanted child, she whispered:

"—Just you and I—That's all that matters—They're all gone now—the whole world's gone—There's no one left but you and I—Do you know," she said in a quiet tone, "that I think about you all the time? All that I do is think about you all the time. When I wake up in the morning the first thought that comes into my head is you—and I. And from that moment on I carry you around inside me all day long. I carry you around inside me—*here*," she laid her hand upon her breast and looked at him like a good child who believes religiously its own fable, "I carry you inside me all the time," she went on in a kind of rapt whisper. "I have an angel that I carry around inside me *here*,"—again she laid her hand upon her breast—"and the angel that I carry around in me is—you. You fill my life, my heart, my spirit, body, and my being," the woman cried. "Oh, do you ever think that there was ever since the world began another love like this—two other people who ever loved each other as you and I? If I could play I'd make of it great music! If I could sing I'd make of it a great song! If I could write I'd make of it a great story—but when I try to play or write or try to sing, I can think of nothing else but you and I—Did you know that once I tried to write a story?" Smiling, she inclined her rosy little face towards his, and put her hand up to her ear and said: "Did I ever tell you the time I tried to write a story? And I was sure that it would make a wonderful story. It seemed to fill me up. I was ready to burst with it. But when I tried to write it all that I could say was 'Long, long into the night I lay, thinking of how I should tell my story.'"—She laughed suddenly, richly—"And that's as far as I could get. But wasn't that a grand beginning for a story? And now at night when I try to go to sleep, that old line of the story that I could not write, comes back to me and haunts me, and keeps ringing in my ears: 'Long, long into the night I lay—thinking about you all the time.' For that's the story." She came closer to him, and lifted her rose face to him—"Ah, dearest, that's the story. I keep thinking of you all the time. And that's the story. In the whole world there's nothing more."

LOVE IS ENOUGH?

· · ·

He made no answer. For suddenly he knew that, for him, at any rate, it was not the story. He felt desolate and tired, weary of all the consuming fury, fire, and passion, the tormenting jealousy and doubt, the self-loathing, the degrading egotisms of possession—of desire, of passion, and romantic love—of youth.

And suddenly it seemed to him that it was not enough. It seemed to him that there had to be a larger world, a higher devotion than all the devotions of this fond imprisonment could ever find. Well, then,—a swift thrust of rending pity pierced him as he looked at the rose sweetness of that childlike and enraptured face—it must be so: he to his world, and she to hers, and each to each—which to the better one, no one could say—but this, at last, he knew, was not enough. There were new lands; dark windings, strange and subtle webs there in the deep delved earth, a tide was running in the hearts of men—and he must go.

The memory of all those years of love, of beauty, of devotion, of pain, of conflict, hate and fear and joy—the whole universe of love, all that the tenement of flesh, or one small room could hold—together with this marvelous tenacity, the determination of the flower face, the resolution of this one small person, the refusal to give up in spite of fate, of rebuff, or repulsion, so often wounded sorrowfully, so often spurned, reviled, and treated cruelly, so often flung away only to return again to try the harness of its love upon the wild horse of spirit—together with all its faith, its tenderness, its noble loyalty—all this returned to rend him in this instant, but he knew that he must go.

They said little more that night. In a few minutes he got up, and with a sick and tired heart he went away.

*   *   *   *   *

Outside, at a side entrance, on the now quiet, deserted street, one of the dark green wagons of the police had slid up very quietly and was waiting now with a softly throbbing motor. No one was watching it. In a few moments a door which gave on to a flight of concrete stairs and led down into one of the basement entrances of the enormous building was opened.

A minute or two later two men emerged bearing a stretcher which had something on it that was very still, completely covered. They slid this carefully away into the back of the green wagon. In another moment two other men, bearing a stretcher with a similar burden, emerged and this also was quietly and carefully disposed in the same way. Then the door of the wagon was securely closed.

The driver and another man walked around and got into the front seat and after conferring quietly a moment with the sergeant of police, they drove off quietly turning the corner below with a subdued clangor of bells. The three policemen conferred together for a moment longer in lowered voices and two of them wrote down notes in their little books. Then the three men said goodnight all around, the two policemen saluted the sergeant and they all departed, each walking away upon the further prosecution of his appointed task.

Meanwhile, at the big front entrance, another policeman was conferring with the doorman, Henry. The doorman answered the questions of the officer in a toneless, monosyllabic and almost sullen voice, and the policeman wrote down his answers in another little book.

"You say he was unmarried?"

"Yes," said Henry.

"How old?"

"I think he was 28," Henry said.

"And where did he live?" said the policeman.

"In the Bronx," said Henry.

His tone was so low and sullen that it was hardly more than a mutter and the policeman lifted his head from the book in which he had been writing, and rasped out harshly: "Where?"

"The Bronx!" said Henry almost furiously.

The man finished writing in his book, put it away into his pocket, and then before he departed, looked up at the facade of the big building with a look of casual, almost weary speculation.

Love Is Enough? 241

"Well," he said, "I wouldn't like to try it. It's a long way up there, isn't it?"

"Yes," the man named Henry answered with the same ungracious sullenness and turned impatiently away—"If that's all you want?" he began.

"That's *all*," the policeman said with a kind of brutal and ironic geniality, "that's all, brother." And with a hard, ironic look of mirth in his cold eyes he oscillated his nightstick behind him and looked at the retreating figure of the doorman as he disappeared.

* * * * *

At this moment, Mr. Jack, wearing his silken dressing gown, and ready for his bed and sleep, had just gone to the window of his room, lowered the sash still farther, and drawn in a good full breath of cool night air. He found it good. The last disruptive taint of smoke had been washed clean and sweet away by the cool breath of April. And in the white light of the virgin moon the spires and ramparts of Manhattan were glittering with cold magic in splintered helves of stone and glass. Peace fell upon his tranquil spirit. Strong comfort and assurance bathed his soul. It was so solid, splendid, everlasting and so good. And it was all as if it had always been—all so magically itself as it must be save for its magical increasements, forever.

A tremor, faint and instant shook his feet. He paused, startled, waited, listened. Was the old trouble there again to shake the deep perfection of his soul? What was it he had felt that morning? What rumor had he heard this night? . . . Faint tremors, small but instant, and a talk of tunnels—what was it? What?—This talk of tremors in the tunnels there below?—Ah, there it was a second time! What was it?—

TRAINS AGAIN!

—Passed, faded, trembled delicately away into securities of eternal stone, and left behind it the blue helve of a night, and April, in the blazing vertices of all that sculptured and immortal peace.

The smile came back into his eyes. The brief and troubling frown had lifted from his soul. And his look as he prepared to sleep was almost dulcet and cherubic—the look of a good child who ends the great adventure of another day and who knows that sleep and morning have come back again—

* * * * *

"Long, long into the night I lay" she thought—"and thought of you—"
Ah, sleep.